It was well a̶̶̶̶̶̶̶̶̶̶̶̶ waiting,

. It had a fashionably high
buttons down its neat, close-fitting bo̶̶̶̶,
the smallest of waists and a long flowing skirt.
She wore it when she left the shop, her primrose
dress in one of the shop's white paper carrier
bags. Her boater sat on her well-dressed wealth
of chestnut hair.

Daniel issued a soft whistle as she walked up to
him.

www.booksattransworld.co.uk

Also by Mary Jane Staples

The Adams Books

DOWN LAMBETH WAY
OUR EMILY
KING OF CAMBERWELL
ON MOTHER BROWN'S DOORSTEP
A FAMILY AFFAIR
MISSING PERSON
PRIDE OF WALWORTH
ECHOES OF YESTERDAY
THE YOUNG ONES
THE CAMBERWELL RAID
THE LAST SUMMER
THE FAMILY AT WAR
FIRE OVER LONDON
CHURCHILL'S PEOPLE
BRIGHT DAY, DARK NIGHT
TOMORROW IS ANOTHER DAY
THE WAY AHEAD
YEAR OF VICTORY
THE HOMECOMING
SONS AND DAUGHTERS
APPOINTMENT AT THE PALACE
CHANGING TIMES
SPREADING WINGS
FAMILY FORTUNES
A GIRL NEXT DOOR
UPS AND DOWNS
OUT OF THE SHADOWS
A SIGN OF THE TIMES

Other titles in order of publication

TWO FOR THREE FARTHINGS
THE LODGER
RISING SUMMER
THE PEARLY QUEEN
SERGEANT JOE
THE TRAP
THE GHOST OF WHITECHAPEL

and published by Corgi Books

THE
SOLDIER'S GIRL

Mary Jane Staples

CORGI BOOKS

THE SOLDIER'S GIRL
A CORGI BOOK: 9780552154444

First publication in Great Britain

PRINTING HISTORY
Corgi edition published 2006

7 9 10 8 6

Copyright © Mary Jane Staples 2006

Set in 11/13pt New Baskerville by
Kestrel Data, Exeter, Devon.

Corgi Books are published by Transworld Publishers,
61–63 Uxbridge Road, London W5 5SA,
a division of The Random House Group Ltd

Addresses for Random House Group Ltd companies outside the
UK can be found at: www.randomhouse.co.uk

Printed and bound in Great Britain by
CPI Cox & Wyman, Reading, RG1 8EX

The Random House Group Limited supports The Forest Stewardship Council (FSC), the leading international forest certification organisation. All our titles that are printed on Greenpeace approved FSC certified paper carry the FSC logo. Our paper procurement policy can be found at:
www.rbooks.co.uk/environment.

To all those readers who wished to know more about Chinese Lady's first husband, Corporal Daniel Adams of the West Kents

The Adams Family

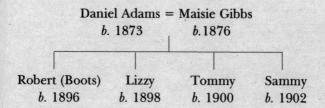

Daniel Adams = Maisie Gibbs
b. 1873   *b.* 1876

Robert (Boots)	Lizzy	Tommy	Sammy
b. 1896	*b.* 1898	*b.* 1900	*b.* 1902

Chapter One

She was born on a very pleasant September day in 1876, her parents being Annie and George Gibbs of Brandon Street, Walworth, the cockney heart of South London. They named her Maisie, and watched over her with care and anxious attention, for two previous children had both died of diphtheria when only one year old.

From the start, however, little Maisie showed an aptitude for survival, throwing off the symptoms of ailments that were forever creeping up on children whose less than salubrious environment in the poverty-stricken back streets of Walworth bred a multitude of germs. By the time she reached five she was a child of endurance and determination, a healthy answer to the prayers of her parents.

Her mum was a slender and upright woman, with a belief in the mercies of God. Her dad was sturdy and hard-working, a classic example of a man poor but honest. In fact, he was honest enough one day to say, albeit with a twinkle, that he'd have preferred to be rich and a bit crooked.

Maisie's church-going mum at once told him never to say things like that in front of a growing girl. Only a joke, he said. Well, I don't hold with jokes like that, said her mum, but not without a twitch of her lips.

Maisie's dad worked as a railway porter, and if his wages were low there were times when he brought home welcome tips. He and his wife saw to it that little Maisie received the kind of affection and attention that a child was entitled to. She also received talks about good behaviour. Good behaviour, her dad told her many times, would make sure she'd get a respectable job when she left school. And it would also make sure, he said, that she didn't turn into one of Walworth's many young perishers. Although he said that with a good-natured grin, it left little Maisie seriously determined not to become a young perisher.

They sent her to St John's Church School in Larcom Street, and there she was a model of endeavour and very good behaviour. She applied herself to reading, writing and arithmetic, although she was never going to be educationally outstanding.

'Maisie Gibbs, how old are you now?'

'Please, miss, I'm eight.'

'Yes, so can you tell me what is four added to three and multiplied by two?'

'Please, miss, I dunno just now, but it must be a lot,' said Maisie.

'What is four added to three?'

'Oh, that's seven, miss.'

'Good. So what is twice times seven?'

Maisie did some silent counting.

'Twice seven is fourteen, miss.'

'Which you know from your twice times table, and which you now know is the answer to four added to three and multiplied by two.'

'Oh, I believe yer, miss, honest I do,' said Maisie with typical earnestness.

The teacher smiled. Young Maisie Gibbs was a plodder, but a conscientious one. Meanwhile, her attendance at church and Sunday school increased her appreciation of all that was right and proper.

Tragedy struck when Maisie was ten. Her mum died of pernicious anaemia. Her dad was sorely grieved, and so was Maisie. They both shed tears at the funeral. But in the way of their kind, they resumed the struggle with their hard-up existence, and Maisie turned into her dad's comfort and housekeeper, doing all the necessary shopping, and mostly down the East Street market, known as The Lane. Having frequently shopped there for her mother, she knew the market and its stallholders as well as she knew her home and her neighbours in Brandon Street. And the stallholders knew her. Little Miss Proper, they called her, because of her prim neatness of dress and her air of seriousness.

''Ello, 'ello, Maisie me little duck, 'ow is yer today, eh?'

'I'm very well, thanks, but would yer mind not being familiar? I ain't yer little duck.' If her cockney accent was unmistakable, she at least never gabbled. 'Kindly give me five pounds of pertaters.'

'I can't actu'lly give 'em to yer, me lady.'

'Well, fancy that, but I want a penny off for buying five pounds all at once.'

'Five pounds for a tanner, that's me reg'lar price, young Maisie, and I don't see no notice on me stall saying I'll knock a penny orf.'

'Look, mister, make it an 'apenny, then.'

'Blowed if you ain't touched me Christian heart. All right, an 'apenny it is, bless yer.'

She was soon making a sixpence do the work of a shilling, and she frequently came home with her shopping basket heavy with specked fruit given by stallholders who had an affection for the slim and upright young girl. Maisie had the carriage of her late mum, who had always taken pride in her straight back.

When she left school at fourteen with an excellent character reference, if not a glowing tribute to her standard of learning, Maisie managed to find a part-time job from eight in the morning until two in the afternoon in a steam laundry. It wasn't her idea of bliss, far from it, but she was paid five bob a week and able to do her housework and to cook the supper before her dad arrived home. She and her sturdy dad were great pals, and he regularly let her know what a treasure she was.

'Dad, I like looking after your wants and wishes, don't I?'

'And don't I know it, me angel? You're yer mum all over again, that you are.'

'Dad, I like yer for saying that.'

'You're a deserving gal, Maisie, bless yer heart.'

At sixteen she was a neat and pleasant-looking girl, with a wealth of dark brown hair close to chestnut, and slightly almond-shaped brown eyes. One day a boy who'd come to the laundry to collect his family's washing asked her if her mum was Chinese. Or her dad.

'Blessed cheek, course not. Me mum's in her Christian grave, and nowhere near China, and me dad was born of 'is Old Kent Road parents.'

'I was only—'

'Be off with you.' That was the sort of thing her mum would say to a ragamuffin who knocked on her door on the fifth of November and asked for a penny for the guy. She could always find a penny for carol-singers at Christmas, but she knew a penny for the guy would be spent buying a firework which, when it went off, would frighten her cat.

Maisie always sighed whenever she thought of her hard-working and upright mum, and how she showed pride in being respectable in an area where some blowsy women, wearing their husbands' flat caps, could be seen on their way to a pub, to the Jug and Bottle entrance, coming out with a jar of beer which would make their red faces redder before the evening was over. They'd even go in their slippers, and kind of slopped along. Slummocky, her dad would say. Then there were the families who bawled and hollered at each other fit to wake the dead as far off as Southwark Cemetery. Maisie knew her mum had belonged to the other kind of Walworth people, the resilient and resolute kind, who were forever struggling for a better life. Maisie told herself that that was what she and her dad would do, work hard to improve their lot.

She was not interested in boys, not in any romantic way. The ones she knew were all good-natured in the fashion of most Walworth boys, but a bit loud, and a bit daft too, in her opinion. Besides, she had her good old dad to look after.

Unbelievably, when she was only a month past her seventeenth birthday, life struck her another cruel blow. Her dad went down with the flu, and pneumonia followed. It killed him off in November 1893. Maisie was devastated, and alone, her grandparents having passed on years before. She had no savings, and only enough money to pay the rent for a few more weeks. The workhouse loomed. A kind lady customer of the laundry came to her rescue, recommending her to a domestic agency always on the lookout for suitable girls willing to enter service. Because Maisie was so presentable and well-mannered, the lady thought her very suitable. A live-in servant's job would provide her with a home and board.

Maisie called on the agency, whose offices were

in the Strand. Neatly turned out, with a black armband to show she was in mourning for her dad, she produced her school reference, the document that paid tribute to her character. Her appearance, her good manners and the character reference resulted in her being offered service with a rich elderly gentleman, Mr Charles Fairfax of Kensington.

It was the gentleman's housekeeper, Mrs Iris Carpenter, who interviewed Maisie. The lady, a widow, was fifty, buxom and dressed in black. She had handsome features and the air of one who must be obeyed. Mr Fairfax, she said, had just lost a housemaid. The foolish girl had left to get married to a City clerk. Much good that would do her.

'Do you have a young man?'

'Me? Oh, no, ma'am,' said Maisie.

'Mr Fairfax won't want to engage you if you're thinking of going off to get married.'

'I'm not thinking of anything like that,' said Maisie.

'Well, you seem a sensible girl, so come with me and I'll introduce you to Mr Fairfax.'

The house seemed enormous to Maisie as she followed the formidable housekeeper. It was typical of that part of Kensington which excelled in Georgian grandeur. Mr Fairfax turned out to be seventy and slender, with a mane of silvery hair. He was seated in a heavily upholstered armchair, had a look of fragility, but was kindness personified.

'So, we have found a new housemaid?' he said.

'Yes, I think this girl will do,' said Mrs Carpenter. 'Her name is Maisie Gibbs. Young lady, you may make yourself known to Mr Fairfax.'

'Oh, how d'yer do, Mr Fairfax, sir,' said Maisie, and executed a little bob.

'I'm as well as can be expected, although I'm told I'm a little unsteady on my feet,' said Mr Fairfax with a delicate smile. 'But I refuse to accept that. I'm merely not as young as I was. Do you care to take on employment with us?'

'Oh—' Maisie nearly said 'not 'alf'. (She dropped aspirates, like any cockney.) But instinct changed the impulse to make that cockney response. 'Yes, sir, very much, thank you.'

'Excellent. Mrs Carpenter will instruct you in all your duties.' Mr Fairfax exhibited another faint smile, which Maisie thought showed a kind of courtesy towards her. But she also thought the poor gentleman probably wasn't in the best of health.

'Thank you, sir,' she said.

So she took up a new life as a housemaid. She was supplied with a servant's outfit, a dark blue dress, a white front and a lacy cap, and given her own room in the basement, the living quarters of all the other servants apart from Mrs Carpenter. The housekeeper had her own suite on the first floor, directly adjacent to Mr Fairfax's suite. Maisie could hardly believe just how many rooms there were in this handsome, three-storeyed house. There were even three tiled bathrooms.

She was allowed to take a bath once a week. Indeed Mrs Carpenter expected her to. Maisie, who had always used a galvanized tin bath on Friday nights, found a real bath the height of civilized luxury, even if it nearly swallowed her up.

Obedient, willing and never afraid of hard work, Maisie began her new life happily, although one of her duties was to rise at six every morning and attend to the fires. This meant stoking up those still slowly burning, cleaning out all that were dead and building new ones. But at least the houseboy, Alexander Beavis, was responsible for refilling the coal scuttles and disposing of the collected ash. A perpetually grinning lad, he was asked by Maisie where he got such a posh name.

'From me mum and dad,' he said, 'they give it me, and without asking, so I'm stuck with it, ain't I?'

'It's a nice name, so you should be proud of it, and of yer mum and dad,' said Maisie.

''Ere, suppose your mum and dad 'ad called you Honoraria instead of Maisie, would yer be proud of that?' asked Alexander.

'Honoraria?' said Maisie. 'There ain't no such name.'

'There y'ar, then, you'd be stuck with a label what no-one ever 'eard of afore,' said Alexander.

'I just don't know why boys are so daft,' said Maisie. 'Go and fill this scuttle.'

'Never mind what you don't know,' grinned

Alexander, picking up the scuttle, 'what I know is that gals are all the same.'

'All the same what?'

'Bossy,' said Alexander.

'Cheeky saucebox, be off with you,' said Maisie.

'Tell yer what,' said Alexander, tapping his nose, 'don't get on the wrong side of the dragon.'

'What dragon?' asked Maisie.

'Her.' Alexander jerked a thumb.

'Her?' said Maisie.

'Mrs Carpenter.'

'It ain't me desire, nor me nature, to be impudent to anyone, least of all Mrs Carpenter,' said Maisie.

'That's it, use yer loaf,' said Alexander.

'Hoppit,' said Maisie, already aware that the other servants, all female except for Alexander and Bill Townley, the coachman, took pains to keep on the right side of the formidable housekeeper. Mr Townley kept out of the way by spending all his time in the nearby mews, where Mr Fairfax's carriage and horses were housed. He appeared only on the occasions when the carriage was needed, not by Mr Fairfax, who never went out, but by Mrs Carpenter.

'Boy,' she would say to Alexander, 'go down to the mews and inform Townley that the carriage will be required at two this afternoon.'

Alexander would run all the way.

There was, however, one person who did not seem intimidated by the housekeeper, and that was Mrs Fanny Blisset, the cook, who had been taken on ten months ago, subsequent to her predecessor being dismissed for insolence. In her twenties, she had a baby daughter who was now eleven months, the circumstances of the child's existence being a bit of a puzzle to everyone. Although the cook wore a wedding ring, there seemed to be no husband or father around, and no talk of one. Still, no-one said anything. Maisie thought Mrs Carpenter must have shown a kind heart in persuading Mr Fairfax to engage a woman with a child. Acting as nursemaid to the infant became a frequent part of Maisie's duties. She took this on happily and competently, and often gave the child an airing in the four-wheel bassinet, a forerunner of the perambulator.

All in all, Maisie was content in her work. She felt it had saved her from the workhouse, and that it was a consolation for the loss of her mum and dad. In her night-time prayers, she thanked the Lord for looking after her.

She rarely saw Mr Fairfax. He dined in his suite and spent most of his time in the library, reading books. And when she did see him, usually on the few occasions when she was required to help Milly, the parlourmaid, dust and clean the suite, he had a strange way of being plural when talking of himself as employer.

'Maisie, my dear girl,' he would say, 'we are delighted with your efficiency.'

It was Alexander who told her the old gent was under the thumb of Mrs Carpenter, and that he meant her and himself whenever he said 'we' or 'us'.

'Oh, well, I suppose the poor gentleman has to rely on her for everything,' said Maisie.

'Not half he don't, and you'd think she was his trouble and strife, wouldn't yer?' said Alexander.

'I ain't thinking that at all,' said Maisie.

'Well, don't be surprised if one day she don't manage to get 'im to the church and up the aisle,' said Alexander. ''Ere, Maisie, I'll walk out with yer when yer free times coincide with mine, if yer like.'

'Oh, honoured, I'm sure,' said Maisie, 'but I don't like.'

She certainly didn't, for Alexander was not only a mere fifteen, he was also a saucy young perisher, artful enough to convince Mrs Carpenter he was as angelic as a cherub.

Chapter Two

July, 1894. A Sunday afternoon.

The sun was shining on London, capital of the British Empire, now at its mightiest, even if the Boers of South Africa were growling with resentment at the increasing influx of British settlers, and the Dublin Irish as troublesome as ever.

In the bright light of Hyde Park, young men and young women were riding their new two-wheeled velocipedes, soon to be known as bicycles, up and down Rotten Row. In Kensington Gardens people were strolling around the pond, boys were sailing their boats, governesses were walking their charges, nursemaids were wheeling infants in their prams, and off-duty soldiers in their colourful walking-out uniforms were on the lookout for feminine company, mostly in the shape of flirtatious servant girls.

Young ladies wearing long dresses that hid their feet seemed to be floating along in company with young gentlemen. Boaters predominated among the men, and hats as large and fanciful as decorated birdcages adorned ladies' heads.

A slim servant girl, wheeling a bassinet containing an infant clutching a toy rattle, stopped to watch a boy using a long thin cane in an attempt to reach his boat that was sailing away. The infant in the pram, fractious, threw the rattle to the ground. A tall soldier in the uniform of the West Kent Regiment came smartly up to retrieve the toy. The servant girl turned. The soldier, a corporal, gave her a little bow, then regarded her with a smile.

Maisie Gibbs blinked. She had never seen a soldier as handsome as this one. His features were firm and tanned, his eyes a deep grey, his smart dress helmet showing a glimpse of hair as darkly brown as her own, his moustache thick and well trimmed, his red-jacketed uniform close-fitting around his tall, muscular frame. For his part, he saw a young lady dressed in dark blue with a white front and the white cap of a servant. Her eyes were an instant fascination to him, luminous brown and almond-shaped. Her looks were wholly pleasing, with the freshness of a girl not more than eighteen. Maisie, in fact, was in her eighteenth year.

He spoke.

'Afternoon, miss.'

'Beg yer pardon?' said Maisie.

'Might I introduce meself?'

'No, you might not,' said Maisie. 'What d'you mean by accosting me?'

'Accosting? Not at all, miss. It's a grievous offence, and chargeable.'

'So it should be,' said Maisie, 'and I 'ope you get charged for doing it to me.'

Corporal Daniel Adams whistled soft and low.

'What a regular terror,' he said. 'Anyway, is this yours, miss?' He held out the rattle.

'Mine?' said Maisie. 'No, it ain't, it's—' The infant, a girl, interrupted with a yell. 'Now see what you've done, put her in a temper.'

Corporal Adams leaned over the pram, smiled at the infant and tickled her. She stopped yelling and gurgled happily. He returned the rattle to her. She beamed.

'She's all right now,' he said. 'Might I walk with yer ladyship?'

'Well, you got a nerve,' said Maisie, not given to being picked up, especially by a soldier. Soldiers had a reputation for leading respectable servant girls astray, and the last thing Maisie wanted was the ruination of her own respectability. 'Kindly go away.'

'It's marching orders, is it?' said Corporal Adams, who had joined the army as a drummer boy to escape the depression of the back streets of Camberwell. He'd seen service overseas in burning climates and against warlike rebels with no respect for the Empire. He was now twenty-one, a soldier whose years of campaigning had given him a handsome mature appearance. 'You sure you wouldn't like me to walk with you?'

Maisie, sure at least she didn't want to be regarded as a common young lady, put her nose in the air.

'Go away,' she said.

'Right, marching orders definite, is it?' he said. 'Well, good afternoon to your pretty self.' He saluted her and left, which somehow didn't please Maisie.

The infant howled.

'Now what you howling about, little Rosemary?' she asked of Mrs Fanny Blisset's child. Little Rosemary put the handle of the rattle between her lips and sucked on it. 'That ain't nice,' said Maisie. 'Still, like me dear old mum and dad used to say, a little bit of dirt didn't 'urt no one. And me dad always said it toughens up our impunity.' She meant immunity. 'You listening, me pet?'

The infant sucked happily away. Time I wheeled her home, thought Maisie, and did so, heading for the Queen's Gate exit and Kensington Gore. She saw that soldier again. He was talking to a fellow corporal. He gave her another salute as she passed. About to put her nose in the air again, she did something else, something that surprised her and Corporal Adams as well. She cast a smile, then went hastily on as if she'd committed an offence.

'Who's she?' asked the other corporal.

'A sweetheart,' said Daniel Adams.

'Eh?'

'The girl I'm going to marry.'

'I didn't know you were in line for getting wed.'

'I didn't know it meself until fifteen minutes ago, and that young lady don't know it at all.'

'Blind me, come off it, Danny, you're talking pie in the sky, and you know it. One look at a gal and you want to marry her? You've got bees in yer bonnet.'

'Maybe,' said Daniel. He smiled, eyes following Maisie and the bassinet. 'And maybe not. See you back at barracks, Johnny.' Off he went.

Maisie was sure there were eyes on her back a minute later. And she was pretty sure she knew who they belonged to, for the sounds of footsteps were of a smart military kind.

Daniel Adams was not the sort of man to change his mind once it was made up. He came to a halt when his fancy, leaving the Gardens by the Queen's Gate to cross the road, stopped outside a grand flat-fronted Georgian house in Kensington Gore. So, that was where she worked, the pleasing poppet. He smiled again, turned about and retraced his steps.

Maisie lifted the child from the pram. The door of the house opened and out came blue-liveried Alexander, the houseboy.

'Hello, hello, you're back, then, Maisie,' he said, coming up the steps and taking hold of the bassinet.

'Well, seeing I'm standing right 'ere,' said Maisie, 'I must be back.'

'Ain't you a smart one?' said Alexander. ''Ow's the little terror?'

'She ain't a little terror, she's a little dear,' said Maisie. 'And she's asleep now, bless her.'

Alexander took the bassinet into the house,

and Maisie followed with the sleeping child in her arms. She carried her through to the kitchen where Mrs Blisset had just made up a tray of tea and biscuits for Mr Fairfax and Mrs Carpenter. The housekeeper had taken it up herself. Now the cook was brewing a large pot for the staff. Maisie thought that Rosemary's mother was a pretty woman, but perhaps a little shallow. She didn't give her child a lot of attention, even though she was allowed to keep the cot in a corner of the kitchen. It was always, 'See what she's crying about,' to one or other of the housemaids. She seemed a lot more devoted to her cooking accomplishments than her infant. Well, it had to be said she was a very good cook and made it more of an enjoyable recreation than a duty.

'Here's Rosemary, Mrs Blisset,' said Maisie.

'Is she asleep?' asked the cook.

'Yes, ain't she sweet?' said Maisie. 'She's been ever so good. D'you want to take her?'

'Not now, not now. Put her in her cot, then you can join us for tea.'

Maisie placed the child in the cot, tucked her in, saw she was well asleep, then sat down at the table of the huge kitchen. It had two large ranges, and stoking those was a part of her morning duties every day.

The other servants were at the table. There were two housemaids, Prudence and Agnes. Prudence was thin, Agnes buxom. There were also two scrubbers and cleaners, Edie and Daisy.

Then there was the parlourmaid, Milly, young and attractive. Lastly, but not so anyone would notice, there was Alexander, the houseboy. The women, apart from Mrs Blisset, were all gossiping, mainly about the soldiers who were always to be seen in the parks in this area of London. They're all soppy about uniforms, thought Maisie, drinking her tea. Her upbringing kept her cautious and reserved about flirty young men, soldiers especially.

One of the indicator bells jangled. The indicator was S1. That was Mr Fairfax's suite.

'You go up, Maisie, and quick,' said Mrs Blisset, which Maisie thought a bit much considering she hadn't long been back from her dutiful outing with the pretty woman's baby. But in her willing way, up she went smartly.

The door to the suite was open, and Mrs Carpenter appeared as soon as Maisie reached the landing.

'Maisie, run and fetch Dr Graham, and be quick,' she said, her brisk, commanding voice containing a note of urgency. 'Mr Fairfax has had a fall.'

'Oh, the poor gentleman,' said Maisie. Mr Fairfax had suffered previous falls, the last one a month ago, and Mrs Carpenter had sent her to fetch the doctor on that occasion. 'But will Dr Graham be in, seeing it's Sunday?'

'Don't argue, girl, go. If he's not in, his housekeeper will tell you where he is. Go.'

'Yes'm,' said Maisie, and away she went, flying

down the stairs and out of the house. Dr Graham's surgery, in Queen's Gate, wasn't far, and Maisie ran all the way, although it was against her nature to make a spectacle of herself in public. Certainly, people stared at her as she ran with the long skirt of her dress whipping around her legs.

The doctor's homely housekeeper answered the door to her. Yes, Dr Graham was in, but having his Sunday afternoon tea. Maisie said she was ever so sorry about disturbing him, but could he come and see her employer, Mr Fairfax, who'd had a fall? The housekeeper called the doctor, a handsome widower of forty-eight who, as a general practitioner, had a courteous manner and a professional conscientiousness. As soon as Maisie gave him her reason for disturbing him, he said he would come at once.

'You can accompany me, young lady.'

And Maisie did, in his pony and trap, which sped all the way. Pulling up outside the house, he tied the reins and alighted with admirable agility. Maisie jumped down, and Dr Graham, carrying his bag, advanced with her to the front door. It opened as if by magic, and Alexander's voice was heard.

'Come in, come in, if yer please, doctor.'

Maisie led Dr Graham into the hall and up the stairs. Mrs Carpenter met them on the wide landing.

'It's so good of you to come, Dr Graham,' she

said, 'but Mr Fairfax has had another fall, and I thought I ought to let you know.'

'Of course,' said Dr Graham, 'I'm glad you did. How is he now?'

'Complaining that I didn't need to send for you,' said Mrs Carpenter. She followed the doctor into Mr Fairfax's suite, while dismissing Maisie with a flick of her hand.

Oh, crikey, thought Maisie as she descended the stairs, I hope the old gentleman is all right. I mean, suppose he just faded away? I'd lose me job before a year was up.

She said a little prayer for Mr Fairfax and herself.

Mr Fairfax, seated in a deeply upholstered armchair that might have comfortably accommodated two elderly gentlemen as slender as himself, had his jacket and waistcoat off. Dr Graham was using his stethoscope to test his patient's heartbeats.

'Fuss, fuss,' said Mr Fairfax, as the stethoscope disengaged from inside his unbuttoned snowy white shirt.

'Now, now, Mr Fairfax,' said Mrs Carpenter, her handsome face wearing an expression of concern, 'it's very kind of Dr Graham to come.'

'My dear lady,' said Mr Fairfax, 'there's nothing wrong with me except the onset of old age.'

'Well, your heartbeat is perhaps a little slow,' said Dr Graham.

'There, you see,' said Mrs Carpenter, hovering in her raiment of soft black.

'A little faster or a little slower, what does it matter as long as my heart is generally sound?' said Mr Fairfax.

'I'll test it again in a few minutes,' said Dr Graham. 'Meanwhile, exactly how did you come to fall?'

'Didn't I say? Yes, I did say.' Mr Fairfax was definite. 'I tripped.'

'Oh, dear.' Mrs Carpenter shook her head.

'Fuss, fuss,' said Mr Fairfax again.

'You perhaps caught your foot in one of the rugs?' suggested Dr Graham.

'Yes, I must have.'

'You were present at that moment, Mrs Carpenter?' said Dr Graham.

'Yes,' said Mrs Carpenter, 'I always take afternoon tea with Mr Fairfax. I'm afraid that when he came up from his chair, he simply fell.'

'Did I?' Mr Fairfax looked uncertain for a moment. 'No, no, I tripped.'

'Well, either way, it has done you no real harm, fortunately,' said Dr Graham. He used his stethoscope again, Mr Fairfax muttered. Mrs Carpenter shook her head again. Dr Graham concentrated. 'Good,' he said in a while.

'Good?' said Mrs Carpenter.

'Remarkably good for his age,' smiled Dr Graham. 'But tripping up could cost you a broken bone, Mr Fairfax, so I beg you not to make a habit of it.'

'I'm so relieved that he's come to no harm,' said Mrs Carpenter, 'and I shall see he takes extra care in future.'

'That means more fussing,' said Mr Fairfax.

'Let me see,' murmured Dr Graham, replacing the stethoscope in his bag, 'I believe on the previous occasion, you stumbled, is that right?'

'Yes, stumbled,' said Mr Fairfax.

'I think you must beware of your floor rugs,' smiled Dr Graham.

'They're my friends, they keep my feet warm,' said Mr Fairfax, buttoning up his shirt. If he was not physically robust, he was never helpless.

'I wonder, are you able to do a little walk around the room?' asked Dr Graham.

'Able? Certainly, certainly.' Mr Fairfax stood up. Mrs Carpenter at once took helpful hold of his right arm. 'My dear lady, that isn't what our good doctor requires of me, an assisted walk.'

'Very well, but please be careful,' implored his housekeeper.

'I shall walk as I normally do,' said Mr Fairfax, and began. Mrs Carpenter kept close to him. His walk was quite steady, if not brisk, and Dr Graham looked on as his patient returned to the armchair without any kind of faltering. 'There, you see, nothing wrong, just a little too many years and a lot of fuss,' said Mr Fairfax.

'I'll prescribe a tonic,' said Dr Graham, 'and perhaps your young housemaid will collect it from the dispensary tomorrow morning.'

'Young Maggie, you mean?' said Mr Fairfax.

'Maisie, not Maggie,' said Mrs Carpenter, gently corrective.

'Yes, splendid girl, splendid,' said Mr Fairfax who, if a little vague at times, never let it bother him any more than his seventy years did. He was happy enough, existing as he did, in his library of hundreds of books. He had lived his time in the world outside but reached the point where it no longer interested him, except through his history tomes and his newspapers.

Dr Graham said goodbye to him, and made his exit from the library in company with the housekeeper. She pulled the door to.

'One can understand his reluctance to admit to a weakness, doctor,' she said, 'but the fact is, he fell on this occasion and others. He didn't trip.'

'Yes, I suspected so,' said Dr Graham, 'although I can find no real reason for it. As I've mentioned before, his heartbeat is a little slow, but that's no great problem. His sense of balance may be failing a little. I'd like you to keep a close eye on him and to get in touch with me whenever you think it necessary. He mustn't be allowed to overexert himself. With care, he still has more than a few years in front of him.'

'Dr Graham, I'll do everything I can for him,' said Mrs Carpenter earnestly. She smiled wryly. 'Neither I nor any of my staff can afford to lose him.'

'I understand that,' said Dr Graham, 'and I'm sure I can rely on your experience as a nurse to give him all the necessary care.'

'Those experiences were longer ago than I like to remember,' said Mrs Carpenter, her smile softening her. 'But one doesn't forget the basic principles.'

'Very true,' said Dr Graham, and bid her good-bye.

'Goodbye, doctor, and thank you so much for coming,' said Mrs Carpenter.

Chapter Three

Maisie was able to see Mr Fairfax a little later. She was called up to his suite by Mrs Carpenter to collect the tray of tea things. He was still in his library, his favourite room. He looked his usual elderly self, but not actually unwell.

'Hello, Maisie, have you come to fuss over me too?' he asked with his faint smile.

'Oh, no, sir, just to collect the tray,' said Maisie. 'I'm ever so sorry about yer fall, but ever so glad the doctor found you didn't come to no harm.'

'Nothing of consequence, young lady, and I can't think how it happened,' said the charming old gentleman. 'I assure you, I'm not as feeble as that.'

'Still, you must take care, sir,' said Maisie, picking up the tray from a table. Mrs Carpenter walked in.

'Hurry with that tray, girl,' she said, 'Mr Fairfax needs rest, not gossiping to.'

'Oh, sorry, mum,' said Maisie, and carried the tray out. As she did so, she heard Mr Fairfax speak to his housekeeper.

'The girl is very thoughtful, Iris.'

'Yes, not many are so pleasing and obedient,' said Mrs Carpenter.

Crikey, thought Maisie, the way he calls her Iris, he must be fond of her.

All the servants were happy that Mr Fairfax hadn't suffered from his fall. They all liked and respected him. Alexander conveyed to Maisie in private his hope that the old gent would live for ever.

'Then we'd all keep our jobs for ever,' he said.

'Well, I like him very much,' said Maisie, 'but I don't know I want to be a housemaid for ever.'

'Got yer mince pies on a bloke that's got ideas of churching you, 'ave yer?' demanded Alexander.

'No, I ain't, not yet,' said Maisie, 'but it's me natural wish to be a married woman some day.'

'Well, I've got natural romantic feelings for gals,' said Alexander, 'and if—'

'You've got what?' said Maisie.

'I mean I like gals,' said Alexander, his grin precocious, 'and if me job 'ere did go up the chimney, I'd like to be a sailor and have one in every port.'

'Oh, you would, would yer?' said Maisie. 'Well, just now you're supposed to be putting that bag of kitchen waste in one of the dustbins.'

'It's like I've always said,' observed Alexander.

'And what's that, might I ask?' enquired Maisie.

'You're bossy,' said Alexander, and went off carrying the bag of rubbish and grinning triumphantly.

Later, after supper, Mrs Carpenter called Maisie up to inform her that she and Alexander could have the rest of the evening off.

'Oh, thanks ever so, mum,' said Maisie.

'Mr Fairfax thinks you deserve it,' said Mrs Carpenter, 'and I'm inclined to agree. It won't count against your usual entitlement.'

The usual entitlement for all servants was eight hours a week.

'Oh, how kind, mum,' said Maisie, a model of good manners, especially in the presence of the household's female overlord. Maisie may not have been a young lady of wit and brilliance, but she was endowed with enough common sense to know how to keep on the right side of Mrs Carpenter.

'Be back before dark,' said the good lady. In many parts of London, dubious characters lurked, none of whom had honest intentions, especially in regard to females carrying purses. 'And let Alexander know that if he returns looking as if he's been in a fight, I'll have something to say to him that he won't like. That boy's a rapscallion at times.'

Maisie knew the houseboy was inclined to charge fists first at young hooligans who jeered at his uniform and shouted insults at him.

'Look at 'im, bet he's the cook's pet.'

'Bet she gives 'im a rattle to play wiv.'

'Bet he kisses the butler's flat feet.'

Alexander would go flying in, and come back looking as if he'd barged his way backwards through a hedge.

'I'll tell him, mum,' said Maisie, and went looking for him. She found him in his basement room, reading the *Police Gazette*, a weekly publication full of lurid accounts and equally lurid illustrations of criminal activity, police action and the vengeance of the law. It wasn't averse to recounting and illustrating a hanging. Alexander lapped it all up.

''Ere, Maisie,' he said, as she entered, 'd'you want to read about that evil bloke that cut another bloke's throat from ear to ear? Look, see the drawing.'

The drawing was hideous, and Maisie averted her eyes.

'You shouldn't be reading that 'orrible stuff,' she said. 'Burn it for your own good. Listen, Mrs Carpenter says we can have the rest of the evening off. So I'm going for a walk to Hyde Park. I don't know what you want to do, but Mrs Carpenter says she'll send you to purgat'ry if you come back looking like you've been in a boxing ring.'

'Maisie, can I come with yer to Hyde Park?' begged Alexander.

Maisie hesitated for only a second. Alexander, like herself, had no home to go to. At this very moment, Edie and Daisy, the scrubbers and cleaners, taking four hours off, were visiting their families in Lambeth, and Maisie thought what a comfort it must be to have a family one could be with now and again. But she and Alexander were orphans.

'All right, Alexander, you can come with me,' she said. 'Wash yer face and put yer cap on.'

Alexander's large cap had a huge peak that overshadowed his perky features and his saucy grin, something Prudence referred to as being a blessing to people that had got sensitive eye-sight.

It was a pleasant walk through Kensington Gardens to Hyde Park, the evening fine and only a few people about. Maisie supposed a lot of families would be at Evensong in the posh churches of this upper-class area. She still went to a morning service whenever she could, knowing her late mum would want her to. In any case, she liked a church service and a rousing sermon from a vicar with a sort of rolling, godly voice. After all, vicars were ordered – she meant ordained – to speak the word of God official, like.

In Hyde Park, there were quite a few more people about than in the Gardens. Most were strolling along the borders of Rotten Row, where some ladies and gentlemen were taking advantage of the balmy evening to enjoy an outing in their horse-drawn carriages.

'Don't they look nice, Alexander, all the

carriages?' said Maisie, as neat as ever in her uniform and lace-trimmed cap.

'Cor, me and you ought to 'ave one of our own when we're older,' said Alexander. 'One for you and one for me, eh?'

There were many different kinds to see, barouches, chaises, gigs, phaetons, dog carts, and even governess carts. Maisie thought it all like an evening gala parade, every vehicle shining with polished fittings, the brasses of reins gleaming, and all the horses or ponies in what she knew was called a spanking condition. Some horses were trotting, some walking and some, pulling the lighter vehicles, cantering.

She and Alexander watched in absorbed fashion, although what they saw wasn't new to either of them. One exciting thing about London was its many free spectacles, like the Lord Mayor's procession every November and the daily changing of the guard at Buckingham Palace.

'Don't it all look posh?' said Maisie.

'Well, it's the pastime of the rich and noble, yer know,' said Alexander. 'I dunno why you and me ain't rich and noble, Maisie. I feel, personal like, that being rich and noble would suit me a lot, and of course, it would suit you no end. You'd be a lady with six maids and a butler.'

'Which wouldn't suit me a bit,' said Maisie, 'and might I mention I'm already a lady? It ain't riches that make someone a lady or someone else a gentleman, it's how they behave. Me mum and dad told me that years ago. Me dad said that a man could be penniless and ragged and hungry, but if he was kind and Christian, then he was as good as any gent.'

''Ello, me darling, 'ow is yer?'

The voice reached her ears from close to, startling her. She turned. A youth in an ancient bowler, tipped at a cocky angle, and wearing a serge suit shiny with age, as well as a feeble attempt at a moustache, was bestowing a grin saucier than any of Alexander's. He looked about nineteen, and as if he was particularly fond of himself.

'Kindly clear off,' said Maisie, neat bosom proudly firm, back straight.

'Come on, I'm Frankie, and I'll take yer to a party at me friend Osbald's digs,' offered cocky bowler.

'I don't know Osbald or any of yer friends,' said Maisie, 'and I don't know you, and I don't want to, neither, so be off with you, d'you 'ear?'

'My, you got pride, you 'ave, darling,' said the cocky specimen. 'I bet you're a real class lady's maid. All right, no party, then, so let's you and me go and sit on the grass somewheres nice and quiet, and I'll tell you what goes on up the back stairs of Buckingham Palace and Windsor Castle.'

Alexander, squaring up, took a turn to speak.

'You heard this 'ere young lady,' he said, 'so do what she wants yer to. 'Oppit.'

''Ello, 'ello,' said Cocky, peering under

Alexander's peaked cap, 'where'd you pop up from, sonny, yer cradle? Well, pop back in, suck yer dummy and don't interfere with me forthcoming friendship with this lady's maid.'

'You got a hope,' said Alexander, sturdy at fifteen, if not as tall as the interloper. 'And you got something else as well.'

'And what might that be?' asked Cocky.

'An ugly mug, yer granddad's bowler and too much lip,' said Alexander.

'Well, strike a light, ain't you a cheeky young sod?' said Cocky. 'How would yer like me boot up yer backside in half a tick, eh?'

'Like to see yer try,' said Alexander.

Maisie intervened.

'Come on, Alexander,' she said, 'let's go and find some place that don't have bits of rubbish walking about.'

'Now don't be like that, Queenie,' said Cocky, 'and never mind Alexander, if that's 'is daft moniker. Let 'im toddle home to his mother, and she'll change his nappy for him. I got a fancy to make yer acquaintance.' With that declaration, he laid a hand on Maisie's arm.

Smack!

Alexander's bunched fist landed on his left eye. He staggered, bawled and went for the houseboy. Alexander, experience having taught him how to come off best in a punch-up, thrust out a foot and tripped him up. He crashed. From a distance, people looked on, genteel ladies in fearful fashion. A bobby in blue materialized,

41

arriving at the scene just as Cocky came up on his feet and aimed a blow at Alexander.

'Got yer,' said the constable, grabbing Cocky by the scruff of his neck.

''Ere, leggo,' bawled Cocky, 'I been assaulted.'

'Officer,' said Maisie, quivering a bit but bravely up to the mark, 'this 'ooligan's been accosting me.'

'Oh, he has, has he?' said the bobby, and fixed Cocky with the stern eye of the law. 'Oh, you have, have yer?'

'Listen, I just said good evening to 'er, didn't I?' said Cocky. 'That ain't a crime, is it?'

'Accosting a female subject of Her Majesty is unlawful, and I ought to charge yer,' said the bobby. 'But it'll upset yer mum, I daresay, so I'm just cautioning you, providing you offer this young lady an apology.'

''Ere, what about that bleedin' young rip that's just give me a black eye?' complained Cocky. But his left optic hadn't yet started to change colour, and the constable was unimpressed.

'I'm cautioning him as well,' he said, and addressed Alexander. 'Now listen to me – half a mo, where's yer face?' He lifted the peak of the houseboy's cap. 'Oh, there you are. Well, at your age, young 'un, you've got to respect the law as much as grown-ups have, so I'm warning you, watch where you put your fists from now on. If they strike a fellow human being, that's an assault and chargeable. D'you hear me?'

'Yes, sir,' said Alexander, wisely refraining from argument.

'Right,' said the bobby, 'now both of you young scallywags get off to where you belong, and mind the pair of you keep the peace, specially Sunday evening peace in this here public park.' At this point, the constable turned to Maisie. 'Sorry you've been bothered, miss.'

'Oh, you've been ever so 'elpful, officer,' said Maisie.

'Pleasure, miss.'

'Come on, Alexander,' said Maisie. There was only blank space where Cocky had been. He'd slipped niftily away from the arm of the law in the hope of finding a raw steak with which to placate his now swelling eye. Maisie and Alexander began to stroll back to Kensington Gardens.

'What a palaver,' said Alexander.

'Yes, and see what you nearly did with that fist of yourn?' said Maisie. 'Nearly got yourself run in.'

'I ain't remorseful,' said Alexander. 'I wasn't going to let the bloke take liberties with you.'

'I know,' said Maisie, 'so I ain't ungrateful. You're a good boy at heart, Alexander, and you'll grow up to be a man a lot quicker than that bit of rubbish, if he ever does.'

'Did yer see what his mince pie looked like?' said Alexander.

'Don't gloat,' said Maisie, 'it's sinful, like vanity.'

'Who said?' asked Alexander.

'Me mum,' said Maisie, and sighed a bit.

One day, she thought, she would have a place and a family to go home to.

Her own place, her own family. One day.

Chapter Four

The following morning, Monday, Mrs Carpenter
sent Maisie to Dr Graham's surgery to collect the
bottle of tonic. On her way back, she made
the turn into Kensington Gore just as a platoon
of West Kent infantrymen came marching along
on the side of the road. Leading the platoon was
a tall, fine-looking corporal. One step behind
him was a lance corporal. Marching bodies of
soldiers from the Knightsbridge barracks were
not uncommon in the area, and they always
looked a handsome sight to susceptible servant
girls.

Maisie turned her head as the platoon
marched by. The corporal in charge spotted her
and smartly detached himself.

'Take over, Lance Corporal Wicks,' he said.
'I'll catch you up on the parade ground.'

'You'd better,' said the lance corporal, and
took the platoon on.

A voice reached Maisie's ear.

'Morning to you, Miss Smith.'

Maisie looked up into the face of the soldier

who had accosted her – well, tried to pick her up – in Kensington Gardens yesterday.

'Well, I'm blessed, it's you again,' she said, as he fell into step with her. 'What d'you mean by calling me Miss Smith?'

'It's like this, d'you see,' said Corporal Daniel Adams. 'I know you, but I—'

'You don't know me,' said Maisie, 'you've just seen me.'

'Well, I kind of know you,' said Daniel, 'but not yer name, so I had to call you something out of politeness, and Miss Smith is more polite than Miss Whatsername.'

'Excuse me,' said Maisie, 'but you're accosting me again.' Still, it wasn't actually unpleasant, not like yesterday evening, when that cocky youth had made a nuisance of himself. She didn't feel this handsome corporal really was accosting her, more like trying it on with her. But she had to put him in his place, so she said, 'I suppose you know accosting's against the law?'

'Don't tell my sergeant major that, or he'll run me in,' said Daniel.

'Good job too,' said Maisie, standing her ground as the respectable daughter of her late mum and dad.

'Might I enquire when you next get time off?' asked Daniel, fixed in his determination to strike up a happy relationship with this slim, straight-backed housemaid of entirely pleasing looks.

'I just can't believe your cheek,' said Maisie,

fighting little vibrations that were impelling her towards dropping her guard. She was slowing in her walk, as if her legs didn't want her to reach Mr Fairfax's house too soon. 'How many girls you had on your arm? Hundreds, I bet.'

'Since I was twenty, I've been looking out for just one girl,' said Daniel.

'What one?'

'One I reckoned I'd like more than any other,' said Daniel.

'What, just by seeing her?' said Maisie.

'That's what I reckoned,' said Daniel. 'And I'm taken with you, I know that.'

'Crikey, you don't half come it with your talk,' said Maisie.

'What's your name?' he asked.

'Maisie Gibbs.' The answer came out just like that, as naturally as the question, and before she could resume her cautious front.

'Maisie?' Daniel smiled. 'I like it. Maisie. I'm Daniel Adams. Well, Maisie, when can we meet?'

'Nowhere,' said Maisie hastily and stopped. She'd reached her place of work. 'Beg yer pardon, I'm sure, but I've got to go in now.' She went down the steps and rapped her knuckles on the door. As was customary, servants entered the house where they worked by the basement door, but Mrs Carpenter didn't seem to mind which entrance Mrs Blisset used. The cook, who appeared to be Mrs Carpenter's favourite, only ever came in by the front door, which was most remarkable.

'I'd still like to meet you,' said Daniel, smiling down at her from the top of the steps.

Maisie heard someone coming. She turned her head, gave Daniel a quick look and said, 'I might be in the Gardens Sunday afternoon, I might be.'

The door was opened by Prudence, and Maisie stepped in. Prudence did not miss the figure of the soldier before he went away, quick-marching to catch up with his platoon.

'Here,' said Prudence, a plain-looking woman of twenty-four, 'is that soldier your walking-out bloke?'

'I don't have any walking-out bloke,' said Maisie.

'Still, that soldier looked like every girl's fancy dream,' said Prudence.

'I didn't notice,' said Maisie, crossing fingers to hold off any reproach from the One Above for her little white lie.

'But you must of—'

'I've got to take this medicine up to Mrs Carpenter for Mr Fairfax,' said Maisie, and up she went. She knocked on the door of the housekeeper's suite. There was no answer, so she knocked on the door of the adjoining suite. It was opened by Mrs Carpenter. 'Here's the medicine, mum,' said Maisie.

'You've taken longer than I expected,' said the housekeeper.

'Oh, ever so sorry – '

'Never mind,' said Mrs Carpenter, 'you can clean my rooms now. Milly's busy elsewhere.

Mind that you use the feather duster in the ceiling corners.'

'Yes'm,' said Maisie. 'Oh, beg pardon, but could I ask how Mr Fairfax is?'

'A little tired, but fairly well.'

'Oh, that's good,' said Maisie.

The week went by in its usual way, with Fanny Blisset coming up with delicious meals but giving her infant daughter less attention than Maisie and Prudence did. They and the other servants applied themselves diligently to their work of cleaning, dusting and polishing, as well as washing and ironing clothes, linen and bedsheets. They also did kitchen chores. Additionally, rugs and carpets were hung on a line in the spacious back yard and beaten free of dust. Maisie and Alexander were usually ordered to do that job, and twice a week. Maisie wore a smock over her uniform and covered her nose and mouth with a clean duster for this chore. Alexander let the rising dust settle where it did, risking being commanded by Mrs Carpenter to go and brush himself down and wash himself under the kitchen tap. The cold one.

Everyone did all they could to keep in the good graces of the ever-watchful housekeeper, whose responsibility was to maintain a clean and orderly establishment on behalf of Mr Fairfax. She also had the power of dismissal. Alexander, who had made Maisie his confidante, suggested to her in so many words that he was glad Mrs

Carpenter wasn't God's wife, or she'd always be busy exercising the power of life and death, and not only over them, but the people next door as well.

'Alexander, I just don't know what I'm going to do with you,' said Maisie. They were in the yard, using carpet beaters, and the dust was springing forth from suffering carpets. Maisie spoke through her mouth-covering duster. 'You get soppier, d'you know that?'

'Eh? What?' said the houseboy.

'Don't say what, it's common.'

'What?'

'I told you, don't say what, say beg yer pardon.'

'What? I can't 'ear a word you're saying.'

'Wash yer ears out, then,' said Maisie.

'What?' said Alexander.

Maisie tittered. Alexander might be a typical grinning boy, and artful as well, but she couldn't help liking him. And she knew that as an orphan, like herself, he needed a job that gave him board and lodging. She stopped beating for a moment and removed the duster.

'Well, don't say "what" to Mrs Carpenter,' she warned.

'Crikey, I did once,' said Alexander, 'and she asked me where me manners was. 'Ere, d'you think she's sweet on our old gent?'

'What, and him old enough to be her dad?' said Maisie.

'You just said "what",' remarked Alexander.

'Oh, it's different when you say it like that.'

'Still, he's well britched, yer know.'

'Mr Fairfax?' said Maisie.

'Yerse, and been a bach'lor all 'is life, so he ain't got no one to leave 'is money to. Blimey, I tell yer, Maisie, if I was a woman instead of a bloke, I'd marry 'im meself and live very 'andsome ever after. I could buy bags of caramels every day, and have me own 'orse and carriage for outings to Southend, and even Brighton. Mind, I ain't actually craving to be a woman, yer know.'

'Thank the Lord for that,' said Maisie, 'you'd look daft in a frock.' She wound the duster around her nose and mouth again.

'But fancy if you and me 'ad been sisters,' said Alexander, beating a fireside rug almost to death.

Maisie smiled. That boy was what her dad would have called a rip.

Mrs Carpenter issued most of her orders from upstairs. The kitchen indicator bell would jangle, mostly for S2, which was her suite. Up would go one of the servants and be advised of what was required.

From her close proximity to Mr Fairfax, Mrs Carpenter kept a caring and watchful eye on the old gentleman, and that included taking all her meals with him, except breakfast.

It was Alexander, of course, who suggested to Maisie that one day when Fanny Blisset went up, she'd find the pair of them enjoying breakfast in bed together.

'You little horror,' said Maisie. Mrs Blisset was the only servant whom Mrs Carpenter entertained for a chat.

'I ain't saying it's what our old gent would want,' said Alexander, 'just something he might wake up to one morning. Mind, for 'is age, he ain't a bad-looking bloke, and some middle-aged female might fancy him genuine.'

'You saucebox, you ought to have more respect for Mr Fairfax, and you ought to watch yer mouth as well,' said Maisie, who thought that talking about a man and a woman in bed together was just about as improper as anyone could get.

Alexander rattled on. He could talk nineteen to the dozen, and did, as if his tongue was powered by clockwork that didn't need winding up.

Maisie slipped away to polish the banister rails of the handsome staircase. While doing so, thoughts of Corporal Daniel Adams entered her busy mind. Crikey, if she took little Rosemary into the Gardens on Sunday, would he really be there, waiting for her?

Of course, if Mrs Blisset didn't ask her to do the outing, he'd wait for nothing. Unless she got time off.

Chapter Five

It was Sunday morning when Mrs Blisset asked
Maisie to take little Rosemary for an outing
in the bassinet, which wasn't what Maisie had
anticipated at all, not the morning, and certainly
there was no sign of Corporal Adams. The West
Kents were on church parade.

However, in the afternoon, she was given two
hours off. The weather was lovely. Winter fogs
had long gone, and the air was clear, the sky
blue, the sunshine warm and bright. Her feet
took her happily into the gardens, where she
sauntered amid the promenading people, an
attractive sight in her one and only Sunday dress.
Its primrose colour was enchanting, and it had
puffed shoulders, a stand-up starched white lace
collar, and a white hem to the long skirt that
flirted around her pretty ankles. It was the only
decent dress Maisie had outside her housemaid's
blue ones. A tipped boater, sat on her wealth of
chestnut hair.

Alexander had caught her slipping out of the
house in her private finery.

'Blimey, Maisie, ain't you a treat?' he said. 'Where yer going in that fancy rig-out. To meet the Prince of Wales?'

'I'm just going out, that's all,' said Maisie, and escaped before the saucebox could get saucier.

Kensington Gardens offered a delightful picture of green expanses and verdant colour, the waters of the Round Pond sparkling in the sunshine. On her right, as Maisie strolled along the Broad Way, the royal palace rose to present its own picture, that of a majestic frontage. There, fifty-seven years ago, the young seventeen-year-old Princess Victoria had been awakened early one morning to be told that on the death of her uncle, the King, the throne was hers. She was now a venerated old lady of seventy-four, but still wielding a monarch's power, still causing her Prime Minister to quake a little if whatever was brought to her for the royal signature displeased her. She might be a constitutional monarch, but had never been a mere cypher. Nor would she ever be. Her subjects admired her for that, even if they thought her a bit dowdy in her eternal widow's black.

Maisie walked on amid the crowds. Children darted, ladies floated under colourful parasols and accompanying gentlemen doffed hats to passing acquaintances.

Corporal Daniel Adams, off duty, was standing by the pond, casting his eyes this way and that. He spotted the young lady he was hoping to see. She came brightly into focus, looking delicious, her walk upright, her bearing prim and proper, a discouragement to young bloods looking for saucy minxes.

Daniel stepped into her path. Maisie stopped.

'Excuse me,' she said, 'but you're standing in me way.'

'How's yourself, Maisie?' smiled Daniel, red jacket close-fitting, blue trousers perfect, helmet adding to his height.

Maisie stared at this fine-looking man and little tingles disturbed her. She had never been bothered by such tingles before, never felt affected by any boy or man. Conventional, she expected that one day she would become a married woman. That was the whole point of life, really, marriage and families. She was sure, however, that the man in question would have to be the one she wanted. She was not in favour of marrying anyone for the sake of it, even if it meant waiting until she was as old as twenty-one before she fell in love.

She cleared her throat, doing the proper thing by putting her hand to her mouth so that the cough did not escape in a common way.

'Oh, it's you,' she said.

'You did say you might be here this afternoon,' said Daniel.

'But I didn't mean I wanted to meet you,' said Maisie. 'We haven't ever met proper.'

'What's meeting proper?' asked Daniel, liking everything about her, her pleasing looks, her brown almond-shaped eyes, her clean neatness of dress and even her air of primness. He guessed that here was a young lady without the flirtatious tendencies of many servant girls. 'Yes, come on, what's meeting proper?'

With people passing by, Maisie said, 'Well, like at a tea party and getting introduced.'

'Good idea,' said Daniel briskly.

'What d'you mean?' asked Maisie.

'We'll walk through to the tea rooms by the Serpentine in Hyde Park,' said Daniel, 'and I'll introduce meself very proper to you over a pot of tea and fruit cake.'

'What?' said Maisie. 'I mean, beg yer pardon?'

'Don't mention it,' said Daniel, 'just let's walk, eh?'

'Crikey, you don't half fancy yourself,' said Maisie. 'Still, all right,' she said. Then she added hastily, 'But don't think I do this with everyone that accosts me.'

'Maisie, I like it that you don't,' said Daniel, grey eyes frank and honest, 'and I'll like it even more if you only ever do it with me.'

'I can't promise nothing like that,' said Maisie, as they began their walk along the path that led to the Hyde Park Serpentine and its tea rooms. Suppose, she said, just suppose she met a really nice and respectable young man that she liked, she couldn't tell him she only walked out with some soldier she didn't hardly know anything about. Daniel said he'd tell her as much as she wanted to know about himself over tea, and that he'd be obliged if she'd keep away from any other blokes, respectable or not. Well, what a blessed cheek, said Maisie. She wasn't, she said, going to take orders from him, nor from anyone else except her employers. (She consciously bracketed Mr Fairfax and Mrs Carpenter.)

'Maisie,' said Daniel, 'it's me fervent wish to be your one and only.'

'Me one and only what?' asked Maisie.

'Feller,' said Daniel.

'What, when I don't hardly know you?' said Maisie, aware of more tiny tingles. Did he really fancy her? He really was ever so handsome. But she could bet he had other girls.

The Serpentine, shimmering, was not far ahead now, and a tall army officer was approaching. He glanced at Daniel. Daniel executed a smart salute. The officer returned it, stopped and beckoned.

'Don't go away, Maisie,' whispered Daniel, who marched crisply up to the officer, a captain. He saluted again. The officer returned it again and eyed the upstanding NCO with suspicion.

'Corporal Adams?' he said.

'As ever, sir,' said Daniel.

'Are you out of barracks on a pass?'

'Well, I can't say I'm not out, sir, seeing I am,' said Daniel. 'I've got time off.'

'With a pass?' said Captain Burnett of the West Kent 10th Battalion. Troops of fighting regiments temporarily stationed in London after a term of active service overseas were subject to strict limitations in regard to passes. For such men, the capital had a wealth of diverse attractions, some enjoyably harmless, some dubious and some, notably hole-in-the-corner brothels, much to be discouraged. They were the fount of disease.

'A pass, sir?' said Daniel. 'Well, I can't rightly say I've got a signed chit.'

'You're absent without leave, you mean,' said Captain Burnett, as gimlet-eyed as the regimental sergeant major.

'Due to circumstances, sir,' said Daniel, as fine a military figure as the officer himself.

'What circumstances?' asked Captain Burnett, glancing at Maisie several yards away.

'Well, very confidential like, sir,' said Daniel, at twenty-one an old hand in such matters as this one, 'I'm in love.'

'You're what?' Captain Burnett's searching eyes looked ready to pop with disbelief. He glanced at Maisie again, who was hoping Daniel wasn't in trouble.

'Yes, that's her, sir, that's me young lady.'

'Good God, thought you were set on winning medals, not a wench,' said Captain Burnett.

'Well, sir, it's me serious belief that medals can take second place at a certain time in a man's life,' said Daniel.

Captain Burnett, a martinet but not an unimaginative one, showed the hint of a smile.

'Damn me, this is your certain time, is it, Corporal Adams?' he said. 'Very well, you're excused, but only if you're back in barracks by five. Right, off you go then, don't keep your lovelight waiting.'

'Much obliged, sir,' said Daniel. He saluted once more and returned to Maisie. Captain Burnett, after a final glance at the attractive young lady in the primrose dress and boater, went on his way, still wearing the hint of a smile. He'd done the same thing himself once when, as a cadet, he'd sneaked out for an hour to meet the young lady who eventually became his wife.

'You're in trouble, I suppose,' said Maisie to Daniel as they resumed their walk. 'Does it mean you'll get punishment?'

'I tell you, Maisie, being shot at dawn is punishment all right,' said Daniel.

'Shot at dawn?' Maisie gaped in shock. 'Oh, me Gawd, what kind of trouble you in, then? You must of sinned something chronic.'

'Only by coming out to meet you,' said Daniel. 'But I've been excused on account of Captain Burnett taking a fancy to you.'

'Well, now I just don't know what's 'appening,' said Maisie, 'but I do know he don't have any right to take a fancy to me.'

'Rightly, I should've said – yes, let's see – that you met with his official approval.' Daniel made the comment with a straight face.

'Oh, I did, did I?' said Maisie, hoity-toity. 'Well, thanks very much, I don't think. Crikey, you soldiers, and officers as well, you've all got the cheek of old Nick 'imself.'

They entered Hyde Park and were greeted by

scenes of Sunday afternoon activity around the Serpentine. They didn't stop, however, they went directly to the tea rooms. Maisie had to be back by four thirty, and Daniel half an hour later. But he had further to go.

Much to their frustration, there was a long queue for tea, and it was hardly moving.

'I don't think we've got time to join the queue, Maisie,' said Daniel.

'Oh, blow,' said Maisie, disappointed, although feeling she shouldn't be.

'Some other time, eh?' said Daniel, also disappointed. He'd been looking forward to what well-educated people would have called a tête-à-tête with this engaging cockney girl. A cockney himself, he reckoned the two of them could suit each other very well, as long as he could persuade her he wasn't after anything that would ruin her respectability. Getting wed, that was it, that was what every respectable young lady wanted.

'We'd best go back to the Gardens,' she said. They'd be nearer then to her place of work and his barracks.

'Yes, let's do that,' said Daniel, and they retraced their steps, still sauntering. Sauntering was more romantic, like, thought Maisie, and then asked herself what was she thinking of?

'I'm losing me sense,' she said to herself, but out loud.

'What's that?' asked Daniel, tempted to put his arm around her slender waist.

'Oh, nothing,' said Maisie.

'Well now, Maisie,' said Daniel, enjoying the colourful spectacle of the Gardens, enhanced by the girls in their Sunday frocks and the ladies in their Sunday finery. And kids in sailor suits. Talk about Old England and Drake's sea dogs. Did Drake ever come to Kensington Palace for a bit of a chinwag with Good Queen Bess? Might have. Anyway, the gardens were just the ticket for a walk with Maisie, as engaging as any other young lady there. 'Tell me about yourself, then.'

'About me?' said Maisie. 'You told me it was going to be about you.'

'Oh, right, me lady,' said Daniel breezily. 'Well, I'm twenty-one, I was born in Camberwell, did me schooling, joined the army as a drummer boy, and I'm now a corporal in C Company of the Royal West Kent 10th Battalion, having served in Africa and won me stripes there. One day I'll be a sergeant. There, that's me life story, so how about yours now?'

'Wait a bit,' said Maisie, 'none of that could mean you're respectable.'

'On me honour,' said Daniel, 'I've only ever been crimed once, and that was when I was a private and got caught helping meself to what didn't belong to me.'

'And what was that?' asked Maisie, trying to tell herself it wasn't actually improper to be seen in company with this soldier. After all, he wasn't one of those that swore like a trooper for people to hear. 'Come on, what was it?'

'A jar of jam from the ration store,' said Daniel, a grin lurking.

'A jar of jam?' said Maisie. 'Well, that wasn't much to get crimed for.'

'You'd think so, wouldn't you?' said Daniel. 'But unfortunate, like, it was the officers' mess ration store. Their jam's always a bit superior, y'know.'

'Well, it didn't ought to be,' said Maisie, 'jam ought to be the same for everyone.'

'You going to tell me about yourself?' said Daniel.

'Oh, all right,' said Maisie, enjoying the saunter and the atmosphere. She was born to her mum and dad in Walworth, she said. Her dad was a railway porter who didn't earn much, except when a toff or two gave him a good tip, so he and her mum were a bit hard up most times. But they gave her lots of love and kindness, and she never really wanted for anything. They brought her up to believe in the Ten Commandments, and to have respect for their neighbours, for old people and for the vicar. Also, her dad was very keen on her being well behaved, and not turning common, like the kind of girls that hung about on street corners with flashy boys.

'I'd gamble on you being a good girl all your life,' said Daniel, highly diverted.

'Bless me soul,' she said, 'you don't suppose I'm going to be a girl all me life, do yer? Girls get to be women, don't you know that?'

'I can rightly say I do,' said Daniel. 'D'you go home to see your mum and dad sometimes?'

'Don't I wish I could,' said Maisie, and sighed a little. 'But me mum passed on several years ago, and last year so did me dear old dad.'

Daniel touched her shoulder.

'Well, I'm truly sorry, that I am,' he said. 'Don't you have any brothers or sisters?'

'No, just meself and me memories,' said Maisie. Not one to go in for self-pity, she added brightly, 'But I do have kind employers and the company of the other servants, so I ain't grumbling.'

'No, you're not,' said Daniel, progressively taken with her. In her neatness, her beliefs and even her primness, she was beyond comparison with giggling little flirts. 'I'd say you're a young lady of spirit, and as for only having other servants for your friends, might I be so bold as to tell you you've got me as well now?'

'Beg pardon?' said Maisie.

'Fact,' declared Daniel.

'Who said?' asked Maisie, tingling again.

'I just did.'

'But I didn't.'

'Well, look at it this way,' said Daniel. 'I'm unattached and you've lost your mum and dad. So it's natural.'

'What's natural?' asked Maisie, aware that passing girls were giving him glances. Well, he really was ever so upstanding in his uniform. 'Come on, what's natural?'

'You and me,' said Daniel.

'D'you mean walking out together?'

'I like that idea, Maisie. D'you like it?'

'How many girls have you said that to?' asked Maisie.

'Just one,' said Daniel.

'I bet,' said Maisie. 'Who's she, then?'

'You,' said Daniel.

Maisie gave him a look. He returned it, half smiling. It came from her then, a little gurgle of laughter.

'You're a bit comical, you are,' she said.

'On me honour, Maisie, I'm dead serious,' said Daniel. They strolled on, chatting away, Maisie now finding it easy to talk to him, and Daniel liking the little rustles from time to time of what was obviously her starched petticoat. Coming to an empty bench, they sat down at Daniel's suggestion, and there they talked some more and watched the people passing by.

Daniel said his battalion would be stationed at Knightsbridge for a decent while, so he'd be able to meet her at least once a week whenever she had time off. Maisie gave that careful thought, then said she supposed meeting him would be all right now that they knew each other properly.

'Mind, don't think I haven't heard about soldiers,' she said.

'You haven't heard about me,' said Daniel.

'Well, no, course I haven't,' said Maisie, 'and if I let you walk out with me, I'll have to trust you.'

'You can trust me, Maisie, I give you me word,'

said Daniel, 'I'm no fly-by-night, I promise you.' His smile made her tingle again. Oh, crikey, she thought, have I met me fate? I can't help liking him, and not just because he's handsome. He's sort of nice and he don't flirt, swear or act common. ·

'Well, I'll take your word for it,' she said.

'Good,' said Daniel, 'you're a fine girl, Maisie. Now I'd better head for the barracks. I don't want to leave you, but any NCO not abiding by an order could lose a stripe, which would make him a cuckoo. Stripes are hard won, y'know.'

'Well, I wouldn't want to be the cause of you losing one,' said Maisie. 'Anyway, it's been nice talking to you, but yes, you'd best get back. Goodbye.'

'Here, hold hard,' said Daniel, 'I'd like to know when we can next meet.'

Maisie hesitated. She was never going to rush into anything, especially what could be a very personal relationship. She would always take her time about important issues. However, she now made up her mind that Corporal Daniel Adams was respectable as well as an upstanding soldier.

'Well, I might just get time off on Wednesday afternoon,' she said.

'In that case,' said Daniel, 'I'll present meself to our company sergeant major, remind him I saved his trousers from being blown off—'

'Oh, go on,' said Maisie.

'Fact,' said Daniel. 'He fell off a parapet when we were fighting in the Sudan. It turned him upside down, and there he was with his legs in the air. The Sudanese had an old cannon, they'd loaded it, and as I jumped down and flattened the sergeant major out, they fired it. So I saved his legs as well as his trousers from being blown off. I'll remind him of that and then ask him for a pass. Next Wednesday afternoon, right, Maisie?'

'You don't think I believe all that stuff, do you?' said Maisie.

'On me Aunt Sally's honour,' said Daniel, but Maisie didn't miss the twinkle in his eyes, a twinkle that reminded her of her dad.

'You and your Aunt Sally, I bet,' she said. 'Still, all right, Wednesday afternoon, then. About two o'clock and just here. Now you'd best go, but don't rush or you might lose yer stripes – they might fall off.'

Daniel, delighted at that, laughed out loud.

'Strike me pink,' he said, 'I like you, Maisie Gibbs, that I do. So long till Wednesday.'

Off he went at a brisk march. Maisie watched his progress for a little while, wondering if her feelings meant anything serious. Then she began her walk back to the grand house in Kensington Gore.

A young man, seated on a bench, followed her with his eyes for several seconds before rising to his feet.

Chapter Six

Alexander came galloping down the stairs just as Maisie opened the door. He looked up over her shoulder in the direction of the Gardens.

''Ere, Maisie,' he said, 'there was a bloke follering you.'

'A soldier?' said Maisie, and turned her head to glance back.

'No, a young geezer in a floppy black hat and a frilly white shirt,' said Alexander. 'I was up in the attic, see, having a spit and a draw—'

'Now you know Mrs Carpenter's forbid you to smoke cigarettes,' said Maisie.

'It was only one of me fag ends,' said Alexander, 'and she wasn't up there with me, anyway.'

'She can smell cigarette smoke,' said Maisie. She was getting a bit motherly towards the house-boy, wanting to do her best to keep the young perisher out of trouble. 'You sure this bloke was following me?'

'I spotted 'im out of the attic winder, didn't I?' said Alexander, standing on the doorstep with her. 'Up there, you can see for a mile. I spotted you first – crikey, you don't half look a picture today, Maisie – and then I saw 'im behind you. He follered you all the way down to the gate, watched you cross the street, then hopped it when you knocked on the door. That's when I come down.'

'He might not have been following me, just doing a walk to the gate,' said Maisie. 'And what would he want to follow me for? Go on, tell me that.'

'Well, ain't I just told you, ain't I just said you don't half look a bit of all right.'

'Here, d'you mind?' said Maisie, very much against being called a bit of all right. If anything was common, that was. 'Just you watch yer tongue, me lad.'

'What I meant was he probably fancied yer,' said Alexander. 'I do meself, don't I?' His grin was sauce personified.

'You'll get your ears boxed in a minute,' said Maisie. 'Can't a girl put her Sunday frock on without little horrors like you talking about her being fancied?'

''Ere, Maisie, don't yer like being fancied, then?' asked Alexander, his head of hair looking like a mop that had been under curlers all night. 'I mean t'say, it's a compliment, ain't it?'

'Never you mind,' said Maisie, as they entered the house. A thought entered her head. Did Corporal Adams fancy her? Seriously, not casual, like? He talked as if he did.

'Let's have some tea,' said Alexander.

Maisie was smiling as they went through to the kitchen. The large pot of tea was on the table, so was a plate on which rested slices of Fanny Blisset's fruit cake. Little Rosemary was sitting up in her high chair and looking rebellious.

'Oh, there you are, Maisie,' said Mrs Blisset. 'See if you can get Rosemary to eat her tea, will you?'

'Yes, course I will, Mrs Blisset,' said Maisie, and sat down beside the child, whose tea consisted of a small dish of bread and warm milk.

'Come on, me pet,' said Maisie, spooning a helping.

Little Rosemary shook her head and burbled something, as if she was to start her speech process.

'There, she don't want it,' said Prudence.

'Still, she ought to have it,' said Agnes.

The child uttered what sounded like a sulky mumble.

'I know what we can do,' said Maisie, and she sugared the bread and milk, then tried again. This time Rosemary slurped it down happily.

Mrs Blisset, pouring tea for everyone, said she didn't want her child to have too much sugar, especially as she was bound to be cutting her teeth in a little while. Prudence said that's right, sugar was bad for new teeth. And for old teeth, said Agnes. Maisie said she didn't think a little a day would hurt Rosemary.

'There, you're a good girl, Maisie, I'm sure you're right,' said Mrs Blisset.

You bet she is, thought Alexander. He was getting fond of Maisie. She was a lot nearer his age than Prudence and the other housemaids, who weren't a very bright lot, anyway. Watching her feed the now happy child, anyone could tell she knew what was best for the infant. She was a born mum, that's what Maisie Gibbs was, and a bit of all right as well.

'What're you grinning about, you boy?' asked Agnes.

'Me?' said Alexander.

'That's him,' said Prudence, 'he doesn't know when he's grinning and when he's not.'

'He's a happy boy, ain't you, Alexander?' said Maisie.

'I don't 'ave nothing to cry about,' said Alexander.

'Well, he's willing, I'll say that much,' said Mrs Blisset. 'Now, I want everyone doing a bit of tidying up in here.'

If Mrs Carpenter was a handsome queen of the household, Mrs Blisset was a pretty queen of the kitchen, although her prettiness was sometimes spoiled by a look of discontent.

A young man, twenty-two, whose appearance was not unlike that of Oscar Wilde in his youth, sat on an old worn sofa in a room on the top floor of a house in Bayswater. He was sketching on the top sheet of a block of drawing paper. The sketch began to take the form of a young woman in a dress and boater.

It was an excellent example of creative talent, although at this stage of his life his aspirations soared a little higher than experienced artists might have said was good for someone not yet conversant with the challenges of painting professionally. Nevertheless, when finished, the sketch was more than commendable, and its subject would have been instantly recognizable to anyone who knew her. Looking at it, his eyes reflected self-satisfaction and pleasure.

He put the sketch block aside, first stripping off the top sheet. He stood up, crossed to his iron bedstead, laid himself down on rumpled blankets and studied the sketch more intently. The light of happy possibilities dawned.

Chapter Seven

Wednesday morning. The weather was fine, a delight to people able to get out and about. Maisie, however, was confined by her duties to four walls. She was dusting and tidying Mr Fairfax's library. The gentleman came in then, his slender figure attired in a black frock coat, grey waistcoat, grey trousers and a grey cravat adorning his white shirt. Well, thought Maisie, he ain't so helpless that he can't dress himself very nice.

'Good morning, Maggie, good morning,' he said, smiling.

'Oh, good morning, sir, but it's Maisie, not Maggie.'

'Maisie, yes, of course, I should know that by now, shouldn't I?' said the charming old gentleman. 'Ah, well, the fault of advancing years, alas. What are you doing?'

'Dusting and cleaning your libr'y, sir,' said Maisie. It was Milly's privilege to attend to his suite and Mrs Carpenter's, but Maisie was occasionally called on to help out. 'I'll be finished in a tick and be out of your way.'

'You're not in my way,' said Mr Fairfax, 'I like to see young people around. Dear me, how busy you are. On a day like this, you should be enjoying the sunshine.'

'Oh, me work comes first, sir,' said Maisie, polishing a large mahogany table.

'Well, that is a very good point,' said Mr Fairfax, 'but you must go out sometime today. Yes, this afternoon. You may take the afternoon off.'

'Oh, that's ever so kind of you, sir,' said Maisie, 'I was going to ask Mrs Carpenter if I could have a few hours off.'

'Free time amounting to a full day off every week is your entitlement,' said Mr Fairfax, running his eye along a shelf of historical tomes, and again Maisie thought the old gentleman wasn't yet in his dotage. 'Yes, on such a fine day as this, young lady, of course you must take the afternoon off.'

'What's that?' Mrs Carpenter had entered the library, her soft black raiment rustling.

'Oh, I was going to ask you, mum, about this afternoon,' said Maisie, who knew the housekeeper governed everything relating to the servants' free times.

'I hope you haven't been worrying Mr Fairfax about that,' said Mrs Carpenter, frowning.

'No, no, of course not,' said Mr Fairfax, selecting a volume, 'let her take the afternoon off, Iris.'

'Have you finished in here, girl?' asked the housekeeper.

'Yes, just finished, mum,' said Maisie.

'Come with me,' said Mrs Carpenter, and Maisie, carrying pail and dusters, left the library with her. The housekeeper halted on the wide landing. 'Maisie, you are not to ask favours of Mr Fairfax, do you hear?'

'Yes, mum, and I didn't, honest,' said Maisie. 'He was just saying what a fine day it was and told me to take the afternoon off.'

'H'm,' said Mrs Carpenter, observing the maid of all work with a critical eye. 'Very well, I believe you. Run along now.'

'Yes'm,' said Maisie. 'Oh, could I have a few hours off this afternoon?'

'Three,' said Mrs Carpenter, 'just three, mind.'

'Thank you, mum,' said Maisie, and went down the staircase with the familiar feeling that the housekeeper liked nobody to get close to Mr Fairfax except herself.

Alexander was one person on the staff who was out in the sunshine. He was hurrying back from the mews after informing the coachman that Mrs Carpenter required the carriage at two thirty this afternoon. Bill Townley, the coachman, had said the old biddy's going shopping, is she? Alexander said he supposed so. Not with her own oof, I bet, said Mr Townley.

'Well, I bet she makes sure there's always a few bob over from the weekly 'ousekeeping,' said Alexander. 'She ain't simple, yer know.'

74

'Nor ain't I,' said Mr Townley. 'Still, I won't say she don't treat me fair and square, and always gives me me wages very punctual.'

'It wouldn't surprise me if she got the old gent to church one day,' said Alexander.

'You still got a lot to learn about Mr Fairfax if you think he'd be that far off his old rocker,' said Mr Townley. 'He's a born gent, a confirmed bach'lor, and she's as common as you and me, me lad, under all them dignified black weeds what she thinks make a lady of her. She knows she'd never get 'im to church. It's his dibs she's after, not his bed.'

'Ta for all that info,' grinned Alexander, 'but I can't stand about, I got to get back to let her know I've give you her orders about this afternoon. Get the gee-gees polished.' And away he went.

It was on his way back that he ran into the bloke he'd seen following Maisie, a young pale-faced man wearing a black floppy hat, a white shirt with a silk scarf tied around the neck and drainpipe trousers. Talk about looking . . . what was it, now? Someone might have told him the word he was searching for was Bohemian, but that wasn't yet in his vocabulary.

'Boy,' said the bloke, 'kindly do me a favour.'

'Eh?' said Alexander.

'I'll give you tuppence.'

'Now yer talking,' said Alexander. 'What favour?'

'There's a young lady who works in the same

house as you. She has a primrose frock and wears it with a boater.'

'What, our Maisie Gibbs?' said Alexander. ''Ere, wait a tick, 'ow'd yer know where I work?'

'I've seen you.'

'You've seen our Maisie as well, ain't yer?' said Alexander. 'I saw yer on 'er tail once.'

'I don't dispute that,' said the young Bohemian. 'I want you to give her a letter. Here.' He produced it in a plain white envelope. Alexander regarded it suspiciously. 'There's nothing wrong with it, boy, it's a very polite missive, you can believe me. Kindly give it to her.'

'Where's me tuppence?' asked Alexander.

Given the two pennies, he took the letter, promised to deliver it and resumed his hurried return to the house. He went up to the first floor and informed Mrs Carpenter that the carriage, as was required, like, would be outside at two thirty punctual.

'You took your time,' said Mrs Carpenter.

'Well, yer see, mum, a poor old lady 'ad a fall just outside the mews, and I 'ad to stop and help 'er to her feet and brush 'er down. She's all right, though, just a bit shook up.'

'A likely story,' said Mrs Carpenter.

'Honest Injun, mum,' said Alexander.

'Very well, get back to your work.'

Alexander wasn't in favour of work at this exact moment. He knew it would be something like helping Prudence to peel potatoes. So he went to find Maisie. He located her down in the basement, where she was making up Fanny Blisset's bed. That was one of her more recent daily jobs, ordered by Mrs Carpenter on the grounds that the cook was always far too busy to do it herself, especially as she had a baby to look after. Maisie might have said the cook didn't look after it all that much, but she kept quiet, of course, while wondering where Mrs Blisset's husband was.

''Ere, Maisie, I got a letter for yer,' said Alexander.

'A letter?' said Maisie, and thought at once of Corporal Daniel Adams, and that perhaps he'd written to say he wouldn't be meeting her this afternoon. 'Give it me.'

'It's from that bloke that follered yer one day,' said Alexander, handing the letter over.

'I don't believe yer,' said Maisie, 'I never saw the bloke, and I don't know him and he don't know me, and what're you grinning about, might I ask?'

'Well, I tell yer, Maisie, he asked very civil, like, for me to give it to yer,' said Alexander. 'What's he say?'

'None of yer business,' said Maisie, and out of curiosity she opened the letter and read it.

Dear Miss,
    Forgive me for writing to you, but I've seen you about and am much impressed. My name is Hubert Smythe, my connections excellent, and I'm an artist. I hope you won't think me

impertinent, but I would very much like you to sit for me, since I'm desirous of painting a full-length portrait of you. I will happily pay you five shillings an hour. My address is as above and I'm in earnest hope of hearing favourably from you.

Yours most truly, Hubert Smythe.

Maisie blushed to her roots.

'Oh, what a blessed cheek, what impudence,' she breathed.

''Ere, come on, Maisie, what's it say, then?' asked Alexander eagerly.

'I can't hardly believe it,' said Maisie, and Alexander took the letter from her nerveless hand and digested its contents for himself.

'Oh, gorblimey,' he said, 'ain't it scandalous? Wanting you to pose for 'im, like for one of them Chelsea artists that paint females in their birfday suits. Crikey, I wouldn't 'ave brought it if I'd known, not even for five bob on top of tuppence. 'Ere Maisie, you ain't half gorn red.'

'Oh, I never read anything more saucy,' breathed Maisie, who had taken it for granted, as Alexander had, that the proposition meant taking off all her clothes and sitting for hours just as God made her. 'Fancy this bloke that I've never seen nor met sending me a letter like this. I could faint, I could, and what me mum and dad would of said, well, I bet they're turning in their graves this very minute. You Alexander, you

78

beastly boy, what d'you mean by letting this bloke give it to you?'

'Maisie, I didn't know what was in it,' protested Alexander, who had lost his grin for once. 'He went and told me it was a very polite letter, so I thought it might just be about inviting you to meet 'im sometime.'

'Well, it ain't, is it?' said Maisie. 'It's scandalous.'

'Yerse, I said that meself, didn't I?' remarked Alexander. 'Tell yer what, Maisie, you could take it to the police station and show it to the flatties, I bet they'd go and arrest the bloke.'

'D'you think I want to show this 'orrible letter to anyone else?' said Maisie. 'They might think I've been flaunting meself in the park and inviting looks from blokes that call themselves artists. No, I ain't showing this letter to no-one else, I'm going to burn it, and next time you see that walking impudence on two legs, hit him with a brick.'

'Well, I dunno about that, Maisie, a brick can do a bit of damage and land the feller in 'ospital and me in clink,' said Alexander. He had a thought, and his grin came back. 'Mind, there's one thing that ain't too scandalous.'

'And what's that?' asked Maisie, recovering a bit, although she was still fairly high on umbrage.

'Five bob an hour,' said Alexander.

'Oh, yer little wretch,' yelled Maisie, 'I'm going to box your ears!'

Alexander didn't wait for that, he escaped at a gallop. From the kitchen, a voice shouted.

'You Alexander, you boy, you come and help peel the taters, you hear?' It was Prudence.

'Coming,' called Alexander, and made his way to the kitchen, where a large bowl of potatoes greeted his resigned eyes.

'Where've you been?' demanded Mrs Blisset.

'Helping Maisie.'

'She doesn't need any help making a bed,' said Mrs Blisset, her looks marred by irritation. 'Before you start on the potatoes, go down and tell her to come up here. Tell her I want her to take my infant off my hands for a while.' Baby Rosemary was grizzling in her cot. She wanted to be lifted out and to test her fat little legs.

Alexander delivered the message, and Maisie arrived. She saw to the fractious child, who stopped making a fuss as soon as she was lifted out and helped by Maisie to toddle around the kitchen. She cooed, her legs unsteady but determined. She was a year old now.

'Oh, you're good with her, Maisie,' said Agnes, and Maisie thought the infant only needed a little attention now and again.

Alexander opened his mouth to deliver a scandalous titbit, that which was contained in the letter to Maisie. However, he thought better of it just in time, and shut his mouth. He liked Maisie too much to embarrass her and make her blush beetroot red again. So he sat down and began peeling the potatoes, grinning to himself. Crikey, Maisie being invited to pose in the altogether at five bob an hour. What a yell, she being such a proper young madam and all. Still, he admired her for turning it down and showing she wasn't like some of them tarty girls that disappeared into dark alleys with soldiers at night. He'd bet they'd do it for a bob an hour.

Chapter Eight

That afternoon it was still warm and sunny, but clouds were building up in the west, threatening to sail up to London and deposit heavy rain on its citizens. July often behaved as if it disliked its place in the calendar, and would have preferred to be close to April, sharing its quirks and showers, instead of existing in the middle of summer.

In the barracks at Knightsbridge, Company Sergeant Major Albert Sawyer addressed Corporal Daniel Adams.

'Corporal Adams, what's going on?' he enquired, handing over a signed pass.

'Nothing you might call detrimental, Sarn't Major,' said Daniel, smartly turned out, his boots gleaming, his moustache faultless.

'I've been hearing things,' said the sergeant major.

'Things are always flying about in barracks, y'know,' said Daniel.

'Like you're courting?'

'That's one of the things, Sarn't Major.'

'If you're aiming to get wed, Corporal Adams, you'll have to talk to the colonel. It's custom'ry.'

'If he asks, Sarn't Major, would yer let him know it won't be tomorrow?'

'Impertinence, Corporal Adams, impertinence. Get marching, then. And that pass runs out at five per the clock.'

'Much obliged,' said Daniel, and off he went in the hope of meeting Maisie Gibbs, a highly respectable young lady, towards whom his intentions were honourable.

When he reached the arranged spot, he halted and waited. There weren't as many people around as on Sundays, but there were nurse-maids, as usual, and servant girls enjoying time off, as well as ladies and gentlemen of leisure. Girls passed by, some aloof and some casting saucy eyes at him. Most people took no notice of his presence. Soldiers in the parks and gardens of Kensington or Knightsbridge were ten a penny. Come to that, so were off-duty servant girls.

Corporal Daniel Adams was oblivious to any girl but one. She appeared, dressed in her primrose frock and boater, the perky tilt of the boater at odds with her prim, straight-backed walk.

Daniel stepped forward to meet her. Maisie stopped. They looked at each other. Grey eyes met brown. Daniel felt that here was his one and only. Maisie simply tingled. Oh, crikey, she said to herself, what's coming over me?

'Hello, Maisie,' said Daniel.

'Hello, soldier,' said Maisie, a little breathless.

'You're a picture, that you are,' said Daniel with feeling. Some people might have said she hardly compared with Helen of Troy, but to Daniel her looks were distinctly pleasing, her manner equally so. And he found her primness intriguing, just as much as her insistence on self-respect. He would bet that as a wife, she would be faithful, loyal and steadfast. His growing affection for her carried his thoughts as far as that. In fact, such thoughts had entered his mind when he first met her. 'Shall we take a stroll?' he asked.

'Look, there's an empty bench, we can sit down for a bit,' said Maisie, feeling wobbly at the knees, which she never had before.

'Come on, then,' said Daniel, and they walked to the bench. He heard the whisper and rustle of petticoats. Real fetching, that was. They seated themselves. 'How are you, Maisie, how's life treating you in your work?'

'Oh, me work's a pleasure,' said Maisie, 'it keeps me busy, and I like being busy.'

'Are you the parlourmaid, or a general maid?' asked Daniel, smiling. Maisie thought he had the kind of smile that could weaken a girl and put her at risk.

'Oh, I'm just the maid of all work,' she said.

'Well, does anything exciting happen in that grand house you work in?' asked Daniel, wanting to know more about her daily life.

'Exciting?' said Maisie. 'Crikey, no, the housekeeper don't allow nothing exciting or disgraceful to take place . . . Oh, there was—' She stopped, checking the impulse to tell him about a scandalous letter she had received from a bloke she'd never met and never even seen.

'What?' said Daniel.

'What?' said Maisie, forgetting her manners.

'Yes, there was what?' said Daniel.

'Oh, nothing really,' said Maisie, pinking slightly.

'Maisie?' said Daniel, noticing her slight flush.

'Ain't it a lovely day?' said Maisie, observing the strolling people. 'It looks as if everyone's come out for the afternoon, and it's only Wednesday, not Sunday.'

'Never mind everyone,' said Daniel, 'it's just you and me as far as I'm concerned. I think you've got something you'd like to tell me.'

'Not much I don't,' said Maisie, 'it's . . . it's . . .' She stopped again, wondering why she hadn't burned that letter, after all, and why she had it with her, in her reticule, which she'd fashioned herself from embroidered cotton and a white cord drawstring. Handbags, a recent innovation for ladies, were now available in shops, but not affordable to her. She saved what she could out of her weekly wage of six shillings, but although her uniforms and her board and lodging were free, there were always things she needed to buy for herself, such as underwear and other personal items. Her savings she stowed away with her modest possessions in an old brass-mounted portmanteau that had belonged to her parents. She kept that under her bed. 'It's private.'

'In what way?' asked Daniel. 'Don't tell me the butler's been chasing you.'

'Oh, we don't have no butler,' said Maisie. 'Mr Fairfax, me employer that's a nice old gentleman, don't need one. He's got a housekeeper.'

'Come on, Maisie, I know you've got something on your mind,' said Daniel, hoping that whatever it was, it wasn't serious. Such a nice young lady didn't deserve to have worries.

'No, it's nothing,' said Maisie, at which point women and girls began to shriek and to run, escorts sweeping some young ladies aside from the rapid advance of a crazed dog. Dogs were not allowed in any of the royal parks, but this one had obviously broken free of its owner somewhere to charge into Kensington Gardens. Like a young bull seeing the red of Daniel's jacket, it was making straight for the bench on which he was sitting with Maisie. It was snarling, lips drawn back, teeth savagely gleaming, white foam spraying from its open mouth.

Maisie shrieked. Daniel sprang to his feet and placed himself in front of her. People watched in horror as the sick dog leapt at the soldier. Daniel, every defensive instinct at a peak, reacted lightning-fast. He aimed a huge kick, and the toe of his gleaming black boot caught the animal forcefully under its throat in mid-air. The blow seemed to paralyse it. It fell like a fur-covered log.

People crept slowly forward, staring at the fallen dog, which lay on its side, exposing its foam-flecked mouth. Its limbs shivered.

'Kill it!' shouted a young man. 'It's diseased, it's got rabies!'

'Oh, me Gawd,' breathed Maisie. She stood up and put herself beside Daniel. Together they looked down at the stricken animal. 'Daniel – ' For the first time she spoke his name. She swallowed. 'Oh, I never saw anything more 'orrible than that charging dog, nor anyone act as quick as you did. But look at the poor thing now, it looks like it's going to die.'

'It has to, Maisie, one way or another,' said Daniel, 'it's infected. It's got rabies, and there's no cure for that. And the disease is contagious, so don't try to touch it.'

'I ain't thinking of doing that,' said Maisie.

The creeping people now formed a crowded circle around bench, dog, soldier and servant girl. Mothers, however, stood well off, keeping their children close to their skirts.

The young man spoke again.

'Someone shoot the beast.'

'Oh, I'll do that if it'll please yer,' said an off-duty postman in sarky fashion, 'only I ain't carrying me blunderbuss, and me old lady 'ere don't 'ave one.'

'Don't that dog look 'orrid?' said his old lady.

'Stamp on its head,' suggested a toff. 'Put it out of its misery.'

'No-one should touch it,' said Daniel, 'nor any animal that's got rabies. Rabies means keep yer distance.' He had come across such infected dogs overseas, in countries where nothing was done about preventing the onset of the disease. The army shot the animals out of hand. In Britain, inoculation had been successful, but there was still the occasional case, mostly affecting a dog that had been allowed to roam far and wide, which subjected it to deadly bites from creatures such as rats and bats. Daniel knew all this. He carried books for reading and learning in his kitbag, wherever he was, and he was also an observant man.

'I say, here's the law,' said the young man.

A constable came hurrying up, accompanied by a boy who, on school holiday with a friend, had rushed to inform the bobby of the incident concerning a foaming dog.

'Now, kindly stand aside, ladies and gents,' said the officer, pushing his way through. He advanced to the spot. 'Stand back, Corporal,' he said to Daniel, and to Maisie, 'Stand back, miss. That animal's still showing foam, which is highly infectious. Who crippled it?'

'This soldier gentleman,' said Maisie, not without a little note of pride, and forthwith explained all that had happened.

'Well, good for you, Corporal,' said the constable, 'I might have broken the hundred-yards sprint record meself. Hundred yards, that's as near as anyone should get to a dog with rabies.

Anyway, you can leave it to me now. I've sent that boy's friend to inform me station sergeant.'

'And then what?' asked Daniel.

'Suitable action,' said the constable. 'A bullet and a sack, gloves for handling, and a removal cart.'

'Good enough,' said Daniel, 'I'll leave you to it. Shall we go, Maisie?'

'If me legs'll carry me,' said Maisie. 'Crikey, I nearly died a death.'

'Come on,' said Daniel, and they left. As they made their way through the crowd, some people clapped. A man slapped Daniel on his shoulder.

'Well done, Corporal.'

Maisie went pink with pride for him.

'Daniel, I feel ever so proud of you,' she said impulsively.

'I feel bloody relieved my boot connected . . . I mean – er – sorry about me French, Maisie,' said Daniel.

'Oh, I've heard a lot worse in me Walworth days,' said Maisie, 'and I can forgive yer for that word.'

The young man who had urged Daniel to kill the stricken animal watched them go. He saw the soldier take the hand of the young lady. He looked a bit of a Bohemian in his floppy black hat, white shirt, loose blue cravat and black drainpipe trousers. His eyes were warm with admiration, though not necessarily for the young lady's soldier companion.

*　　*　　*

Maisie and Daniel walked through to Hyde Park, and this time there was no queue at the tea rooms, so they were able to enjoy a leisurely interval for refreshments. Maisie sat very upright in her chair, for although she was practical rather than shy, she felt self-conscious about the fact that this was the first time she'd been in what she thought of as a restaurant. She'd been in fried-fish and chip shops that had tables for customers who ate on the premises, but didn't see them as restaurants, Here, there was a waitress service.

Up came one, young and pert-looking. She eyed Daniel with interest. His helmet was off, placed on a spare chair, and his dark hair, thick, springy and without a parting, showed a widow's peak.

'Hello, soldier, what can I get you?' The question was accompanied by a saucy glance.

'Kind of you to ask,' said Daniel, at home in any environment. 'How about a pot of tea and some sliced fruit cake?'

'Oh, me pleasure, Captain, I'm sure,' said the waitress, scribbling on her pad.

'What's the idea of promoting me?' asked Daniel with a broad grin.

'Well, if you're not a captain, you ought to be,' said the waitress, and skipped off with the order.

'Well,' said Maisie, 'what a saucy minx.'

'Friendly,' said Daniel.

'She was making eyes at you,' said Maisie.

'She's after a tip,' said Daniel.

'After you, more like,' said Maisie.

'Blow my stripes, d'you think so, Maisie?' Daniel was all good humour. 'Well, I'm not up for the privilege, I'm what you call already committed.'

'Who to?' asked Maisie, avoiding his eyes.

'You don't have to ask that,' said Daniel.

'Yes, I do.'

'No, you don't.'

'Oh, well,' said Maisie, 'now that we know each other more, I suppose it's all right to meet reg'lar.'

'I'm all in favour of reg'lar,' said Daniel, amid the happy sounds of people enjoying afternoon tea.

'Well, don't fall over yerself,' said Maisie, whose natural reservations were still making her react cautiously to Daniel's overtures. At the same time, little vibrations and new feelings weren't doing those reservations any good. They were suffering all kinds of dents. And the incident with the diseased dog had made her regard Daniel as truly heroic. Oh, me heartbeats, she thought, they were going nineteen to the dozen when he was dealing with that poor animal. She asked herself a now familiar question: What's coming over me?

'Penny for yer thoughts, Maisie,' said Daniel.

'Oh, I was thinking ain't it nice in here?' said Maisie. 'It's nearly posh.'

'It's not as posh as your primrose frock,' said Daniel.

'Oh, me frock's not posh, not like ladies' Sunday hats and gents' top hats,' said Maisie.

The waitress returned with a laden tray.

'Here we are, me lord,' she said, and began placing the tea items on the table.

'Now I've jumped from captain to Lord Muck, have I?' said Daniel.

'With me compliments,' replied the waitress, lashes fluttering.

Maisie then said, in as posh a voice as she could summon up, 'Excuse me, but d'you mind not being familiar with me young man?'

'Oh, beg your pardon, miss, I'm sure,' said the waitress, 'it's just that we try to be pleasant to all our customers, like.'

'Kindly go away,' said Maisie.

'Well, really,' said the waitress, but departed with her tray and a muffled giggle. Daniel regarded Maisie as if she'd turned into a music-hall comic. His smile was broad.

'Might I ask why you're grinning?' she said.

'What a performance,' said Daniel. Maisie put her nose in the air. 'Now play mother,' he said.

'That waitress is common,' said Maisie, but she milked the cups and poured the tea, all with very neat turns of her wrist.

'So I'm your young man, am I?' smiled Daniel.

'Listen, I only said that to stop her acting familiar,' Maisie told him.

'It stopped her all right,' said Daniel, 'but personally it tickled me no end.'

Maisie, in a bit of a fluster, opted for the only retort she could think of.

'Oh, that's why you're grinning, is it?'

'You're an original, Maisie, that you are,' said Daniel, and bit into his slice of fruit cake.

'What's that mean?' asked Maisie.

'You're one on your own,' said Daniel, 'which I mention as a compliment.'

'Oh, well,' said Maisie, and a little smile twitched her lips. 'Oh, well,' she said again, 'you're not so bad yourself.'

'I promise you,' said Daniel.

They drank their tea, ate their cake, and as Maisie was refilling their cups, she said in a thoughtful way, 'Daniel?'

'Well, Maisie?'

'I don't mind meeting you reg'lar, I get time off every week, and I think I could be in the Gardens every Wednesday and Sunday afternoon.'

'I like that prospect, Maisie, not half I don't.'

'It won't matter if sometimes you can't get a pass, I'll understand.'

'I'll get my passes, Maisie, the battalion's being allowed to take it easy after our time in Africa, which was a bit hot in more ways than one,' said Daniel. 'If I can't get a pass, I'll be minded to make one out for meself.'

'Daniel Adams, don't you do nothing as silly as that,' said Maisie. 'I don't want you getting into trouble.'

'I'm hearing you, Maisie.'

'Especially not on my account,' said Maisie.

'I won't,' said Daniel.

'It won't make me admire you if you do.'

'I think you admire common sense,' said Daniel, which Maisie did. At least, she had more respect for it than for foolish bravado.

The waitress brought their bill a little later. Daniel took it, looked at it, passed it as fair and square and gave the waitress a silver threepenny bit as a tip. It made her go away happily. Maisie said that was too much, a penny or tuppence would have been enough. Daniel said the occasion having been special, it was only right to fork out handsome, like.

He paid the bill at the desk, and they left. It was time to think of returning to their respective quarters, anyway, and they parted at the point where Hyde Park joined Kensington Gardens.

'So long, Maisie, I'll look out for you on Sunday afternoon, then?'

'Yes, all right, Daniel. Oh, and thanks for me tea and cake.' A pause. 'And for being ever so brave about that dog.'

'Don't thank me, Maisie, thank my boot.'

'Still, not every feller's boot would've faced up to it like yours did. Goodbye, Daniel.'

Daniel smiled as he watched her go. Proper young Maisie had come up with a witty comment.

Chapter Nine

Alexander opened the door as soon as Maisie descended the steps. His perpetual grin was touched with excitement.

'I saw yer coming, Maisie,' he said.

'That nose of yours, you've always got it up against one window or another,' said Maisie. 'You'll flatten it one day and it'll stay flat.'

'Course it won't,' said Alexander, stepping aside to let her walk in. 'Will it?'

'Squashed, that's what'll happen to it,' said Maisie.

'It's only boxers that get squashed noses,' said Alexander.

'And nosy boys,' said Maisie.

''Ere, Maisie, what d'yer think? That funny bloke knocked and give me another letter for you. He said he saw you in the gardens with a soldier, and the soldier done in a dog that 'ad got foaming rabies. Is that right, Maisie?'

'Yes, that's right,' said Maisie, the sounds of the house a kind of peaceful hum. 'Listen, what d'you mean, the bloke gave you another letter for me?'

'Honest,' said Alexander. 'I tell yer, he came right up to the front door and knocked on it, bold as brass. I answered it and there he was, on the doorstep. "Good afternoon, sonny," he says, "we meet again, I see, so be good enough to give this 'ere letter to Miss Gibbs."'

'You shouldn't of took it,' said Maisie crossly.

Alexander, whose scruples had been overcome by another tuppence, said, 'I did tell 'im you wasn't best pleased with 'is first letter, and he told me to let you know 'is intentions was – let's see – yes, sort of hon'rable.' The actual words had been 'purely professional and without ulterior motive'.

'I ain't falling for hon'rable,' said Maisie. 'Have you got the letter?'

"Ere.' The houseboy dragged an envelope from his pocket. It looked a bit creased. Maisie regarded it with distaste.

'I just don't know how he had the sauce to call,' she said, 'and I don't want another letter from him.' She took it, all the same, and went down to her room in the basement. She still had several minutes to spare before she needed to change into her uniform and report her return. Alexander followed like a faithful puppy. She slit the envelope and extracted the letter. She read it, with Alexander trying to get an uninvited peep at its contents.

Dear Miss Gibbs,

I had the pleasure of seeing you this afternoon, in company with a very gallant soldier. I was very impressed with his bravery, but as an artist, I am still much more impressed with you. Your carriage is as excellent as that of a duchess, and I see you as the perfect example of a proud feminine subject of our Glorious Queen. I confess I'm waiting with hope and a prayer to hear from you in regard to my earnest desire to paint you. I've decided it must be in oils. Watercolour is not for you, no, indeed not. With respect, may I request an answer?

I am your inspired admirer, Hubert Smythe.

PS. Perhaps we could meet for a mutually happy discussion?

'Well,' breathed Maisie, flushed with new umbrage, 'if I ever did meet 'im, I'd forget all me manners and box his ears.'

'What's he say, then? Give us a look, Maisie, eh?' said Alexander, his grin expectant of more scandalous stuff.

'Not now,' said Maisie, cooling down a little, 'I've got to change and report me return to Mrs Carpenter.'

'That reminds me,' said Alexander, 'the old biddy wanted to see you soon as you got back.'

'Well, all right,' said Maisie, 'I'll have to get changed straightaway.'

'Would yer like some 'elp?' suggested Alexander, and left at the double as Maisie looked for something to chuck at him.

*　　　*　　　*

'You're back, then,' said Mrs Carpenter, coming out of her suite to eye Maisie in her critical way.

'Yes, mum,' said Maisie, a picture of willing obedience to the rules the housekeeper laid down.

'I want you to trim Mr Fairfax's hair. His personal barber is unwell and can't attend him for a while. I understand you've a talent for hairdressing.'

'Oh, not professional, like, but I can do trimming, mum,' said Maisie. Her mother had had the talent, and had seen to her husband's and daughter's hair to save paying professionals. She had taught Maisie.

'Mr Fairfax is fretting about his hair,' said Mrs Carpenter. 'Do you have the right kind of scissors and comb?'

'Yes'm, and I've seen to Alexander's hair more than once,' said Maisie.

'That boy has got a head like a thatched roof,' said Mrs Carpenter, 'but I've noted recently that it does look tidier at times. You're a good girl, Maisie, and I'm sure Mr Fairfax will give you sixpence for a nice trim. You can do it now.'

'Oh, I'll get me scissors and comb,' said Maisie, delighted at the prospect of earning a whole tanner, and down she went, returning a minute later with comb, scissors, brush, hand mirror and a towel. Entering Mr Fairfax's suite through the open door, she heard Mrs Carpenter talking to him in his living room, so she knocked. 'It's me, mum.'

It was Mr Fairfax who answered.

'Come in, come in, young lady.'

Maisie went in. Mr Fairfax was seated on an upright chair, Mrs Carpenter standing beside him, and Maisie had an impression of a black-clad attendant standing guard over the silver-haired old gentleman.

'Here I am, sir,' said Maisie.

'Charming,' smiled Mr Fairfax, 'charming. See, I'm here too and quite ready. Do forgive me for allowing my hair to turn into a bush.' His abundant hair was a mane that suited his features, and was much admired by Maisie and the rest of the staff.

'Oh, it ain't so bad at all, sir, and only needs a trim,' said Maisie, placing her barbering items on a nearby table, 'not like a short back and sides that some men have.'

'Such as soldiers?' said Mrs Carpenter,

'Some soldiers, I suppose, mum,' said Maisie, thinking that Daniel had a real handsome head of hair which didn't ought to be spoiled by a short back and sides look, although she'd heard that when soldiers were campaigning, their regimental barbers cropped them very short.

'Well, I'll leave you to it,' said Mrs Carpenter. Oh, good, thought Maisie, who didn't want the housekeeper standing guard over her. 'Be careful how you use the scissors, girl.'

'Fuss, fuss,' said Mr Fairfax, and actually winked at Maisie as Mrs Carpenter left. 'Dear me, Maisie, one would think I'm even older than I am.'

'You ain't that old, sir,' said Maisie, wrapping the towel around his neck and shoulders. She knew by now that his look of fragility was deceptive, that he could be an active old gent when searching his library shelves for books. 'Why, I never knew no-one more lively.'

'Ah, well, Maisie, perhaps this is the age of my second youth,' said Mr Fairfax, and Maisie, behind him, began to use the comb and scissors with deft neatness. Little clippings of white hair fell on the towel. 'Who knows, mmm?' he said.

'You'll be going dancing one day,' said Maisie, her scissors working to define a shelving smoothness to the back of his mane.

'Young lady, do you go dancing?' asked Mr Fairfax, relaxing to the comforting feel of scissors and comb.

'Oh, not since I was a young girl and there was dances at our church hall in Walworth,' said Maisie. 'St John's Institute, that's what it was called. It was in Larcom Street.'

'Alas, unknown to me,' said Mr Fairfax. 'But then, many things are unknown to most of us. Indeed, my dear young lady, if I ever come face to face with someone who knows everything, I will assuredly be looking at God Himself.'

'Lor', sir,' said Maisie, 'don't it say somewhere that anyone that sees the face of God is struck down by lightning and thunderbolts?'

'Does it?' murmured Mr Fairfax. 'Perhaps it does, but there, that's something else I don't know. Tell me, did you enjoy your afternoon off?'

'Ever so much,' said Maisie, snipping away. 'Crikey, sir, what d'you think 'appened?'

'Tell me,' said the kind old gentleman, and Maisie recounted the story of the mad dog. Mr Fairfax said it was a brave man who could stand up to the charge of a diseased dog foaming at the mouth. Was the soldier her young man?

Maisie, cautious, said, 'Oh, he's just a friend, sir.'

'Well, we should all have friends, Maisie, but not those who fuss too much, eh?'

'I expect they sometimes mean well, sir,' said Maisie, thinking he had Mrs Carpenter in mind. Well, Prudence and Agnes said she was taking such kind care of him that she was hardly ever out of his suite. Alexander had whispered to Maisie that he hoped the old biddy's kindness wouldn't do the old gent in.

Satisfied that she had trimmed her employer's mane very nicely, she did the same to his sideboards. Had they grown longer, they would have resembled the bushy mutton-chop whiskers sported by the Austrian Emperor, whose photograph she'd seen in newspapers.

Very relaxed, Mr Fairfax murmured, 'How pleasant.'

'Yes, I used to like me mum doing me own hair,' said Maisie. 'It made me feel sort of dreamy.' She snipped away, taking a look every so often, then said, 'Shall I give it a brush now, sir?'

'How kind,' said Mr Fairfax.

Maisie put her scissors and comb back on the table, and reached for the hairbrush. At a little distance she noticed an open document, lying across a long brown envelope. Printed words in script style leapt to her eye. 'Last Will and Testament'. Crikey, she thought, what's he been doing with his will? It was full up with words. She was sure he hadn't meant to leave it lying about for anyone to see. However, she said nothing, feeling it wasn't her business. She took up the brush and applied it to Mr Fairfax's hair. He sighed contentedly.

'There, sir, all done,' she said, and picked up the hand mirror. This time she spotted a sheet of notepaper lying near the will. There were scribbles on it. Oh, he's been altering his last testament, she thought. I hope that don't mean he's going to pass on soon, he's such a nice, kind gentleman, and we'd all get the sack. 'Here we are, sir, you can look now.' She gave him the mirror, and he examined the reflection of his silvery mane.

'Splendid, Maisie, splendid. That will do very well, yes, indeed. You have tidied me up with charm and efficiency.' His gentle smile arrived. 'Thank you.'

'I'm pleased you like it, sir.'

Maisie removed the towel, folding it to keep the fallen wisps contained. Mr Fairfax came to his feet, slipped a hand into his trouser pocket, and came up with a shilling.

'There,' he said.

'A shilling, sir, a shilling?' Maisie was overwhelmed. It was more than any barber would charge for a trim, except the West End barbers, of course. She'd heard they could charge posh gentlemen as much as five shillings. 'That's too much, sir, ain't it?'

'Not for such excellent service, Maisie. There, run along now. Supper will be served in a few minutes, I fancy.'

'Thank you ever so much, sir,' said Maisie. Gathering up her implements, she executed a little bob and left. Going down the staircase, she met Mrs Carpenter coming up, a laden supper tray, covered by a snowy white cloth, in her hands.

'You've finished, girl?'

'Yes'm, and Mr Fairfax said it was fine.'

'Good, but I hope you didn't worry him with a lot of gossip.'

'Oh, no, mum, nothing like that. Me dad always said gossip was the pastime of the idle rich, and I've never been idle, mum, nor rich.'

'Well, at least you're not short of a tongue,' said Mrs Carpenter, but not unkindly.

Then servant girl and housekeeper each went her own way.

Wait till she finds out Mr Fairfax has left his will lying about, thought Maisie. She won't like it that I might have nosed into it, which I didn't and which I wouldn't.

*   *   *

'Really,' said Mrs Carpenter to Mr Fairfax on a chiding note, 'how careless of you to have left your will on the living-room table for everyone to see.'

She was seated at his dining-room table, their suppers in front of them.

'Hardly everyone, my dear lady,' said Mr Fairfax, enjoying roast lamb.

'I hope the girl Maisie didn't read it.'

'Maisie attended only to my hair. What a pleasant girl she is.'

'Well, it was partly my fault that the will was left on the table. I should have reminded you about it.' Mrs Carpenter shook her head at her omission. 'But I must say it's a great kindness of yours to increase the bequests to the staff. Are you sure they should each have a hundred pounds?'

'One must show one's appreciation of faithful service, Iris.' Mr Fairfax spoke in benevolent fashion.

'Well, we must arrange for your solicitor to call.'

'Such a fussy man, yes, indeed, but very helpful. Oh, by the way, I must include young Maisie among the beneficiaries. Yes, I must.'

'But she's only been on the staff for a few months,' said the housekeeper.

'Nevertheless, I shall include her.'

'Very well,' said Mrs Carpenter.

*   *   *

Down in her basement room, Maisie's thoughts returned to the second letter from that scandalous beast, Hubert Smythe. He'd actually suggested a meeting so he could discuss things with her. She couldn't think of anything more shameful than letting any bloke talk to her about taking her clothes off so's he could paint a picture of her in the altogether. Imagine him putting the painting on the wall of one of London's picture galleries for everyone to see.

I'd just die.

What I ought to do, she told herself, is send Alexander round to his address to set fire to his house and all his paints.

That would learn him to respect a girl.

Chapter Ten

Over supper the servants talked to Maisie about her giving Mr Fairfax a haircut. Everyone thought that could mean promotion, everyone, that is, except Mrs Blisset, who said no-one was going to get promoted just for doing one haircut. There wouldn't be a second time, she said, because Mr Fairfax's professional barber would be calling again when he was better.

Agnes didn't think much of that ungracious remark, considering how often Maisie attended to the wants of little Rosemary. The child was now sleeping in her cot in Mrs Blisset's room, and it was Maisie who'd seen to that, with the help of Alexander, who'd carried the cot there.

'Oh, I wasn't supposing Mr Fairfax would want me services any more,' said Maisie, keeping quiet about the shilling reward.

'Me, I appreciate you giving me haircuts,' said Alexander, chewing away at his supper.

'I wish you wouldn't speak with your mouth full,' said Mrs Blisset who, on account of being blessed with pretty looks, and also being in the good graces of Mrs Carpenter, had no right in Alexander's eyes to be complaining.

Swallowing, he said, 'It ain't full now.'

'That's a change,' said Prudence.

'Not 'alf,' said parlourmaid Milly, 'it's either full of food or a lot of babble and bumble.'

'I make so bold as to point out that at the orphanage I was complimented on me wisdom,' said Alexander.

'There you go, you're talking with your mouth full again,' said Mrs Blisset.

Alexander glanced at Maisie. She rolled her eyes in sympathy, although she'd been brought up herself never to speak with her mouth full.

After supper, when the large amount of washing-up had been done by Edie and Daisy, the scrubbers and cleaners, and Mrs Blisset was upstairs on one of her regular visits to Mrs Carpenter's suite, Maisie went down to check that little Rosemary was still sound asleep in her cot. Alexander followed. It had become compulsive, his habit of attaching himself to Maisie as often as he could.

He followed her from Mrs Blisset's room to her own.

'Alexander, stop treading on me heels,' she said.

'I can't 'elp meself,' grinned Alexander, 'I'm getting to fancy yer.'

'You saucebox,' said Maisie, 'you ain't old

enough to do any fancying. Don't I keep telling you that?'

'Yerse, and it pains me ears,' said the irrepressible houseboy. "'Ere, Maisie, would yer show us that letter now?'

Maisie, feeling she needed to talk to someone, even Alexander, took the letter from under her pillow and let him read it. He whistled.

'Blimey,' he said, 'he ain't backward in coming forward, is he? Crikey Moses, he wants to meet you. Maisie, what yer going to do about that?'

'Ignore it,' said Maisie. 'Me mum and dad didn't bring me up to meet impudent specimens like him. Mind, I was thinking of sending you round to where he lives and blowing him to bits.'

'Strike me pink, Maisie, I dunno I could do that,' said Alexander, 'and I ain't got no dynamite, anyways. And if I did 'ave, supposing I got copped? I'd get fifty years in Dartmoor.'

'All right, I'll let you off,' said Maisie, 'but if Rupert Smythe calls again—'

'Ain't it Hubert?' said Alexander.

'If he calls again, or you see him,' said Maisie, 'hit him with a shovel.'

'Maisie, I told yer, hitting him with that kind of thing ain't allowed by the law, it could—'

'Well, writing me letters about posing for him with all me clothes off ain't allowed by the law, neither,' said Maisie, 'it's an unlegal insult to me self-respect. Now what you grinning about?'

'Crikey, Maisie, you with all yer togs off, I

ain't actually crying about that,' said Alexander. Maisie eyed him threateningly. 'Course,' he added hastily, 'I share yer vextiousness, like, it ain't exactly nice getting them kind of letters from a bloke that's got saucy designs on yer body—'

Bang!

Maisie hit his head with her hairbrush. His mop saved him from any real damage, but he did see one or two stars.

'Did yer like that?' asked Maisie.

'Not much, no,' said Alexander, rubbing his mop.

'Well, just remember me respectability,' said Maisie, 'and don't come it.'

'No, all right,' said Alexander. 'What're you looking at?'

'Me hairbrush, to see if your loaf of bread damaged it,' said Maisie. 'Lucky for you it didn't.'

'Is yer mind made up about this bloke?' asked Alexander. 'I mean, you ain't going to meet him?'

'No,' said Maisie decisively, quivering at the very thought. Then she had a sudden idea. If she talked to Daniel, perhaps she and him could meet Hubert Smythe together. She was sure Daniel would know how to put him in his place for good.

It was two days later, on Friday, when Mr Fairfax had another fall. The bell of his suite jangled in the kitchen. It was followed by Mrs Carpenter calling loudly down the back stairs from the first-floor landing.

'Maisie! Maisie Gibbs! You there?'

Maisie, running from the kitchen, called up.

'Yes, here I am, mum!'

'Run and fetch Dr Graham at once. Mr Fairfax has suffered another fall. Quick, now.'

'Yes'm, right away.'

Out of the house she ran. Oh, the poor old gentleman, she thought, I don't know what Mrs Carpenter was about, letting him fall over again.

On she ran, skirts whisking, petticoat rustling, with people looking. Oh, what luck and by the grace of the good Lord, there was Dr Graham, pulling up in his pony and trap outside his house. She flew across the street.

'Dr Graham, sir, Dr Graham!'

'Why, it's young Maisie,' said the doctor.

'Doctor, oh, could you come right away to see to Mr Fairfax?' gasped breathless Maisie. 'Mrs Carpenter says he's had another fall.'

'I've other calls to make,' said Dr Graham, 'but I'll fit Mr Fairfax in at once, of course I will. Jump up, Maisie, and we'll ride together.'

'Oh, that's ever so good of you, sir,' said Maisie, and climbed up to sit beside him. Dr Graham flicked his whip, clucked and away the sleek pony trotted, with Maisie thinking how grand it was to see everything from up on high, except her pleasure was spoiled by worry over what kind of condition Mr Fairfax was in.

Mr Fairfax proved to be querulous, an unusual mood. He was propped up in a comfortable armchair upholstered in dark blue, a cushion at his back, Mrs Carpenter standing guard over him, concern written all over her.

'Here's Dr Graham, mum,' said Maisie.

'Oh, thank you so much for coming so quickly, doctor,' said Mrs Carpenter.

'Piffle,' muttered Mr Fairfax.

'We'll see, shall we?' said Dr Graham, setting down his Gladstone bag, called so in honour of the venerable Parliamentarian, now in his eighty-fifth year. 'What happened?'

'Nothing,' said Mr Fairfax.

'He stumbled and fell,' said Mrs Carpenter, 'and lay unconscious for several minutes.'

'Piffle,' said Mr Fairfax.

'Unconscious?' said Dr Graham to Mrs Carpenter.

'Yes,' said Mrs Carpenter.

'Rubbish, woman,' said Mr Fairfax. Mrs Carpenter quivered a bit and looked hurt. 'I simply took a few minutes to get my breath back.'

'We'll see, shall we?' said Dr Graham, un-buttoning the old gentleman's jacket and waistcoat.

'Girl, what are you waiting for?' asked Mrs Carpenter of Maisie, hovering in the back-ground.

'Oh, I just thought I might be wanted for an errand, mum,' said Maisie, hoping to hear the doctor give out good news on Mr Fairfax.

'Go about your work,' said Mrs Carpenter, and Maisie left to the tune of Mr Fairfax's mutters and complaints concerning all this fuss.

'How is he?' asked Prudence when Maisie entered the kitchen, a place that was the servants' own little world.

'Irritated,' said Maisie.

'Irritated?' said Daisy, a woman whose scrubbing and cleaning routine had reduced her over the years to lean muscle. 'He ain't supposed to be irritated. More wounded, like.'

'Wounded?' said Mrs Blisset, studying an edition of Mrs Beeton's primary cookbook. 'Don't be silly. It's only soldiers who get wounded. Maisie, has Mr Fairfax broken any bones?'

'I don't think so,' said Maisie, 'I think he just 'ad his breath knocked out of him when he fell, but I don't know how he come to fall. Dr Graham's looking at him now, and Mr Fairfax is irritated about it.'

'I ain't surprised,' said Agnes, 'I'd be irritated meself if I kept tripping over carpets or suchlike that ain't laying flat. Milly, you ought to make sure all Mr Fairfax's rugs and carpet strips ain't scuffed up.'

'I do make sure,' said Milly, the comely parlourmaid who had a gentleman friend she kept quiet about. 'I'm not one to skimp my work upstairs, not with Mrs Carpenter keeping both eyes on me all the time.' She glanced at Maisie. 'It's more like you get a bit careless, Maisie, when you're helping out.'

'Excuse me,' said Maisie, 'but I ain't careless in any of me work.'

'You Milly,' said Mrs Blisset, 'Mrs Carpenter's got responsibilities that mean she has to keep her eyes on all of you, the same as I have to watch that the kitchen work is done properly.'

'That's two pairs of eyes watching us,' muttered Prudence.

'What's that, what did you say?' demanded Mrs Blisset.

'Nothing,' said Prudence.

'Just watch—' Mrs Blisset was interrupted by a wail from little Rosemary, who had woken up and was struggling to get out of her cot. 'Maisie, see to her, take her walking round the ground floor, will you?'

'I'm supposed to be beating carpets with Alexander,' said Maisie.

'Let him do it by himself,' said Mrs Blisset.

Maisie was happy enough to take charge of Rosemary and to help her exercise her fat little legs. The child beamed in gratitude.

Down the stairs came Dr Graham, Mrs Carpenter speaking to him from the landing.

'We're very grateful, doctor,' she said, 'Mr Fairfax and myself.'

'He's fine,' said Dr Graham, 'no harm done. Goodbye.' As he reached the hall, he spoke to Maisie and the child. 'Goodbye, Maisie, goodbye, little one.'

'Oh, is Mr Fairfax all right, doctor?' said Maisie.

'Exceptionally so for his age, apart from his dislike of fuss,' said Dr Graham. He smiled. 'He has just told me I'm the biggest fusspot of all.' He smiled again, shook his head and left.

Maisie felt happy and relieved. She was really very fond of Mr Fairfax. He had no wife to comfort him in his old age, having been a bachelor all his life. So he didn't have any children, either. Which made her think again about his Last Will and Testament, and that made her wonder who he'd leave his money to. Then she remembered Agnes had told her he had relatives in South Africa.

Sunday morning.

Maisie finished dusting the framed pictures in the ground-floor reception room. It was a room that didn't see many visitors. Well, Mr Fairfax hardly ever entertained. She looked at the ornate clock on the mantelpiece. It was time to go up to the old gentleman's suite. Mrs Carpenter had told her earlier that she was to tidy his library at nine fifteen.

Maisie had said, 'But don't Milly do his rooms mostly?' She'd asked the question because she knew Milly didn't like it when Maisie was required to help her in Mr Fairfax's suite. Milly was thorough in her work but slow.

'Yes, she does,' Mrs Carpenter said, 'but Mr Fairfax wants you to do his library this morning.'

'Oh, yes'm, I'll be pleased to,' said Maisie. Sunday work was light, but it had to be done.

'You're not to think you'll take Milly's place as parlourmaid,' Mrs Carpenter had said sternly.

'Oh, no, mum, I won't think nothing like that.' Maisie knew that even the possibility would provoke Milly into pulling her hair out.

Now, as she climbed the staircase and arrived at the carpeted landing, she passed the housekeeper's suite on her way to Mr Fairfax's abode. The door was open, and she heard Mrs Carpenter say from somewhere, 'I've done everything I possibly could for you, and you know I'm doing my best to do more, so stop worrying me about it. It's going to take—'

The rest was lost on Maisie as she reached the door of Mr Fairfax's suite. Crikey, she thought, who's the housekeeper talking to? It must be one of the staff, because there were no visitors in the house. That made her words a bit of a mystery. Well, no-one could have said she particularly favoured any of the staff. Except she was a bit friendly with Mrs Blisset. Oh, well, it's none of my business, thought Maisie.

Mr Fairfax's door was also open. She knocked.

'Come in, come in,' called Mr Fairfax from his library.

Maisie entered and went through to the room, where the old gentleman, examining his bookshelves, turned to greet her with a smile.

'Good morning, sir,' said Maisie.

'Good morning, young lady.'

'I've come to dust and tidy your lib'ry, sir.'

'On a Sunday morning as fine as this? No, no.'

'But Mrs Carpenter said—'

'Ah, yes.' Mr Fairfax positively twinkled. Conspiratorially. 'Well, between you and me, Maisie, what I need you for is to go down to the mews and inform Townley that I should like him to bring the carriage to the house in half an hour.'

Maisie blinked.

'Beg pardon, sir?'

'I am going to take a ride on this beautiful morning.'

'But, sir, you don't ever . . . oh, Lor', what's Mrs Carpenter going to say?'

'Dear me, yes, what will she say?' Mr Fairfax twinkled again. 'However, is there any need to inform her?'

'But she'll find out as soon as you leave your suite, sir.'

'We may escape that. If not, then the circumstances may require me to ask her to ride with me. The carriage will be here and waiting, and between us, young lady, we shall have achieved a fait accompli.'

'Oh, 'elp,' breathed Maisie, not sure what a fait accompli was, but certain sure Mrs Carpenter would dismiss her for going behind her back. 'Sir, did you ought to be going out?'

'Goodness me,' said Mr Fairfax, 'you aren't going to fuss too, are you?' His smile became understanding. 'Have no worries, Maisie, I shall take all responsibility. The point is, my invaluable housekeeper will argue me out of it if we let her know beforehand what we are up to. Let us go forth and achieve our fait accompli. That is, go now and alert our coachman.'

'Yes, sir,' said Maisie. 'Oh, Lor',' she breathed again as she slipped out and made a quick and silent descent of the staircase. Her exit from the house was also quiet. Her walk to the mews was quick.

Chapter Eleven

'Eh?' said Bill Townley, ruddy face falling apart, as it were. Well, his mouth gaped wide open. 'Do what, young Maisie?'

Maisie repeated Mr Fairfax's request. Mr Townley scratched his head and his expression changed from disbelief to the highly dubious. He said Mrs Carpenter wasn't going to like it, no, she wasn't, as sure as eggs is eggs and not bananas. Maisie said Mr Fairfax was going to take all responsibility.

'He said so to me face, Mr Townley.'

'Fair, young Maisie, fair, but what about me own phizog, eh? Will the old gentleman take responsibility for what Mrs Carpenter might do to it when she finds out?'

Maisie studied his face, which was very homely, owing its ruddy colour, she suspected, to a regular intake of coachmen's favourite tipple, a pint of porter.

'Oh, Mr Fairfax said that if she does find out, he'll invite her to go with him. He said it would be her fate, or something like that.'

'Meaning she might fall off on the way and get run over?' said Mr Townley, sorrowful at the thought.

'No, I don't think he meant that,' said Maisie, 'more like she'd have to go with him out of good grace.'

'Blind me, the old gentleman's standing a bit lively on his feet, is he?' said the coachman. 'Well, we'll have to risk Mrs Carpenter's umbrage. She's a good woman in her way, but I ain't sure her mercy falls like the gentle rain from heaven above. Shakespeare said that, did yer know?'

'Oh, I know he said to be or not to be, that's the question,' Maisie offered brightly.

'Good on yer, Maisie, so he did, and I never heard nothing that fits you and me and our old gentleman better right now. To be bold or not to be, eh?'

'And we can pray a bit, Mr Townley,' said Maisie.

'So we can.' Mr Townley squared his broad shoulders. 'Tell yer what, best if you don't get back till I arrive with the carriage. You can ride with me, and it'll be done then, and all you'll have to do will be to pop up to inform our old gentleman that his carriage awaits. Make sure you give Mrs Carpenter the slip, or she'll come out and drop a spanner in the works afore you get to prime him. She'll order me to take the carriage back again. She's got concern for our old gentleman, and she's likely to think a ride out of doors after all this time might make him catch a cold and be his death.'

'Oh, me Gawd,' breathed Maisie, 'no wonder she fusses about him so much.'

'Come on,' said Mr Townley, 'come and meet Chippy and Chirpy.' Those were the names of the carriage pair, Maisie knew that. She also knew through Alexander's informative tongue that neither horse had ever been known to break into more than a trot. Dignified, that was what Chippy and Chirpy were, he said. So how did they get names like that, Maisie wanted to know. They was born like it, said Alexander, but when they was growing up they come up against a couple of them great big shire horses one day, the kind that pull loaded beer drays round the City, and they'd been sort of quiet ever since.

Now Maisie met the carriage pair in the stables, which smelled of leather, liniment, soap and horses. Mr Townley offered Maisie two lumps of sugar to give to them.

'Oh, crikey, I don't know I could,' she said, a bit faint at being so close to gleaming horsey teeth. Although horses were part of everyday life, she had always been a little nervous of their largeness.

'Go on, Maisie, they ain't going to bite,' said Mr Townley, 'and once they take sugar from yer they'll have kind mem'ries of yer.'

Maisie took her life bravely into her hands and made the gift offering. Large lips and tongues accepted the gifts, and the teeth made no attempt to bite her head off. Maisie, not far short of eighteen, had made her first really close acquaintance with two members of the animal fraternity that provided the main engine power for carts, vans, trams, buses, carriages, coaches and hansom cabs.

'Oh, ain't they gentle really?' she said.

'Noble, Maisie, that's what horses is, noble,' said Mr Townley, and proceeded to make ready for the drive to the house.

From a window, Alexander watched in astonishment as Bill Townley pulled up outside the house with Maisie beside him, the sun shining down on the equipage. Blimey, he thought, so that's where Maisie's been. No-one told me, but of course, no-one tells me nothing. I sometimes feel I ain't here. Well, here but sort of invisible.

He rushed to open the front door. Maisie descended from the carriage very ladylike, and then darted down to the basement door, opened it and disappeared.

"Ere, Bill, what's a-going on?' asked Alexander of the coachman.

'Mr Townley to you, me cock sparrer, and there ain't nothing going on that you ought to know about. Just keep quiet and kindly put your head in a sack somewhere.'

'Crikey, something's up,' said Alexander. He closed the door and disappeared.

Maisie arrived on the first-floor landing by the back stairs, and hastened to Mr Fairfax's suite.

'Girl!'

Oh, me heartbeats, thought Maisie, it's her. She turned, and to her nervous eyes the formidable housekeeper looked like the messenger of doom.

'Yes'm?'

'What are you doing and where are you going?'

'Please, mum, I ain't finished tidying Mr Fairfax's lib'ry yet,' said Maisie.

'Well, you should have.'

'Oh, I would of, mum, only Mr Fairfax didn't want me to start when I first come up,' said Maisie, stretching the facts a little on account of the circumstances.

'Why are you so flushed, girl?'

'Well, I just been running up the stairs—'

'That will do. Finish your work in the library. The time is ten o'clock, and all the basic housework should be finished by now. Go along.'

'Yes'm, thank you.' Maisie hurried. She knocked on the door of Mr Fairfax's suite, Mrs Carpenter watching her. Mr Fairfax opened the door.

'Ah, Maisie,' he smiled. He saw his redoubtable housekeeper.

'I can finish me work now, sir?' said Maisie.

'Yes, indeed, come in, young lady, come in.'

Maisie entered and he closed the door.

'Oh, Lor', sir, me pulse is running all over the place,' she breathed, 'but it's outside, the carriage, and Mr Townley's waiting.'

'Splendid, Maisie, splendid. My word, what a

morning. I'll come down at once. Ah, a moment first.' He opened the door a fraction and peeped. 'There, the coast is clear and fuss is absent. The dear lady will be quite happy with her Sunday newspaper and a glass of lemonade. Certainly, one doesn't wish to provoke fuss or argument on such a beautiful day.'

'Sir, you sure you'll be all right?' said Maisie. 'Only you haven't been out of doors for ages.'

'It's time I did, yes,' said Mr Fairfax, producing a light panama hat and placing it on his head. 'Come, Maisie, let us go down while the coast is still clear.'

Maisie walked with him out of the suite. From her own suite, Mrs Carpenter emerged.

Oh, I'm done for now, thought Maisie.

'Mr Fairfax, what's this?' said the looming housekeeper. 'Where are you going?'

'Ah,' said Mr Fairfax ambiguously.

'Maisie, what is going on?' asked Mrs Carpenter.

'Beg pardon, mum?' said Maisie, presenting herself in upright fashion, her back straight. It was an attempt to suggest that any implication of misbehaviour hurt her pride.

'Mr Fairfax, you are wearing your panama hat,' said Mrs Carpenter, accusation the partner of reproach.

Mr Fairfax sighed.

'Iris, dear lady, I am going to enjoy a jaunt in the carriage,' he said. 'Townley is here and waiting, and—'

'Waiting?' said Mrs Carpenter. 'Who sent for him?'

'I confess I did,' said Mr Fairfax, 'and Maisie, you see, has come up to tell me he's arrived, with the carriage.'

'Mr Fairfax, you're surely not going out,' protested Mrs Carpenter. 'You will put me in a state of worry and alarm. I really can't permit it.'

Crikey, thought Maisie, she must be worried to tell her employer she can't permit his outing.

'My mind is made up,' said Mr Fairfax gently, 'and I should be delighted if you will accompany me. Yes, an excellent idea. An hour's ride on this beautiful morning will do wonders for our health and your nerves. Put your hat and gloves on, Iris, and join me outside. Maisie, take my arm, escort me down the stairs, and then ask Mrs Blisset to take charge while Mrs Carpenter and I are out.'

'Mr Fairfax, really, this is most reckless of you,' said Mrs Carpenter. For once, however, she was floundering. And for once, thought Maisie, Mr Fairfax was acting like he ought to, as the boss. 'Oh, very well,' continued the housekeeper, 'I know I simply must not let you go on your own.' She hastened back to her suite to collect her hat and gloves, and Maisie descended the staircase arm in arm with the triumphant old gentleman. Alexander, lurking, saw them coming. He gaped, then ran to open the front door, since it was obvious that the wearing of the panama hat meant Mr Fairfax was actually going out. Cor, what a palaver, and where was the old biddy?

The lady herself came rustling down the stairs and sailed like a black-feathered, fine-bosomed swan in the wake of Maisie and Mr Fairfax.

'Boy,' she said as she passed Alexander, 'I shall speak to you later.'

'Me, mum?' he said. 'I ain't done nothing.' His words passed into thin air. He was to find out that Mrs Carpenter suspected he was the one who had carried Mr Fairfax's request to Townley. He stayed at the open front door, watching as Mr Fairfax and Mrs Carpenter climbed up into the carriage, with Maisie standing by. Crikey, look at them, sitting up there together, like an elderly nob with his middle-aged fancy piece.

'Walk on,' said Mr Townley, and the carriage moved off.

Maisie came back into the house.

''Ere, Maisie, what's been going on?' asked Alexander.

'Well, you saw, didn't you?' said Maisie. 'Mr Fairfax and Mrs Carpenter have gone for a morning ride.'

'Blimey, I saw all right,' said Alexander, 'but I ain't believing it. Suppose Mr Fairfax has one of 'is falls?'

'Lordy, I hope he don't,' said Maisie, blanching. 'Still,' she said, perking up, 'he can only fall into Mrs Carpenter's lap.'

Alexander chortled at that, then said he'd like to know who got Bill Townley to bring the carriage, and who gave the order, the old gentleman or the old biddy? Maisie said he'd better ask them, and that she couldn't stay talking because she'd got to tell Mrs Blisset to take charge while their employer and housekeeper were out. Alexander said he wasn't going to ask no questions of either the old gent or the old biddy, not likely, and anyway, he probably wouldn't get no answer because no-one ever told him anything.

'I'm sort of invisible,' he complained.

'Well, fancy that,' said Maisie. 'Still, you can always be heard, and a bit much most times.'

The other servants were astonished, of course, to hear of the outing, Mrs Blisset more so than anyone.

'Well,' she said, 'well, I just don't know I can believe it. Mr Fairfax going out when he's such a feeble and tottery old man?'

'Oh, I don't think he's all that feeble, like,' said Maisie, 'and I honestly ain't ever seen him tottery.'

'He wouldn't keep having falls if he wasn't a bit unsure of his balance,' said Mrs Blisset, mixing dough. 'And you, Maisie, where've you been all this time?'

Maisie said she'd been told by Mrs Carpenter to dust and tidy Mr Fairfax's library on account of Milly being too busy. Milly said what a sauce, the library didn't need tidying. Maisie said that Mr Fairfax himself asked for it to be done, and Milly said that was out of his absent-mindedness. Don't you start crossing my path, Maisie Gibbs, she said.

'I wouldn't do that,' said Maisie.

'Never mind who did what,' said Mrs Blisset, 'I need Maisie to take Rosemary for a bit of a walk out in the sunshine.'

Rosemary at the moment was clinging around her mother's skirts. Maisie gladly took charge of the child, and walked with her up and down the street, holding her hand, Rosemary chirping happily, her little legs going all ways.

Maisie was a bit chirpy herself. She had a whole four hours off later, and a happy anticipation of meeting Daniel.

Oh, help, she said to herself, something must have come over me.

The carriage returned at eleven twenty. Alexander opened the door to the old gentleman and his housekeeper. Mr Fairfax looked fresh and pink from his excursion, Mrs Carpenter looked as if she was still trying to work out how the morning had turned upside down for her. Alexander looked as if he was hiding a grin.

'Welcome back, sir,' he said.

'Thank you, my boy,' said Mr Fairfax.

'I wish to see you, Alexander,' said Mrs Carpenter.

'Yes, mum,' said the houseboy.

Mrs Carpenter advanced to the handsome staircase in close, attentive company with Mr Fairfax. They ascended together, Alexander following at a distance. Mrs Carpenter made sure Mr Fairfax reached his suite safely, her concern for him quick to surface as he entered his living room. She grabbed his arm to prevent what might have been a fall.

'There, I knew it,' she said, her chiding self overtaking her concern, 'I knew going out would exhaust you.'

'Not in the least,' said Mr Fairfax, 'I feel regenerated, my dear madam.'

'And I feel you're deceiving yourself,' said Mrs Carpenter. 'Sit down, do, and I'll have a refreshing drink prepared for you. '

'Not hot milk, no, certainly not,' said Mr Fairfax, removing his panama hat. 'A glass of sherry, I think.'

Alexander, waiting at the open door of the suite, heard the housekeeper say, 'Good heavens, you never take sherry in the mornings.'

'I shall this morning, and pour it myself,' said Mr Fairfax, 'while you go and enjoy your lemonade.'

Mrs Carpenter said something Alexander didn't catch. The good lady emerged from the living room some moments later, and noticed Alexander standing at the open door of the suite.

'Boy, what are you doing there?' she asked.

'Well, mum, you said you wanted to see me, so I come up after you,' said Alexander.

'Yes, I do want to see you. Follow me.' Mrs Carpenter led the way into her own suite where, in the living room, she turned to face the mop-haired youth. 'What did Mr Fairfax say to you when he told you to inform Townley the carriage was required?'

'He didn't say nothing, mum.'

Mrs Carpenter, who had been gently requested by Mr Fairfax to ask no questions during the drive, at once accused the lad of not telling the truth. Alexander responded by assuring her Mr Fairfax didn't say nothing to him at all, which was because he and the old gentleman hadn't seen anything of each other until the carriage arrived.

'Who did go down to the mews, then?' Mrs Carpenter spoke like a woman whose responsibilities had been undermined from below stairs.

Alexander, pretty sure by now who it was, nevertheless said, 'I dunno, mum, on me honour. Mind, someone could've done.'

'Of course someone did,' said Mrs Carpenter. 'Go down and inform all the staff that should Mr Fairfax ever ask again for errands to be done, I'm to be told at once. At once. Our gentleman's welfare must be our first consideration always.'

'Yes, mum.'

'Do you understand?'

'Yes, mum.' Alexander understood all too well that if the old gent went off to his Maker, everyone would lose their jobs.

'Very well, you may go.'

Alexander made fast going down to the kitchen, where preparations for Sunday dinner were underway. He informed the rest of the staff of Mrs Carpenter's instructions, but said nothing about her wanting to know who'd been down to the mews.

'But Mr Fairfax don't ever ask any of us to do errands, anyway,' said Edie, 'he always leaves it to her.'

'That's because she has to concern herself with his good,' said Mrs Blisset, 'so just make sure you all bear that in mind.'

'What was Mr Fairfax like after 'is drive?' asked Prudence inquisitively.

'Oh, he looked like 'imself, like always,' said Alexander. 'I mean, he 'adn't started to look like someone else.'

'That boy gets worse,' said Agnes, shaking her head. 'Worse,' she insisted.

'Alexander, I meant did he look a bit under the weather?' said Prudence.

'No, he didn't look under nothing,' said Alexander, 'he looked a bit over the top.'

'What d'you mean, over the top?' asked Maisie, busy shelling peas.

'All pink and perky, like,' said Alexander, 'as if he'd had a nip or two of Dutch gin during his outing.'

'If you don't show more respect for our employer,' said Mrs Blisset, 'I'll let Mrs Carpenter know.'

'I beg yer won't, Mrs Blisset,' said Alexander, 'I was only joking, like.'

'Do some work,' said Mrs Blisset, 'help Maisie shell the peas. '

'Oh, right,' said Alexander, and sat down next

to Maisie to share the task of shelling a large bowlful of the green pods. Maisie glanced at him. He winked. Maisie's lips twitched.

Rosemary, worn out by her walk, lay asleep in her cot. At the Knightsbridge barracks, Daniel was receiving a pass for an outing in the afternoon. In his studio, Hubert Smythe was still waiting for an answer from Miss Maisie Gibbs, the young lady whose upright walk was as impressive as that of a duchess, and who had put the scandalous artist out of her mind to look forward to seeing her soldier this afternoon.

Chapter Twelve

They met, they strolled, Maisie in her one and only best Sunday outfit, the primrose frock and straw boater. And of all things, Milly had had a moment of Christian generosity and lent Maisie something very elegant, a pink parasol. Maisie, owning no airs, graces or affectations, wasn't sure she suited a parasol, but decided that – well, that such things did suit Kensington Gardens.

She used the parasol to gain some shade from the sun. Daniel, of course, thought her on a par with the spirit of summer, except that she was still prim, still cautious about letting his compliments go to her head.

They halted to regard the Albert Memorial, the imposing monument erected eighteen years ago to honour Queen Victoria's late consort.

'D'you know, Daniel,' said Maisie, 'I keep reading in newspapers that our Queen still mourns him, even though he died over thirty years ago. Poor woman, don't you feel sad for her that she still can't get over her loss?'

'Well, frankly, Maisie,' said Daniel, 'I feel that for over thirty years the old lady has been ruling us with one foot in Prince Albert's grave.'

'One foot in 'is grave?' said Maisie. 'Now what sort of sense does that make?'

'It's a kind of – well, a figure of speech,' said Daniel, smart as ever in his uniform, and a little more learned than Maisie because he did so much reading.

'D'you mean she acts as if she does?' asked Maisie. 'Have one foot in his grave, I mean?'

'That's it,' said Daniel.

'It's a kind of reverent monument, I suppose,' said Maisie.

'And a lot bigger than a gravestone,' said Daniel. 'Now let's go and see Tower Bridge, eh?'

'Crikey, you serious?' said Maisie.

Tower Bridge, a mighty structure over the Thames, was the nearest bridge to the sea, and spanned a great stretch of water. It had been officially opened only a month ago, and people were still flocking to see it.

'We've got time to get there,' said Daniel. 'That's if you'd like to go.'

'Oh, I would,' said Maisie, 'but it's a long way to walk.'

'Walk?' Daniel laughed. 'We're not going to walk, you simpleton, we're—'

'Simpleton?' said Maisie. 'Excuse me, but you better take that back, Daniel Adams, or I won't ever meet you again.'

'Sorry, fell over me foot,' said Daniel.

'Over your tongue, more like,' said Maisie.

'We'll go on two wheels,' said Daniel, 'so come on, me summer maiden.'

Summer maiden? Oh, help, thought Maisie, I never heard nothing more romantic, he could go to a girl's head, he could, talking like that.

'What two wheels d'you mean?' she asked.

'This way,' said Daniel, and as good as marched her out of the Gardens into Bayswater Road, a busy thoroughfare even on Sundays.

'Here, d'you mind not dragging me?' said Maisie, while liking his air of command. She didn't think a lot of men who dillydallied so much about making up their minds that they got left behind. Her dad, being a railway porter, had told her once that they were the kind of blokes who always missed their train.

Daniel put two fingers in his mouth and whistled up an ambling hansom cab.

'This'll do us, Maisie,' he said.

'A cab?' said Maisie. 'Daniel, it'll cost two bob at least to Tower Bridge. We can wait for a horse bus.'

'It'll take too long,' said Daniel, 'and besides, you look like a hansom-cab fare, not an ordin'ry bus passenger. But you'll have to close yer parasol.'

'We're going to pay as much as—'

'You're not going to pay anything,' said Daniel, 'it's a feller's privilege to do the honours.'

Maisie considered that right and proper, actually.

The cab pulled up. From his perch on high, the top-hatted cabbie addressed Daniel.

'Where to, soldier?'

'Tower Bridge,' said Daniel, 'and at a gallop.'

'If I ask me Nelly to gallop, who's going to pay for 'er funeral?' enquired the cabbie with a grin.

'All right, we'll settle for a lively trot,' said Daniel. Maisie closed her parasol and he helped her aboard.

Crikey, she thought, it's me first ride ever in a hansom cab, and I'm going to feel all swish. Daniel settled beside her, the cabbie flicked his whip and away they went at a frisky trot, passing a horse-drawn bus as if it was standing still.

'Daniel, ain't this lovely?' said Maisie.

'A lot better than a coal cart,' said Daniel.

'D'you mean you've rode on coal carts?'

'More than once when I was a growing kid,' said Daniel.

'Didn't it make you all black?'

'Only me face and hands.'

'Crikey, what did yer mum say?'

'That if she had one more like me, she'd drown us both.'

'Well, I'm glad she didn't have to.'

'How glad, Maisie?'

'Oh, I just spoke out of the goodness of me heart.'

On went the cab towards Oxford Street, where it turned right into Park Lane, an elegant thoroughfare dotted with leisurely moving carriages both handsome and stately, in which sat people who looked to Maisie as if they belonged to London's aristocracy. In open carriages, parasols shielded seated ladies from the sun. Such ladies considered a tanned complexion deplorably rustic, and aimed for a pure white pallor. Hence in summer, not only parasols, but hats with huge brims were the thing. Maisie, while being a loyal subject of the Queen and respectful of the aristocracy, felt almost triumphant as the trotting horse whisked the hansom cab past the regal vehicles.

'Enjoying the ride, Maisie?' asked Daniel.

Maisie, impelled to say not half, rose to the occasion and said, 'Oh, my word, yes, ever so much, thank you, me lord.'

'What?' said Daniel.

'Don't say what, it's common.'

Daniel, who always had a smile close to the surface, let it appear. Young Maisie Gibbs might be prim and proper, but she was also droll, without realizing it.

The cab turned east towards Piccadilly Circus and the Strand, and with an absence of the commercial vans and carts that usually cluttered up the streets, progress was lively. Shops were shut, pavements devoid of crowds. Sunday, thought Daniel, was a good day for the journey of two people whose time was limited. For his part, he'd have liked the whole day to belong to Maisie and himself, and to have the cab carry them out of London into the countryside, where summer offered them fields of golden buttercups and lazy dalliance. Even kisses.

What would happen if he did kiss her? He suspected she'd box his ears. Or clout him with her parasol.

'Daniel, now what're you smiling about?'

'Oh, funny thoughts, Maisie.'

'What funny thoughts?'

'I once saw a large Sudanese woman pick up a grown man and dump him in thorn bushes.'

'That's funny?'

'Well, she laughed.'

'And what did he do?'

'Oh, he went to the witch doctor and got himself plucked.'

'Plucked?'

'You bet he did, Maisie me girl, he had as many thorns in his hide as a chicken's got feathers.'

'Oh, you spoofer, Daniel Adams, you don't think I believe these daft stories of yours, do you?' said Maisie.

'Would I tell you fibs?' asked Daniel.

'You've just told me a whopper,' said Maisie. 'Still, me dad would of enjoyed it.'

'I'd have liked to meet your dad,' said Daniel, 'and your mum.'

Maisie gave a little sigh.

'Yes, ain't it a shame, Daniel, that we both lost our parents?' she said.

'You're right, Maisie, but you and me, we've both got to get on with life,' said Daniel, 'including using the afternoon to take a look at Tower Bridge.'

The cab travelled freely through the Strand, Fleet Street, then up Ludgate Hill and into the City, Maisie enjoying every passing scene. The City was even quieter than the West End, with not a single clerk or office boy to be seen.

'Well, I must say it's faster than any horse bus, Daniel,' said Maisie, 'except I don't like to think what it's going to cost you.'

'Worth the time it's saving,' said Daniel, and Maisie liked that. She liked the attitude of any man who didn't act stingy when taking a girl out, especially if he was hard up, which she was sure most soldiers were, even corporals. Her dad had been hard up for as long as she could remember, but somehow he could always find her a penny with which to buy sweets of a weekend when she was a little girl.

They passed the Monument that commemorated the Great Fire of London, entered Eastcheap and then Tower Street. At that stage, people began to appear. Maisie saw families all in their Sunday best, walking towards Tower Hill.

'Look, Daniel.'

'They're going to the bridge, Maisie, for a bit of sightseeing,' said Daniel. 'It's been a fav'rite place for a Sunday outing since it was opened. But I don't suppose any of these people realize they're on the same road that condemned men took on their way to the Tower of London and the execution block.'

'Crikey, is that right?' said Maisie. 'Daniel, you don't half know a lot of things.'

'It's books, Maisie, and what reading learns a bloke,' said Daniel. 'There ain't many times when I don't have a book in me kitbag.'

'Oh, I've read some books meself,' said Maisie, 'but they didn't learn me about where prisoners had to walk to the Tower. Didn't they ride in police carts? I mean, going to have their heads chopped off and having to walk there, I don't think that was very nice. Oh, now look at the people, there's crowds.'

'We're almost there,' said Daniel.

The cab passed a stationary horse bus that was disgorging a full complement of passengers. The cabbie brought his vehicle to a stop as it reached the top of Tower Hill. People were swarming and there was a perceptible air of excitement. Daniel alighted and gave Maisie a hand down. He looked up at the cabbie, seated behind and above the passenger compartment.

'You're 'ere, soldier.'

'Much obliged,' said Daniel, 'and now tell me what we owe yer.'

'Two honest bob,' said the cabbie, and Daniel handed up two shilling coins with a threepenny bit as a tip.

'Obliged to yer, Colonel,' said the cabbie affably.

'If you could be here in an hour,' said Daniel, 'you could take us back.'

'I note that,' said the cabbie, 'and seeing

Sunday fares don't come too frequent, I might just see you again, and yer young lady. An hour, eh? Yes, I note that.'

With the co-operation of his willing nag, he turned his cab around and away he went, leaving Daniel and Maisie to join the throng of people who had decided to spend this Sunday afternoon admiring the spectacular architecture of mighty Tower Bridge.

'Daniel, I never saw nothing like this before,' said Maisie, eyes wide. She and Daniel were at a standstill, just looking.

There it was, its footbridge nearly a hundred and forty feet above high water, its roadway a hundred feet below the footbridge. Its massive structure was based on twin towers of awe-inspiring majesty.

'It's an original, eh, Maisie?' said Daniel.

'Oh, yes,' said Maisie, 'one on its own.'

'There's no other bridge in the world like it,' said Daniel.

'Did you learn that from a book?' asked Maisie.

'No, from me company sergeant major's newspaper, which happened to be lying about and asking to be borrowed,' said Daniel. 'Well, he only reads the horse-racing page.'

They moved on, reaching a point where vendors of balloons, flags, sweets, drinks and hokey-pokey were offering their wares. Hokey-pokey was a cheap imitation of ice cream, and kids could buy a helping for a ha'penny. A small helping, true, but large enough in the eyes of

East End kids. Aside from these vendors was an Italian with a suitably constructed barrow in which reposed a galvanized metal container surrounded by ice. In the container was real ice cream, such as only London's immigrant Italians could produce. It was sold between two wafer biscuits, and this was called an ice-cream wafer.

'Who'll buy my fine ice-a d' cream, eh?' called the vendor.

'Maisie?' said Daniel.

'Crikey, you offering?' said Maisie. 'Yes, please, not half.'

Daniel joined three other people at the barrow and watched as the vendor used a rectangular scoop to dig out a block of glistening ice cream half an inch thick. This he deposited on a wafer biscuit, and slapped its twin on top.

'Tuppence, eh?'

The customers paid up and so did Daniel when he was served with two.

'Here we are, Maisie.'

'Daniel, oh, thanks ever so,' said Maisie, lifting brown optics to grey, and they looked each other in the eye as they had once before. A discerning person might have said there was a momentary spark of communicative electricity. Be that as it may, the fact was Maisie experienced a little breathlessness, and Daniel told himself that if he didn't get to marry this lovely-looking, well-behaved girl sometime in the near future he'd end up deprived.

'You're the nicest girl, Maisie.'

'Oh, you ain't half bad yourself,' said Maisie, hiding flutters.

They walked together over the footbridge, enjoying their ice-cream wafers, which Maisie thought a real treat. They stopped now and again to look down at the lazy low-water flow of the sunlit Thames. The river seemed so far below that Maisie thought anyone who fell off the bridge would take all day to make a splash.

'It's a long way down,' said Daniel, reading her thoughts. Well beneath the footbridge, some Sunday traffic moved along the roadway that could be opened and raised by hydraulic power to allow the passage of shipping to and from London's docks.

'Daniel, look at the view,' said Maisie, lifting her head. From this side of the bridge, the rooftops of the City and its eastern neighbourhoods were visible on this clear day. Church steeples sprouted amid arrays of chimney tops, and here and there one could just glimpse what looked like the green of a park. London, for all its built-up areas, had many parks.

'It's a rare old sight,' said Daniel.

'Lor',' breathed Maisie, 'London looks as if it's got no end to it. '

The footbridge was alive with sightseers, parents holding onto excited sons and daughters quite capable of climbing the ramparts and toppling over. Maisie and Daniel made a dawdling crossing of the footbridge, which spanned three hundred yards, before turning back. Their return was just as leisurely, and marked by the fact that Maisie had her parasol up. It made some people think her a well-off young lady chaperoned by a corporal instead of her mother. Lucky old corporal.

They were very easy with the nuances of their relationship now. No awkward pauses, no searching for something to say, no wish on the part of either to be with someone else. Daniel recounted more stories of army life, and Maisie informed him she didn't believe any of them. She told him about her employer, Mr Fairfax, what a kind old gentleman he was, and how he regarded his housekeeper, Mrs Carpenter, as a fusspot. Still, she did care for his welfare.

'Well, I'm right pleased you work for a kind old gent, Maisie,' said Daniel, 'but I'm certain sure it ain't going to be for much longer.'

'What d'you mean?' asked Maisie.

'I've got plans,' said Daniel.

'What plans, might I ask?' Maisie's flutters came back.

'Some day I'll tell you,' said Daniel. The day when she first accepted a kiss from him, a moment when she looked willing.

'Oh, I can't hardly wait, can I?' she said, but in light, throwaway fashion.

They were back then, back at the top of Tower Hill, and there was the hansom cab waiting, the cabbie lifting his top hat as he saw them.

''Ere we are, young lady and escort, ready and willing, me and Nelly,' he said.

'What an obliging bloke,' said Daniel.

The return journey went all too quickly. The cabbie deposited them in Bayswater Road, adjacent the gardens, and Daniel gave him another two and threepence, for which he doffed his top hat again, and informed Daniel he was very much obliged.

Back in Kensington Gardens, Daniel and Maisie finally parted for the day, Daniel saying that if she could get time off again on Wednesday afternoon, he'd break his neck in his efforts to get a pass.

'Oh, I'll do me very best on me own account,' said Maisie, 'but I won't be daft enough to break me neck. Daniel, thanks ever so much for a lovely afternoon, and the ice-cream wafer, and the posh rides, oh, and everything.'

'I'm tickled we now know each other good and proper,' said Daniel. Resisting the temptation to kiss her, for he felt she still wasn't ready for that familiarity, he saluted her and went on his way.

Maisie, in a kind of happy glow, returned to her place of work.

Chapter Thirteen

Maisie entered the house by the basement door and made straight for her room. With several minutes to spare before her free time was up, she changed into her working outfit, then pulled her trunk out from under the bed. She fished among its contents for a little leather bag with a drawstring. She opened it and quietly spilled its contents onto the counterpane that covered her bed. Halfpennies, pennies, silver bits, silver tanners, bobs and florins, and even a banknote for ten shillings, made a happy little pile of savings. She knew the pile amounted to something between five and six pounds, a useful sum if she lost her job. She'd be able to live for ten weeks on that, by paying three and six a week for a rented room in Walworth, and spending the same amount on food.

The point now was could she afford a new Sunday frock? She just couldn't keep wearing her primrose one. How much would a really nice new frock cost? Crikey, as much as half a crown, and even more if she bought it in a posh shop.

Whiteleys, yes, that was the place. Whiteleys catered for modest customers as well as well-off ones. Half a crown? Yes, out of her savings she could afford that, and even sixpence more if she had to.

Oh, Lor', I think I know what this means, it means I want to look nice for Daniel, she thought.

She returned her savings to the bag, put the bag back among her belongings and pushed the portmanteau out of sight under the bed again.

Just in time.

'Oi, Maisie, you there?' Alexander knocked on her door.

She stood up, opened the door, and there he was, his face decorated with his permanent grin.

'Alexander, what d'you want?' asked Maisie.

'Oh, I just come to see if you're back,' said Alexander. 'I been out meself, and what d'yer think I saw?'

'Something funny, I suppose,' said Maisie, 'or you wouldn't be grinning like that.'

'No, it wasn't nothing funny,' said Alexander, 'it was that bloke that admires you and wants to paint yer.'

'Oh, him,' said Maisie. 'He don't have any right to admire me, the cheeky beast, nor to paint me. I hope you told him off.'

'Well, I did tell him you wasn't exactly falling over yerself to sit for him,' said Alexander, 'but he didn't seem to take a blind bit of notice. He just said he'd been in the Gardens for an hour, 'oping to spot you so's you and him could have a talk. Course, I said you didn't want nothing to do with 'im, and he asked me to tell you again that 'is intentions was hon'rable.'

'I bet,' said Maisie. 'What's he up to, spending all his time in the Gardens waiting to accost me? Don't he do any work?'

'I don't think artists do any proper work,' said Alexander, 'I think they just paint and end up starving.'

'Well, it's time he got an honest job instead of trying to get me to sit for him,' said Maisie. 'End up starving, did you say? More like he'll end up haunting me and stop me sleeping at night.'

'You still ain't keen on meeting him?' said Alexander.

'I should say not,' said Maisie, 'he'd haunt me more than ever if I did.'

'Where you been with yer soldier this afternoon?' asked Alexander.

'None of yer business,' said Maisie, 'but if you must know we went to see Tower Bridge.'

'Crikey,' said Alexander, 'I'm going to see it one day – 'ere, that reminds me, Mr Fairfax said he wanted to see you when you got back from yer time off.'

'What does he want to see me about?' asked Maisie.

'He didn't say, but you could go up now,

Maisie. Mrs Blisset's up with the old biddy, having tea and biscuits wiv 'er. And they've got Rosemary wiv 'em.'

Maisie came out of her room, closing the door behind her. Alexander watched as she climbed the back stairs to the first floor. All was quiet on the wide landing, and she knocked on the door of Mr Fairfax's suite. After some moments, the old gentleman appeared.

He smiled at her.

'Ah, Maisie, my dear young lady,' he said, 'come in, do.'

He took her into his library, where books from the shelves lay on the table. They represented his ideal way of passing the time. Maisie thought of Daniel's interest in books, and wondered if she should do a lot more reading on her own account, and get to know more about life. Well, she knew some books were supposed to educate readers. Old Walworth neighbours might have told her she didn't need any educating, that her years of coping with the hard facts of life had done more for her than a roomful of books.

'D'you want me to tidy up, sir?' she asked.

'Tidy up? No, no, indeed not. It's Sunday, isn't it?' Mr Fairfax smiled again, and Maisie thought what a really charming old gentleman he was. 'Did you enjoy your outing?'

'Oh, ever so much,' said Maisie, and told him about her visit to Tower Bridge with her soldier friend.

'How delightful,' said Mr Fairfax, 'and how coincidental. I have a book on that bridge. Did you know it took eight years to construct, and that it's unique?'

'Sort of original?' said Maisie.

'Exactly.' Mr Fairfax positively beamed at her. 'What a pleasing young lady you are. Now, what I would like you to do for me concerns tomorrow week.'

'Monday week, sir?'

'Precisely. August Bank Holiday Monday. Sometime between now and then, when you aren't too busy, I would like you to go to the mews again, and request Townley to bring the carriage here at ten in the morning of the bank holiday.'

'Beg pardon, sir?'

'I know I can trust you to keep quiet about it,' murmured Mr Fairfax. 'Alexander, alas, although a fine boy and very willing, is – ah – apt to let his tongue run away with his discretion. You see, Maisie, I am going to do what you did today, I am going to see Tower Bridge. That is the coincidence. I shall go on Bank Holiday Monday, when flags will be flying.'

'Lor', Mr Fairfax, sir, there'll be enormous crowds,' breathed Maisie, 'and I'm sure Mrs Carpenter will worry herself sick about you being in a crush.'

'Ah, well,' said the old gentleman, 'we shall overcome the good lady's concern as we did before, by inviting her to accompany me. But we shan't speak to her today, indeed not, no, or there will be a whole week of fussing and argument, all to do with the risk of my going out at all, with or without her company. Dear me, Maisie, a good woman's concern can sometimes be a little – um – trying. There now, do you and I understand what is to be done?'

'Yes, sir, I'm to go to the mews sometime and let Mr Townley know about August Bank Holiday Monday,' said Maisie. 'And tell him not to say anything to no-one.'

'Excellent,' said Mr Fairfax. I shall inform Mrs Carpenter of my proposed outing on the evening before the bank holiday, and I shall reduce her fuss by inviting her to join me on the ride to our wonderful Tower Bridge. Also, I shall speak to her about Milly, my parlourmaid.' The old gentleman was rattling on, his expression quite mischievous, and Maisie was all receptive ears, if quivering a little. 'Yes, I shall tell her that after Milly's morning duties on the bank holiday, she must have the rest of the day off for her excellent attentions to my suite.'

'Oh, Milly will like that, sir, the bank holiday and all,' said Maisie.

'Then, as an afterthought, I shall tell Mrs Carpenter that our maid of all work must also have a free bank holiday.'

'Me, sir? Me?' Maisie's eyes opened wider. Bank holiday free? Oh, corks.

'Yes, you, Maisie, but it must sound like an afterthought, since nothing should be said that points to you as my confidante. One must not let the good lady feel she is anything but my only confidante. She's a sensitive woman.'

'Oh, I suppose so, sir,' said Maisie, who couldn't see the housekeeper as sensitive. 'But, sir, if you want to go out now and again, and not to have any fuss about it, you could always go with Mrs Carpenter when she uses the carriage for shopping.'

'Maisie, my dear girl,' said Mr Fairfax, looking pained, 'shopping for groceries and fripperies with Mrs Carpenter? Would you impose such an ordeal on a man of my age?'

'Oh, beg yer pardon, sir, I forgot meself,' said Maisie. 'I think I was thinking too much about having bank holiday free. It's ever so kind of you.'

'Perhaps,' said Mr Fairfax, his smile gentle, 'perhaps you and your soldier friend will be able to enjoy it together.'

Maisie almost wanted to kiss this lovely old gent.

'Oh, perhaps we might, sir,' she said.

'Splendid,' said Mr Fairfax. 'I shall leave it to you to go to the mews at a time of your own choosing, a time convenient to your circumstances.'

'Yes, sir, I'm sure I'll be able to find the right time,' said Maisie.

'Good,' said Mr Fairfax. He smiled, and Maisie departed, feeling she and the old gentleman were sort of partners in a plot.

*   *   *

Monday.

At the Knightsbridge barracks, the morning parade of the 10th Battalion, Royal West Kents, was over, and Corporal Daniel Adams was having a word with C Company's sergeant major.

'I'm hearing rumours, Sarn't Major.'

'Rumours, Corporal Adams, don't amount to much except to old women,' said Sergeant Major Albert Sawyer.

'I still keep hearing them,' said Daniel.

'Time you knew that rumours ain't the same as official information.'

'I've known rumours to turn official.'

'What's in these here present rumours, Corporal Adams?'

'Ireland,' said Daniel. Ireland, governed by the British, was a permanent hotbed of troubles on account of a demand by the Catholics for Home Rule. The Protestants, mainly those of Ulster, were ferociously against this. British troops hated a spell in Ireland. They were constantly being shot at from dark corners.

'In my lifetime,' said Sergeant Major Sawyer, 'Ireland never was my idea of fairyland. You've heard of Irish leprechauns, have you?'

'Now and again,' said Daniel.

'Well, even them little creatures eat each other.'

'Point is, Sarn't Major, the rumours tell me the battalion's going to be posted there in the near future,' said Daniel.

'What the rumours tell you, Daniel,' said the sergeant major in friendly fashion, 'don't count as official.'

'But if they turn out official,' said Daniel, 'I'm not going to like it.'

'There's a reason, is there?' said the sergeant major, one of Daniel's many comrades-in-arms over a period of several years. 'You've got something going, have you? All these passes you keep asking for don't happen to be on account of your fancy female, I suppose?'

'My fancy female is a respectable young lady, Sarn't Major.'

'Then I wish you luck, but you're still in the army, and in the top infantry regiment, and when orders come along you obey them and go where you're sent.'

'I still ain't keen on Ireland.'

'If it happens, Daniel, you'll do your bit, same as you always do, same as we all do.'

'Talking of passes,' said Daniel, 'I'm officially requesting one for Wednesday afternoon.'

'Well, you get a smart turnout of your platoon on Wednesday morning, and I'll arrange the pass.'

'Much obliged,' said Daniel.

'I won't say it won't cost you a packet of Gold Flake,' said the sergeant major.

Gold Flake was a popular brand of cigarettes.

'Hearing you, Sarn't Major,' said Daniel, willing to fork out for two packets in return for the privilege of being able to meet up with Miss Maisie Gibbs.

He hoped for sunshine.

It was beginning to rain today.

Maisie, polishing the banisters and rails of the handsome staircase, drew aside as Mrs Carpenter ascended. The housekeeper had been down in the kitchen giving the staff orders for the week. She never allowed them to run things for themselves. She was always in touch with her responsibilities.

She stopped to observe the effects of Maisie's work.

'Very good, miss, very good,' she said.

'Thank you, mum,' said Maisie, and seized the opportunity to make a request. 'Oh, could I have some of me free time on Wednesday afternoon?'

'Wednesday again, girl, and then Sunday?' queried the good lady.

'Well, it's Wednesday and Sunday afternoons I like best,' said Maisie. 'If you please, mum.'

'Very well. Four hours on Wednesday, and four hours on Sunday.' Mrs Carpenter's mood was benevolent.

'Thank you, mum,' said Maisie, and the housekeeper moved on upwards. Maisie noted that she went directly to Mr Fairfax's suite, knocked lightly and then went straight in without waiting for an answer.

Oh, well, it's not my business, thought Maisie.

But four hours off on Wednesday, wasn't that kind of her? I could spare time to go to the mews first and speak to Mr Townley, and then to buy a new frock before meeting Daniel. If he's there about the usual time of half past two, he won't mind waiting a bit for me. Will he?

Chapter Fourteen

Wednesday afternoon, cloudy but dry. The time was just after two o'clock.

'Eh? Eh, what?' Mr Bill Townley registered the same kind of shock as before. 'Are you having me on, young Maisie?'

'No, honest,' said Maisie, 'you're to bring the carriage to the house by ten on Bank Holiday morning, to drive Mr Fairfax to see Tower Bridge, and you ain't to say anything to no-one.'

'Now look you 'ere, young Maisie,' said Mr Townley, and went on about his life not being worth a brass farthing if Mrs Carpenter got to know that these kind of arrangements were going on outside her eyes and ears.

Maisie said that like before, Mr Fairfax would invite her to join him and calm her down according. Mr Townley shook his head, and said the old gentleman was getting a bit too frisky, and would give Mrs Carpenter a fateful heart attack well before anybody would want him to have one himself. Mind, he said, on the previous outing, they both came back in the pink. Still, doing it again, and going all the way to Tower Bridge, what was Mr Fairfax thinking of?

Maisie said she supposed he was thinking of enjoying the sights.

'Well, if he takes a fall off the bridge,' said Mr Townley gloomily, 'I hope I don't get the blame.'

'Oh, Mrs Carpenter will make sure that don't happen, Mr Townley,' said Maisie, 'and if you'll excuse me, I've got to go now.'

'All right,' said Mr Townley, 'ten o'clock Bank Holiday Monday, is it? But I ain't sure what Chippy and Chirpy is going to make of that there Tower Bridge.'

'Oh, you could buy them an Italian ice-cream wafer each,' said Maisie, and left the coachman thinking her prim and proper self was getting a bit perky just lately.

It was well after two thirty when Daniel, waiting, saw her arrive. Strike a light, he thought, here's a poppet.

Maisie had bought a new dress in a shop in the Brompton Road, one that catered for the lower middle classes. In apricot, which the proprietress assured Maisie was a new colour for cottons, and accordingly a bit more expensive, it had a fashionably high collar, pearl buttons down its neat, close-fitting bodice, the smallest of waists and a long flowing skirt. Maisie had taken a whole five bob out of her savings, just in case, and she found she needed it, for the cost was four shillings and fourpence three farthings. She paid up with a little sigh, and wore it when she left the shop, her primrose dress in one of the shop's white paper carrier bags. Her boater sat on her well-dressed wealth of chestnut hair.

Daniel issued a soft whistle as she walked up to him.

'Is that you, your own self, Miss Maisie Gibbs?' he asked.

'Don't I look like me own self, then? Oh, d'you mean I'm a bit late?' Maisie was a little flushed. 'I'm ever so sorry, but I had to go to the mews first to see Mr Fairfax's coachman about something.'

'You're never late, Maisie, as long as you arrive,' said Daniel. 'We're both in service, we both know we can't be exact in our times. What I do know is that you look a rare treat again, not half you do. Is that a new frock?'

'Oh, I've had it for a little while,' said Maisie, which was true in its way. And, naturally, she didn't want Daniel to know she'd bought it in a rush on account of wanting to make sure she had an alternative to her primrose frock. Well, the same frock every time could get to look boring to him, couldn't it?

'Well, I tell you, Miss Maisie Gibbs, it's as pretty as your primrose frock,' said Daniel. 'They both make you look like a May queen.'

'Oh, flattered, I'm sure,' said Maisie, although

thrilled by the compliment. She knew she wasn't the greatest beauty ever to be seen in Kensington Gardens, but she wasn't discontented with her looks or with her firm figure. 'D'you really like this one?'

'Love it,' said Daniel, his smile warm.

'Oh, help,' said Maisie, familiar flutters rising.

'What d'you want help for?' asked Daniel, tempted to kiss her.

'It's me modesty,' said Maisie.

From a distance, a young man was watching them. It was Hubert Smythe, the artist who was craving to create a painting of Maisie in oils. Her new apricot frock drew his eyes. If she parted from the soldier in a while, he would speak to her. Yes, he must.

However, she moved off with her uniformed escort towards Hyde Park, holding a white paper carrier bag. He was tempted to follow, but his mother was arriving at his lodgings within the hour to drink tea with him and give him his monthly allowance, an allowance that subsidized his penurious existence as an artist. A fellow could sometimes avoid being at home when his mother was expected, but not when she had money for him.

'Maisie, would you like to go to the tea rooms again?' asked Daniel.

'Daniel, you've got nice ways for a soldier—'

'Hold up,' said Daniel, 'soldiers don't happen to be natural ruffians, yer know.'

'Oh, I didn't mean to be rude,' said Maisie

hastily, 'I only meant you hear stories that ain't very compliment'ry.'

'What you hear about soldiers is the same you can hear about all blokes,' said Daniel. 'So all blokes, as well as soldiers, like girls and a bit of slap and tickle.' He said that with a saucy grin.

'Excuse me, Daniel Adams,' said Maisie, 'but I know what a bit of slap and tickle means, so how much of it have you done with girls?'

'Not much,' said Daniel, 'I've never been that keen on tarty females. What I know to me sorrow is that the army don't mean a lot to people until it has to go to war. Then everyone wakes up a bit sudden to cheer soldiers marching off to battle.'

'Daniel, I'm ever so sorry.' Maisie was contrite. 'I'm sorry I didn't give you respect.'

'No hard feelings, Maisie. Shall we go to the tea rooms?'

'Oh, I was going to say about your nice ways that I don't want you to keep on spending money on me. It's being friends that counts most, don't you think?' She was earnest about that as they entered Hyde Park.

'It counts most, you're right, Maisie,' said Daniel, 'but I ain't empty of pocket, and I've got savings. I've always got savings. Rainy days come for soldiers just like they do for civilians, and I ain't disposed to be found wanting.'

'Oh, I've got savings too for a rainy day,' said Maisie.

'Then you're a wise girl, Maisie, and I admire you for yer good sense,' said Daniel. 'Will it be the tea rooms now, for a pot and currant buns this time?'

'I'd like that, Daniel, ever so much,' said Maisie, and they set off for refreshments.

They arrived, found the place only half full and collared a table. Daniel doffed his helmet, and they sat down. Maisie's apricot cotton and her starched petticoat rustled as she seated herself, which made Daniel take another look at her in her new frock and her familiar boater.

'One day, Maisie, I'm going to have to talk serious to you,' he said.

'Oh, crikey, how serious?' asked Maisie.

'Point is, will it be to your liking?'

'Not if it means you're going off to war,' said Maisie. British troops always seemed to be going off to one trouble spot or another.

Daniel thought about the Irish troubles and the rumour that the battalion might be heading for Ireland in the near future.

'No, it won't be—'

'Good afternoon, sir, what can I get you?' A waitress, not the same one as before, much to Maisie's relief, had materialized

'How about a gold mine?' suggested Daniel.

'Sorry, sir, but we don't serve gold mines.'

'Don't you get a call for them?' asked Daniel.

'Only from saucy soldiers.'

'In that case, we'll have a pot of tea for two and two currant buns,' said Daniel.

'Very good, sir.' The waitress, a homely young woman, bustled away.

Maisie, mouth twitching, said, 'Daniel, one day you'll get a black eye for the way you tease waitresses.'

'Oh, a bit of a laugh takes the weight off their feet,' said Daniel.

Subsequently they enjoyed their tea and buns, and what with that and their earlier visit to the place, together with their hansom cab ride to and from Tower Bridge, Maisie felt she was living a bit posh lately. She reminded Daniel he hadn't said what he was going to talk serious about. Daniel said it wouldn't be about going off to war. Maisie asked what, then?

'D'you feel you'd like me to kiss you?' asked Daniel.

'Beg pardon?' said Maisie, startled.

'D'you feel you'd like me to kiss you?'

That confused her.

'What a question,' she said. 'Daniel Adams, eat up your bun.'

Daniel smiled.

'I'll wait,' he said.

'Wait for what?' Maisie was pink.

'Oh, for what comes along,' said Daniel.

'Like a tram?' said Maisie. Talk of kissing was deep water for her. She saw it as something that was sort of exclusive to engaged couples. Soldiers kissing flirty girls in alleyways wasn't proper kissing.

Daniel didn't pursue the subject. He really

was willing to wait. In his opinion, a feller would be an idiot to press a clean-living girl like Maisie Gibbs. A kiss had to be her wish as much as his.

'How's your currant bun?' he asked.

'Nice and fresh, with lots of currants,' said Maisie. 'Oh, what d'you think, Daniel, I'm going to get Bank Holiday Monday off.'

'So's the battalion, except for duty personnel and blokes on CB,' said Daniel.

'What's CB?'

'Confined to barracks for breaking the Queen's Regulations,' said Daniel. 'Which means something like getting drunk and obstreperous while in uniform. Can't have too much of that, yer know. Listen, Maisie me girl, have you ever been to the Happy Hampstead fair on a bank holiday?'

'No, never,' said Maisie, 'only to Peckham Rye with me mum and dad sometimes.'

Daniel reached across the table and lightly patted her hand. It was a touch that communicated something of his feelings for her.

'Right,' he said, 'put your glad rags on next Monday and I'll take you to Hampstead.'

'Honest?' said Maisie, her brown eyes lighting up.

'You can bet on it,' said Daniel.

A soldier, a private of the West Kents, came in then, with a young woman. They sat down at a table in a kind of aggressive way and at once began a whispered argument. Daniel looked, and frowned slightly. A waitress approached the table, and the young woman said, 'Oh, not yet, go away.' Then she and the soldier went at each other hammer and tongs. Everyone in the restaurant turned their heads.

'Well, I never knew such bad manners,' said Maisie.

They were positively rowing with each other, the private and the young woman.

'Excuse me, Maisie,' said Daniel. He came to his feet and performed a brisk advance on the couple. Maisie watched. Reaching the table, he interrupted their angry exchanges and addressed the private quietly.

He's using his corporal's stripes to give that silly soldier what for, thought Maisie. What did he mean exactly, talking about being serious with me one day? Oh, help, I think he meant something ever so personal. That made her think of her job, and her assurance to Mrs Carpenter that she didn't have a young man and wasn't thinking of getting married. Well, she had to admit it, she did have a young man now, a young man that was going to talk serious to her one day. Oh, Lor', what's best for me to do she wondered.

On the other side of the restaurant, the private and the young woman had subsided into silence while listening to what Daniel was saying to the former. Suddenly, however, the young woman said something hot-temperedly to Daniel, then got up and walked out. The private hesitated.

Daniel spoke a few more quiet words to him, and the soldier followed the woman out.

Under the intrigued eyes of tea-taking customers, Daniel returned to Maisie and sat down.

'What did you say to them?' asked Maisie.

'Nothing to the lady, plenty to Private Goodbody about getting the West Kents a bad name,' said Daniel.

'You did right, Daniel.'

'You think so, Maisie?'

'Yes, I do. I'm never going to like people behaving like that in public. What did the woman say to you?'

'Nothing fit for your ears. Would you do something for me, Maisie?'

'Only if it's right and proper.'

'Would you pour me another cup of tea?'

Maisie looked at him, and was sure that the smile in his eyes had the kind of twinkle her late dad showed so often.

'Oh, a pleasure, Daniel,' she said.

After this, the time passed quickly for them, there at the table and later back in the Gardens, where they eventually came to a parting.

'Sunday?' said Daniel.

'Oh, I don't know I can get time off Sunday,' said Maisie, 'not when I been promised a free bank holiday.'

'Well, if I get another pass, I'll look out for you,' said Daniel, 'but not to worry if you can't manage it yourself. So long for the time being, Maisie me girl.'

'So long, Daniel.'

Daniel waited a moment in the hope she would invite a kiss, but it didn't happen, so he said, 'It's a peach, your new frock, Maisie,' and went on his way.

Chapter Fifteen

Alexander opened the door as Maisie approached.

'Saw yer coming, Maisie,' he said. 'Crikey, where'd you get that?'

'That?' said Maisie, stepping in.

'Yer new frock. Cor, it don't half suit yer. I ain't seen it afore, 'ave I?'

'Well, you're seeing it now,' said Maisie.

'What's in yer carrier bag?' asked Alexander, closing the door.

'A nose-grinder,' said Maisie.

'A whatter?'

'It's for shortening the beaks of nosy boys,' said Maisie.

'Well, it ain't for my beak, then,' said Alexander. ''Ere, Maisie,' he said, following her towards her room, 'I spent me free time making a visit to me old home, the orphanage, to show 'em how smart I look in me uniform. The staff didn't half make me welcome, and invited me to partake of tea and cake. I got friendly with one of the girls that's an orphan 'erself. Well, course, they're all orphans there, like me. Patty Cuckoo, that's her name.'

'Patty Cuckoo?' said Maisie. 'Alexander, you're hopeless. No-one's got a name like that.'

'Well, it's Cook, actu'lly,' said Alexander, 'only all the other orphans call her Cuckoo on account of she sings like a bird.'

'Cuckoos don't sing,' said Maisie.

'Well, Patty does, I 'eard her perform to the orphanage joanna,' said Alexander.

'She ought to be called Nightingale, then,' said Maisie.

'I can't say she sounds like one of them,' said Alexander. 'She's me own age, except a year younger, and the head bloke said I could take 'er out if I honour the orphanage with me presence again. What d'yer think of that, Maisie, me with a girl?'

'You're not old enough,' said Maisie, 'and she wants her head examined. Still, I wish yer luck, Alexander. Now hoppit, I've got to get changed.'

'Wait a tick,' said Alexander, 'I only got back half an hour ago, and first thing Milly told me was that Mr Fairfax 'ad another fall. But it wasn't fateful, like, and Mrs Carpenter was with him at the time. He wouldn't let 'er call the doctor, he said he was all right. Ain't it lucky the old biddy's always with him when he has a fall?'

'Oh, she does keep a caring eye on him, which is just as well,' said Maisie.

'Second thing, Maisie, there's another letter for yer,' said Alexander. 'I picked it up off the mat when I come up from me room after resting me plates of meat for a bit. Well, it's a long walk to me old orphanage.' He produced the letter and gave it to her. Maisie handled it gingerly. 'You know who it's from, don't yer?' said Alexander.

'Yes,' said Maisie, looking at her written name, 'but I ain't going to open it, I'm going to get changed, so be off with you.'

Alexander went.

She did open it, after she'd changed. Mr Hubert Smythe expressed his compliments and begged her to reply to him, since her silence was causing him grief. If she couldn't meet him in the Gardens, might he have the pleasure of calling on her at her place of work?

Not likely, the blessed pest, thought Maisie, and went up to let Mrs Carpenter know she was back.

The good lady wasn't in her own suite, so Maisie knocked on Mr Fairfax's door. Mrs Carpenter showed herself.

'I'm back, mum,' said Maisie.

'Yes, very well.' Mrs Carpenter wore a frown. 'See if Mrs Blisset has any work for you.'

'Oh, could I ask how Mr Fairfax is? Only Alexander told me he'd had another fall.'

'Much to my alarm,' said the housekeeper. 'Fortunately, however, it was only a slight tumble, and he refused to have the doctor call. But, of course, these falls worry me, and far more than they worry Mr Fairfax.' Mrs Carpenter spoke on a confiding note, which Maisie thought very human of her. 'Well, go and see Mrs Blisset, there's a good girl.'

'Yes'm,' said Maisie, and went down to the kitchen. Mrs Blisset wanted her to take Rosemary off her hands for a while, so Maisie treated the child to a walk up and down the street, as before. Rosemary expressed her pleasure by cooing. She wasn't yet up to making conversation, and any words she tried to speak emerged only as bubbles. Maisie thought her a little darling, and wondered if she'd have children like her. Eventually.

How serious was Daniel going to be one day?

Milly had the day off on Friday to go and see her family in Wanstead. Prudence whispered to Maisie that it was also to see her gentleman friend. Parlourmaids could have gentlemen friends, kitchen servants only had blokes.

Mrs Carpenter asked Maisie to clean and tidy Mr Fairfax's suite, and Maisie went up with pleasure. Mrs Carpenter came out of his suite as Maisie arrived with her cleaning materials.

'Just do the work, girl, and don't worry Mr Fairfax with chatter,' she said, speaking curtly this time.

'No, mum,' said Maisie dutifully.

But the old gentleman, in his library, his favourite retreat, was delighted to see her. He said she brightened his morning.

'Yes, indeed, and how are you, young lady?'

'Oh, in the pink, sir.'

'In the pink? Charming. Charming.'

'But I was sorry to hear you'd had another fall on Wednesday, sir.'

'Was it Wednesday? Well, what does it matter which day it was, mmm, Maisie? It was nothing to alarm anyone, just a slip as I attempted to sit down, and Mrs Carpenter was close by, close enough to break the fall. But, oh, dear, the fuss, Maisie.' Mr Fairfax shook his head.

'It's because she's caring of you, sir.'

Mr Fairfax smiled.

'Yes, indeed, and I couldn't do without her,' he said, 'although between you and me, young lady, I confess that such caring makes me feel I'm a hundred, not a mere seventy.' He chuckled. 'Ah, by the way, have you anything to tell me?'

'Tell you, sir?' Maisie was already at work. 'Oh, d'you mean about the carriage?'

'Yes, have you seen Townley?'

'Yes, I saw him Wednesday, when I had some time off,' said Maisie, thinking what a palaver it was that a gentleman who owned this house and paid all his servants, including Mrs Carpenter, to run it for him, had to be secretive about going for outings in his own carriage. Well, of course, he was a nice old gentleman, and Mrs Carpenter, being a strong-minded woman, was able to order his life like she ordered the lives of the servants. He was just too nice to put his foot down. 'Mr Townley's going to bring the carriage round at ten on Bank Holiday morning, like you said, and he ain't going to say anything to no-one.'

'Good. Splendid.' Mr Fairfax looked delighted and slightly triumphant. 'The cat must stay in the bag until Sunday evening, Maisie, when I shall then advise our invaluable housekeeper of my proposed jaunt the following day.'

Lor', thought Maisie, I hope it don't give her a heart attack.

'And you're going to invite her to ride with you, sir?'

'Yes, I must, as soon as she becomes alarmed at the thought of my going by myself. That, I think, was what we proposed, Maisie.'

'Oh, did we, sir?'

'Everything will be quite all right, you'll see.'

Crikey, I hope so, thought Maisie.

She made an excellent job of cleaning, dusting and tidying his rooms, and when she'd finished, Mrs Carpenter came to inspect the results. Maisie waited for some critical comments, but the house-keeper expressed generous approval.

'Yes, I'm pleased,' she said. 'Is Mr Fairfax satisfied?'

'I think so, mum,' said Maisie.

'Well, now you can have your morning refresh-ment, and then help Alexander beat the rugs from this suite and mine.'

'Yes,'m, thank you,' said Maisie, although beating rugs wasn't high on the list of jobs she liked. It wasn't on the list at all, in fact. But it had to be done. And Maisie had the kind of resolute approach to life that enabled her to take the rough with the smooth.

She was allowed free time on Sunday afternoon. She said nothing about her prospect of having Bank Holiday Monday off, since she wasn't supposed to know.

Alexander caught her on her way out of the house. She was wearing her new frock.

'Lumme, don't yer look posh again, Maisie? Where yer going?'

'Out,' said Maisie.

'Who with?'

'The cat,' said Maisie. Mrs Carpenter had a cat, mainly for the purpose of decimating any encroaching mice.

'I bet,' grinned Alexander. 'Listen, I got free time meself, so can I come with yer?'

'Not this afternoon, Alexander,' said Maisie. 'Why don't you do another visit to your old orphanage and take Patty Cuckoo for a walk?'

''Ere, I might just do that,' said Alexander. 'Can yer lend me tuppence for a bus fare?'

'All right,' said Maisie. She took out two pennies from her purse and gave them to him.

'Ta,' said Alexander, 'and blowed if you ain't me best friend.'

'Well, make sure you pay me back, then,' said Maisie.

'Corporal Adams,' said Company Sergeant Major Albert Sawyer, stopping Daniel on his way to the

173

Knightsbridge barracks gates, 'might I enquire as to where you're going this time?'

'To the Gardens, Sarn't Major,' said Daniel, pulling up smartly. 'With me pass.'

'And what's in the Gardens for you, might I also ask?'

'Well, as ever, there's the Round Pond, the Albert Memorial, the Palace—'

'Seeing my grandmother taught me to suck eggs, don't you try it on. What I hear is that you're done for definite.'

'In what way, Sarn't Major?'

'You're thinking of getting wed definite.'

'Now where'd you get that idea from?' asked Daniel.

'Dicky birds,' said the sergeant major. At forty, he was one of the old school, with a waxed moustache and a voice like thunder, when thunder was called for.

'Dicky birds carry rumours,' said Daniel, 'and I've heard some meself, Irish ones.'

'Irish dicky birds get shot,' said the sergeant major. 'All right, Corporal Adams, don't keep the lady waiting, get marching. And don't forget the colonel will want to see you if a wedding's definite and you'll require married quarters.'

'Hearing you, Sarn't Major,' said Daniel, and departed, wondering if Maisie had managed to get time off.

Maisie, entering the Gardens, was spotted by young Mr Hubert Smythe, who had an artist's fixation on her upright, straight-backed carriage, and her exemplary neatness of figure. He was seated on a bench in the hope she'd appear, and he came to his feet to intercept her.

He raised his floppy black hat.

'Miss Gibbs, Miss Maisie Gibbs?'

Maisie, finding him in her way, stopped.

'Excuse me, if you don't mind,' she said, 'but who are you, might I ask?'

'It's a great pleasure for me to introduce myself, Miss Gibbs. My name is Hubert Smythe, your humble servant and devoted admirer.'

'Oh, you're him, are you?' said Maisie. 'You're the bloke that keeps sending me disgusting letters. Well, take that!' She boxed his left ear. His hat, restored to his head, fell off. Other than that, his reaction was one of thrilled admiration.

'Oh, by Jove,' he said, 'a young Queen of the Amazons, an Hippolyte, by all that's wonderful.'

'You're barmy,' said Maisie, 'and I'll box your ears some more if you ever come near me again. Be off with you, d'you hear?' And she went on her way. Hubert Smythe called after her.

'I shall never stop hoping, never give in!'

Maisie walked on, leaving poor old Hubert dreaming of a canvas on which a modern Hippolyte rode a winged Pegasus against the background of a radiant sky, her white robe and auburn hair streaming. Yes, he'd make her hair auburn and tip it with fire. It was unfortunate that Hippolyte, in the form of Maisie Gibbs, suspected he meant to paint her in the altogether, and equally unfortunate that he was unaware of this. Mind, her streaming robe did mean her legs would show.

On went Maisie. Daniel entered the Gardens from the direction of Knightsbridge, and amid the Sunday promenaders they saw each other. Each made a beeline for the other, very much like two people in love.

'Maisie me girl, strike a flag if you don't look more of a treat every time I see you,' said Daniel.

'And you look a real smart soldier all the time,' said Maisie, impulsively responsive.

'I was never made of lead,' said Daniel.

'Well, no, you couldn't march about if you was,' said Maisie. 'Daniel, let's find a bench for a sit-down, I want to talk to you about something.'

'Hold up,' said Daniel, 'you haven't found a job up in bonny Scotland, have yer?'

'No, it's nothing like that,' said Maisie, and they walked until they found a vacant bench. They sat down, and Maisie told Daniel all about a dubious bloke called Hubert Smythe, and his scandalous desire to have her sit for him, like one of them brazen Chelsea models, she supposed. She also recounted how she had just met the rotter and what had happened.

Daniel stared, twitched and roared with laughter. People looked. It made no difference. Daniel simply laughed his head off.

'Maisie, you actu'lly did that, you boxed his ears?'

'Yes, so I did,' said Maisie stiffly, 'and it ain't funny.'

'I tell you, Maisie, the thought of you clouting the bloke is a right old rib-tickler,' said Daniel.

'Thanks very much, I don't think,' said Maisie. 'What about me self-respect, and being invited to pose in me birthday suit?'

'Now that's different,' said Daniel, 'I take offence at that.'

'So what would you have done, then?' asked Maisie.

'Knocked his block off,' said Daniel, 'but you, a slip of a girl at what – five feet six? With not a bulging muscle in sight? And you box a bloke's ears? What happened to him?'

'His hat fell off,' said Maisie.

Daniel looked at her. Her lips twitched and she actually giggled. If there was something she had never been, it was a giggler, but she giggled now.

'Oh, help,' she said, 'you should of seen his face, it was like he didn't know where he was. But I still feel it didn't pay him out properly for insulting me self-respect.'

Daniel asked if she still had the letters he'd sent. Maisie said yes, she had them in her reticule. Daniel asked if he could see them, so she took them out and let him read them. It surprised her that he didn't seem to think them scandalous.

In fact, Daniel said, 'Well, I must say he sounds like a polite bloke.'

'Polite?' said Maisie indignantly. 'What's polite about inviting a respectable girl to take her clothes off? Go on, tell me that.'

'You've got a point, Maisie,' said Daniel. 'His politeness could hide the evil in his mince pies.'

'Lord above,' said Maisie, 'd'you think he could actu'lly be evil, then?'

'Well, I'm minded to say it's a bit evil of any bloke to invite a well-behaved young lady to take all her clothes off,' said Daniel. 'Not that he actu'lly says so.'

'Well, them Chelsea painters don't, do they?' said Maisie. 'They just expect it of their models. Here, d'you know what he shouted after me when I walked away from him? That he'd never stop hoping, he'd never give in.'

'Saucy blighter,' said Daniel. 'Well, I tell yer, Maisie, he's got to stop pestering you. I'll get an hour off one evening, with the co-operation of me sergeant major, and I'll give him a call at this address of his.'

'Oh, would you do that for me, Daniel?'

'It's me bounden duty, Maisie, to sort him out,' said Daniel, stowing Hubert Smythe's letters inside his red jacket. 'Now, about tomorrow, and taking you to Happy Hampstead. What time d'you think you'll be ready?'

Maisie thought about what Mr Fairfax had said. It meant she and Milly would be free after the old gentleman had started his drive to Tower Bridge, which would probably be a bit after ten.

'I think, well, say about half past ten.' She'd have to change into one of her frocks first.

'Right,' said Daniel. 'I'll be in the Gardens at that time and wait for you.'

'Oh, I ain't 'alf looking forward to 'appy 'ampstead,' said Maisie, dropping all her aitches in her excitement.

'That's my girl,' said Daniel, and they spent the rest of their free time strolling, lingering and talking amid the familiar atmosphere of sauntering people and lively children.

They were watched by Hubert Smythe, trailing them at a distance, while committing to his artistic imagination further impressions of the young lady. Such a canvas would surely be accepted by the Royal Academy as the work of a genius.

Chapter Sixteen

Sunday evening.

'What? What?' Mrs Carpenter looked alarmed. She was with Mr Fairfax in his suite, where she had just finished eating supper with him.

'Yes, I intend to see Tower Bridge, Iris,' he said. 'A remarkable architectural creation, which everyone should see.'

'No, no, I protest,' said Mrs Carpenter, 'you will be crushed by a horde of common, barging people who'll give no thought to your frailty.'

'My condition, dear lady, is not as frail as that,' said Mr Fairfax, looking, indeed, very much in the pink. 'No, my mind is made up, I simply must see this bridge.'

'Again I protest,' said Mrs Carpenter, 'and I should be failing in my duty if I let you go.'

'Then you must come with me.' Mr Fairfax nodded genially. 'Yes, we will go together, and you can intercede should I be in danger of large bodies barging me about.'

'I tremble for you,' said the black-clad house-keeper. Black suited her. It gave a dignified air of command to her full-bodied person. And one could have said she knew it. Certainly, she was an awesome figure in the eyes of her servants at times. 'But very well, if you must, you must. And since I can't let you go on your own, I shall most definitely come with you. Otherwise, I shall worry about you having another fall.'

'Well, now you need not worry,' said Mr Fairfax. 'It's settled, then. Good. I can't remember when I was last out on a bank holiday. Ah, by the way, Milly has been looking after my rooms so well that I think she should have the bank holiday off.'

'The whole day?' Mrs Carpenter frowned.

'The whole day? Yes, why not?' Mr Fairfax, smiling, seemed to infer his housekeeper had made a suggestion. 'Splendid, yes. I agree, we must offer extra rewards occasionally. Maisie can dust and clean my suite. That young lady is an excellent worker. I'm delighted you found her.' As an apparent afterthought, he added, 'Oh, and yes, after she's finished here, she can take the rest of the bank holiday off.'

'Well, really.'

'Come, let us be generous, Iris.'

'Very well, but too much generosity can make servants slack,' said Mrs Carpenter.

'Well, there must be limits, of course,' said Mr Fairfax, nodding wisely, 'but for tomorrow, let generosity prevail, mmm?'

'If you wish,' said the housekeeper, 'but we shall have to make it up to the other servants. It won't do, you know, to favour two at the expense of the rest. There'll be jealousy and backbiting.'

'I shall leave it to you, Iris, to tell the others they may have a full Sunday off in addition to their usual free times,' said Mr Fairfax who, having won over his housekeeper, could now have asked her to send Alexander to prime Mr Townley in the morning. But that deed had already been done. By Maisie. It had tickled the benevolent old gentleman to engage in another conspiratorial arrangement with the pleasing maid of all work.

As it was, Mrs Carpenter took up the point in question, saying she would tell Alexander to instruct Townley first thing in the morning. Mr Fairfax smiled gently and said Townley had been advised earlier.

'Well, really,' said Mrs Carpenter, 'it's up-setting to have you do these things without telling me.'

Mr Fairfax begged her to forgive him these oversights. She must know, he said, how much he appreciated all she did for his comfort.

That soothed her rumpled black feathers.

Later, Edie and Daisy were scrubbing the surface of the large kitchen table. It was their last duty every Sunday, Tuesday and Thursday night. Mrs Blisset, who had been upstairs on one of her visits to the housekeeper's suite, came down to tell the staff that they were going to get a full day off extra to their official free times. An extra full day? Edie and Daisy nearly fell into their buckets of soapy water.

Continuing, Mrs Blisset said that Milly's and Maisie's day off would be tomorrow, Bank Holiday, although Maisie was required to dust and clean Mr Fairfax's rooms first.

Maisie, elated, knew Mr Fairfax had kept his word, bless the old gent. And on top of that, he'd thought of Prudence, Agnes and the others. Prudence and Edie grumbled a bit about not being given the bank holiday themselves, but Alexander said he didn't mind, and that he could spend his extra free day at the orphanage whenever it was.

'What, with that girl that's cuckoo?' said Edie.

They'd all heard about the girl. Alexander's non-stop tongue had a habit of spilling out every detail of his life, private or working, except where it concerned Maisie. His tongue was faithful to Maisie.

'Now did I say she was cuckoo, meaning daft?' he said. 'No, I didn't, I just said it was what the other orphans called 'er. Patty Cuckoo, that's what I said, on account of her being on song when the orphanage joanna is playing.'

'On song? You're a character, you are, Alexander,' said Agnes, and Alexander said he prided himself on his musical ear.

Mrs Blisset said he could sail through low clouds with ears like he had.

Alexander grinned. The lively houseboy never

took offence. Maisie gave him a friendly glance, and Edie and Daisy finished scrubbing the table. All was well with the staff. Mrs Blisset even went to her room to watch over her sleeping child for a while.

In a house in Bayswater, the landlady called up to one of her tenants.

'Mr Smythe? Mr Smythe?'

The young gentleman came out of his room to answer the call.

'Hello, yes?'

'There's a visitor to see you.'

'My mother?'

'No, it's a gent in the Queen's uniform.'

'Really? I'm not expecting anyone like that. Oh, well, send him up, Mrs Loveday.'

Up went Daniel. He had about fifteen minutes to spare before time made it necessary to perform a quick march back to barracks. On the second-floor landing, he came face to face with Mr Hubert Smythe.

'You're Smythe?' he said, a hint of steel in his grey eyes.

'Yes,' said the aspiring painter, 'and I think I've seen you around.'

'Corporal Adams. Let's talk.'

'In here,' said Hubert, and led the way into his bedroom, which also served as a studio because of its favourable light. The easel was by the window, paints, palette and brushes on a table. 'It's not much, but it's private,' he said. 'Might I have the honour of knowing the reason for your call?'

Daniel went to work on behalf of Maisie, dressing the offending artist down with some no-nonsense language mixed with some choice army stuff. He made it very clear to Hubert that any more unwanted letters or further accosting of Miss Gibbs would cause a hundredweight of Welsh coal in a chain-mail bag to fall on his head.

'Oh, I say, have I offended her?' asked Hubert.

'What do you think?' said Daniel. 'She's a very respectable young lady, and you've been inviting her to pose stripped, haven't you?'

'Good gracious, no,' said Hubert, looking a bit offended himself. 'My original idea was to depict her as a perfect example of a proud well-dressed young subject of our Glorious Majesty. My present wish is to depict her as Hippolyte riding winged Pegasus through the heavenly sky.'

'Eh what?' said Daniel.

'In a robe of white purity,' said Hubert.

'Who the hell's Hippy?'

'Hippolyte, legendary Queen of the Amazons.'

'Have I heard of her?' asked Daniel, whose reading hadn't embraced Greek mythology. But he had a vague idea he had heard of the ancient Amazons and some queen or other.

'I won't say everyone is familiar with her feats and her encounter with Theseus—'

'Hold up,' said Daniel, 'you're losing me.'

'I've a book telling various tales of legendary Greece,' said Hubert. 'It's called *Myths of the Gods*, and is frightfully compelling reading. It includes the myth of Hippolyte and Theseus, and Hippolyte and Hercules.'

'It does, does it?' said Daniel, seeing the bloke in a new light. 'Listen, while I've still got a couple of minutes to spare, show me some of your work.'

'Willingly,' said Hubert, not inclined to bandy harsh words with this long-legged, muscular corporal, obviously capable of pulverizing a fellow. 'Here we are.' His portfolio lay on the table, and he opened it up for Daniel's inspection. Daniel went through a selection of watercolours and pencil sketches, and was frankly impressed.

'Well, I'll admit it, sunshine,' he said in friendly fashion, 'these look a bit of all right. I'm no artist meself, but you seem a genuine one. Hello, what's this?' He was looking at a very fine pencil sketch of a distinctly recognizable young lady.

'That,' said Hubert, 'I modestly present as an outline of Miss Gibbs, sketched from memory.'

'Well, strike up the band if it ain't a blinder,' said Daniel.

'A blinder?'

'A real pleasure to my optics,' said Daniel. 'It's Maisie all right. Damn good.'

'I'm delighted you think so,' said Hubert, 'and I'll be happy for you to give it to her, if you wish.'

'Much obliged, I do wish,' said Daniel, so Hubert rolled up the sketch, put a light elastic band around it and gave it to him.

'There, with my compliments,' he said. 'I can always make another.'

'Thanks,' said Daniel. 'All right, no hard feelings, Mr Smythe, I believe all you've told me, except I've got serious doubts about Miss Gibbs posing for you in a white robe.'

'And with Greek sandals, of course,' said Hubert.

'They'll do it, will they?' said Daniel. 'Well, I doubt it. I don't think Miss Gibbs will pose in any white robe, with or without Greek sandals.'

'Believe me, I shall be bitterly disappointed,' said Hubert.

'Well, I'll at least tell her you're a genuine artist,' said Daniel, 'but leave her alone and I won't have to call again.'

'I'd appreciate it if you'd put in a good word for me,' said Hubert.

'This sketch will do that for you,' said Daniel. 'By the way, I'd like to borrow that book you mentioned. Any chance?'

'A pleasure, Corporal Adams,' said Hubert, 'it's here.' He examined a row of books on a shelf, plucked one free and handed it to Daniel.

'Much obliged,' said Daniel. 'I'll let you have it back. Well, I'm off now, glad to have met you and put things right. You're a good bloke. So long.'

'Goodbye,' said Hubert, sighing as his unexpected visitor departed. But there was still hope, there was always hope, especially now that Corporal Adams would undoubtedly let Miss Gibbs know she was to be depicted as a fully robed Hippolyte, Queen of the Amazons. Good heavens, how remiss he had been in not making it clear to her that he had no intention of painting a nude. Nude in art belonged mainly to the Renaissance era, the subjects extraordinarily fleshy women. Such women must have found it difficult to keep everything tidily in place, and could not compare with the slender form of Miss Gibbs, which was very tidy indeed. Yes, hope must stay eternal.

Daniel slipped smartly through the gates of the barracks as dusk gave way to encroaching night.

'Sergeant Lee's looking for you, Corp,' said the guard.

'Hearing you,' said Daniel, striding briskly on. He ran into the looming figure of his platoon sergeant.

'Hold up,' said Sergeant Jack Lee, 'I've got news for you.'

'Irish news?' said Daniel.

'Forget the Irish,' said Sergeant Lee. 'I'm trying to. Guard commander duty for you tomorrow, Corporal Adams. Stand to at five forty-five, as per usual, and mount the guard at six.'

'That's for Corporal Thomas,' said Daniel, 'he's on the roster tomorrow.'

'Corporal Thomas has gone sick with tonsillitis.'

'Silly sod,' said Daniel, 'and highly inconvenient. I've got a pass for tomorrow.'

'Just lately, Corporal Adams, passes have rained down on you like wedding confetti. Be back here for duty tomorrow, as per my orders.'

'Noted, Sarge.'

Chapter Seventeen

August Bank Holiday Monday, 1894.

Cockney families were enjoying the sea breezes at Southend and Margate, and lapping up shrimps, winkles and jellied eels. Parliament was in recess, Queen Victoria was at Balmoral, and Maisie Gibbs and Corporal Daniel Adams were sitting on a bench in Kensington Gardens.

Daniel had wanted to talk to Maisie before they caught a horse bus to Hampstead Heath from Bayswater Road. He was now telling her of his call on Hubert Smythe, and how his time with the bloke had convinced him he was a genuine artist who hadn't ever intended to paint her in the altogether. Maisie said what a relief that was, it would stop her having shocking dreams about finding herself posing on a couch in her birthday suit, with an evil-looking painter leering at her out of wicked eyes. Still, she said, she wasn't actually sorry she'd boxed Hubert Smythe's ears. After all, he'd never had no right to send her letters and to accost her. It just wasn't complimentary to her respectability.

Daniel, hiding a smile, said he thought the bloke was harmless, even if he did have a bee in his bonnet about painting her as a young Queen of the Amazons.

'Beg pardon?' said Maisie.

'Well, I think I've heard about female Amazons and their Queen,' said Daniel, 'but he had me off balance when he called her – what was it now? Hippopollity, or something like it.'

'Crikey, who wants to be painted with a name like that?' said Maisie. 'It ain't a proper name at all, it's more like a sneeze or a hiccup. And a hiccup's bad manners if you don't put your hand over yer mouth.'

'He lent me a book about them ancient Greeks and their gods, which I'm going to read,' said Daniel. 'And what d'you think of this, Maisie? It's his own work and it's yours. He asked me to give it to you.'

The rolled sketch was in his hand. He unrolled it and passed it to Maisie.

She looked, she stared and she blinked.

'I don't believe it,' she said.

'It's a winner, Maisie.'

'It's me, then?'

'It's you, and all done in pencil. When we get to Hampstead Heath, let's see if there's a stall selling picture frames. If so, we'll buy one and frame that sketch.'

'Crikey,' breathed Maisie, 'I suppose I've got to be a bit sorry now that I hit him.'

'If he did paint you, he'd put you in a white robe,' said Daniel.

'Like a bathrobe?'

'I suppose so.'

'I ain't posing for no-one in a bathrobe.'

'Whatever you say, Maisie. Right, shall we go and catch a horse bus now?'

'Yes, let's, Daniel.'

'I need to be back at barracks by five, I've been copped for guard duty, but we've still got plenty of time for Happy Hampstead and the funfair.'

By the time they were on their way in the bus, Maisie's employers, Mr Fairfax and Mrs Carpenter, were well into the pleasure of inspecting Tower Bridge along with a horde of people. They were arm in arm, Mrs Carpenter giving the old gentleman firm support. Mr Fairfax relayed statistics concerning the building of the bridge. Mrs Carpenter said as many statistics as that were worrying, since the weight of them might collapse the bridge while they were on it. Mr Fairfax said one should be capable of happier thoughts on a bank holiday.

The old gentleman was in fine fettle.

Hampstead Heath and its funfair provided a typical London bank holiday festival for cockneys and the lower middle classes. Swings, roundabouts, coconut shies, hoopla, shooting booths, roll-a-penny, guess-your-weight, strike the bell and other fairground entertainments had crowds around them. Balloon-sellers were raking in pennies, and ice-cream merchants were beginning to think that a week of sunny bank holidays would enable them to start a useful bank account.

On a swingboat that was going higher and higher to the vigorous pull of a laughing soldier, a young lady was shrieking.

'Daniel! Stop it! Oh, me skirts!'

The skirt of Maisie's dress was billowing, and so was her petticoat each time her half of the swing whooshed downwards. Her legs in black cotton stockings were caught by the sun. Worse, even the frilled, pink-ribboned lace hems of the legs of her white drawers kept showing above her knees. Her self-respect kind of blushed all over, and her dignity was falling to pieces.

Daniel, the shocker, was all delighted eyes. Maisie, by Holy Joe, not only had legs, she had a very good-looking slender pair.

'Higher, Maisie?'

'Oh, I'll kill yer!' shrieked Maisie. No respectable girl should be put in the position of showing her legs and drawers, especially not in public. 'Daniel, stop it! Oh, me Gawd, there's people coming to look!'

Daniel eased his grip on the tasselled rope, and the swingboat began to slow down. Flushed, she covered her legs, and gave Daniel a look that carried the threat of boxing his ears.

Daniel, the saucy devil, only said, 'Another ride, Maisie?'

'Oh, you wait,' said Maisie, 'I'll take that silly grin off yer face.'

Daniel brought the swing to a stop, and eased himself out with a lithe movement of his long-legged body. He helped Maisie to alight by taking hold of her slim waist between both hands, lifting her free and putting her on her feet. Breathless, she gave him another lethal look. He winked.

'Maisie me girl,' he said, 'I never saw anything prettier.'

'Oh, I'm going to—' She stopped as reaction took a different turn, and suddenly her rare laugh broke through. 'Oh, you,' she said.

'Pink ribbon's very pretty,' said Daniel, quite definitely in love, and lost to the sounds and spectacle of multiplying crowds.

'Daniel Adams, don't you dare mention what you saw,' blushed Maisie. It really was a blush. 'I've a good mind to box both your ears for not respecting me person.'

'Maisie, I respect your person honest and genuine,' said Daniel.

'You've got a funny way of showing it,' said Maisie, giving him another look. He was wearing a blue peaked cap today, not his helmet, and looked handsomer than ever. His ever-present smile was in his eyes, teasing her. 'Daniel?' Compulsively, she turned her face up. Impulsively, Daniel put his lips to hers, and there, close to the swings, with people passing by and kids darting about, Maisie received the first romantic kiss of her life, and on a day when she was still five weeks short of eighteen.

She went giddy, and her knees faltered a little.

'Maisie?'

'Oh, Lor',' she breathed.

'Maisie, walk with me.'

'Yes, all right,' she said faintly.

He took her arm and they left the noisy, rumbustious fairground. They found an unhindered spot on the Heath and sat down on the grass.

'Maisie?' said Daniel again.

'Yes, Daniel?'

'Exactly how old are you?'

'Eighteen next month.'

'Maisie, will you marry me?'

'Will I what . . . ? Oh, beg pardon, what did you say?'

'Will you marry me, you sweet girl?'

Maisie quivered, then steadied herself.

'Daniel, is that what you wanted to talk serious about?' she asked.

'You bet it is,' said Daniel. 'Well, I love you, don't I?'

Maisie flowered.

'Oh, ain't it a lovely day, Daniel?'

'Might I ask what that means?'

'It means yes, I'll marry you.'

'You will?'

'Yes, Daniel.'

'You darling,' said Daniel and kissed her with ardour. Maisie clung in heady response.

The kiss broke and she gasped, 'Daniel, there's people looking.'

'Let 'em,' said Daniel, arm around her waist and sitting warmly close to her. 'Shall we get churched when you're eighteen, say?'

'That's only next month, in September.'

'Say in October, then?' Daniel put rumours of a spell in Ireland out of his mind.

'Could we talk first about things?' said Maisie, who had always had very definite ideas of what marriage should mean.

'Say whatever you want to say, Maisie.'

Maisie said she hadn't ever thought about marrying a soldier, so what would it be like? Daniel said they could live in married quarters. Maisie said no, she didn't want that, she wanted a proper home where they could bring up a family in private, like, even if he was away at times. She was sure married quarters wouldn't be a bit private. So could Daniel afford to rent a house? Daniel said he'd get an allowance as a married man, so where did she fancy living? Maisie said at once that a nice three-up, three-down house in Walworth, where she was brought up, could be rented for nine shillings a week. There was a lovely market in East Street, where she'd be able to shop ever so cheaply.

'I'd feel really at home in Walworth,' she said.

'Walworth it'll be, then,' said Daniel. 'I know it well meself, seeing I was brought up in Camberwell. I've got savings, yer know, Maisie, which'll give us a good start.'

196

'Oh, I've got some too,' said Maisie. 'I've got as much as a bit more than five pounds. I've saved it out of me wages since last year.'

'You're a wise girl,' said Daniel, ecstatic on account of having had her say yes. 'It's what I call useful money for a rainy day.'

'I don't call a wedding a rainy day,' said Maisie.

'I stand corrected, me young love,' said Daniel, 'and I'm letting you know my own savings add up to just over a hundred pounds right now.'

'A hundred pounds?' gasped Maisie.

'Put aside out of me army pay since I signed on,' said Daniel. 'Well, I don't live reckless, like a sailor who's always rolling out of one pub into another. I just buy the occasional pint of beer and necessary odds and ends.' He had, he said, always had in mind a time when a bit of a nest egg would be more than useful. Once they were married, and he'd paid for some necessary things, they could put the rest of the money into a Post Office savings account in the name of Mrs Maisie Adams, and it would be hers to draw on whenever she needed a bit extra to the allowance she'd get as a corporal's wife.

'Daniel, you'd give it all to me?' said Maisie, eyes wide.

'It's a man's duty to see his wife is provided for as best as he can manage,' said Daniel.

Maisie believed, as her mum had, that every man was born to be a provider and protector as a husband, and a woman's obligation as a wife was to see to her man's comfort and keep him in order.

'Daniel, you're a good man,' she said earnestly, 'and I'll never take anything out of the savings except when we might be a bit desp'rate on account of extra expenses.'

Daniel said there'd be expenses at first, like furniture and all kinds of other things. They'd shop for them at the right time. Maisie said she knew places in Walworth where they could get real bargains. By the way, she said, would Daniel be able to live at home or in the barracks? Daniel, knowing his time in the barracks was of a temporary duration, said he'd live at home whenever he could. Other than that, as a married man he'd get a regular weekend pass.

They talked on and on, making their plans, with Daniel kissing her every now and again, and Maisie telling him that people were looking. But she didn't actually object. Kisses from Daniel were new and exciting, exciting enough to arouse all kinds of pleasurable flutters.

They didn't go back to the funfair. They'd bought a frame for the sketch, which Maisie carried together with it in a paper carrier bag. And they'd bought fruit for lunch.

She was happy sitting on the Heath with Daniel and just talking. The afternoon seemed to rush by, and they left in time for him to get back to barracks by five o'clock. Maisie actually accompanied him to the gates, where the guard looked on with a grin as Daniel kissed her goodbye for the time being.

'Daniel, when I've put the picture in the frame, would you like to have it and keep it?' she asked.

'Would I. You bet I would,' said Daniel.

'I'll write on it first,' said Maisie.

'What'll you write?' asked Daniel, thinking about buying her an engagement ring.

'To Daniel, with love from Maisie, August Bank Holiday, 1894.'

'You sweet girl,' said Daniel. He kissed her again and they parted. He stood at the gates to watch her go, delightful as ever in her primrose frock and perky boater.

She's my girl, and she's a jewel.

Maisie took her time going back to the house. She sat on a bench in Kensington Gardens to lose herself in dreamy thoughts about marriage to Daniel. What would it be like as a soldier's wife? It shouldn't be too worrying, because the country wasn't at war. There hadn't been any war for years, not since the Crimea, which she knew from her history lessons at school had been forty years ago. So had the Indian Mutiny. Well, nearly forty. Of course, there were always nuisance uprisings in various parts of the world. And so there were in the Empire as well, but the British army soon settled those little bothers.

No, she wouldn't have any serious worries

about Daniel being in the army. She was sure she'd be as good a wife to him as her mum had been to her dad. She supposed he could have found someone a lot more like Lillie Langtry than she was. Still, she wasn't actually plain, she knew that. If she had been, that funny bloke, Hubert Smythe, wouldn't have begged to paint her, would he? Fancy him wanting her to sit for him in a white bathrobe. Mr Fairfax had a bathrobe, a blue one. She'd seen it hanging up on the occasions when she'd helped Milly clean his suite, and when it had to be parcelled up with other items for collection by the laundry van from Bayswater Road. Lots of things had to be properly laundered and not put in the Monday washtub.

She thought then about Mrs Carpenter, who had let her know right at the beginning that she wouldn't be given the job if she was thinking of getting married. If she told the housekeeper now that she was going to marry Daniel in two months' time, would she get sacked immediate, like? She didn't want that, she didn't have anywhere to live except in a rented room somewhere, which would mean using some of her savings. No, she'd best keep quiet about it for the time being.

If that was a bit of a problem, it didn't affect the little vibrations of happy excitement, which were still with her when she reached Kensington Gore at half past six.

There, however, she came to a startled halt.

Standing at the foot of the steps of Mr Fairfax's handsome residence was a policeman, a tall uniformed constable with a firm official look about him.

Oh, me Gawd, thought Maisie, what's happened?

Chapter Eighteen

'No callers being admitted, miss, ' said the constable, as Maisie hurried up.

'But what's happened?' asked Maisie. 'I work here, only I've been out all day. What's happened?'

'I'm not allowed to give information, miss,' said the constable, grave of face. 'But you work here, you say?'

'Yes, I'm the gen'ral maid, I'm Maisie Gibbs.'

'Well, that being the case, miss, you can go in. You'll find the other servants in the kitchen.'

Maisie hastened down the basement steps, opened the door and hurried through to the kitchen. Outside the closed door was another constable, looking as if he was standing on guard. Maisie explained who she was. He looked her over and nodded.

'You can go in, miss,' he said. He opened the door for her.

Prudence, Agnes, Daisy and Edie were all sitting around the table, shoulders hunched. Agnes and Edie were crying, Prudence and Daisy pale-faced and red-eyed. Alexander was there too, standing with his back to the pantry door, his countenance devoid of any single aspect of its usual perkiness, his body stiff.

'What's happened, what's happened?' gasped Maisie.

'Oh, you're back,' sighed Prudence, 'but you'll maybe wish you 'adn't ever returned. Milly's still out, and I could wish 'er to stay out. You'd best sit down.'

'But I don't want to sit down till I know what's 'appened,' said Maisie desperately.

Alexander spoke, in a strangely tight voice.

'I'll tell yer, Maisie.'

The story came out then from the houseboy, aided by occasional interjections from Prudence, the most sensible of the women. It was a story that gradually petrified Maisie.

At about four in the afternoon, Alexander, who'd been smoking a cigarette up in the attic, heard a loud shriek from the first floor. He descended the stairs at a run. Going down, he glimpsed Mrs Blisset entering Mrs Carpenter's suite. She was carrying something. Further shrieks assailed his ears. They were coming from Mr Fairfax's suite. He took the rest of the stairs in leaps and rushed into the suite, where he immediately came up against Mrs Carpenter, face wild, eyes wild and hair wild, her hands and the sleeves of her dress sopping wet.

'The doctor, the doctor, run for Dr Graham, Mr Fairfax has had another fall – in his bath! Run, run!'

Alexander, scared out of his wits, ran like the wind. Dr Graham was in, entertaining a friend to tea. As soon as he learned that Mr Fairfax had had a fall in his bath, he took up his bag and excused himself to his friend. With his pony and trap in the mews, he followed Alexander back to the house at a run. Up they rushed to the first floor, where the other servants were gathered in a frightened huddle on the landing, Rosemary in Prudence's arms, the bewildered child cuddled to her protective bosom. Into the suite ran Dr Graham, Alexander on his heels. There, Mrs Carpenter was in a collapsed state on Mr Fairfax's bed, Mrs Blisset standing at the bathroom door, hands tightly clasping her suffering face.

On the bathroom floor lay Mr Fairfax, and on top of his body lay his bathrobe. His exposed face was turned to one side, his eyes closed.

'I covered him up, I covered him up!' gasped Mrs Blisset. 'It seemed only decent. Is he dead, doctor, is he dead?'

Dr Graham went down on both knees beside the old gentleman. He pushed the robe off Mr Fairfax's chest and began a hurried and critical examination.

Alexander, eyes wide and horrified, looked on from beside the shocked Mrs Blisset. He knew, he just knew, that his employer was dead. Indeed, after only a few short minutes, Dr Graham pronounced him so. He covered him up and came slowly to his feet. He turned to Mrs Blisset.

'Can you tell me what happened?'

'He's dead, doctor, he's really dead?' was the cook's painful rejoinder.

'I'm afraid so, and there's no chance of reviving him,' said Dr Graham. 'What happened, do you know?'

Mrs Blisset, drawing breath, first of all said Mrs Carpenter was in a terrible state of collapse after what had happened. She went on to say the old gentleman had taken a ride to Tower Bridge in the morning, in company with Mrs Carpenter, who had a responsibility to make sure he didn't have a fall while he was out. He was a little tired when he got back about midday, and later this afternoon he decided to take a refreshing bath. Well, he usually did bathe before supper, every other day.

Mrs Blisset said she was with Mrs Carpenter in the living room of his suite, talking. Mrs Carpenter wanted to stay nearby, to make sure she would hear him if he called. He wouldn't, of course, allow anyone in his bathroom when he was using it, and Mrs Carpenter did worry sometimes about what might happen to him if she wasn't around.

Anyway, he did call out. They heard him, and Mrs Carpenter hurried to the bathroom. Worried, she knocked on the door and asked if he was all right. There was no answer. More worried, she knocked again and called to him. There still wasn't any answer, so she went in, the door not being locked. He never did lock it, being sensible enough to know that at his age he might be in a fix one day.

Mrs Carpenter could hardly believe her horrified eyes. Mr Fairfax was lying full length in the large bath, his whole body under water and his head too. For a brief time of terrible shock, she was transfixed, then in a panic she called for Mrs Blisset to come.

Mrs Blisset, continuing her agitated account to Dr Graham, with Alexander listening horror-struck, said she rushed in, and that she couldn't believe what she saw, either. Desperately, she and Mrs Carpenter reached into the bath. It was a terrible job trying to lift the old gentleman out, with his body a dead weight, as well as wet and slippery. But they managed it, and then Mrs Carpenter screamed for help, while Mrs Blisset tried to revive Mr Fairfax. Nothing happened, and Mrs Carpenter screamed again, and Alexander appeared.

'You know the rest, doctor,' said Mrs Blisset, looking exhausted. 'Oh, poor Mr Fairfax, he must have hit his head on the edge of the bath when he fell. It must have been as he was getting in. Oh, he should never have gone to Tower Bridge, it's always so crowded there, and more especially today, with it being a bank holiday.'

'I wonder,' said Dr Graham, looking down at the dead man, 'did he call when he knew he was going to fall, or at the moment when his head struck the bath, if it did? Did it sound like a cry of pain? I found no bruise.'

'It was just a cry out,' said Mrs Blisset.

Alexander managed to speak at last.

'D'you think he 'ad an 'eart attack, doctor?'

'Alexander, my boy,' said Dr Graham gently, 'there'll have to be a post-mortem and an inquest.'

'Oh, it's awful, the poor old gentleman,' said Alexander.

'Mrs Blisset, touch nothing,' said Dr Graham. 'I must arrange for an ambulance to take the body away. Close the door. I'll see Mrs Carpenter now.'

'She's in Mr Fairfax's bedroom, lying down and suffering,' said Mrs Blisset. She closed the bathroom door, entombing the old gentleman for the time being, and went with the doctor into the bedroom. Alexander followed and stood at the open door, watching. Dr Graham was kindness itself to Mrs Carpenter, staying with her for several minutes, asking questions. She replied incoherently. Alexander, in a terrible state himself, thought her right over the top. Dr Graham gave her a sedative powder to take before he left.

Alexander went down the stairs with him, while Prudence, Agnes and Edie poured into the suite to bombard Mrs Blisset with agitated questions. Daisy had taken charge of Rosemary, and she stayed on the landing with her.

Reaching the front door, Alexander opened it for the doctor, only to suddenly push it to without closing it.

'Doctor, could I talk to yer for a minute?' he asked.

'You've something to say, my boy?' Dr Graham was very grave.

'Well, it's like this, doctor,' whispered Alexander. 'Mrs Blisset said Mr Fairfax was tired when he got back from 'is morning outing. But he wasn't. Well, I opened the door to 'im, didn't I, and he was as jolly and lively as he could be.'

'He may have felt tired later,' said Dr Graham.

'Well, he might, yes,' said Alexander, 'but he was still lively when I went up to get the tea tray. Milly's been off for the day, yer see, so 'as Maisie, so Mrs Blisset told me to go up and bring the tray down.'

'Tiredness could still have affected him at the time he took his bath,' said Dr Graham.

'Doctor, when you was talking to Mrs Carpenter just a bit ago,' said Alexander, 'she was lying on Mr Fairfax's bed, wasn't she?'

'Yes.'

'Well, didn't you notice there was one pillow missing?'

'One pillow?'

'Mr Fairfax always 'as two, doctor, I know that.'

'What are you getting at, young man?'

'Well, I tell yer, doctor, when I 'eard Mrs Carpenter first scream, I come out of the attic and started to gallop down the stairs. From the top flight, I caught a glimpse of Mrs Blisset going into Mrs Carpenter's suite. I noticed she was carrying something.'

'She'd left the scene to enter the housekeeper's suite?' Dr Graham's interest increased to a keener level.

'Honest, doctor, I saw her, didn't I?' said Alexander, his whispering voice intense. 'And d'yer know what I think she was carrying? A pillow.'

Dr Graham stiffened. Alexander could imagine what he was thinking.

'Alexander, come with me into the reception room,' he said. Alexander closed the door, and they entered the reception room. The other servants were still upstairs, and there was a suggestion of women in hysteria. Dr Graham said, 'Do you realize what you are trying to make me believe, Alexander? Please be very careful what you are about.'

Alexander said all the servants often mentioned that whenever Mr Fairfax had a fall, Mrs Carpenter always happened to be close by. Dr Graham asked him what he meant by that.

'Well,' whispered Alexander, 'Edie said something to me one time when Mr Fairfax had had a fall. She was scrubbing some Monday washing, and she said, "Did he fall or was he pushed?" She giggled, like, but she looked as if she'd been doing some thinking.'

'Alexander, this is entirely fanciful and not to be taken seriously,' said Dr Graham.

'Well, downstairs some weeks ago, doctor,' said Alexander, 'we all 'eard the rumour that Mr Fairfax 'ad made a new will. So who's he left 'is money to?'

'Good God, boy, this is nonsense, dangerous nonsense,' said Dr Graham, eyeing Alexander with severity. All the same, after a moment or two, he said, 'Are you sure it was a pillow Mrs Blisset was carrying?'

Alexander made a practical suggestion, that they should go up to Mrs Carpenter's suite now and see if it was there and why. He said Mrs Blisset's dress and apron were sort of wet all over. Dr Graham said that was to be expected, since she'd assisted Mrs Carpenter in lifting Mr Fairfax out of the bath.

'Yes, I know that, doctor,' said Alexander, a pale and troubled boy. 'But what did she want to take a pillow into Mrs Carpenter's rooms for?'

They looked at each other.

The doctor said, 'I repeat, Alexander, you must be very careful what you are about. But very well, let us go up to Mrs Carpenter's rooms, where I expect to be able to scotch your suspicions and your imagination.'

Up they went. All the women servants, except Daisy, were still in Mr Fairfax's rooms, trying to come to terms with this horrible tragedy, as Prudence said later in so many words. Daisy had gone down to the kitchen by the back stairs, taking Rosemary with her to find her a quietening biscuit.

Alexander led the way into the adjoining suite, and there he and the doctor searched for a surplus pillow, urgently on the part of the house-boy, worriedly on the part of the medical man. It was Alexander who found it, for he'd gone straight to the bedroom, while Dr Graham looked around the living room. The boy struck lucky, if one could use such a word on such a day. It was there, the pillow, under Mrs Carpenter's bed. He pulled it out, took it into the living room and showed it to Dr Graham.

It was sopping wet.

Chapter Nineteen

Dr Graham, now a very troubled man, had despatched the housemaids down to the kitchen, with a request for them to stay there. In Mr Fairfax's living room, with Alexander beside him, he forced himself to begin new questioning of Mrs Carpenter and Mrs Blisset, both of whom had recovered somewhat. Seated, they were pale of face, and seemed resentful of the doctor's declared intention to ask for clarification of the facts.

'I am unsure now of exactly what happened,' he said. 'According to you, Mrs Blisset, when you joined Mrs Carpenter in the bathroom, Mr Fairfax was lying quite still under the water. That is the truth?'

'Really,' said Mrs Blisset, 'I can't give you a different version, since that was how it was.'

'Mrs Carpenter, you and Mrs Blisset then managed to lift him out, and Mrs Blisset tried to revive him?' Dr Graham put that question quite gently to the housekeeper, whose black garments still looked damp.

'Dr Graham, I'm still unable to take in this

terrible accident,' said Mrs Carpenter, 'and must confess to an inability to think clearly. But at least I think I can confirm Mrs Blisset is right, and that the poor gentleman was fully immersed. I can't, however, clearly remember what followed, only that I became aware Mr Fairfax was on the floor of the bathroom and that I was at the mercy of a nightmare.'

'You screamed?' said Dr Graham.

'I must have,' said Mrs Carpenter, 'it would have been an automatic cry for help.'

'Did Mrs Blisset leave the suite at any time during these traumatic minutes?'

'I've no idea, my mind was reeling,' said Mrs Carpenter.

'Dr Graham,' said Mrs Blisset, 'I stayed with Mrs Carpenter, of course I did. May I ask why the houseboy is here?'

'He has something to show you,' said Dr Graham, a professional need to establish the facts increasing his worry. 'Alexander?'

The houseboy, stricken with a terrible sadness, disappeared for a few moments before returning with the pillow, still clearly in a soaked condition. He held it up for everyone to see. Mrs Carpenter and Mrs Blisset visibly stiffened, then eyed Alexander with suspicion.

'Boy,' said Mrs Carpenter, 'what are you doing with that?'

'Showing it,' said Alexander out of a dry throat. Only his innate resilience kept him sane and capable.

'Why have you taken it from your bed, and why is it so wet?' asked Mrs Blisset. 'Have you been fooling about on a day as terrible as this one?'

'Mrs Blisset, Mrs Carpenter,' said Dr Graham, 'it distresses me beyond all imagination to tell you this is one of Mr Fairfax's pillows, that the pillow slip bears his embroidered blue monogram. It distresses me even more to tell you it was found under Mrs Carpenter's bed only fifteen minutes ago.'

Mrs Carpenter looked disbelieving, Mrs Blisset looked angry.

'Then that wretched boy put it there himself,' she said.

'I have never known a more precocious boy,' said Mrs Carpenter. 'Yes, he must have put it there himself.'

Dr Graham was a doubly troubled man. His suspicions, fostered by Alexander, had been of a reluctant kind at first. Now they were positively alarming him, since he could understand only too well what the pillow might have been used for. That was too dreadful to contemplate easily, but he had to continue his questioning.

'Ladies,' he said, 'can either of you suggest why Alexander should have done such a thing?'

'He's capable of the worst kind of mischief,' said Mrs Blisset.

'That ain't true!' Alexander blurted the denial.

'Alexander, kindly say nothing,' warned Dr Graham. 'Mrs Carpenter, would you have any idea of when Alexander might have procured the pillow for the purpose of soaking it and hiding it under your bed? Might it have been before Mr Fairfax took his bath, or while you and Mrs Blisset were examining the fatal immersion? You must understand how necessary it is for me to be sure of all facts before a death certificate is signed.'

'Dr Graham,' said Mrs Carpenter, 'I'm not responsible for what gets into that rascal's mind, and I've no idea when he removed that pillow. Or why he did what he did do with it. I only know a terrible tragedy has struck this house, and that you are asking questions which make no sense to me. Or to Mrs Blisset, either.'

'You may believe me, Mrs Carpenter, that every question is as painful to me as I imagine it is to you and Mrs Blisset,' said Dr Graham. 'Frankly, I cannot believe Alexander was responsible either for the removal of the pillow, or for soaking it and hiding it. What could possibly have been his purpose? I must now tell you he informed me that when he began his descent of the stairs from the attic, he caught a glimpse of Mrs Blisset entering your suite carrying something he thought was a pillow.'

'That boy is a liar as well as a rascal,' said Mrs Carpenter.

'Mrs Blisset, can you state again that at no time during these frightful circumstances did you leave Mr Fairfax's suite and go to Mrs Carpenter's rooms?'

'I do state so,' said Mrs Blisset, 'and I'd like to

point out you're a doctor, not a policeman. You've no right, none at all, to insinuate by these questions that Mrs Carpenter and I did anything except what we felt we must do for Mr Fairfax.'

'You would be much better off asking questions of that dreadful boy,' said Mrs Carpenter. Both she and Mrs Blisset were showing a defiant front, their indignation very apparent.

'It grieves me, Mrs Carpenter, to tell you I'm not satisfied,' said Dr Graham. That was an understatement. His suspicions appalled him, and made him think of Alexander's reference to the old gentleman's will. God Almighty, could it be? 'Alexander,' he said, 'come with me. Ladies, excuse me for a moment, and bear with me.'

He and Alexander went into the library.

'Oh, ain't it awful, doctor?' said Alexander. 'I can't 'ardly believe what's been going on – '

'Don't think about it. Place that pillow on the table. Good. Now, I'm afraid I must ask you to go to the police station. I'll write a note for you to take.'

'Oh, today's going to see the death of me,' groaned Alexander, 'and I don't mean no disrespect to our old gentleman that's dead already.'

'Alexander, you have acted courageously in all you've done and said. Now you must brace yourself further and go to the police station for me.'

'Oh, Gawd 'elp us all,' said Alexander, knowing what that meant. An inquiry into possible murder, and the loss of jobs to all the staff, in any case.

*   *   *

'So there you are, Maisie,' he said when he had finished recounting all he could remember, 'that's everything as far as I know, like.' His summation had been good, even if he sounded hoarse at times, and Maisie's imagination, and a word or two from Prudence now and then, had filled in the occasional blank.

Maisie had almost collapsed into a chair under the weight of such unbearable news. As Alexander had said, everything was too awful to believe. Worst of all was the terrible fact that that kind old gentleman was dead. Oh, Lord above, and how did he die? By drowning in his bath, yes, but how? That wet pillow, which Alexander had made so much of, what did that mean?

Maisie almost fainted thinking about it.

Alexander just stood there, his back to the pantry door, his expressive features now a mask of grey. He was a boy who, during these last few hours, had taken on a responsibility that only a hardened man could be expected to bear.

The police presence in the house was a heavy one. As well as the constable outside the kitchen door, there were two upstairs, following an official inspection of the body. They were there to ensure it was not disturbed until Dr Graham received permission to arrange for it to be taken to the mortuary. On the ground floor, in the reception room, a Detective Inspector Rawlings and his sergeant, who had already interviewed Alexander, and taken a statement from him, were interrogating Mrs Carpenter and Mrs Blisset.

Soon the two women would be separated and then questioned singly.

In evidence the whole time was a sodden pillow.

Maisie dwelt in misery. She and the other servants wondered, of course, exactly what was going on between the police and the two women. Maisie shuddered at what the questions might be like, and what kind of answers were being given.

Prudence, Agnes, Edie and Daisy were numb now. Rosemary, fortunately, was fast asleep in her cot, in her mother's room. No-one mentioned what might lie in store for the child.

Huskily, Maisie said, 'I'm going to my room.'

Alexander at once said, 'I'll come with you, Maisie.'

'Yes, all right, Alexander,' said Maisie.

Prudence said, 'I'm going to make a pot of tea, I'll go off me head if I don't do something normal.'

'Give me and Maisie a call when you've made it, eh?' said Alexander.

Prudence said she would, and Alexander and Maisie left the kitchen. Outside the door, the constable allowed them to go to Maisie's room, his nod sympathetic, although he did warn them they were not to leave the house in case they were called.

'Including me?' said Maisie.

'No, not you, miss, more like the boy,' said the constable.

'I've already been talked to,' said Alexander.

'You'll get treated kindly, sonny,' said the constable.

In her room, Maisie turned to Alexander. They exchanged the glances of two young people devastated by events.

'I feel awful and helpless,' breathed Maisie.

'I ain't never going to forget this day, and nor don't I think I'm going to forget what might come next,' said Alexander.

'Alexander, d'you think – d'you think Mrs Carpenter and Mrs Blisset – oh, Lor', I just can't say it,' whispered Maisie.

'I know what you mean,' said Alexander.

They sat down on the edge of Maisie's bed. Somehow, her primrose frock had lost its brightness, and her boater, still on her head, looked out of place.

'Whatever happens, we're going to lose our jobs,' said Maisie.

'Yes, and what're we going to do then?' said Alexander.

Maisie thought of Daniel and their wedding. That would take care of her, but Alexander would have to go looking for a place in some other big house, and him still only fifteen. He'd been fourteen when he started here.

'You'll find something,' she said, 'I'll help, you'll see.' She would have liked to have made a firm promise of successful help to a boy who was suffering the worst day of his life. 'I think I'll have nightmares tonight.'

'I've 'ad mine, yer know, Maisie, I've 'ad a baker's dozen all rolled into one.' Alexander brooded. 'The worst was when I found that pillow all soaking wet. Well, I mean, soaking wet, it made me—'

'Don't talk about it,' said Maisie, shuddering. She knew what she wanted most at this moment: for her day with Daniel to be reborn, and for the afternoon at the house never to have happened. She longed for Daniel, for his strength and comfort. Her resilience, however, was greater than she knew. Daniel could have told her she had strengths of her own. And she did.

Edie appeared with a tray, two cups of tea and some biscuits.

''Ere we are, you two, I've brought yer tea for yer,' she said.

'God bless yer, Edie,' said Alexander, taking the tray.

'Milly still ain't back,' said Edie. 'When she does come in, I hope I ain't going to be the one to 'ave to tell 'er the awful news.'

Alexander squared his sturdy shoulders.

'I'll tell 'er, Edie, I might as well.'

'Oh, you're a good boy, Alexander, you been real manly about all this,' said Edie, and went back to the kitchen.

Maisie and Alexander drank their tea. Alexander managed to eat one biscuit. Maisie ate none.

'Constable Pritchard?' A voice from above, the voice of Detective Inspector Rawlings.

'Sir?' called the policeman on duty at the kitchen door.

'Come up here.'

'Yes, sir.' The constable made his way up to the ground floor. Alexander slipped out of Maisie's room and followed him up, keeping his distance. He stopped. He listened to what was being said. He blanched. The constable was being instructed to return to the station and arrange for a Black Maria to be driven to the house to collect Mrs Carpenter and Mrs Blisset. They were to be detained at the station and questioned further. Alexander heard the constable say, 'Jesus Christ.'

'Never mind the Lord, Constable, just get going,' said the inspector.

Alexander returned noiselessly to Maisie.

'Try to believe this, Maisie,' he whispered, 'the police are going to give 'em a ride to the station.'

'Give who?' breathed Maisie.

'Why, Mrs C. and Mrs B., who else?' said Alexander. 'And when they get 'em there, they're going to ask 'em more questions. I dunno, I was ever more knocked sideways.'

'I can't believe it, I just can't,' gasped Maisie.

'What can't yer believe, Maisie?'

'You know what I can't!'

'Nor me, Maisie, except about that pillow.'

'It's dreadful, dreadful.'

'Maisie,' said Alexander quietly, 'what's going

to come out when the old gentleman's will is read?'

'Shut up, Alexander, shut up, d'you hear?'

They heard the basement door being opened then, and the sound of clicking footsteps. Milly appeared, wearing her best dress and hat. She looked in on the young couple.

'Here, what's going on?' she asked. 'There's a copper outside, and he wouldn't let me in till I told him who I was. What's up?'

'Shall I tell her, Maisie?' asked Alexander, his face a grey mask again, such was his feeling that their world had come to an ugly and heart-breaking end.

'You've got to,' said Maisie. 'I'm going for a walk. I'll go out of me mind if I stay here.'

She left. Climbing the basement steps, she was addressed by the policeman still on duty.

'Where you off to, miss?'

'Just for a walk, that's all.'

He knew she had not been present all day, He looked at her face. She was suffering. He understood.

'Well, all right, miss, but would you stay in sight?'

'I'll only walk up and down the street, I promise,' said Maisie.

'Good enough, miss.'

Maisie set off, her footsteps slow, her body lagging, her thoughts running wildly. A hurrying soldier approached in the dusk, a soldier of the West Kents, a private. She stopped him.

'Excuse me—'

'Now now, girlie, I'm spoken for, and I'm in a hurry.'

'Oh, give me a minute, would yer, please? Could you tell me if you're at Knightsbridge barracks and if you know Corporal Daniel Adams?'

'Everyone knows Corporal Adams. He's . . . here, half a mo, you don't happen to be his fancy, do yer? There's rumours he's going to get wed.'

'Yes, it's me,' said Maisie. 'Could you ask him if he could come and see me tomorrow, could you tell him it's urgent?'

'Urgent?'

'Serious. I must see him, if he could manage it. Tell him to come to the house.'

The soldier studied her, her face pale in the dusk, her eyes dark.

'I'll tell him, but I've got to get a move on now, I've got ground to cover or I'm for it. I'll tell him, don't you worry. Good luck.' On he went at a quick pace, flitting in and out of light and shadow. The street lamps were on, gas mantles glowing.

Maisie stood watching him, then slowly walked back, thoughts still running wildly. She passed the duty constable. He gave her a nod, feeling sympathy for the pleasant-looking girl in her obvious need to be out of this house for a while. Although the body had been taken away in a horse-drawn ambulance, the atmosphere couldn't be anything but grim.

Maisie's thoughts were on Daniel. She prayed he would come tomorrow, so that she could draw comfort from his presence.

Traffic was desultory, and held no interest for her until, suddenly, she was aware of the approach of an ominous-looking vehicle drawn by a pair. It was shapeless at first, until caught by the light of a street lamp. She knew what it was then. A Black Maria, a police vehicle for transporting criminals or suspected criminals. Her heart beat fast. She stopped as it passed her, and turned to watch it. It pulled up outside the house.

For a few moments she stayed watching. She glimpsed the figure of an alighting policeman. Then she resumed her walk, this time at a quick, agitated pace.

She thought of Mr Fairfax, she thought of that fine old gentleman drowning in his bath. He did not deserve that, however it had happened. He was a man who deserved to pass peacefully away in God's good time.

Maisie's tears seeped.

A little later, she had her back turned to the vehicle as it made its return journey, her body stiff as it passed her again. She refrained from looking.

Were they in this Black Maria, Mrs Carpenter and Mrs Blisset? If so, she just couldn't imagine what they were feeling. Oh, Lord.

She turned about and walked back to the house.

Alexander was still in her room, waiting for her. On the bed was a carrier bag. In it was a picture frame, together with a pencil sketch. They were promised to Daniel, and somehow, that made her feel he would come tomorrow.

'They've gone, Maisie, they've been taken away,' said Alexander.

'Have they? Yes, I suppose they have. I saw the Black Maria.'

'The police have gone too, and so 'as Dr Graham,' said Alexander. 'Maisie, I ain't very happy, and nor is Prudence. The police took a statement from her before they left. It didn't 'alf upset her. And Milly, she ain't a bit happy now, neither.'

'And nor am I, Alexander.'

Chapter Twenty

At ten o'clock, Dr Graham returned to the house to talk to the suffering servants.

'I'm going to give all of you a sedative powder to take in water before you go to bed,' he told them kindly.

'Oh, that's good of you, doctor,' said Prudence, drained of colour.

'It's the very least I can do,' said Dr Graham, a little haggard himself. 'In the morning, I shall go and see Mr Fairfax's solicitor during my rounds, and ask him to call on you. He's the executor of Mr Fairfax's will. He will know what to say to all of you.'

'You mean he'll know how to give us notice,' said Milly a little bitterly.

'No, Milly, I don't know that,' said Dr Graham. 'But I do know this house must still be looked after until it's sold, as I imagine it will be. I hope that will give all of you time to find new positions.'

The servants launched into a round of emotional talk that turned into a babble. All, that is, except Alexander and Maisie. They stood beside each other, Alexander now a stalwart, Maisie with her natural resilience as her present strength. She and the houseboy were one in their fortitude.

'Doctor,' said Maisie above the babble, 'd'you know what's happening to Mrs Carpenter and Mrs Blisset?'

'Only that they're at the police station,' said Dr Graham. He hesitated. 'Perhaps I should tell you something now that you will probably learn in the near future, in any case.' He hesitated again. The babble stopped and all eyes travelled to regard him intently. 'Mrs Blisset is Mrs Carpenter's niece, the daughter of her sister.'

There were sucked-in breaths, and then noisy exhalation.

'Oh, I always knew there was something between them two,' said Milly.

'Mrs Carpenter always treated that cook a bit special,' said Edie.

'Made a fav'rite of her,' said Agnes.

'And let her bring young Rosemary with her when she took on the job,' said Daisy.

'Which was something I ain't ever 'eard of before,' said Prudence.

'Where is the child?' asked Dr Graham.

'Doctor, she's sleeping in Mrs Blisset's room, in her cot,' said Maisie.

Dr Graham looked sad.

'Poor child,' he said, 'I must give her some thought. Ladies, is it possible she can be left in your care for the time being?'

'Maisie will keep an eye on her,' said Prudence. 'I tell yer, doctor, Maisie's been more of a mother to the mite than ever Mrs B. was. Could I ask you a private question, doctor?'

Dr Graham could have said it was hardly going to be private under these circumstances. However, he said, 'Ask away, Prudence.'

'D'you know if Mrs B. was married?'

'The answer, I'm afraid, is no,' said Dr Graham.

'Oh, didn't I say that more'n once?' said Edie. 'Didn't I?'

'You didn't say she wasn't,' said Daisy, 'you just thought so.

'The information came out during the interrogation,' said Dr Graham, 'and Inspector Rawlings mentioned it to me. Well, I must leave you now. There's little I can say that will comfort you. I'm dreadfully, dreadfully sorry for all of you. I shall call again in the morning. Make sure you take the sedative powders.'

A babble began again. Alexander and Maisie escaped it by seeing Dr Graham to the front door.

'Doctor, you've been ever so kind,' said Maisie.

'I echoes that,' said Alexander.

Dr Graham showed the faintest of smiles.

'Chin up, Alexander, chin up, Maisie, the worst of storms eventually blow over,' he said, and left, emerging with his bag from the house and walking into the dark night.

'That's left me sort of bereft,' sighed Maisie.

'Maisie, you still got me,' said Alexander.

'Alexander, you're a love,' said Maisie, 'and we'll stick it out, you'll see.'

She slept quite well, considering everything. The sedative probably helped. Next to her bed was little Rosemary. She and Alexander had transferred child and cot from Mrs Blisset's room.

There were dreams, but not unpleasant ones, far from it. They featured her walking hand in hand with Daniel over a heath to which there was no end. They walked on and on into a pool of mellow sunlight that softly swallowed them up.

It was different for Alexander. He suffered a nightmare in which he was running into darkness, a black-clad witch behind him, leaping in pursuit, a huge white pillow in her hand. His legs began to feel like lead weights, slowing him. Boggy ground grew beneath his feet, dragging at him. With the red-eyed witch almost on top of him, he fell, plunging down into a black pit and jerking awake as swirling water came up to engulf him.

Alexander lay sweating.

Maisie was up by half past six. She checked on Rosemary. The child lay quietly, a picture of content in her cot. Maisie let her sleep on. The little girl rarely came awake before eight. Maisie went into the kitchen and stirred the hot embers of the range fires into life. Someone was going to have to prepare breakfast if food was wanted. She was still not hungry herself, but she longed for some hot tea. She half-filled one of the large iron kettles and placed it on an open hob. Flames leapt to lick at it.

Alexander came in, carrying two scuttles, both laden with coal.

'Oh, you're up too, Alexander.'

'Force of habit and not enjoying me sleep, Maisie.'

Maisie looked at him. His eyes were dark hollows. The lad had shouldered an awful burden, right from the moment when he had heard Mrs Carpenter shriek. What sort of a shriek had that been? Had it been natural or put on?

'Oh, I'm sorry, Alexander, I can easy guess what an awful night you had,' she said.

'That's all right, Maisie. Who's going to get breakfast? I don't suppose poor old Prudence and the others feel like jumping out of bed a bit sharpish.'

'I'll do the breakfast,' said Maisie, 'just some porridge and toast.'

'Good on yer, Maisie, I never knew no gal more willing than you.'

'Alexander,' said Maisie, bringing china to the table, 'I've been thinking.'

'What about?' said Alexander. 'As if I don't know.'

'I was thinking about the falls Mr Fairfax had, and Mrs Carpenter always being close to him at them times.' Maisie drew a long breath.

'Alexander, d'you think it was because she made them happen?'

'Well, didn't one of them females make a remark about did he fall or was he pushed?' said Alexander. 'I tell yer, Maisie, the more I think about it meself, the more I get cold shivers down me back.'

'Oh, it all gets worse,' said Maisie.

'You and me, Maisie, we've got to stop thinking about it,' said Alexander, 'or we'll 'ave nightmares for years.'

'Yes, we've got to get on with our lives and with our work,' said Maisie, slicing bread. 'That'll stop us doing too much thinking.'

She wondered if Daniel would be able to get time off to come and see her.

Morning parade at the barracks was over. Company Sergeant Major Sawyer was regarding Corporal Daniel Adams like a man whose ears were deceiving him.

'What was that you asked, Corporal Adams?'

'A favour, Sarn't Major.'

'Was it to do with more time off?'

'I can't tell a porkie,' said Daniel. 'It was. Sometime this morning.'

'State the reason.'

'I've had a cry for help.'

'You've what?'

'From me young lady.'

'Bloody hell,' said Sergeant Major Sawyer, 'don't tell me you've put her in the fam'ly way.'

'Which I haven't,' said Daniel, 'which I wouldn't have, and which suggestion offends me, Sarn't Major.'

'See that?' The sergeant major put a hand to his chest. 'That's my bleeding heart. Now listen, battalion's expecting a delivery of new Enfield rifles this morning, on which weaponry all officers, warrant officers, NCO's and other ranks will be given instruction from time of arrival until five of the clock on Saturday, when arrangements will then be made to travel to the rifle ranges on Salisbury Plain for testing of self-same weaponry on account of not being able to fire 'em in these here barracks. Her Majesty won't allow it. Why am I telling you all this when you already know it? I'm telling you, Corporal Adams, because you've forgotten.'

'Sarn't Major, I'm heart and soul in favour of these new Lee-Enfields, seeing I've heard the kind of reports about 'em which are uplifting,' said Daniel, 'but if I could have, say, half an hour with me young lady, I'll be back in good time to get me platoon standing to attention around the delivery cart which, if I've got permission to say so, ain't due here till twelve noon at the earliest.'

'Blind my Aunt Fanny if I don't have a feeling you're trying to out-talk me,' said the sergeant major. His waxed moustache twitched. 'All right, if I can believe it, your young lady needs you, so get going. Give you an hour. But do me a favour on me own account. Remind your young lady you're in the army, not the land of the fairies.'

'Much obliged, Sarn't Major.'

Dr Graham was in the office of Mr Fairfax's solicitor, Mr Samuel Burnaby. And Mr Burnaby was staring at the good doctor in horror and disbelief. Mr Fairfax was dead, drowned in his bath, and his housekeeper and cook were under suspicion of causing his death?

'I beg you, Dr Graham, to tell me none of this is true.'

Sadly and unfortunately, said Dr Graham, it was very true, as was the unpalatable fact that the ladies were in police custody. Before they were taken away last night, they had asked if he could arrange for a solicitor to represent them, and Mrs Carpenter had mentioned Mr Burnaby. Would Mr Burnaby be willing to do so?

Mr Burnaby said he was not himself at the moment, that his mind was reeling, his morning shattered. The news alone that Mr Fairfax was dead grieved him, the possibility that his demise was not accidental nor the consequence of a heart attack, appalled him. He was caught in a conflict – but realized that the trial would cause a sensation, and it would be difficult for the women to engage unbiased legal representation. With some reservations, he said he would travel to the police station, talk to them and find out if they would wish him to engage a competent barrister in the event of their being charged with . . .

'No, impossible, Dr Graham, impossible, and I cannot bring myself to utter the word.'

'I have not uttered it myself, not at any time since I was brought to the scene,' said Dr Graham, 'and I've no intention of doing so now. Mr Burnaby, you are the executor of Mr Fairfax's Last Will and Testament, I believe.'

Mr Burnaby, stiff white collar clasping his neck a little unkindly in view of his difficulty in breathing normally, said with an effort that yes, he'd completed the formalities of a revision only a short time ago.

Dr Graham regarded the troubled solicitor with sympathy. Would it be unethical, he asked, for Mr Burnaby to reveal the name of the main beneficiary?

'To you, sir, to you?' said Mr Burnaby, attempting a loosening of his collar.

'Mr Burnaby, I am as troubled as I think you are by certain possibilities,' said Dr Graham, consulting his pocket watch. He had broken into his round to call on the solicitor.

Mr Burnaby said details of the will would have to be revealed to interested parties consequent on the tragic death of Mr Fairfax, in any case. But to outsiders in advance? Yes, that would be most unethical. Dr Graham said he believed the police would probably request that information quite soon.

'Dear God,' said Mr Burnaby, 'I beg you not to tell me the reason why.'

Dr Graham said his hope was that a certain

lady was not the main beneficiary, since that would remove the possibility of an incriminating motive. Mr Burnaby, aghast, appealed to the doctor to say nothing more and ask nothing more.

'I can stay only a minute longer,' said Dr Graham, his whole demeanour painful, 'and you may or may not confirm my suspicions, just as you wish.'

Mr Burnaby was silent for a few moments, then, like a man in crisis, he said, 'I will tell you, Dr Graham, that the main beneficiary is Mrs Carpenter, on whose care and devotion he relied so much, that she has been the main beneficiary for over a year, and that should she have predeceased Mr Fairfax, the bequest would have passed to his cousin in South Africa. The estate, including the worth of the house, will amount to a fortune. There is also a bequest of a thousand pounds to Mrs Blisset, and a hundred pounds each to all the other servants.'

For a few telling moments, Dr Graham bowed his head as if in prayer.

'I have to tell you, Mr Burnaby, that Mrs Blisset isn't married and is Mrs Carpenter's niece,' he said.

'You are devastating my morning,' breathed Mr Burnaby.

'I'm sorry, Mr Burnaby, desperately sorry for Mrs Carpenter and Miss Blisset,' said Dr Graham.

'Dreadful, dreadful, Dr Graham,' said the appalled solicitor. His professional instincts managed to surface. 'But we can say these facts don't amount to proof.'

'The police will see the terms of the will as an irresistible motive,' said Dr Graham sadly. He straightened himself. 'One last thing before I go. I'm sure you'll agree that in some way Miss Blisset's child must be taken care of, and that the servants need instructions, which perhaps, as executor, you'd be kind enough to give them.'

'Yes.' Mr Burnaby spoke like a ghost of a man. 'Yes. I'll call in on my way back from the police station.' He hardly noticed the doctor's departure, simply that when he came to and looked up there was only empty space.

A dark cloud hovered above.

Chapter Twenty-one

Breakfast was long over, and the servants were doing their best to attend to their usual rounds of work. Milly, however, did not want to see to Mr Fairfax's suite. She just couldn't stand the thought of taking broom, dusters, brush and pan around the rooms of the dead old gentleman who had never been unkind to anyone. His ghost was sure to be there, all restless and fitful.

Prudence, who had taken charge, said the whole house was suffering and that Mr Fairfax's rooms had got to be seen to out of respect for him. It was Milly's duty to get on with it. Milly said she couldn't, she just couldn't. Prudence sighed and said all right then, you can leave it for a day or two. Help Agnes to do Mrs Carpenter's rooms instead. Milly wasn't too keen on that, either. Nor was Agnes. Prudence, weary-eyed, put her foot down.

Daisy, cleaning and dusting the hall, had a sudden thought. She left her work to go to the kitchen and ask Prudence a relevant question.

''Ere, who's going to pay our wages come Friday?'

'We'll ask Dr Graham when he calls,' said Prudence. 'He said he would. Go on, finish doing the hall.'

Maisie was working on the staircase, Alexander polishing the brass knocker and decorative letter box of the front door, applying himself vigorously in an attempt to take his mind off what might be going on at the police station.

He looked up at the sound of crisp footsteps. Approaching the house was a soldier, surely Maisie's friend, as upstanding a military bloke as Alexander had ever seen.

Daniel turned in at the foot of the steps and took them briskly to come face to face with a sturdy-looking boy, whose mop of curly hair and honest features would have been youthfully engaging were it not for the fact that his eyes were shadowed by dark blue rings.

'Hello, sonny,' said Daniel.

''Ere, have you come to see our Maisie?' asked Alexander.

'I'm standing right here for just that,' said Daniel.

'Crikey, she's going to like that,' said Alexander. If Maisie needed a fine pair of shoulders to cry on, this corporal had them. 'Come on, come in, but I've got to tell yer she ain't exactly 'appy, nor is anyone else 'ere.'

'Why?' asked Daniel, following the boy into the hall.

Alexander, closing the door, said, 'Maisie'll tell yer. Half a mo while I call her.' He went to the foot of the stairs. Maisie was on the landing, polishing the top of the banisters. 'Maisie?'

'Yes?' called Maisie.

'It's yer soldier friend, he's come to see yer.'

Maisie, elation supplanting depression for the moment, came running down the stairs, skirts whisking. She swept past Alexander and ran to meet Daniel.

'Daniel, oh, I'm so glad to see you,' she breathed. 'Come into this room.' She took his hand and they went into the reception room, dusted and cleaned by Agnes. She closed the door.

'Maisie?' said Daniel.

Maisie gave in to her feelings. She put herself into his arms and clung. She might have burst into tears, but she was made of sterner stuff than that.

'Daniel,' she whispered into his shoulder, 'it's been awful, awful – oh, I still can't hardly believe it.'

Daniel, conscious that her warm body was communicating shivers, said, 'Maisie, you're alarming me. What can't you hardly believe?'

Maisie drew a shuddering breath and told him. It took time, and during the telling, Daniel held her tighter and closer. He didn't interrupt except to say once, 'God Almighty.' He let her spill out everything. In any case, his reactions were numbing. He could only begin to guess just how frightening and plain bloody awful it had

239

been for her and the other servants. At the end, he drew her to the comfort of a red and gold sofa, made her sit down and seated himself beside her, arm around her.

'Daniel,' she whispered, 'oh, you don't know how glad I am to see you and to be able to talk to you.'

'Maisie love,' said Daniel, 'I can't stay long, but if it's been a help for you to pour it all out, then that's something. I hope to God those women can be cleared, and that it'll come down to the old boy having had a heart attack.' From all she'd told him, he didn't think this was likely, but something had to be said to cheer her up a little.

'Oh, it might, it might,' said Maisie, which was a piece of compulsive wishful thinking. What stood between hope and despair was that pillow. 'Daniel, we're all going to lose our jobs.'

'Well, that's coming down to earth at least,' said Daniel, 'but don't you worry too much about that, Maisie. We'll put the banns up for a day in October, shall we? I'll leave the exact date to you, and in between, I'll try to get time off to look around Walworth for a house to rent.'

'If you can't manage,' said Maisie, perceptibly brightening, 'I could get a free day off easy. Prudence – she's the one in charge now – she'll give me a free day all at once, and p'raps every week while Mrs Carpenter and – no, I won't talk about them any more. Daniel, I know Walworth ever so well, and I could ask old friends and neighbours if they know of any house to rent.'

'You do that, Maisie, you go,' said Daniel, 'and if I'm able to go with you, I'll let you know. How's that, eh, me love?'

'Oh, it's so good talking to you,' said Maisie. 'Daniel, I'm ever so worried about Alexander.'

'That's the houseboy, the lad I've just met, and the one that gave himself a ruddy hard time yesterday, poor young perisher?' said Daniel.

'Yes, and he' s such a fine boy,' said Maisie. 'A bit cheeky and a reg'lar saucebox at times, but I just know he'd never let anyone down. He's an orphan, and this job's all he's got, and none of us know how long that's going to last.'

'Well, he can do what I did at his age,' said Daniel, 'he can join the army as a drummer boy. He's sturdy and he's bright, and I tell yer, sweetheart, the army'll be mother, father, uncle and granddad to him, as long as he fits into the life. He won't starve and he won't be alone, he'll have comrades the whole time he's in uniform. I ain't going to say it'll make him rich, but it'll keep him healthy.'

'Daniel, oh, have you still got a bit of time to talk to him?' asked Maisie, eager with hope for the houseboy.

'Five minutes, say,' said Daniel.

Maisie came to her feet, hurried to the door, opened it, and there was Alexander, lingering in the hall.

'Alexander, come in here.'

'What for?' asked Alexander, crossing the hall.

'My friend, Corporal Adams, has got something to say to you.'

'Maisie, you look a bit cheered up,' said Alexander, entering the room.

'Oh, you might get a bit cheered up yerself now,' said Maisie.

''Ello again,' said Alexander to Daniel, who was on his feet.

'Hello, lad,' said Daniel. 'You're fifteen, so Maisie told me. And likely to be out of work soon.'

'I ain't looking forward to that,' said Alexander.

'Right,' said Daniel, 'let's have a good look at you, Alexander. Come on, square yer shoulders and hold yer head proud. That's it. Blowed if I ever saw a likelier recruit.'

'What?' said Alexander.

'Say beg yer pardon,' said Maisie.

'All right, beg yer pardon, soldier,' said Alexander, 'but what're you talking about?'

'You're going to join the army,' said Daniel.

'Eh?'

'As a drummer boy, as I did meself,' said Daniel. 'I'll get you enlisted in the Royal West Kents, top infantry regiment and pride of the line.'

'Crikey.' Alexander's dark tired eyes came to life. 'Would they 'ave me?'

'They'll have you.'

'And I'd get a uniform?'

'You would, and a shilling a day, and a lot

242

of drill, and a lot of discipline,' said Daniel, 'and it'll make a man of you before you're even eighteen.'

'What do I do to get in?' Alexander was eager.

'Come to the Knightsbridge barracks sometime next week, ask at the gates for me, and I'll see you to the recruiting office at Chelsea meself. Right, that's all, Alexander me lad, you're going to be a drummer boy. About turn, quick march, dismiss.'

Maisie opened the door, and Alexander marched straight through, shoulders back, head high and eyes bright, a boy already dreaming of bugles, trumpets and drums. Maisie closed the door and turned to the man who had put warmth back into the lives of herself and Alexander.

'Daniel, oh, I've never been more glad I met you that day,' she said. 'You're a good man, as good as me dear old dad ever was, and I know one thing for sure now, which I want to tell you before you go.'

'And what's that, Maisie?'

Maisie swallowed. She was not a demonstrative person. She was always going to hold her deeper emotions in check, just as her mum had. But she spoke from her heart now.

'I know I'm always going to love you, Daniel.'

Daniel arrived back at the barracks ten minutes late. Company Sergeant Major Sawyer dressed him down a bit. But they were old comrades,

243

and Daniel took him into his confidence. The Sergeant Major actually winced.

'That's one of the most Godalmighty liver-shaking stories I've ever heard,' he said, 'and I've heard plenty in my time, and seen things. Army cock-ups and the like, with blood running red and useless. Now listen, I can't give you special privileges, but I'll see you get a few extra passes come off-duty times.'

'Like Sunday?' said Daniel.

'Sunday, is it, and meaning all day?'

'Just before I left, I promised I'd do me best to be with her then.'

'Sunday. Right. Treat her gentle, Corporal Adams. And see the colonel sometime.'

Who was going to cook the midday meal? The housework had been done, if not as painstakingly as usual. Well, no-one could apply any enthusiasm to their tasks, and Prudence was sensibly understanding of this. It'll get better, she said. It can't get no worse, said Daisy. Yes, it can, said Agnes. Oh, me shaking nerves, said Edie. Stop thinking about it, said Prudence. No great cook herself, she asked again who was going to do a bit of dinner.

'I will,' said Maisie, who was holding the hand of Rosemary, perched in her high chair. 'I cooked a lot for me and me dad, and he never complained.'

'Good on yer, Maisie, you're a sport,' said Alexander, feeling much better, even if he couldn't get two certain women out of his mind.

'I don't know why you're chirpy all of a sudden,' said Agnes.

'We've got to be a bit cheerful,' said Alexander. Neither he nor Maisie had mentioned his prospects of being a drummer boy. They'd agreed it was best not to talk about it for the time being, especially as everyone would want to know everything about Maisie's soldier friend, which she wanted to keep to herself for a while.

She asked what was in the pantry, and she and Prudence inspected it. There were enough ingredients for a light meal. Someone sometime had got to do what Mrs Carpenter had always done, go shopping, if someone supplied them with the necessary money. Prudence said she thought the solicitor would do that, seeing he'd done Mr Fairfax's will and would be in charge of everything, including all the money. And Dr Graham had said the gent would call.

It was the doctor himself who called first, at the end of his morning round, and when Maisie was getting on with the meal. Alexander let him in.

'Oh, 'owdyerdo, doctor,' he said, 'is there any news?'

There was, the news that Mrs Carpenter was her late employer's main beneficiary. Dr Graham, however, had no intention of landing the houseboy or any of the other servants with that unwelcome information. It pointed to a motive and to premeditation.

'I've no idea, Alexander, of what is happening at the police station,' he said. 'I would simply like to know how all of you are facing up to the unhappy situation.'

'We're all in the kitchen,' said Alexander. 'Come down, sir, if you please.'

The arrival of the kind doctor was welcomed by all. He noted evident strain and supplied them with more sedative powders, to be taken just before bed. And he found a sweet for the child.

Prudence asked him if he knew who might supply them with housekeeping money, and their wages. He said Mr Burnaby, the solicitor, would definitely be calling. As the executor of Mr Fairfax's Last Will and Testament, he had the authority to supply all necessary monies, including their wages.

It was Edie who asked the doctor if he knew what was happening to Mrs Carpenter and Mrs Blisset – no, Miss Blisset. He said he knew nothing, and that he supposed the unfortunate ladies were still being questioned.

'But that's been going on ever since yesterday evening,' said Agnes. 'Don't the police know yet if – well, if . . .' She gave up.

'Now 'aven't I told all of you not to think about it?' said Prudence, rattled. 'Best if we take every rug and carpet strip out in the yard this afternoon, so we can all beat 'em silly and forget what the police are up to.'

'That might not be such a bad idea,' said Dr

Graham. 'I really must go now.' He glanced at Alexander and Maisie, close together as usual. His faint smile was encouraging, and Alexander saw him to the front door.

'Kind of you to come and see us, sir,' he said.

'Oh, I almost forgot,' said Dr Graham. 'Tell Prudence I mentioned to Mr Burnaby that something must be done for the care of the child. Perhaps he will hire a nurse. I can help in that direction.'

'I'll tell Prudence,' said Alexander, and the doctor left. He was making no charge for prescribing and supplying the sedative powders.

Returning to the kitchen, where Agnes was keeping Rosemary content with a biscuit, Alexander informed Prudence that she was to talk to Mr Burnaby, the solicitor, about the child's welfare. Prudence said she would when he arrived.

Alexander then smacked himself on his forehead.

'Oh, blimey, we've forgot about Mr Townley, Maisie,' he said. 'He don't know nothing about all this. Who's going to tell 'im? I ain't keen on doing it all over again.'

'And you shouldn't have to,' said Maisie, busy frying bacon, which they were going to have with scrambled egg and grilled peppered tomatoes. And buttered toast.

'So who's going to?' asked Alexander.

'Mr Burnaby, the solicitor,' said Prudence, a loyal and hardworking servant presently shocked to her core. 'It's only right he should, so don't you worry, Alexander. You've done your share, and more, that you 'ave.'

'Which I didn't enjoy one bit,' said Alexander. His nose twitched and he added, 'Don't that bacon smell good?' And Milly, still brooding, looked at him as if he'd profaned the altar of St Paul's Cathedral.

Chapter Twenty-two

Mr Burnaby arrived at two. A very professional middle-aged gentleman who rarely attired his body in anything other than clerical grey, he had a reputation for integrity. To the liking of his clients, he was correct rather than pompous, modest rather than self-important.

He braced himself on being admitted into the house and the presence of the staff, most of whom he knew. He had been acting on behalf of Mr Fairfax for years.

'Alas, my dear ladies,' he said, by way of greeting, 'such a terrible event.' He had had an extremely trying time at the police station in his interview with the detained women. They vehemently declared themselves innocent of any suspicion, and insisted the incriminating pillow must have been placed under Mrs Carpenter's bed by the houseboy, a malicious young wretch.

Mr Burnaby went through the traumatic incident with them, feeling as much bewildered as unhappy. Everything became repetitive, Mrs Carpenter beside herself, and Mrs Blisset outraged. Miss Blisset, that is. Mr Burnaby asked why she had kept secret her relationship with Mrs Carpenter, and the fact that she was unmarried. To save unpleasant gossip among the other servants, of course, said Miss Blisset, and now it's nobody's business but my own whether I was married or not.

It was uncomfortably prolonged, the interview, and it turned into a welter of indignation and the occasional interludes of apprehension. Mr Burnaby assured them that if matters resulted in a trial—

A trial? A trial?

One hopes not, one prays not, but if the worst happened, said the discomfited solicitor, he would brief an excellent barrister on their behalf.

Mrs Carpenter said of all things, there was simply no proof that would enable the police to charge them with any kind of crime. Mr Burnaby was to see that they were either released or granted bail. Mr Burnaby said yes, yes, of course.

At the end he said goodbye for the time being, and then found that Detective Inspector Rawlings wished to talk to him. Mr Burnaby knew what might be coming, and it did: a request to be informed of the chief beneficiary of the deceased gentleman's will. He had no option but to deliver the information. He was then told that Mrs Carpenter and Miss Blisset would be charged with murder, and was asked to be present while this was done.

Mr Burnaby left the police station in a daze, having watched Mrs Carpenter collapse and Miss Blisset reduced to hysterics when formally charged. His job now was to consider which barrister to brief. He doubted if bail would be granted at the preliminary hearing, but it was his duty to ask for it.

Being in the house and speaking to the staff was another ordeal, but not of the same proportions, thank God. Daisy was absent. She was walking Rosemary up and down the stairs, the child eager for activity.

Mr Burnaby enquired after everyone's health in this debilitating time. Prudence said they were all trying to stay on their feet, and that Dr Graham was letting them have sedative powders to help them relax at night. What everyone wanted to know, she said, was how long they could keep their jobs, and who was going to supply them with housekeeping money and pay their wages.

Mr Burnaby said it would take a considerable time to settle the affairs of the estate, and that the house would probably not be sold for some months. Until then, he would be grateful if they looked after it, although he would understand if any of them obtained work elsewhere. He would supply all housekeeping money, and pay their wages each Friday, they could be assured of that.

Having called on his bank during his return from the police station, he extracted twenty pounds from his wallet and handed the bank-notes to Prudence.

'There, that is a beginning in respect of house-keeping,' he said, 'and any bills received from the Gas Board and other creditors can be sent to me for settlement.'

'Well, we thanks yer, Mr Burnaby,' said Prudence, 'and we'll look after the house. Oh, and would yer kindly tell Mr Townley, the coach-man, about everything?'

Mr Burnaby, whose stiff collar had felt like a chain round his neck since the moment when Dr Graham had begun to recount yesterday's disastrous events, sighed and said, 'Yes, one must, I must. And I must also do something about the child.'

'Ain't its mother going to be released?' asked Edie.

Mr Burnaby's collar tightened.

'One hopes she will, one hopes so indeed,' he said, 'but until then I must do something about the child's welfare.'

'You don't 'ave to worry too much just now, sir,' said Prudence, glad to have twenty pounds in her hand. 'Maisie's being a real mother to her.'

'That is so?' said Mr Burnaby, glancing at Maisie. She offered a faint smile. 'Then sup-posing she looks after the child full-time? I assume there's not quite so much work to do in view of the – mmm – unhappily depleted house-hold.' He could have put that in stronger terms, but could not bring himself to do so. As it was, Prudence and Agnes winced. 'I trust that means Maisie could be excused all duties except for taking care of the child.'

'Oh, we'll excuse 'er, sir,' said Prudence, 'except there's always dust around, in every room. I don't know where it comes from, but it lays about in every corner from one day to the next, and has to be got rid of. But we can still excuse Maisie.'

'I understand,' said the solicitor, and looked at Maisie again. 'Will you do that, Maisie, will you take care of the child for the time being?'

'Oh, I'd like to,' said Maisie.

'Maisie's a natural, sir,' said Alexander, and Mr Burnaby took a professional glance at the boy who, if a trial took place, would be a key witness. He looked sturdy and capable.

'Then that at least is settled for the time being. Good.' The solicitor felt some relief. 'You know where my office is, Prudence. Don't hesitate to contact me in the event of any difficulties arising. I shall keep in touch, in any case. I must thank you all for everything you are doing and have done. Ah, yes, before I forget, and before my official reading of Mr Fairfax's Last Will and Testament, I can tell you he left all of you a hundred pounds each. You will receive it in the near future.'

'A whole 'undred pounds?' gasped Agnes.

'Oh, crikey,' gasped Edie.

'Oh, the lovely old gentleman,' said Prudence,

tears in her eyes. 'A hundred pounds'll keep us going for ages if we don't get new jobs.'

'Crikey, ain't it bliss?' said Alexander. 'It'll keep meself going till I get to be— Well, whatever I'll get to be.'

'I never knew a kinder old gentleman,' said Maisie, thinking of a hundred pounds added to her savings and Daniel's. It would make them almost rich for a while.

It was she who saw Mr Burnaby out. At the front door, she spoke to him.

'Mr Burnaby, sir, I think I ought to tell you I'm getting married in October, but Mrs Blisset – I mean Miss Blisset – she'll be back here well before then, won't she?'

Mr Burnaby was prone to the same kind of hesitation as Dr Graham in dealing with the servants on unpleasant matters.

'We'll see, Maisie, we'll see,' he said after a few moments.

'Me soldier fiancé said the police have to release her and Mrs Carpenter unless they charge them.' Daniel had said that.

'Yes, we'll see, we'll see. Ah, are there daily papers delivered here?'

'Yes, Mr Fairfax always had *The Times* and the *Morning Post*,' said Maisie, 'and no-one's cancelled them yet.'

'Well, perhaps there'll be some information in them tomorrow,' said Mr Burnaby, silently damning himself for this cowardly evasion. Like Dr Graham, he simply had no heart for delivering a body blow to this pleasing young lady and the rest of the staff. But he must. It was his duty, his professional obligation. 'No, I must tell you myself. Much as it will distress you and the others, and much though it distresses me, I have to advise you that the police have charged Mrs Carpenter and Miss Blisset with a capital crime, and I'm afraid you will not see them back here until they've been found not guilty.'

'Oh, dear Lord,' gasped Maisie, 'supposing it ain't not guilty?'

'That, my dear young lady, we must believe to be impossible.' Mr Burnaby experienced painful twinges of despair at the look in Maisie's brown eyes, a look of horror. 'We must pray, Maisie.' He departed then, to climb aboard his pony and trap.

Maisie carried the dreadful news to the others. Morale, which had been boosted by news of the bequest, sank heavily and collapsed. Alexander went and sat on the front steps and looked into nothing.

At the brief preliminary hearing on Wednesday, Mrs Carpenter and Miss Blisset were remanded in custody to await trial at the Central Criminal Court. Bail was refused.

On Friday, Maisie received a letter from Daniel.

Dear Sweetheart,
    I'm feeling for you all the time, especially

now. I've seen a morning newspaper. Maisie, I frankly thought this might happen, and I think you did too. Well, try not to take all the worries on your shoulders, I daresay you'd come to respect those women, but it's a fact that respecting people don't always mean all of them are entitled to it. There's many a clean label hiding a twisted mind. Having met Alexander, I believe everything he told you, like you believed it yourself, but come what may you've got your own life to live.

Maisie love, I'm looking forward to living it with you, I've got our wedding day prime in my mind, and that's the truth, so help me. All my life I'm going to stand on my belief that God made you like one of His very own, and that He favoured me like nobody else when you said yes on Hampstead Heath. If that sounds like I've been reading books, well so I have and I couldn't speak fairer. I'll be coming to see you Sunday morning, and I'll be carrying an all-day pass as well as all my love.

Yours forever, Daniel.

In her room, with Rosemary toddling happily about, Maisie wrote an immediate reply.

Dear Daniel,

Thanks ever so much for writing, it was my first love letter which I'll keep, it was such a lovely one. I'm trying not to be down in the dumps but of course everyone's feeling awful.

Still, I won't go on about it, it won't do me any good, anyway. I'm so glad you'll be free on Sunday as I will too, Prudence has said so, except I'll have little Rosemary with me, I told you about her when I was talking to you about everything. So can we meet in the Gardens at the usual place at ten o'clock, and you can help me keep Rosemary happy, which I'm sure you won't mind. Yes, I just can't wait for the wedding day, I've now told all the others about it and Alexander as well, and it kind of cheered everyone up a bit, and Prudence said I can be married from here because she knows a chef that will do the wedding breakfast. She said she was sure Mr Burnaby the solicitor wouldn't mind, oh and would you believe it, Mr Fairfax the dear old gentleman left us all a hundred pounds each, so I'm going to a dress shop in Bayswater Road this afternoon to order my wedding gown. Daniel, I'd like the date to be the second Saturday in October which will suit me fine and I hope it will you too.

Love and kisses, your Maisie.

Daniel, receiving this on Saturday, thought the whole letter came alive to his reading of it. What a grand young lady she was.

Dr Graham in his kindness had called in at the house every day to concern himself with the staff. Having known and attended Mr Fairfax for many years, he was sure this was what the considerate old gentleman would have wanted of him, particularly since the new blow had demoralized them. However, in talking to them at midday on Saturday, he found they were now bearing up and investing their interest in the coming marriage of Maisie to a soldier of the Royal West Kents. And having already learned that Maisie was free to be with her fiancé on Sunday, he told her she would be completely free. He had arranged for a district nurse to come and take care of Rosemary for the day. He did not say he would see to the expenses himself.

Maisie was so delighted she almost hugged the doctor, especially as the arrangement meant she could make a very practical suggestion to Daniel.

Mr Burnaby visited the prisoners on remand to let them know he had briefed a barrister, Mr J.G. Clark, QC, to conduct their defence. If the two women were still insistent on their innocence, they were at least not so loud and aggressive. Mr Burnaby assured them that if anyone could conduct an effective defence, it was Mr Clark, renowned for his aptitude on behalf of clients in any court of law in the land.

Mrs Carpenter wanted to know whether effective was the same as successful. Miss Blisset said if justice was done, she'd have no worries. Mrs Carpenter asked if Mr Burnaby had seen anything of that wicked rascal, Alexander the houseboy. Mr Burnaby countered in hopeful avoidance of a tirade by saying yes, he had seen the boy and noted he wore an air of innocence. Oh, he can put on that kind of look right enough, said Mrs Carpenter, which made Mr Burnaby think that if the lad was so much of a rascal, why had the all-powerful housekeeper not dismissed him months ago?

Some questions left one very uncertain of mind, although at the same time he was impressed by the women's unchanging protestations that Mr Fairfax's death could not be laid at their door.

The post-mortem, incidentally, had ascertained that the death was caused by drowning, not asphyxiation, such as might have been achieved by a pillow being pressed down over the victim's face.

Detective Inspector Rawlings, however, was of the opinion that the old gentleman had been kept fully immersed by a pillow pressing down on his chest. At his age he would not have had the strength to resist. Further, a pillow would have avoided bruising by hands.

Maisie went shopping on Saturday afternoon for a wedding gown and accessories, taking Rosemary with her, and Prudence went shopping for the household in the carriage and pair, for heaven's sake. Mr Townley, having been given the grievous news of the tragic events, told Prudence he was bearing up remarkable, considering.

Chapter Twenty-three

Sunday morning, cloudy but dry.

Daniel, striding through the Gardens, saw the young lady of his dreams. She was sitting on a bench, and talking to her was the artist character, young Hubert Smythe. Maisie didn't look offended, she simply looked herself, composed and tidily arranged, and fetching as well, for she was wearing her engaging boater and her apricot frock.

Up came Daniel. Hubert turned and Maisie looked up. Gladness brightened her eyes.

'Oh, Daniel, here's Mr Smythe wanting to know if I've thought any more about posing for him,' she said.

'I assure you, Corporal Adams, mine is a humble suit with no desire to press Miss Gibbs,' said Hubert. 'I've merely been suggesting to her that sometime in the near future she might perhaps be interested in sitting for me.'

'Well, I tell you, Mr Smythe,' said Daniel, 'Miss Gibbs's near future kind of belongs exclusive to me.' Then he had a thought. 'Would you mind stepping aside?'

'Oh, not I trust for exchanging blows,' said Hubert, perturbed.

'Now, Daniel,' said Maisie.

'No, it's not for that, perish the thought,' said Daniel. 'Excuse me, Maisie.' He drew Hubert aside and informed him he was marrying Maisie on the second Saturday in October. If Hubert would care to attend the wedding at the Kensington church, and the reception at Maisie's place of work, could he then perform from memory? Hubert said perform? Paint her in her wedding gown, said Daniel, like you sketched her in her frock.

'Well,' said Hubert, 'I'd do my very best, but—'

'Good, that's the ticket,' said Daniel breezily, 'but don't put her on – what was the name of that horse?'

'Pegasus.'

'That's it, I think I've come across it in that book of yours now I'm reading it,' said Daniel.

'Well, as I say, I'll do my best.'

'Good man. I'll let you know the time of the wedding and you let me know your charge for the painting, which I hope won't be more than a fiver, nor more than twelve inches by eight in size, eh?'

'I see, yes, for a mantelpiece frame,' said Hubert. 'For myself, although it won't be as arresting as if she sat for me, I shall paint a large canvas of Miss Gibbs in the pure white of her wedding gown.'

'Lovely,' said Daniel, 'well, nice to have talked to you. So long for now.'

Hubert blinked, sighed and departed, wondering how he had been talked into attempting a masterpiece from memory and for a mere fiver.

Daniel sat down beside Maisie and forthwith kissed her on her lips.

'Daniel, there's people!'

'There always are, specially on a Sunday, Maisie love. Talk about the lights of London, if you ain't the brightest light of all. It's good to see you. How you feeling?'

'Better,' said Maisie. And she was entirely free for the day. A district nurse had arrived at the house to look after Rosemary, as Dr Graham had promised. 'I'm just not thinking about nothing except our wedding. Daniel, I've got an idea, as we're both free all day. Why don't we go to Walworth and look around to see if there's a house for rent?'

'On a Sunday?' said Daniel.

'Well, if there's a notice in some house window saying it's for rent, the landlord won't take it down just because it's Sunday, will he?' said Maisie on a practical note.

'No, that he won't,' said Daniel, 'so we'll go, eh, sweetie?'

They rose from the bench, Maisie picking up a carrier bag that had been resting there, and off they went. Subsequently, a horse-drawn tram took them to Westminster Bridge, and along Westminster Bridge Road to the busy and populous junction of the Elephant and Castle, quieter on this Sunday morning. There they caught another tram that carried them down Walworth Road, where Maisie surveyed the old and familiar.

'Look, Daniel, there's Hurlocks, the drapery store where me mum bought me dad a new shirt once for Christmas.'

'I had a clockwork train set for one Christmas, which me dad said he had to clean the soot off first on account of Santa Claus dropping it down the chimney with no box round it. And I believed him. Well, I was only eight and believed anything me parents told me, didn't I?'

'That was what made you grow up nice, Daniel. Look, there's the Town Hall. Ain't it handsome? Oh, and there's Larcom Street coming up. It's where St John's Church is and the church school, which I went to.'

'That was what made you grow up a regular sweetheart, Maisie.'

'Oh, let's get off here,' said Maisie, as the tram came to a stop.

They alighted, Maisie colourful in her apricot, and Daniel an eyeful to females in his red jacket and peaked blue dress cap. They both brightened the quiet Sunday morning scene in this cockney heart of South London, and entered Larcom Street hand in hand, Maisie carrying her paper bag. They walked slowly, casting glances at house windows in search of a notice. They reached the school, immediately next to the church, and Maisie peered through the gates at the deserted playground.

'Memories, Maisie?' smiled Daniel.

'It's where I did me skipping,' said Maisie. 'I think I was better at skipping than learning. Still, I did the three R's very competent, the teachers said.'

'They're singing in church,' said Daniel, as the melodious sound of a hymn reached their ears.

That made them discuss what hymns they'd like for their wedding service, and Maisie said that personal, she'd like 'Onward, Christian Soldiers', and 'O, Valiant Heart'. Daniel asked was there something special about 'Valiant Heart'?

'Yes,' said Maisie, 'it reminds me of me mum and dad. But, of course, if you'd—'

'If they suit you, Maisie, they suit me,' said Daniel, 'specially as "Valiant Heart" fits you as much as it does your mum and dad.' He felt her hand squeeze his fingers as they walked on. 'By the way, second Saturday in October's fine for me. I've been up before our colonel, told him all about you and received his blessing.'

'Oh, that's lovely,' said Maisie. They were walking the short little path between the church and the vicarage, and from there they turned into Walcorde Avenue. On each side of this street stood a row of well-built, quite good-looking terraced houses, all with bay windows and railed-off frontages, and some with their front doors open. There were a few children about, little girls in their Sunday frocks, little boys in their Sunday sailor suits. Here and there, frocks and sailor suits showed patches. Most of the people in Walworth were hard up, and open front doors were no temptation to burglars.

'Daniel, you look in the windows that side, I'll look the other side,' Maisie told her fiancé.

'Hearing you, Sergeant Gibbs.'

'No sauce,' said Maisie.

They had no luck until out of her open front door a woman emerged to call to one of the little girls.

'Jane, you come in now, your dad's finished heeling yer Sunday boots and wants you to put them on.'

'Coming, Mum.' A little girl, separating herself from her playmates, darted past her mother into the house. The mother, a woman in her early thirties, stared as she spotted Maisie. Maisie stopped and stared back.

'Lor', is that you, Maisie Gibbs?' said the woman, hair in a comfortable bun, white blouse covering a homely bosom.

'Oh, bless me,' said Maisie, 'it's you, Mrs Godsby.'

'Maisie, I ain't seen you since I don't know when – near two years, I should think,' said Mrs Godsby. 'My, ain't you a smart young lady now? And who's yer soldier friend?'

'He's me fiancé,' said Maisie, not without a little touch of proud possessiveness. 'Daniel, this is Mrs Godsby that me mum and dad knew since she was young.'

'Well, how's yerself, Mrs Godsby?' said Daniel, giving the lady a salute.

'My, you're an 'andsome feller,' said Mrs Godsby, 'pleased to meet you. What brings you back here, Maisie?'

Maisie, seeing possible help in the offing, explained that she and Daniel were getting married in October and were thinking of renting a house in this neighbourhood. Would Mrs Godsby know of one that was up for renting? Mrs Godsby said she would and did. There was a house in the next street, Caulfield Place, where the tenants were leaving in three weeks to emigrate to Australia, which was all right for some, but she wouldn't never go all that way herself. Why didn't Maisie and her soldier go round to the house now and give the tenants a knock. It was number four.

'Oh, I don't know we ought to disturb people on a Sunday,' said Maisie.

'Maisie, the tenants are Mr and Mrs Russell,' said Mrs Godsby. 'Just tell them that Flo Godsby sent you.'

'Shall we do that, Daniel?' asked Maisie.

'Why not, if it's only in the next street and they're friends of Flo?' said Daniel.

'Oh, you saucy devil,' said Maisie, 'you didn't ought to be as familiar as that when you've only just met Mrs Godsby.'

The lively cockney lady laughed.

'Any soldier as 'andsome as yours, Maisie, can be as familiar as he likes as long as me old man ain't listening,' she said. 'I hope I'm going to have the two of you as near neighbours. Go on, off you go. The Russells won't be having their Sunday dinner just yet.'

'Thanks ever so,' said Maisie.

'Good luck, Maisie, good luck, soldier.'

'Much obliged, Flo,' said Daniel.

Mrs Godsby laughed again.

'Daniel Adams, if you're going to show me up, I'll have to talk to you,' said Maisie, as they went on.

'Maisie me love, it's me fond hope to have you talking to me now and again for the rest of me life,' said Daniel.

'What d'you mean?' They were in York Street now, destined to be renamed Browning Street in memory of Robert Browning, the poet, a native of South London. 'Yes, what d'you mean, now and again?'

'Well, marriage is a partnership, yer know,' said Daniel, 'so I'm hoping we get to take turns in—'

'Oh, you're really saucy this morning,' said Maisie, but her lips twitched in that familiar semblance of a smile.

They turned right into Caulfield Place. Maisie knew it well. It was a homely cul-de-sac that backed onto part of St John's Church School. On the left side was a printing works, closed for Sunday, then a row of six terraced houses. On the right was a row of a dozen. All were of solid Victorian construction, three up, three down, each with a scullery and an adjacent toilet with a second toilet upstairs. Maisie knew all that.

There was no notice in the window of number four. There were curtains, a sign of occupation. Maisie asked if they really ought to knock. Up came a street kid in a ragged jersey and patched shorts.

'Who yer looking for, soldier?' he asked.

'Old Nick,' said Daniel.

'Oh, he don't live 'ere, more like in Marshall's coal yard,' said the kid. 'Well, me mum says he's as black as Satan. I'll take yer there for a penny.'

'Here's a penny,' said Daniel, who had known years as something of a penurious kid himself. He gave the urchin a copper coin. 'Now buzz off before I call me sergeant major.'

'Crikey, don't he like kids, then?'

'Oh, he likes them all right,' said Daniel, 'he has one for breakfast every morning.'

'Oh, blimey, I'm off.' The boy scampered, clutching his penny.

'Daniel Adams, you're acting shocking this morning,' said Maisie.

'Let's knock,' said Daniel. He opened the iron gate to number four, advanced to the door and knocked. It was opened by a large, good-looking bloke of about forty, in shirt, braces and trousers. From the kitchen travelled the aroma of a Sunday dinner cooking.

'Hello, got the army on me doorstep, have I?' said the bloke. 'Where's the war, then, cully, and who's the lady?'

'The lady's Maisie Gibbs, my intended,' said Daniel. 'Apologies for disturbing you, but Flo Godsby recommended us to call. We're looking for a house to rent.'

'Flo, eh?' said the bloke, genial enough. 'Well, this one is full up at the moment. With me, me wife and me four kids.'

'Flo said you were leaving for Australia in three weeks,' said Daniel, with Maisie wanting to box his ears for bandying Mrs Godsby's Christian name about.

'So we are. The kids want to keep kangaroos instead of white mice. I'm Barney Russell, and if you're after renting this here quality abode when we leave, come in and write a note to the landlord and I'll see he gets it.'

'That's friendly of you,' said Daniel.

'Don't mention it.'

'You sure we're not disturbing you?' said Maisie.

'You will be if you get as far as the kitchen, which is crowded with me family, so let's use the parlour.'

They used the parlour, which was typical of its kind in that it contained, among other items, matching sofa and armchairs, a mahogany table with upright chairs, an old piano and a shiny-leafed aspidistra. The hospitable Mr Russell supplied a sheet of notepaper and a pen for

Daniel's use, as well as the name and address of the landlord. Daniel, seated at the table, began writing.

'Mr Russell, I just don't know how to thank you,' said Maisie.

'Well, to start with, wish me and the wife luck on our voyage,' said Mr Russell. 'We'll need it if the kids get seasick. They'll want to come back and keep rabbits. I can't stand rabbits except skinned and in a stewpot. Also, being frank, the furniture's all ours, and seeing we're not carting it with us, we'd like to sell the lot at one go. So if you two are thinking of buying the necessary, suppose I invite you to make an offer for ours? It's all in good condition, even if the joanna looks a bit ancient.'

Daniel, finishing the letter, put the pen down and looked up at Mr Russell, whose offer had an obvious advantage to it. Neither he nor Maisie had the freedom to go shopping whenever they wished.

'We'd need to look it all over,' he said.

'You'd be daft if you didn't,' said Mr Russell, and went on to assure them he was on the level, that none of the furniture belonged to the landlord, and he'd let them have the lot for twenty quid, which ought to make it affordable for them to chuck out what they didn't want. Seeing it would cost them six or seven quid at least to furnish each of the six rooms, twenty quid was a knockdown price, but preferable to selling the stuff chair by chair, bit by bit.

Maisie looked at Daniel. Daniel looked at Maisie. Then they both looked at the parlour furniture with new eyes. Yes, it was in good condition and it suited the room. Maisie gave Daniel a little nod. So Daniel asked when they could look at the rest. Mr Russell said Connie, his trouble and strife, was taking the kids to their granny's that afternoon for Sunday tea, while he got on with what he had to get on with in respect of leaving in three weeks.

'So if you and your young lady could get back here, say, at four, you'd be welcome to look everything over then. Could you manage that?'

'Yes,' said Maisie.

'Well, that's just the ticket,' said Mr Russell. 'Finished the letter?' he enquired of Daniel.

'All done,' said Daniel. He folded the letter and handed it over.

'Give you my word, I'll see the landlord gets it. I know George Hackett, and I'll talk turkey to him on your account, you can bet.'

'Thanks, hope you and yours make a fair old go of it down under,' said Daniel. 'We'll be back at four.' He shook hands with the genial and very obliging bloke, who saw him and Maisie out.

'Daniel,' said Maisie, as they made their way back to Walworth Road via York Street, 'ain't some people grand?'

'Well, I tell you, Maisie,' said Daniel, 'no-one could say the streets of Walworth and Camberwell are paved with gold, but there's many a nugget hiding its light behind a front door.'

'Did you learn that from a book?' asked Maisie.

'And from knowing the people of this area,' said Daniel.

'Mind,' said Maisie, 'you don't suppose Mr Russell's too good to be true, do yer?'

'It crossed my mind until I remembered the friend of your mum and dad,' said Daniel.

'Mrs Godsby?' said Maisie. They were in Walworth Road.

'That's her,' said Daniel. 'Flo. She'd have warned us if Barney was a bit of a fly cove.'

'Yes, she would,' said Maisie. Then, 'Don't I keep telling you it ain't polite calling her Flo when you don't hardly know her?'

'Can't help it, I like Flo,' said Daniel. The road was still Sunday-quiet except for a horse bus approaching from Camberwell. 'Now, where can we get something to eat?'

'On a Sunday? You'll be lucky,' said Maisie. 'But we could ride to Ruskin Park and eat our sandwiches there, then have tea and cake at the refreshment rooms.'

'Sandwiches, what sandwiches?' asked Daniel.

'I've got them in a biscuit tin in this carrier bag,' said Maisie. 'I made them first thing this morning.'

'Maisie, you sweetheart.' Daniel performed another impulsive act of appreciation. Maisie's blushing reaction was predictable.

'Daniel – oh, you kissed me right in the middle of Walworth Road!'

'No, on the pavement, Maisie.'

'Don't you care about people looking?'

'There aren't any, Maisie, they're all home and about to have Sunday dinner. Except a few in that horse bus. And here's a tram coming. We'll ride it to Ruskin Park. What sandwiches are they?'

'Ham with a bit of mustard.'

'I prize you, Maisie, that I do.'

'Still, you didn't ought to keep kissing me in public.'

'Can't help meself, Maisie.'

They boarded the tram, Maisie hitching her skirts. Trim ankles in black stockings showed for a moment.

Daniel smiled. Maisie had pretty limbs, that she did.

Chapter Twenty-four

Ruskin Park, Sunday dinnertime. They almost had the place to themselves, and the sun had come out. The sandwiches, kept fresh by the biscuit tin, were delicious. Two thick ones each, the bread crusty. Some sparrows arrived in the hope of crumbs, often a nice change from worms, and a bit of a breather for the wriggly fraternity.

Maisie asked how many guests Daniel was going to invite to the wedding, so she would know for the wedding breakfast. Say six army comrades and my company sergeant major, replied Daniel. Maisie asked wouldn't there be any relatives? Daniel said the only relatives he had were an aunt and uncle and their family in Canada. Maisie said she didn't have any here, either. Her mum and dad had both been only children, which wasn't very usual, but there it was. Mind, she did have a distant cousin called Tom, but they hadn't seen each other for years. So she'd be inviting some old friends from Walworth, and of course there'd be Alexander and the other servants. Daniel said all told that ought to make enough for a knees-up.

'Daniel, we can't, not in the house, not when – well, you know.'

'Understood, Maisie.'

They spent hours in the park, mingling with the usual Sunday afternoon promenaders, and enjoying tea and cake in the refreshment rooms. Maisie found everything such a welcome change from being confined to the house, where the atmosphere was hardly enlivening, which you couldn't expect, anyway. Being in this park with Daniel was, well, almost joyful, especially as it would be their local park if they did come to live in Walworth.

They were back at the house in Caulfield Place at the agreed time of four. Mr Russell let them in and took them into the parlour again. There were papers spread on the table.

'All to do with emigration and leaving everything in order,' said Mr Russell. 'Look, the house is yours, the kids are at their granny's with Connie. Best, I'd say, for you to look at all the furniture by yourselves. I'd just be in the way. You can go into every room.'

'Oh, thanks,' said Maisie, and as she knew the geography of these houses, she and Daniel were able to make their tour an easy one. They saw a lot that they really liked, and what didn't appeal to them, well, they could gradually replace. It all depended on the landlord accepting them as tenants.

They spoke to Mr Russell, and Daniel said he'd let him have payment as soon as the landlord agreed their tenancy. Could Mr Russell tell them what the rent was? Ten bob a week.

'That'll do us,' said Daniel.

'Did you put your address on the letter?' asked Mr Russell.

'I did. Corporal D. Adams, C Company, Royal West Kent Regiment, Knightsbridge Barracks.'

'Good. Pleased to have met you both. Would you like a cup of tea?'

'It's ever so nice of you, Mr Russell,' said Maisie, 'but we had two cups each only a little while ago. In Ruskin Park.'

'Right you are,' said Mr Russell, and his callers parted from him on very amiable terms.

By horse buses, Maisie and Daniel travelled all the way to Green Park, and from there sauntered into the evening and towards Kensington Gore. Daniel saw her right to the door of the house.

'Maisie, it's been my best Sunday ever, and that's a fact,' he said.

'Oh, mine too,' said Maisie, 'and look, I brought something else in me carrier bag as well as the biscuit tin.' She took out a picture frame. Fitted neatly into it was the charming pencil sketch. She'd trimmed it to fit without clipping anything from the sketch, and at the bottom she'd written, 'To Daniel from Maisie with love August Bank Holiday 1894'. 'There, it's for you, Daniel, like I promised.'

'Maisie, you're my girl and the best I'll ever

know,' said Daniel. The door opened then, and Alexander appeared.

'Oh, pleased to see you again, soldier,' he said, 'can I come and see you at the barracks tomorrer or the next day? I'll get some free time off for it.'

'Not at any time this week, Alexander,' said Daniel, 'which reminds me to tell you, Maisie, the battalion's off to Salisbury Plain tomorrow, and we'll be there till next Saturday.'

'Well, thanks for telling me now, I'm sure,' said Maisie.

'Lucky for me I remembered in time,' said Daniel. 'Alexander, come to the barracks sometime the week after next.'

'I can't hardly wait,' said Alexander, and showed he actually owned a bit of tact by disappearing. That allowed Daniel a private moment to kiss Maisie again. A snooty lady passing by in company with a gentleman viewed the act on the doorstep with pinched-mouth disapproval.

'Daniel Adams, you've gone and done it again,' said Maisie, blushing, 'kissed me in public with people looking. And don't tell me you can't help yerself.'

'Well, as God's me witness, Maisie, I can't,' said Daniel.

'All right, I forgive you, seeing we've had a nice day,' said Maisie.

'I'll write to you from Salisbury,' said Daniel, 'and be in touch when the battalion gets back. Goodbye, sweetie.'

Maisie quivered. She had reason to, because he kissed her yet again.

Still, as she watched him go, handsome and upright, the framed sketch in his hand, she didn't actually feel put upon.

Down to her room she went, put the carrier bag aside, took off her boater, touched her wealth of piled hair, and glanced in her wall mirror. Oh, Lor', she was flushed. That Daniel. The little tingles arrived, pleasurable tingles. She waited a few minutes, then went to the kitchen, where the other servants were having a cold supper of sliced ham and a tomato salad. Enjoying it with them were District Nurse Maud Galloway and little Rosemary.

'Oh, you're back,' said Agnes, the champion of the obvious.

'Well, I told yer she was, didn't I?' said Alexander.

'That boy's getting cheekier,' said Edie.

'He'd 'ave to watch hisself if – if – ' Daisy didn't finish. She didn't need to. They all knew she meant if Mrs Carpenter was there and hovering. Remarks like that, touching on what they tried to avoid mentioning, were frequent.

'Sit down, Maisie,' said Prudence. 'There's plenty for you if you ain't had any supper yet.'

'Oh, ta,' said Maisie, not at all minding more ham. She was hungry. 'How's Rosemary been?'

The child burbled. She was being fed by the district nurse to make sure most of the food went into her mouth.

'She's been sweet and good.' Maud Galloway, a fine-looking woman of thirty-five, spoke cheerfully. 'She's a dear little mite.'

'I'll take her off your hands as soon as you've had your supper,' said Maisie, sitting down and helping herself to ham and salad.

'That will suit me just fine, Maisie,' said the friendly district nurse.

'Oh, good,' said Maisie, 'and I'm ever so grateful for you looking after her all day.'

'A pleasure.'

'Maisie, where you been all day?' asked Agnes.

'Oh, all over,' said Maisie, 'on trams and buses.'

'With yer soldier sweetheart?' said Prudence.

'Yes,' said Maisie, and told them that she and Daniel had managed to find a nice house for rent in Walworth, where she'd been born and brought up. They had happy hopes that the landlord would let them have it, and then they'd buy all the furniture and save themselves having to shop for it.

'Wish yer luck, Maisie,' said Daisy. Like Prudence, Agnes and Edie, she'd been in service since the age of fourteen and never had the chance to go courting.

'Yes, do have a lovely wedding,' said Nurse Galloway. She left after supper, calling in on Dr Graham on her way home. He received her kindly, and asked how her day with the child had gone.

'Satisfactorily, I hope, Maud?'

'I had no trouble with her,' said Nurse Galloway. 'Hasn't her mother asked to see her?'

Dr Graham said he'd been told by Mr Burnaby, solicitor for the detained women, that Miss Blisset was bitter about the father, who had apparently disappeared during the final stages of her pregnancy. Nurse Galloway said she supposed that had affected her attitude towards the child. A man ought to do the decent thing with a woman who was going to bear his child, otherwise the woman had a bad name all her life.

'True,' said Dr Graham.

'And some widowers ought to marry again,' said the extrovert district nurse.

'I think you've said that before,' murmured Dr Graham, paying her out of his pocket at a Sunday rate for her excellent day's work.

Nurse Galloway, advancing to the door, turned and said, 'It's about time you asked me.'

'Pardon me?' said Dr Graham.

'You know you'd like to,' smiled Nurse Galloway, not a woman hidebound by the strict social mores of the era. 'Cheerio, Charles.'

She disappeared, leaving the good doctor slightly flummoxed in a pleasant kind of way.

Well, Nurse Galloway was a fine figure of a woman, with a most likeable disposition.

On Monday afternoon, a sergeant and a constable in plain clothes arrived to check Alexander's statement. They went through it with him in the reception room, while the other servants suffered for him in their retreat, the kitchen.

'Oh, that poor boy,' whispered Daisy, 'up there with two coppers and all.'

'It ain't right at his age,' whispered Edie.

Alexander, however, was surpassing himself. His radically upset nerves had calmed down. He was now made of stern stuff rather than precociousness, mainly by seeing himself proudly uniformed as Drummer Alexander Beavis of the Royal West Kent Regiment. His chest was stuck out, his back straight, his image of Corporal Daniel Adams his inspiration.

The policemen couldn't fault him. He stood by every word of his original story, even if he had signed the statement with a nervous flourish that made his name look like a whirligig.

'That's a name?' said the sergeant, but with a grin.

'It's me official moniker that I got from me parents,' said Alexander, 'and if they could rise up from their Peckham churchyard, they'd tell yer so.'

'Fair, fair,' said the sergeant, 'and if you can speak up on the witness stand like you have now, I'll be admiring of you.'

'I ain't going to faint,' said Alexander, 'I know me duty. Listen, when's it happening, the trial?' He asked this question much more bravely than he would have done earlier.

'We'll let you know.'

'Well, I hope I ain't too busy learning drums at the time,' said Alexander.

'Drums?'

'I could be,' replied Alexander, and said no more.

Mr Burnaby had been visiting the prisoners often, making notes to pass to the barrister. If Mrs Carpenter and Miss Blisset were much quieter and more reflective, they were still able to show hot resentment of their detention and what it meant. Mr Burnaby did his best to soothe them, particularly as the barrister had offered the opinion that the evidence was primarily circumstantial.

On Wednesday afternoon, the solicitor called at the house to let the staff know the trial would take place earlier than expected. It would commence on the 6th of October at the Old Bailey. The servants' reactions ranged from dead silence to noisy emotion. Maisie winced, and Alexander said no-one was going to like it. Daisy wailed.

Prudence came out of numbed silence to say, 'Well, we all knew it 'ad to come and we'd best put up with it.'

Maisie knew none of them had anything against the housekeeper and the cook, but if they were found guilty of causing the death of the kind old gentleman, then there wouldn't be a good word spoken about them. On the other hand, there'd be fainting fits at what could happen next. Women could be hanged if their crime was wicked and premeditated, and the jury didn't ask for mercy to be shown.

Lord, the trial starting on October the 6th. That was ten days before her wedding to Daniel. Her special day could be horribly blighted.

The forlorn household brooded. Prudence shook herself and made everyone go and do some work, even if it didn't need doing. Do it again, she said, out of respect for Mr Fairfax. Make everything shine.

His suite, however, still hadn't been touched. It was as it had been left on that dreadful day. Milly was adamant about not going in there. So Prudence said she'd do it herself. And she did, with Maisie's help. Rosemary toddled about in their wake.

On Thursday, Maisie received a letter from Daniel headed 'Somewhere in the wilds of Salisbury Plain'. He wrote that he'd rather be in the wilds of Kensington Gardens, which would always be special to him, seeing they were where he'd had his very first meeting with a certain young lady who gave him his marching orders on account of not knowing him properly. His legs wanted to take him back there, he said, but his company sergeant major ordered them to stay where they were, and being an NCO it was always best to accept an order. He hoped she was in the pink and not worrying too much about what had been so upsetting to her. Life's like that, Maisie, it's full of hard knocks, he wrote. He was thinking of her all the time, and that house in Walworth. He'd get in touch with her when he got back, and sent her love and kisses, which he underlined. Underlining was a habit of Queen Victoria herself in her addictive letter-writing, so Daniel was in right royal company.

Maisie kept the letter, putting it with the first one she had received.

As for Rosemary, the longer the child was in her care, the more Maisie dreamed about a daughter of her own. And a boy, of course. Say two girls and two boys. That was what life was all about, families. Mind, there were always some families that raised the roof with their yelling and hollering, even on Sundays sometimes. No self-respect, that was what her mum had said about them. And in her time, Maisie had heard irate, put-upon wives hollering at backsliding husbands, and using language which made her dad put his hands over her ears. Still, when real trouble hit a quarrelsome family, they all stood together as one.

Our family, mine and Daniel's, won't yell and holler, and have no self-respect, I'll see to that, thought Maisie.

All her hopes for her future with Daniel kept at bay the unwanted thoughts, those concerning a dreadful outcome to the trial of Mrs Carpenter and Miss Blisset.

The daily papers enjoyed by Mr Fairfax had been cancelled. Accordingly, the staff missed the headlines concerning the indictment of two women for the murder of their rich employer. They were glaring and sensational, those headlines, and the staff were well off in not having them drop on the mat every morning.

Chapter Twenty-five

Mr Burnaby called in on Friday to pay the staff their wages. He was good enough to extend his remit as executor to add a bonus of five shillings each for all they'd gone through, which delighted them. He was also wise enough to avoid answering too many questions about Mrs Carpenter and Miss Blisset. Yes, they were bearing up, that was his general response. When asked what he thought their chances were, he only said we shall see, we shall see. He escaped further questions by drawing Maisie out of the kitchen and talking to her concerning the welfare of Rosemary.

Could she possibly manage to continue caring for the child until the result of the trial was known?

Maisie understood. It was a question she had to think about carefully, because it considered the possibility that the women might be found guilty. She stood up to it bravely, replying that she would look after Rosemary with pleasure right up to her wedding day if necessary. It was no hardship because the little girl wasn't ever difficult or troublesome.

'Thank you, Maisie, thank you,' said Mr Burnaby, a harassed man, but not lacking hope in what the defence might achieve for Mrs Carpenter and Miss Blisset.

'Oh, that's all right, sir,' said Maisie.

'I'm delighted, Maisie, that your wedding is such a happy event to think about in the midst of what we all know is a terribly unhappy time,' said Mr Burnaby. He smiled, then sighed, gave her shoulder a little pat, and left.

The following morning, Dr Graham made another of his regular calls. As ever, he did his best to raise the morale of the servants, and he did cheer them up a little. He also told Maisie that District Nurse Galloway would again take care of Rosemary all day tomorrow, Sunday.

'You deserve one full day off a week, young lady,' he said. 'You have much to do, I'm sure, in regard to your wedding.'

'Oh, thanks ever so, doctor,' said Maisie, and he noted how well she was coping with everything. There was something admirably resolute and resilient about her. They were all pretty resilient, the other servants, but Maisie, he thought, stood on her own, young though she was.

'May I hope you'll invite me to the wedding?' he said on an impulse.

'Crikey, would yer really like to come, doctor?'

'Indeed I would,' said Dr Graham, 'and I've a feeling Mr Burnaby would also like to.'

'Oh, my,' said Maisie, 'I don't know I was ever more complimented.

The 10th Battalion of the Royal West Kents, travelling on a special train, were back in their barracks by mid-afternoon. Every platoon had mastered the capabilities of the new rifles. What they hadn't become acquainted with was the reason why the battalion was being equipped with these highly efficient weapons from the renowned Enfield Ordnance factory.

Ireland. That was the guess of some old sweats.

'Is it?' Daniel had asked of Sergeant Major Albert Sawyer. It was when they were sharing the window view in the corridor of the train, the sergeant major smoking a clay pipe so antique that an archaeologist might have labelled it a Stone Age artefact. Its smoke was pungent, but it was the sergeant major's boon companion in peace and adversity. The fact that it was still in one piece was a tribute to the care he took of it.

'Is what, Corporal Adams?'

'Is it going to be Ireland? I've got a personal interest in hoping it won't be.'

'Now look here, this here battalion's not being run to suit your private affairs, but to keep Her Majesty's Empire quiet and peaceful.'

'Must point out, Sarn't Major, that the Irish ain't quiet, nor peaceful, not by a long shot.'

'And might I point out, Corporal Adams, that

a battalion of the Middlesex Regiment is presently knocking them off and locking them up?'

'So what I'd like to know is when do the Middlesex get relieved and who's going to relieve 'em?' asked Daniel, who had Maisie and the wedding permanently on his mind.

'Once and for all, I ain't been informed,' said the sergeant major, blowing smoke that Daniel's nose would have preferred to escape.

'Well, I tell you, Sarn't Major, it's me intuition that's bothering me,' he said.

'Your what? Don't talk like a female with a headache, Corporal Adams.'

'I appreciate you care, Sarn't Major.'

The sergeant major blew more smoke, showed a bit of a grin, and the train thundered on towards London.

At nine that evening, a private of the West Kents knocked on the door of the late Mr Fairfax's residence. Alexander answered the summons.

'Oh, 'ello, soldier, you after me?' he asked.

'Only hif you happen to be Miss Maisie Gibbs,' said the private, 'which Hi can see you ain't.'

'What d'yer want her for?' asked Alexander.

'To give 'er this here missive.' The private produced a letter.

'I'll take it to her,' said Alexander.

'Me hinstructions was to hand it to her personal.'

'Is it from Corporal Adams?'

'That it is.'

'Half a mo,' said Alexander. He turned and called. 'Oi, Maisie, here's a letter for yer.'

Maisie came out of the reception room, Rosemary toddling after her.

'Might you be Miss Maisie Gibbs?' asked the private.

'That's me,' said Maisie.

''Ere we are, then, miss, with the compliments of Corporal Adams.' The private handed her the letter, which was thick.

'Oh, the battalion's back?' said Maisie.

'Punctual, as ordered. Good evening, miss.'

'Thanks, goodbye,' said Maisie, and went back to the reception room with Rosemary. The house was theirs, and wherever the child wanted to wander, Maisie wandered with her.

'Maisie, can I come and read yer letter for yer?' called Alexander.

'Not likely,' said Maisie, 'go and play on your drum, there's a good boy.'

'I ain't got a drum, not yet,' said Alexander.

'Well, use a saucepan, but not so's anyone can hear,' said Maisie, and disappeared with Rosemary.

'Women,' mused Alexander, 'I dunno I'll ever make any of 'em out.'

Daniel's letter was brief but very welcome.

Maisie love,
   We're back, glad to be near you again. A

letter from the landlord of that house was waiting for me. We're accepted as tenants from the day the Russells move out. So if you can get tomorrow off, which I can't, sorry, do you think you could go to Walworth again and pay Mr Russell for the furniture as agreed. I'm enclosing the necessary, twenty quid. Hope to see you sometime next week. Thinking of you always.

Love, Daniel.

'Oh, blow,' said Maisie, her pleasure in getting the house offset by her disappointment at not being able to see Daniel tomorrow. 'Oh, blow,' she said again.

Rosemary burbled something.

'Well, ain't you a little love, learning to talk when you're still only one?' said Maisie. Rosemary beamed, gurgled and sat her little fat bottom on the floor, which gave Maisie time to take the money out of the envelope and count it. It was all in ten-shilling notes, forty of them. She saw them as savings Daniel had managed to wrest out of his beggarly army pay, and she thought of what her dad had once said, that governments everywhere that paid men a miserly few bob for facing up to death ought to be compelled by law to be in the front lines themselves. They paid their civil servants more than soldiers, didn't they, and civil servants only had to face up to their desks. Her mum had said it was governments that made the laws, wasn't it? I know that, said her dad, which is why they make safety-first laws for themselves, which ain't popular with me, nor the soldiers, I bet. A hundred to one, he went on, that if the Prime Minister had had to lead the Charge of the Light Brigade, there wouldn't have been no charge, nor hundreds of deaths, neither.

A little smile touched Maisie's lips as she remembered that. Her dad often spoke what she felt was a lot of sense. It still hurt sometimes to realize he and her dear mum had gone.

I'll go to Walworth tomorrow, Daniel, she said to herself, I'll pay Mr Russell. And thanks ever so much, Daniel, for taking the money out of your savings.

She arrived at the Walworth house in the middle of the morning. Urchins with fairly clean faces were playing in the street. Clean faces abounded on Sunday mornings, but didn't always last up to Sunday dinnertime. Still, clean faces first thing showed that there were caring mums and dads around, respectable mums and dads. There always had been, however poor some families were.

Mr Russell himself opened the door to her, and insisted she come and meet his wife, seeing the kids were at church.

'Oh, d'you send them to church, Mr Russell?' said Maisie.

'It's one more way of making sure they don't

turn into cannibals,' said Mr Russell. 'Me and Connie go with 'em sometimes. Well, you've got to believe in something or what's the point?' He turned and called. 'Connie, come and meet one of the new tenants.'

Mrs Russell turned out to be nice-looking, hard-working and soft-hearted. Maisie took to her at once, and she made such a good impression herself that when she came to hand over the money for the furniture, the good lady said, 'Now, Barney, you don't mean to take all that twenty pounds, do yer, when the young lady's fiancé is only a soldier?'

'Oh, but me and Daniel thought the amount was very fair,' said Maisie.

'Well, it might be, ducky, it might be,' said Connie, 'but you've saved us all the bother of selling it bit by bit, and there was some things we couldn't sell until the day we left, like the kids' beds and our kitchen table. Them and other things we might never have sold at all. Barney, take just fifteen pounds.'

'Oh, no, honest,' said Maisie.

'Connie's right,' said Mr Russell, 'you and yer soldier have saved us a lot of bother.'

'Yes, and we've got more than enough to see us all the way to Australia and longer,' said Mrs Russell, 'and Barney's got a job as a building worker waiting for him. Here, d'you know what a neighbour offered us for our kitchen table and the six chairs? Four mouldy bob, and he said he was doing us a favour taking them off our hands.

Barney told him to go and fall down a coalhole. No, we'll take just fifteen pounds, love, and you tell yer soldier fiancé that me and Barney are grateful.'

So when Maisie left, she still had five pounds in her purse, the good wishes of the Russells echoing in her ears and a bit of a song on her lips.

She was back at the Kensington house in time for Sunday dinner, which came as a very nice surprise to her, roast leg of lamb, roast potatoes, tender runner beans and onion sauce. And who was doing the carving but District Nurse Maud Galloway, with Rosemary sitting up at the table and beaming.

Knowing Prudence and the other women were indifferent cooks, Maisie asked who had done the roast.

'Maud,' said Prudence.

'Maud?' said Maisie.

'Nurse Galloway,' said Agnes.

Nurse Galloway smiled.

'Me myself, Maisie,' she said, 'with Rosemary helping, didn't you, pet?'

Rosemary burbled in apparent acknowledgement. She was a child who responded to anyone who gave her attention and a cuddle or two. She burbled some more as her slice of lamb was cut up for her by Daisy. Nurse Galloway heaped other plates with the lamb, and everyone helped themselves to the vegetables from tureens and the thick creamy sauce from a bowl.

'Well,' said Maisie feelingly, 'I must say you're a blessing, Nurse Galloway.'

'Maud,' smiled the district nurse, 'I'm professional but not stuffy.'

She was indeed a friendly soul and an attractive woman. Her attitude towards that which troubled the staff was wholly sympathetic, but she did not go on about it.

Maisie was out again during the afternoon, walking in the Gardens, which she was always going to remember as special to herself and Daniel. She strolled in dreamy fashion, but still retained her appearance as an upright and respectable young lady. There were soldiers of the Queen about, as usual, making their forays into the ranks of servant girls. Hubert Smythe was also there, as he often was, hoping to see Maisie. Spotting her from a bench, he made no move to talk to her. He was content to view her from afar, as it were, inspiring him to picture her on winged Pegasus, white wedding gown and gauzy veil streaming, on her ride to Olympus as a proud bride of Zeus. That was to be a small canvas for Corporal Daniel Adams. For himself, it would be a large canvas depicting Maisie as Hippolyte, young Queen of the Amazons, riding through a crimson sky to become a bride to Hercules, as legend had it. He was confident that when he saw her at her wedding he would be able to commit her to canvas from memory, since she was far too sensitive to sit for him. His inspiration took him as far as seeing his canvas hung at the Royal Academy's summer show next year.

Maisie, dreaming her dreams of the future, passed him without being in the least aware of his presence in the well-patronized Gardens.

District Nurse Maud Galloway, having returned her young charge to Maisie that evening, again called on Dr Graham. He expressed his gratitude and pleasure for her day's care.

'You know,' she said, 'it's as well for Maisie Gibbs to be separated from the child more often, or the little girl will come to regard her as her mother, making the ultimate parting unhappy for both.'

'We can do nothing definite until the trial is over,' said Dr Graham.

'No, but I thought I'd mention the possibility of the child becoming too attached to Maisie,' said Maud.

'I've seen that possibility myself, but we must wait,' said Dr Graham, and paid her what was due. Again out of his own pocket and at a Sunday rate.

'You know, these monies should come out of the estate, from the bequest to Fanny Blisset,' said Maud.

'I told you about that, did I?'

'Yes, you did. You're not yourself, Charles, or you wouldn't have forgotten,' smiled Maud. 'Well, I'm always ready to help sustain you. Meanwhile, treat yourself to a glass of port. Cheerio.'

*   *   *

With Rosemary tucked up in her cot, Maisie wrote to Daniel, telling him that Mr and Mrs Russell had insisted on taking only fifteen pounds for the furniture. She also told him that her free Sunday would have been more enjoyable if he'd been with her. She sent him her love.

Chapter Twenty-six

In consideration of the fact that the battalion was mostly engaged in keeping fit in expectation of an eventual posting either at home or overseas, C Company's OC, Major James, conceded that Corporal Adams could be allowed some favours. Accordingly, Daniel received regular passes for the purpose of seeing his fiancée.

And since Maisie was free to take Rosemary out whenever she liked, she and Daniel met two or three times every week. On one outing he bought her an engagement ring, much to her delight. On another, he walked Rosemary up and down the Bayswater Road while Maisie tried on her wedding gown and veil in the dress shop. They fitted so well that when she emerged she was carrying a large white box.

'I won't ask to see what's in it,' said Daniel, Rosemary up in his arms by then.

'You can ask, but I won't show you,' said Maisie, now minus two pounds, six shillings and eleven pence of her savings, a heart-stopping amount of money, but at least spent in a young lady's best cause.

As to their wedding, they had both made their invitations to certain friends. The banns were being called, and Daniel had dropped a line to Hubert Smythe to let him know the time of the marriage service, twelve noon.

Alexander had made his call on the barracks, and Daniel received permission to accompany him to the recruiting centre, where he was interviewed by an old-time infantry sergeant who decided this young and perky cock sparrer was of the right stuff to become a drummer boy.

'You say you're an orphan, me lad?'

'Yes, I been unfortunate, like,' said Alexander.

'He's an orphan?' The recruiting sergeant looked at Daniel for confirmation.

'He's an orphan,' said Daniel, 'and he's got my personal recommendation as a drummer boy recruit for the Royal West Kents.'

'Hold on a tick.' The sergeant knocked on a door, opened it and went in. He reappeared a minute later, accompanied by an elderly officer, a captain, who asked Alexander some pertinent questions, such as was he sound in wind and limb. Alexander said he was, and the officer said he would have a medical, anyway.

'D'you have a guardian?'

'No, sir, I don't 'ave no-one like that.'

'Well, we'll need the signature of a sponsor, say a lawyer, a priest or a doctor.'

'Oh, I can get Dr Graham to do that, sir,' said Alexander.

'Right. Sergeant Foulkes will give you a form to fill in, which your doctor will need to sign. Then bring it back here at your convenience.'

So when Alexander left with Daniel, he had the form. Daniel said to fill it in, get the doctor's signature and then take it back to the recruiting centre as soon as that blamed trial was over.

'Crikey, yes, I got to be at the Old Bailey, ain't I?' said Alexander.

'Best if you get it over with before you join up,' said Daniel.

In September, Maisie celebrated her eighteenth birthday on the very day that the Russell family vacated their Walworth house to begin the first stage of their move to Australia. Daniel, having received a pass for the afternoon, arrived at Kensington Gore to pick her up. So, of course, when Maisie herself opened the door to him, he helped himself to a kiss. On the doorstep, with people passing by. Maisie would have berated him for this saucy habit had it not been her birthday. He gave her a present, a very fine cameo brooch, in return for which Maisie gave him a kiss on her own initiative. In the hall.

Then, taking Rosie with them, they travelled to Walworth to see the landlord and get the keys from him. Square, solid and heavily-moustached, the landlord proved co-operative if businesslike. That is, he handed over the keys with a request for a month's rent in advance, seeing they weren't going to take up occupation until October. Daniel forked out two quid, and was given a rent book.

Then they went to the house itself, Maisie on tenterhooks in case the Russells might just have defrauded them over the furniture, after all.

'I'm putting my trust in Flo,' said Daniel.

'Oh, you and your Flo,' said Maisie.

Daniel's instincts were right. Every stick of furniture was in place and, moreover, all the bed linen and overlays were still there. Everything had been left spotless, including lace curtains, and that, of course, made Maisie declare no people were more reliable than nice, respectable ones.

'It strikes me, Maisie, that we could move in right now,' said Daniel, 'and eat our first meal off our bedroom floor.'

'Oh, you saucy devil, and us not married yet?' said Maisie. 'Daniel Adams, don't you say things like that in front of little Rosemary.'

'Little Rosemary, how d'you feel about what I said?' asked Daniel. The child issued what sounded very much like a bubbly giggle. 'There we are, Maisie,' said Daniel, 'she's broad-minded.'

'We're still not moving in till we're married,' said Maisie.

'That's when I've been promised weekend passes,' said Daniel.

'Daniel, I'm sure we're going to be happy here,' said Maisie.

'More so than in married quarters,' said Daniel.

Returning to Kensington Gore, they were in time for a treat, a birthday tea prepared by Prudence and the rest of the staff. There was bread and butter, shrimps and winkles, blackcurrant jam and an iced cake from the local baker. Prudence didn't trust herself or any of the others to accomplish successful baking.

Maisie was quite overcome, more so when she found little wrapped presents from the staff beside her plate. A string of beads, a lace-edged handkerchief, a posh hatpin for when she wore a proper hat and not a boater, a pair of knitting needles and, from Alexander, a dainty little box containing a powder puff.

A bit choked, Maisie thanked them, one and all.

'Well, you're a good girl, Maisie,' said Prudence.

'We all likes yer,' said Daisy.

'Not half,' said Alexander.

'Bless yer, Maisie,' said Edie.

'You're a lucky soldier,' said Milly to Daniel.

'Tell me something I don't know,' smiled Daniel, and there were sighs all round at how handsome he was.

'Come on, everyone, 'elp yerselves to shrimps and winkles,' said Prudence, 'everything's out of the 'ousekeeping by permission of Mr Burnaby.'

'He ain't a bad bloke, yer know, for a solicitor,' said Edie. 'And so say all of us,' said Agnes.

Time went by, with District Nurse Galloway giving up all her Sundays to take care of Rosemary, which endeared her to Maisie and made Dr Graham very appreciative of Maud's good nature.

Maisie's savings were down to a few pennies because of the cost of her wedding gown and items she had bought for her trousseau, so Daniel gave her ten pounds from his own diminishing savings. Maisie didn't want to take it, but Daniel said what was his was hers as well. Maisie said that was supposed to be when they were married. Daniel said she deserved some of it in advance, and made her take it. Overcome, Maisie kissed him. On a bench in the Gardens, with Rosemary and some passing people looking.

'Oh, I just don't know what you're making me do sometimes, Daniel.'

'Love you, Maisie.'

'Corporal Adams, come here,' said Sergeant Major Sawyer after morning parade one day.

Daniel planted himself smartly in front of C Company's warrant officer.

'Sarn't Major?'

'I'm getting a feeling you ain't here most of the time,' said the sergeant major, waxed moustache stiffly correct.

'Which reminds me to thank you for all the passes,' said Daniel.

'Which reminds me to ask how many times have you sloped off without a pass?'

Daniel said there was one time when he didn't have a pass, the time when he took an orphan lad to the recruiting centre, for which he received permission from Captain Burnett.

'Are you thinking of that, Sarn't Major?'

The sergeant major eyed Daniel thoughtfully. He knew him as a stalwart campaigner in times of trouble overseas, a natural soldier who could stand up to shot and shell with the best of them, the kind of NCO who did the army proud and could keep the lead-swinging old sweats of his platoon with their feet marching around the parade ground instead of plonked on their cots. But lately, there was a difference, a kind of unmilitary spring in his step as if he was about to do a high jump or cavort about on a flying trapeze.

'What's on your mind, Corporal Adams, as if I don't know?'

'I can't tell a porkie, Sarn't Major, it's my young lady.'

'Which I know, don't I, like I said. Well, if I catch you absent without a pass, I'll read you a certain paragraph of the Queen's Regulations. It'll be me duty.'

'Permission, Sarn't Major, to point out I've spoken my gratitude for all the passes I'm getting, which means I don't need to push off without one.'

'Happy in your life, are you, Corporal Adams?'

'Just like you were, Sarn't Major, when you were courting Mrs Sawyer, I fancy.' The sergeant major and his wife lived in the warrant officers' quarters.

'Impertinence is chargeable,' said the sergeant major. 'Well, don't let me receive a report that you've jumped over the moon, because I'll be waiting for you on your way down. Dismiss.' A fleeting grin made his moustache twitch as he watched Daniel stride away. Sod me, he thought, he looks like he's dancing. It's criminal what love can do to a fine soldier. And what did he mean when he talked about me going courting? He was only a drummer boy when I took up with Annie. Had eyes in the back of his head even then, I suppose.

The staff's interest in Maisie's forthcoming wedding began to be affected by their dread anticipation of the trial, which Alexander and Prudence had to attend as witnesses. Alexander would be called to deliver to the court his first-hand account of events, Prudence would appear as chief representative of the staff who had been present on the landing after the body had been lifted from the bath.

Prudence had the shakes, Alexander had self-confidence. Dr Graham and Mr Burnaby, during their frequent visits, did what they could to soothe Prudence, although they themselves were dreading the trial. Dr Graham, of course, would deliver his evidence as the medical officer who had examined the body.

Maisie just hoped the trial wouldn't run on over her wedding day, 17 October, and that the outcome would be acceptable to all, although how that might be, she had no idea. Daniel refrained from mentioning the worst.

Chapter Twenty-seven

October arrived, and with it the trial at the Old Bailey.

In the awesome atmosphere of the court, presided over by the judge in his majestic gown and wig, the prosecution counsel, Mr Gregory Pitt, outlined the Crown's case against the defendants, who sat rigidly stiff in the dock, flanked by uniformed constables.

The case against the defendants was self-evident, said counsel. There was the fact that they were both on the spot, that they did not call for help until after their employer was already dead. And how did he meet his death? Undoubtedly by being held under the water until he drowned. They had spoken of him hitting his head when they claimed he must have fallen. The court would hear, however, that no bruise was found anywhere on his body, least of all on his head. There was no question of heart failure. The post-mortem had confirmed Dr Graham's diagnosis that drowning had been the sole cause of death.

The motive? The deceased's Last Will and Testament, by which the defendant, Mrs Iris Carpenter, stood to gain the whole estate, apart from some minor bequests, and one of a thousand pounds to the second defendant, Miss Fanny Blisset. The court would hear medical evidence to the effect that the deceased, although seventy, could have confidently looked forward to many more years of life.

There was also the odd fact that the deceased had suffered falls that could not be satisfactorily explained, since his housekeeper, the senior defendant, had been close by on each occasion. Close by, repeated counsel, glancing at the jury. He then referred to the discovery of a wet pillow belonging to the deceased under the bed of defendant Mrs Iris Carpenter, a widow. The discovery had been made by the houseboy, Alexander Beavis. If anything pointed to an item that could be used to smother the struggles of the deceased without leaving pressure marks, a pillow could. What other explanation could be offered for its soaked condition and the fact that it had been hidden? Prosecution would seek to prove it had been placed out of sight under the bed by the second defendant, Miss Fanny Blisset.

Mr Pitt enlarged on his outline before giving way to the defence counsel, Mr J.G. Clark, QC, renowned for fastening onto any weakness in the opposition.

Everything in the prosecution case, said Mr Clark, was based on hearsay and circumstance.

His learned friend had not offered one shred of factual evidence. In any criminal case, the Crown must provide clear-cut proof of a defendant's guilt before a jury could convict, and in this case such proof would be found to be non-existent. It was possible, indeed, that the gentlemen of the jury would come to wonder why the Crown had proceeded with a prosecution at all. As for the introduction of the wet pillow, that was a red herring of convenience.

There was an adjournment for lunch, and when the court resumed in the afternoon, Dr Graham was called to give his version of events following his arrival on the scene. He did so concisely and calmly, beginning with his examination of Mr Fairfax and diagnosing death by drowning, and ending with his questioning of Mrs Carpenter and Miss Blisset about the exact nature of events. He was then asked by Mr Pitt what led him to question them.

'I could not dismiss that which the houseboy, Alexander Beavis, told me.'

'And what did he tell you, Dr Graham?'

'That he had seen Miss Blisset entering Mrs Carpenter's suite carrying a pillow almost immediately after he heard a scream for help.'

'Do you know of anything about this boy's character that would have made you doubt this assertion?'

'No. As far as I was aware, neither Mr Fairfax nor Mrs Carpenter found anything untrustworthy about any of the staff.' For this statement the good doctor received an icy look from Mrs Carpenter, whose black-clad presence in the dock drew constant glances from all quarters of the court.

'You had fair reason, then, to believe the houseboy?'

'I had no reason to disbelieve him,' said the doctor. 'In further regard to his insistence that the pillow had been taken into Mrs Carpenter's suite, I searched the rooms with him. It was then that the pillow, belonging to Mr Fairfax by virtue of an embroidered monogram, was found under Mrs Carpenter's bed.'

'Is this the pillow, Dr Graham?'

The clerk of the court held up the exhibit.

'Yes. And let me say that when it was found it was wet through and through.'

'Ah, yes. Um, did either of the defendants question your belief in the houseboy?'

'Both did, vigorously.' Dr Graham's calmness hid his distress. 'But I felt it necessary to call in the police.'

'Thank you, Dr Graham.' Mr Pitt sat down. Mr Clark rose. 'Dr Graham, do you know the age of the houseboy?'

'Fifteen.'

'Fifteen. H'm. Very tender. Did the defendants deny any knowledge of the pillow and how it came to be where it was found?'

'Both denied any knowledge.'

'But you decided the word of a fifteen-year-old boy was more believable than that of a lady known to have devoted herself to the welfare of her employer?'

'What concerned me was the soaking condition of the pillow.'

'Yes, I see,' mused Mr Clark. 'One might wonder whether it was soaked by bath water or by being held under a running tap.'

'I suggest it would take quite some time to become soaked through and through by a running tap,' said Dr Graham.

'However, you were content to accept the word of a young lad in all he said about the pillow?'

'I believed him, yes.'

'Belief is very satisfying to the believed. Thank you, Dr Graham.'

'You may stand down, Dr Graham,' said the judge with a courteous nod.

Mrs Carpenter's eyes followed the doctor's departure from the stand, her expression that of a woman who had found him despicably wanting.

The spectators in the gallery were rowdy in their reactions, and the unmannerly uproar prompted the judge to silence them with threats to have them removed.

Detective Inspector Rawlings was called next. Referring to his notes he gave an account of his interview with the defendants, with Dr Graham, with the houseboy and with the senior member of the staff, Miss Prudence Bird. He was precise and exact. Mr Pitt asked no questions of him. Mr Clark asked him how the defendants reacted to his interrogation.

'They were distressed, resentful and indignant.'

'That would be natural, wouldn't it, Inspector, in persons respectable, conscientious and innocent?'

'In my experience, innocence even in persons of the nobility can hide more than a peck or two of guilt,' said the inspector.

Laughter erupted. Only a month ago, a noble lord, slightly impoverished, had been found guilty of paying a large bill with forged banknotes, despite his protestations of complete innocence.

The judge called for order, with the threat once more of having offenders summarily removed if such a disturbance happened again.

Dr Graham and the detective inspector had taken up the full day's session in giving their evidence, and the court adjourned until the morning.

On the second day in court, Master Alexander Beavis was called to the stand as a witness for the prosecution. The lad had never thought about such an ordeal on the fatal day of Mr Fairfax's death. He had simply confided all he had seen and heard to Maisie and Dr Graham. As nervous as a volunteer entering a lions' den, he nevertheless entered the stand with his shoulders squared and his resolution intact. He took the oath quite clearly.

Prosecuting counsel asked him to tell the court all that was in his signed statement, and to address His Honour, the judge.

Alexander, clearing his throat, said, 'Well, Yer Worship—'

'Your Honour.'

'Yes, on me honour I'm going to tell the truth,' said Alexander, and began to recount the relevant details while keeping his eyes off the figures in the dock, which was just as well for his nerves, since Mrs Carpenter was fixing him with a livid glare. Her niece, Fanny Blisset, did not seem to care much for him, either. If he gave some details in a slightly rambling way, that was to be expected of a fifteen-year-old boy standing in the intimidating atmosphere of one of the Old Bailey's courts of high and mighty justice. It was a whole lot different from recounting details to Dr Graham within the familiar walls of his late employer's house.

Now and again he was a little irrelevant, but counsel for the defence, Mr Clark, did not intercede. He contented himself with the kind of smile that gently suggested well, here is a witness so young that he's liable to wander into fairyland.

It was Mr Pitt who interceded eventually.

'Young man—'

'Objection,' said Mr Clark languidly.

'How so?' asked the judge.

'The witness is not a young man, m'Lord, far from it.'

'I'm going to overrule you, Mr Clark,' said the judge, 'I'm certain the court considers the term appropriate.'

Mr Pitt smiled and turned his attention to Alexander again.

'Young man, have you ever been in trouble?'

'In trouble? Me?' said Alexander, nerves not so bothersome by now.

'For a lack of truthfulness, for disobedience or an act that had brought you to the attention of the law?'

'Me?' said Alexander again. 'No, sir, I ain't, never.' He didn't consider his punch-up with that lout in Hyde Park a real law-breaking act.

'Thank you. Carry on.'

Alexander had reached the stage of explaining why he and Dr Graham went into Mrs Carpenter's suite together to search for the pillow. He described how he had found it under her bed, and how that led to Dr Graham talking to Mrs Carpenter and Mrs Blisset for a long time.

'Mrs Blisset?' Mr Clark let that murmur float into the stuffy air of the court.

'Eh?' said Alexander. 'Well, at the time—'

'Quite so, you've forgotten.'

'Mr Clark?' said the judge sternly.

'My apologies, m'Lord.'

'Kindly confine yourself to objections and don't offer comments during the prosecution's examination of the witness.'

'I stand corrected, m'Lord.'

'The witness may continue.'

Alexander came to the end of his account by saying that after the police arrived at the house, he was interviewed by the chief bloke.

'What, Mr Pitt, does your witness mean by the chief bloke?' asked the judge.

'Detective Inspector Rawlings, m'Lord.'

'Really? How odd. But very well.'

Alexander was then allowed to explain that he told the inspector everything he had just told 'Yer Worship'.

'Your Honour,' said Mr Pitt, gently corrective again.

'Yes, on me honour I've told the truth,' said Alexander.

Mr Pitt smiled and passed the witness over to defence counsel, who rose to eye Alexander in fatherly fashion. At the house in Kensington Gore, Maisie was thinking of the houseboy and wishing him well. At the barracks, so was Daniel.

'Master Beavis, my boy,' said Mr Clark, 'have you ever been reprimanded by Mrs Carpenter for misbehaviour or slackness or, shall we say, impertinence?'

'Well, not serious, like,' said Alexander. 'I mean, only for being a bit noisy or 'aving a smoke.'

'You smoke cigarettes?'

'I only did it now and again, and up in the attic out of 'er way.'

'Mrs Carpenter forbade you to smoke?'

'She said I was too young and that, anyway, she wouldn't allow it.'

'But you disobeyed her and accordingly you were dressed down on the occasions when she caught you?'

'Well, she did tell me off a bit.'

'Which you resented?'

'I just told her sorry, like.'

'But you still continued to sneak up to the attic with a cigarette?'

'It was only a bit of a spit and a draw.'

'I suggest you did it out of resentment and defiance.'

'I dunno what you mean.'

'I think you do. Tell me, how was it that you found the missing pillow so quickly?'

'Eh?'

'I suggest you went straight to Mrs Carpenter's bed because you knew where the pillow was, that you had hidden it yourself.'

''Ere, half a mo,' said Alexander, 'that ain't true. It was a guess, that's all.'

'A guess. A perfect guess, apparently. Did you hold a grudge against Mrs Carpenter for her attempts to keep you in order?'

'I ain't got no grudges against anyone.'

'Did you soak that pillow yourself before you placed it under Mrs Carpenter's bed?'

'Eh?'

'Objection.' Mr Pitt rose. 'My learned friend is indulging in absurd accusations in an attempt to intimidate the witness.'

'Objection sustained,' said the judge. 'Keep to what you know is correct, Mr Clark.'

'Very good, m'Lord. Master Beavis, I suggest you came to dislike and resent Mrs Carpenter—'

'No, I didn't,' said Alexander. 'The old— Well,

she might've been a bit bossy at times, but it didn't make me dislike her.'

'The old . . . ?' Mr Clark smiled encouragingly. 'You were going to say what exactly?'

'What I did say, that I didn't dislike her.'

'Come, my boy, the old what?'

'Lady,' said Alexander in an inspired moment. 'Well, she ain't young, is she?'

A basilisk glare travelled from the dock to the witness stand.

'I suggest that in some way, Master Beavis, you contrived use of that pillow in an attempt to incriminate Mrs Carpenter.'

'Dunno what you're talking about,' said Alexander, remembering that Corporal Daniel Adams had told him to stand up, square his shoulders and stick to his guns.

'M'Lord,' said Mr Pitt, 'must we continue to listen to these fanciful suggestions?'

'I think the suggestions are sustainable,' said the judge.

'I have two final questions,' said Mr Clark. 'Master Beavis, did Mrs Carpenter ever reprimand you for downright insolence?'

'No, course she didn't,' said Alexander, 'she'd 'ave sacked me if I'd been as bad as that.'

'What made you forget Miss Blisset was unmarried?'

'Well, I . . .'

'Never mind, it's understandable that at your tender age you can't be expected to have the memory or the maturity of an adult.'

Which, of course, implied his memory was unreliable, and his credibility not to be trusted.

Mr Clark sat down.

Mr Pitt rose.

'Before you stand down, Alexander,' he said, 'would you like to tell the court when the Battle of Hastings was fought?'

'1066,' said Alexander, not a dunce during his schooling.

'Have I or anyone else asked you this question recently?'

'No, sir.'

'Thank you.'

'Master Beavis, you may stand down,' said the judge.

The relieved houseboy did so, his movements followed by stone-faced Mrs Carpenter.

That ended the day's session.

Mr Burnaby took Alexander back to the witnesses' waiting room, where Prudence had been suffering the shakes all day in anticipation of being called by defence counsel. She didn't know what she was expected to do to help Mrs Carpenter and Miss Blisset, but she was willing to try.

'Oh, me Gawd,' she said, 'you've been in the court for hours, Alexander.'

'Phew, don't I know it,' said Alexander.

'He did very well, Prudence, very well,' said Mr Burnaby. 'I need to consult with Mr Clark for a few minutes, then I'll take you both home.'

He did so, in his pony and trap, Alexander

talking all the way about having to put up with a lot of bullying.

'But I stood me ground and stuck to me guns, like Maisie's soldier told me to.'

'Meself,' said Prudence, 'I'll probably faint.'

On arrival at the house, they were at once besieged by Milly, Maisie, Agnes, Edie and Daisy, who all wanted to know how they had got on. Mr Burnaby said only Alexander had been called, and that there hadn't been time for Prudence. She'd be called tomorrow.

'Well, how did he do, Mr Burnaby?' asked Milly, voice rising above the tongues of the others.

'Splendidly, yes, indeed,' said Mr Burnaby.

'But against Mrs Carpenter and Miss Blisset?' said Maisie, hoping everything wasn't going to turn into another nightmare, a worse one.

'Not necessarily, no,' said Mr Burnaby, knowing that Mr Clark had pointed up the extreme youth of the boy, and the possibility that the jury would find his story concerning the pillow a little hard to swallow. 'Be of good heart, ladies. I must go now. However, I'll pick you and Alexander up again tomorrow morning, Prudence.'

'I'd feel a lot better if I didn't 'ave to be picked up at all, and could get Mr Townley to take me shopping instead,' said Prudence.

'I'm sure you'll bear up,' said Mr Burnaby, and left.

'Come on, Alexander, tell us all about what it

was like,' said Maisie, Rosemary clinging to her skirts.

Alexander entertained them for half an hour, although it was a morbid kind of entertainment.

The next morning, the daily papers headlined the trial, giving Alexander column inches to himself. Fortunately for the frayed nerves of the female members of the staff, they were still having no papers delivered.

'The answer's no,' said platoon Sergeant Jack Lee.

'Wait a bit,' said Corporal Daniel Adams, 'I ain't made any request yet.'

'You don't have to. I know what it's going to be. A request for me to ask Sergeant Major Sawyer if you can have another pass.'

'I think you're what's called psychic,' said Daniel.

'Never heard of it,' said Sergeant Lee, 'which I ain't bothered about, seeing I don't like the sound of it.'

'You ought to do more reading,' said Daniel.

'You're still not getting another pass. It's the platoon's day in the stables, cleaning out the ammunition wagons. You're in charge.'

'Where will you be, then?'

'I've got an all-day pass to see me old Lambeth granny.'

'Is that the granny who's only twenty and known as Lambeth Lily?'

'Who said that?'

'Just another rumour, Sarge. '

'Take over the platoon, Corporal Adams.'

'Well, I've got to, I suppose,' said Daniel, whose devotion to the army was still sound, but not as fixed these days as his devotion to Maisie. 'Give me fond regards to Granny.'

Chapter Twenty-eight

At the opening of the third day's session, Prudence was called to the witness stand by defence counsel. Prudence, in a white pearl-buttoned blouse and long black skirt, a brown straw hat with a spreading brim on her head, looked what she was, a homely woman beset by nerves. She took the oath quaveringly. Then she did that which Alexander had willed himself to avoid. She glanced at the defendants. She received encouraging looks from both.

'Now, Miss Bird,' said Mr Clark with a smile, 'you are the senior servant of the staff still working in the deceased gentleman's residence in Kensington Gore?'

'Yes, that's me,' said Prudence.

'Prior to Mr Fairfax's regrettable demise, you were working under the housekeeper, Mrs Carpenter?'

'Yes, sir, I was,' said Prudence.

'You may address the judge and call him—'

The judge interrupted with a gesture that waived the formality, and Mr Clark asked the witness how long she'd been working under Mrs Carpenter's authority.

'Oh, ever since she took over more'n four years ago,' said Prudence. 'The 'ousekeeper before went and got married to a gentleman from—'

'So you've known Mrs Carpenter for over four years?'

'Yes, sir.'

'And how long have you known Miss Blisset, formerly the cook?'

'Oh, a year and a bit.'

'Would you like to give the court your impression of Mrs Carpenter?'

Prudence gulped, then her words came at a nervous rush, causing the court scribe to scribble at a fast rate. She said she had always found Mrs Carpenter a fine lady, ever so good at her job, always very caring of Mr Fairfax and kind to the staff, a real lady that was fair even when she was a bit firm on account of making sure the house was run very proper and kept in good order for their employer that she couldn't hardly believe had gone to his grave so sudden.

'I just 'aven't got over it, and I don't know I ever will.'

'Do you have any criticism of Mrs Carpenter at all?'

'Beg pardon?'

'You have said she was fair and kind, but were there perhaps some moments when she was neither kind nor fair?'

Prudence, nervously eager to please this man, handsome in his wig and gown, who was asking her questions that weren't frightening her, poured out more words.

No, Mrs Carpenter never had any unkind moments, just a bit firm now and again, which was, well, natural. Everyone respected her, and admired her for how well she looked after Mr Fairfax, and it was no wonder she collapsed when she knew the poor gentleman was dead, it nearly collapsed everyone.

'I never knew a more dreadful day, and I 'ope I never know another one like it.'

'Would you say, then, that you believe Mrs Carpenter to be incapable of any kind of malice, spite or wrongdoing?'

'Oh, she wouldn't do no real harm to a soul, sir.' For that reply, given in the hope that the questions wouldn't get difficult, Prudence received warm looks from the defendants.

'Simply put, a woman of Christian values?'

Now that was difficult. No-one on the staff would have called Mrs Carpenter a kind Christian. Bossy but fair, more like. Still, perhaps being fair was a bit Christian-like.

'Yes, that's it, sir.'

'Now, what is your opinion of Miss Blisset?'

'Oh, ever such a good cook that always made us keep the kitchen in nice order.'

'Was she critical in her attitude towards the kitchen staff?'

'Beg pardon, sir?'

'Did she ever complain about any of you to the housekeeper?'

'Well, if she did, we never 'eard about it, she was just a bit fussy about everything to do with 'er cooking, that's all.'

'Would you say she too was incapable of any wrongdoing?'

'Oh, yes, sir, we wouldn't ever have thought that about her.'

'Does it surprise you that both these ladies are in the dock?'

'I can't 'ardly believe it, that I can't.'

'Thank you, Miss Bird.' Mr Clark sat down. Mr Pitt rose.

'Miss Bird,' he said in a pleasant fashion, 'I understand Mrs Carpenter spent much of her time with your unfortunately deceased employer in his suite. That is so?'

'Oh, yes,' said Prudence, still nervously eager to please, 'she 'ardly ever stopped seeing to 'is welfare.'

'Behind closed doors?'

'Beg pardon?'

'Mrs Carpenter and Mr Fairfax virtually – um – existed together in the privacy of the suite for most hours of each day?'

Prudence hastened to say it was only because the old gentleman needed someone kind to keep an eye on him. Mr Pitt asked why. Well, he was old, he was seventy, and not in the best of health, said Prudence. Mr Pitt pointed out that Mr Fairfax's medical adviser, Dr Graham, had said his patient was capable of living many more years yet. Accordingly, he was not a failing gentleman.

'Oh, but he 'ardly ever went out,' said Prudence.

'Really? Isn't it true that on the last day of his life he actually went to see Tower Bridge and to mingle with the crowds there?'

'Well, yes, he did,' said Prudence, 'but it worried Mrs Carpenter. And Mrs . . . Miss Blisset.'

'What was Mr Fairfax's general time to retire at night?'

'Oh, he was never in bed early, more like close to eleven.'

'And Mrs Carpenter was with him, keeping a careful eye on him until he retired?'

'She was always that kind about his health and comfort, sir.'

'Did you consider it proper for them to be alone together until late at night – um, every night?'

'Proper?'

'Come, Miss Bird, I'm sure you know what I mean.'

'Objection,' said Mr Clark. 'Learned counsel is trying to lead the witness.'

'I think the question relevant, Mr Clark,' said the judge, 'and the witness may answer.'

'But I didn't think about it not being proper, just the way Mrs Carpenter did 'er job very conscientious, like,' said Prudence.

'Did it surprise you when you heard Mr Fairfax had left a thousand pounds, a small fortune, to

326

Miss Blisset, considering she had only been in his service for a year?'

'Like I said, she was a wonderful cook, and Mr Fairfax always enjoyed 'is meals. And he left me and the others a hundred pound each, which was a nice surprise.'

'And what kind of a surprise was it when you learned the bulk of his fortune had been left to Mrs Carpenter?'

'Well, we was all a bit flabbergasted, but being a bach'lor all 'is life, he didn't 'ave no children or grandchildren, so I suppose he felt so grateful for all Mrs Carpenter's care and for the way she ran the house that she deserved it.' Prudence's nerves were beginning to show again.

'He had a cousin in South Africa.'

'Well, he didn't ever come to see Mr Fairfax.'

'Unlike Mrs Carpenter, who saw him every day, keeping him close company up until late at night. Oh, by the way, is it true that Miss Blisset has a child?'

'Yes,' said Prudence, uncomfortable, 'a little girl.'

'But she's unmarried, isn't she?'

'Well, yes.'

'Thank you, Miss Bird.'

And Mr Pitt sat down to allow the jury to contemplate the unpalatable fact that Miss Blisset had fallen from grace like a common wench. People in the public gallery whispered together in shock, and the judge adjourned proceedings. The court scribe, a lady, relaxed at last.

So did Prudence, who received more warm looks from the defendants for all she had said in praise of them.

Maisie, while keeping her usual careful eye on Rosemary, was cooking the midday meal. For once, very little work had been done in the house. Alexander and Prudence were at the Old Bailey, where the trial was in full flow, and Agnes, Edie, Daisy and Milly were in a state of nervous worry, unable to concentrate on anything for more than a couple of minutes.

'I bet Prudence is near fainting,' said Daisy.

'And what's Mrs Carpenter doing, and Fanny Blisset?' said Milly.

'Worrying theirselves sick,' said Edie, 'which they would be, wouldn't they, if they—'

'Shut up,' said Milly.

'But if they did—'

'Will you shut up?' said Agnes.

That was what they still couldn't come to terms with, the unmentionable.

Maisie, resolutely refusing to contribute to the atmosphere of worry and gloom, made a practical suggestion.

'Could someone lay the table? Dinner's nearly ready.'

'Is Maisie giving orders?' asked Edie of Agnes.

'No, I'm just asking if someone'll lay the table,' said Maisie, whose one wish was to be with Daniel. Daniel would lift her spirits and give her comforting affection. It simply wasn't easy not to worry about that awful trial, and what it might be doing to poor Prudence and young Alexander.

Edie and Daisy laid the table.

Rosemary toddled about, a child whose mothering was a collective act by the servants, with Maisie in the forefront.

It was early evening when Mr Burnaby again brought Prudence and Alexander back to the house. Prudence was at least relieved her ordeal was over, Alexander at least happy that he hadn't been recalled to the stand. Mr Burnaby informed everyone that Prudence had been splendid, quite splendid, in that she had refused to say anything unkind about Mrs Carpenter and Miss Blisset. He said the afternoon session had seen Mr Clark produce two friends of Mrs Carpenter, friends who assured the court she had always been a good woman. He did not say that Mr Pitt, in cross-examining them, had brought to light the fact that both had only known Mrs Carpenter for a comparatively short time. Mr Clark had also produced two witnesses to testify to Miss Blisset's exemplary character, first her old schoolteacher, and secondly a close friend. Again, Mr Burnaby did not mention that Mr Pitt had revealed to the court that the close friend had known Miss Blisset for only a few months.

Alexander couldn't hold back a pertinent question.

'D'you think they'll get off, sir?'

'Of course they will, my boy, of course they

will,' said Mr Burnaby. 'The counsel will address the jury tomorrow morning, and the judge will sum up the evidence. I'm sure we can all look forward to the verdict being the right one.'

Maisie wasn't at all sure what the right one should be, but didn't say anything more.

Chapter Twenty-nine

Friday morning, the fourth day of the trial. Counsel for the prosecution and defence addressed the jury in turn in the packed and noisy court. *The Times* was critical of the atmosphere, declaring a criminal court trial was not in the nature of a matinee to which fashionable ladies might go in search of the latest sensation, actors to pick up a striking gesture and writers to look for good copy.

Mr Pitt, for the prosecution, suggested that the jury would probably agree with him that the case was a simple one in that the sudden demise of their employer meant the defendants would benefit at once from his Last Will and Testament instead of in five years, six years, seven or even ten or twelve. An irresistible motive. And who was to know whether or not Mrs Carpenter would further reward her niece for the part she had played in their collective act of murder? They were both in Mr Fairfax's suite when he took his bath. Why both? Surely Mr Fairfax would not want both women hanging around at that time. It could be reasonably assumed that, by pre-arrangement, Miss Blisset had entered the suite when Mr Fairfax was in the bath.

The jury had been made aware that Mrs Carpenter's relationship with her employer was a very close one, and seemingly intimate enough to suggest she had enticed him into drafting his will in her favour. The clearest indication of the act of murder was the discovery of the soaked pillow under her bed. Defence had suggested the houseboy, Master Alexander Beavis, was responsible for placing it there, but had not explained how he had done so without being noticed, merely implying that its wet condition came about by being held under a running tap. Which tap? The implication was patently absurd. It suggested the houseboy was aware that the murder of his employer was about to take place. Yet at the time it happened he was up in the attic smoking a cigarette. On all these facts, the jury must conclude the defendants were guilty.

Mr Clark, shaking his head, and murmuring, 'Dear me, I have never heard so few facts,' began his address. In all his learned friend had placed before the jury there had not been one shred of real evidence. Everything was based on hearsay and amounted to no more than circumstantial evidence, never a sound basis for a conviction. Apart from the defendants, there had been six other servants in the house at the time. None of these had seen a crime being committed, they had only heard Mrs Carpenter's frantic cry for help, and later become aware of her grief and collapse. Not the behaviour of a scheming woman who had planned murder. Prosecution had mentioned the inheritance as a motive, but had produced no evidence that Mrs Carpenter and Miss Blisset knew they were to benefit. 'Indeed,' he said, 'we have a declaration from the executor to the effect that the deceased never mentioned to him that he had made his bequests known to any of the benefactors. Members of the jury will note the prosecution had not called on the executor to confirm this.

'As to witness Master Beavis, will the jury take the word of a young and mischievous boy against the denials of the defendants, two ladies of admirable character? Prosecution tried to make something of Miss Blisset being an un-married mother, but it isn't for the court to judge her in respect of her misfortune.

'Gentlemen of the jury, defence rests its case.'

The judge then summed up quite briefly. He pointed out that both prosecution and defence had relied heavily on assumption. There were only two salient questions to consider. One, was the pillow discovered in a soaked condition be-cause it was used to hold the victim down under the water without leaving such bruises as hand pressure might have caused? Two, was there a clear motive in that the terms of the deceased's will were indeed known to the defendants? You have heard how close Mrs Carpenter was to her employer, and that she was with him until late at night. That, however, could be put down to what has been described more than once as her care for his health and welfare.

'You must judge these vital points for yourselves, and must find the defendants guilty or not guilty according to your unanimous conclusions.'

The jury retired and the sitting was adjourned.

'Corporal Adams, come here!' barked Sergeant Major Sawyer of C Company. Two defaulters had been up before the company OC after parade that morning. They'd staggered back to barracks dead drunk the night before, and the moment they reeled in through the gates, they came up against Sergeant Major Sawyer himself, who promptly charged them with disorderly conduct. An hour ago, they'd each been given seven days CB. They claimed they'd been celebrating the wedding of their platoon corporal.

'Want me, Sarn't Major?' said Daniel, coming smartly to attention in front of He Who Had To Be Obeyed quicker than the OC himself.

'Yes, I bloody do. D'you know about Privates Potter and Patter of your platoon?'

'Potter and Paynter, Sarn't Major?'

'Don't split hairs with me. I want to know if you knew those two lumps of last year's bully beef got a pass to celebrate your wedding last night and rolled back here like a couple of cross-eyed camels up to their ears in gin. Answer up smart, Corporal Adams.'

334

'If that's what they celebrated, Sarn't Major, they got the date wrong.'

'So it's still tomorrow week, is it?'

'With a week's leave.'

'Sergeant Lee informed me you haven't been seen around much these last few weeks, as if I didn't know.'

'Well, I've had a few passes – '

'More like fifty.'

'Permission to dispute that, Sarn't Major.'

'Stop sounding like you went to Oxford and Cambridge. It's exclusive to officers.'

'It's book-reading that does it,' said Daniel. 'By the way, Sarn't Major, any chance of a pass for this afternoon?'

'Bloody hell,' said the sergeant major, 'you're trying me patience now. What are you after, a special afternoon out?'

Daniel confided in him again, letting him know his young lady and the rest of the staff were suffering the jim-jams on account of the trial. The sergeant major nodded. He'd read the daily papers supplied to the warrant officers' mess.

'All right, go and give your young lady a cuddle this afternoon, but be back here by six, no later, and for Christ's sake stay clear of newspaper reporters or we'll have 'em mounting an attack on the barracks gates and bombarding us with inkpots.'

'Much obliged, Sarn't Major.'

*   *   *

By the time Daniel was making his way to Kensington Gore sometime later, newsboys were on the streets, bawling the headline of an early edition of an evening paper.

'Jury out, jury out! Read all about it!'

Well, that's something at least, thought Daniel, it'll all be over by tomorrow at the latest. Or even before this day's out, if the jury can make up its mind by then.

Daisy opened the door to him.

'Oh, hello, soldier, pleased to see yer,' she said. 'D'you want to talk to Maisie? She's in the reception room with little Rosemary. The child likes it there, she can bounce about in the armchairs. Come on, you can go in. Mind, we've all got the shakes about the trial.'

'Did you know the jury's out?' said Daniel, stepping in.

'Oh, me Gawd,' gasped Daisy, 'we never know nothing till Mr Burnaby gets back with Prudence and Alexander, like every evening so far.' She lifted her apron and fanned herself. 'Oh, me Gawd,' she gasped again, 'I'd best tell the others while you tell Maisie.'

Off she went on shaky legs. Daniel entered the reception room, where Maisie was seated in an armchair watching Rosemary, and worrying about what was going to happen to the child's mother. She looked up and saw Daniel.

'Hello, Maisie love.'

'Daniel . . . oh.' Maisie came to her feet, Daniel put his arms around her and kissed her. Rosemary, sitting on a cushion on the floor and playing with a colourful rag doll, looked up at them, her eyes bright.

'The jury's out, Maisie,' said Daniel.

'Is it?' Maisie came to. 'Well, we'll know soon then, won't we?'

'It'll depend on how long the jury will take to make up its mind,' said Daniel, noting she was as neat and pleasing as ever in her servant's outfit, her white lacy cap enhancing the deep chestnut tints of her hair.

'Oh, Lor',' she said, 'I just hope it won't take till tomorrow, or I'll have it on me mind all night. Alexander and Prudence had to go to the court again with Mr Burnaby in case they had to do more witnessing, so the rest of us are here worrying, and hardly doing any real work. Daniel, it's ever so good of you to come and see me.'

'Would you like a walk in the Gardens?' asked Daniel.

'Oh, would I, not half,' said Maisie. 'But we'll have to take Rosemary with us.'

'Suits me,' said Daniel, 'we'll look like a family. You play Mum and I'll play Dad.' His ready smile made its appearance. 'It'll be good practice.'

Maisie, catching on, said, 'We won't have no intimate talk, Daniel Adams, not in front of a growing child, if you don't mind. '

'Are you blushing, Maisie?'

'No, course I'm not.'

'Well, you've turned a very nice shade of pink.'

'No, I haven't.'

'You're a grand girl, Maisie, pink or not.'

There was a sudden movement on Maisie's part. She kissed him.

'Daniel, you're good for me,' she said. Well, he was. He never went on about the ugly world she and the other servants were living in day after day. He just said a few words, that was all, kind or practical words, and then talked about their own little world, the world of their future. 'Come on, then, let's go out, and you can bring the bassinet up from the basement for me.'

Not long after they were in the Gardens, and it really tickled Maisie that Daniel was pushing the bassinet, little Rosemary sleepily tucked up.

The day was cloudy but mild, the air soft, and although the light wispy smoke produced by ever-burning kitchen ranges blew from neighbouring chimneys, the sootiness of winter skies was absent.

They stayed out for ages, Maisie and her soldier and her charge, and not until Rosemary woke up and indicated she was hungry did Maisie suggest they go back to the house and have tea.

'I'm invited?' said Daniel.

'Well, of course you are,' said Maisie, 'and you've earned it, pushing the bassinet all the time.'

'Well, I don't need to get back to barracks till six,' said Daniel, 'and tea will go down a treat.'

Maisie then mentioned that which suddenly leapt to the front of her mind, something they'd been keeping out of their conversation.

'Daniel, by the time we're having tea, I wonder if – well, if the jury . . .'

'Will have given its verdict?' said Daniel. 'If it has, Maisie, the newsboys will be on the streets with special editions, and letting everyone know they can read all about it.'

'Oh, Lor', I feel I don't want to know,' breathed Maisie.

'It's time everything was over, sweetie, one way or the other,' said Daniel. 'It's a blessing that the one person most affected, our infant here, doesn't know about it.'

'Daniel, I've just got to ask,' said Maisie, as the Queens Gate came in sight, 'd'you think they'll be found guilty?'

'Maisie, I only know the facts that you gave me.'

'Yes, but what d'you think?'

'That I don't like all you told me about the pillow.'

'Oh, that's what's most worried me,' said Maisie. 'Mind, Mr Burnaby did say we could look forward to a verdict that was the right one.'

'Question,' said Daniel.

'Question?'

'Yes, what's the right one, Maisie?'

Which made Maisie worry again about Fanny Blisset's lovable child.

Crossing from the Queens Gate, Daniel listened for the possible sound of a newsboy calling along Kensington Gore. But there was neither sound nor sight of one.

They entered the house by the basement door, Daniel carrying the bassinet, Maisie with Rosemary in her arms. They went through to the kitchen. There at the table sat Milly, Agnes, Edie and Daisy, simply doing nothing. They perked up at the arrival of Maisie and her soldier.

'Ain't no-one getting tea?' asked Maisie. It was twenty to five.

'No-one felt like it,' said Milly.

'Well, we ought to start something now,' said Maisie, fitting Rosemary into her high chair. 'I've invited Daniel, and I know Rosemary's hungry.'

'Oh, yes, come on, let's get some tea,' said Milly, and they all came to their feet.

Mr Burnaby had been supplying regular housekeeping money, and there was plenty in the larder to provide a real spread for themselves and their guest, even if everyone was thinking more about the jury than something like a tea party.

Daniel, after thanking them all for a handsome tea, departed for the barracks at five thirty. Maisie saw him out.

'I'll be thinking of you, Maisie love.'

'Yes, we'll know by tomorrow at least, won't we?'

'Chin up, sweetheart.' Daniel kissed her and left, and Maisie thought what a very nice man he was, and woe betide anyone who called him a common soldier in her hearing.

When Daniel was only a minute away from the barracks, a newsboy came running into sight.

'Verdict, verdict, read all about it!'

Daniel stopped him and bought a copy of the evening paper. The headline, seemingly in extra-large type, leapt at his eye.

The verdict had been delivered forty-five minutes ago, and the presses had rushed into action.

Chapter Thirty

It was six thirty, and Rosemary was asleep in her cot in Maisie's room.

''Ere, I can't wait no longer,' said Daisy, 'I'm going up to the street to see if there's any newsboys about.'

'Yes, go on,' said Milly, 'let's see what's in an evening newspaper. Have you got a penny?'

'Yes.' Daisy headed for the kitchen door, but her proposed exit coincided with the entrance of Prudence, followed by Alexander and Mr Burnaby. 'Oh, crikey,' gasped Daisy, 'is it all over, Prudence, did the jury come back?'

'Ain't you 'eard?' said Alexander, face slightly flushed under the huge brim of his cap.

'No, what did the jury say, what did it say?' begged Milly.

'Tell us, for goodness sake,' said Maisie, body stiff, nerves tense.

'Ladies,' said Mr Burnaby, removing his hat, 'the jury returned a verdict of not guilty.'

A strange silence fell. Maisie knew why. All along none of them had really known what verdict they wanted. All along they hadn't been able to get that pillow out of their minds, while at the same time were unable to believe the housekeeper and cook really had drowned that kind old gentleman in his bath. They had inwardly shuddered at the thought of a guilty verdict that would hang the housekeeper and cook, and leave Rosemary motherless in the most dreadful kind of way, unless the jury asked for mercy to be shown.

'Didn't you hear?' asked Prudence, relieved that everything, including her own ordeal, was over.

'They didn't do it, then?' said Edie.

'Not according to the jury,' said Mr Burnaby, and Maisie wondered if the solicitor wasn't sure if that verdict was the right one, after all.

She glanced at Alexander. He made a face.

'They're coming back 'ere later,' he said.

'Yes,' said Mr Burnaby, 'Mrs Carpenter and Miss Blisset are staying at the Cavendish Hotel, ostensibly for the night. Newspaper journalists are besieging the place, and would have followed them here if they hadn't sought refuge in a hotel. I shall pick them up later, by the rear of the hotel to elude the journalists, whom I can only describe as bloodthirsty. Ladies, I do hope you can now relax a little. Dear me, what a time we have all had, to be sure. Maisie, how is the child?'

'Oh, she's in her cot, asleep,' said Maisie.

'I'm sure Miss Blisset will be most grateful for the care you've given her little girl,' said Mr

Burnaby. 'And now, Maisie, you can look forward to your wedding with worry lifted from you. I shall look forward to attending.' He had accepted an invitation from Maisie. 'Now I must be on my way and travel back to the Cavendish Hotel later.'

The moment he left a babble of talk broke out. Maisie, however, did not join in. She said she must see if Rosemary was all right. Alexander followed her to her room, where the child was sleeping peacefully in her cot. The houseboy and Maisie looked at each other.

'Alexander,' said Maisie, 'I just don't know what to say.'

'I ain't going to say anything,' replied Alexander, 'I'm going to keep all me thoughts to meself.'

'Yes, that's best,' said Maisie. 'Now, have you filled in that army form and got Dr Graham to sign it?'

'He's coming 'ere this evening,' said Alexander, 'and I'll ask him to sign it then.'

'That's good,' said Maisie, 'the army's the best place for you now.'

Dr Graham called at nine, expressed his relief to the staff that the ordeal was over, said he understood the extent of the worry and confusion they had suffered, and hoped there would be no further need of sedative powders. As ever, he was kindness itself, but did not stay to discuss the verdict with them, or indeed any aspect of the trial. Maisie thought he was like all of them in wanting to put the whole dreadful thing behind him.

She and Alexander saw him out. On the way, he stopped in the hall to accede to Alexander's request for his signature on the army form. He knew about the lad's wish to join up as a drummer boy.

'I hope they accept you, Alexander,' he said, 'it would be as well if they did.'

'I bet I know why,' said Maisie. 'Dr Graham, sir, will you be calling again?'

'I'm afraid, Maisie, that from now on this house is closed to me.'

'Oh, that ain't fair,' said Maisie.

'I've no quarrel with it, except that it means I shall probably see none of you again,' said the good doctor. 'You two are the bravest young people, and I wish each of you a long, happy and healthy life.'

'I got enormous respect for you, doctor,' said Alexander. 'And liking.'

'We both have,' said Maisie. 'Doctor, won't you be coming to me wedding?'

'I'll be at the church for the service, Maisie.'

'But not here for the reception?' said Maisie.

Dr Graham hesitated, then said, 'That may alter for you, Maisie, yes, it may.'

'Oh, Lor',' breathed Maisie.

'Look here,' said Dr Graham, 'if it should come to that, then let me offer you use of my own house. I have a dining room ridiculously large. It could accommodate your guests very well, and you are very welcome to use it. If it becomes necessary.'

'Oh, ain't you good to me?' said Maisie, eyes quite misty.

'Let me know,' said Dr Graham, 'and I'll call upon the excellent services of my housekeeper, and perhaps of Nurse Galloway too. Goodbye now, Maisie, goodbye, Alexander.'

They watched him leave the house and disappear into the night.

'Ain't he a lovely bloke?' said Alexander.

'And ain't we lucky, Alexander, that there's more nice people around than bad ones?' said Maisie.

'You're nice yerself, Maisie,' said Alexander. 'There ain't a nicer gal nowhere.'

It was a few minutes after ten, in the darkness of the October night, when Mr Burnaby brought Mrs Carpenter and Miss Blisset back to the house. Prudence, hearing their arrival, came up into the hall. She gulped and stared.

There they were, Mrs Iris Carpenter, a handsome woman in a sombre black coat and a black hat, and her niece, Fanny Blisset, a pretty woman in a feathered hat, hip-length brown jacket, long matching skirt and white blouse. To Prudence, the housekeeper seemed formidable, her niece triumphant. Mr Burnaby seemed sort of hardly noticeable, a figure in the background

'Oh, welcome back, mum,' said Prudence

hoarsely, and asked in a desperate way, 'would you all like a pot of hot tea?'

'We dined at the hotel,' said Mrs Carpenter. 'Kindly arrange for you and the rest of the staff to come up to the reception room in ten minutes.'

'All of us, mum?'

'All of you,' said Mrs Carpenter, and entered the reception room with her niece, Mr Burnaby following with a sigh.

They were all there, ten minutes later, Prudence, Agnes, Milly, Edie, Daisy, Alexander and Maisie, nerves on edge.

'So,' said Mrs Carpenter, 'here I am and here are all of you. Does anyone wish to say anything?'

'Well, we all welcome you back, mum,' said Milly.

'All of you?' said Mrs Carpenter.

'Yes, all of you?' echoed Miss Blisset, and Maisie thought it just wasn't natural, not having asked after Rosemary yet, or made any attempt to see her.

'Mum, we've all been feeling for you and Mrs . . . Miss Blisset,' said Prudence.

'I'm sure,' said Mrs Carpenter drily. 'Now, as you probably all know, the sad and unfortunate passing of Mr Fairfax leaves me as the new owner of this residence.'

Mr Burnaby coughed.

'Nominally at the moment, Mrs Carpenter,

legally and officially only when probate is granted,' he said gently.

'That is understood, of course,' said Mrs Carpenter. 'However, as the housekeeper I must inform you all that I shall be making changes.' She turned her steely glance on Alexander. 'You, boy, are dismissed and will leave this house first thing tomorrow morning, with a week's wages.'

Maisie made a courageous protest.

'That just ain't fair, Alexander's got nowhere to go, nowhere to live,' she said.

'That's his misfortune. The rest of the staff are given a month's notice. That will give them enough time to find other jobs. Oh, except you, Maisie. You will stay on as nursemaid to the child Rosemary. How is she?'

'Yes, how is she?' asked Miss Blisset.

'Well, I'm glad you asked,' said Maisie, 'and I hope you'll be pleased to know she's fine.'

'I'll see her in a moment,' said Miss Blisset.

'Wait a bit,' said Prudence, 'is Mrs Carpenter giving us all the sack?'

'My aunt thinks it will be best for everyone,' said Miss Blisset.

In the background, Mr Burnaby sighed. He understood only too well why Mrs Carpenter wanted to rid herself of the staff. She did not wish to live in daily contact with women whose presence would always remind her of the unpleasant.

However, she relented somewhat. The staff,

after all, could stay on, she said, until she sold the house. She had in mind the purchase of a property in Brighton, to which she would retire. This new arrangement still excluded the house-boy, a creature of wickedness and designed for perdition, she said.

''Ere, I ain't standing for that,' said Alexander, 'it's—'

'No, don't say anything.' Maisie pressed his arm.

'That's all,' said Mrs Carpenter. 'Tomorrow I shall inspect the house to see if you've all been doing your work as you should have.'

'I'd like to see my child now,' said Miss Blisset.

The servants, resentful, went back to the kitchen to talk heatedly together. Maisie and Alexander went down to her room, Miss Blisset following. She looked at her sleeping daughter, and lightly touched her face.

'Well, she seems fine, Maisie,' she said, 'and I'm sure you'll be a very good nursemaid to her.'

'Don't you want to sit with her for a bit?' asked Maisie.

'I've too many things to do just now, I'll see her again in the morning. Thanks for taking such good care of her.' And the child's mother left.

Alexander said, 'She ain't much of a mother, Maisie.'

'P'raps she'll be better now she's got no worries,' said Maisie. 'Alexander, what're we going to do about finding you somewhere to live till you join up?'

349

'Oh, I'll find somewhere,' said Alexander.

A thought struck Maisie.

'I know,' she said, 'you can use our house.'

'What d'yer mean?'

'The house me and Daniel are already renting for our marriage,' said Maisie. 'It's in Walworth. I'll take you there.' She'd write a note to Daniel, she said, which Alexander was to take to the barracks in the morning, and another one to Dr Graham, because she didn't want her wedding reception here, not now. He was to wait at the barracks for an answer from Daniel, and should also wait for an answer from Dr Graham.

'I got yer, Maisie.'

'Try to get a good sleep tonight.'

'I'm nearly asleep standing up, I tell yer.'

But it was a restless night for almost everyone, except Rosemary.

The following morning, Alexander did his errands, while Maisie and the rest of the servants did their usual work under the supervision of Mrs Carpenter, once more a hovering figure in black, as if nothing untoward had happened. Miss Blisset actually took charge of her child.

When Alexander returned by way of the basement entrance, both Mrs Carpenter and Miss Blisset were in the housekeeper's suite drinking their mid-morning cup of tea. Maisie entertained Alexander in her room, where he gave her a letter from Daniel and the verbal reply from Dr Graham, which was yes, his promise for the reception to be held in his house was good.

Daniel's letter contained twenty-five pounds.

Dear Maisie love,

That's my girl, you do that, you open up our house for Alexander, and I suggest that if things get difficult for you, then you go and live there too, why not? Here's some money to keep you going with expenses and shopping for a few months. I can't get away myself, not until Friday, when I'll be starting a week's leave that will take in our wedding. It knocked me, that verdict, but at least it worked in favour of that little girl you've been taking care of, you sweetie. No wonder I can't help loving you. Let me know if anything gets awkward for you. Thinking of you every minute. A hundred kisses.

Love, Daniel.'

Maisie made up her mind then.

'Alexander, pack your belongings,' she said. 'Mrs Carpenter thinks you've already gone, anyway. Now we'll go together.'

'Crikey, you mean you ain't coming back?' said Alexander.

'No, Alexander, I ain't coming back,' said Maisie.

'The old biddy won't like it,' said Alexander,

'she'll 'ave her own back by not letting Prudence and the others come to yer wedding.'

'She might try, but Mr Burnaby promised me,' said Maisie, 'and he's in charge till the will's been – um?'

'Executed?' said Alexander knowingly.

'That's it,' said Maisie.

Forty minutes later she went up to see Mrs Carpenter in her suite, Mr Burnaby was there. He gave Maisie a smile.

'Yes, Maisie, what is it?' asked Mrs Carpenter.

Maisie said she was leaving and was giving immediate notice according. Mrs Carpenter, astonished at first, did not take long to recover.

'Ungrateful girl, you'll get no reference, d'you hear?'

Mr Burnaby intervened, gently but firmly.

'As executor with full knowledge of Maisie's work here, I will give her a reference.'

'She doesn't deserve one.'

'Indeed she does, Mrs Carpenter, and I think you know that. Maisie, are you quite sure you wish to leave at once?'

'Yes, sir.' Maisie had her coat on, with her one and only hat.

'Then if Mrs Carpenter will allow me, I'll see you out,' said the solicitor.

'You may please yourself,' said Mrs Carpenter, plainly put out.

'Goodbye, Mrs Carpenter,' said Maisie.

'You are a great disappointment to me.'

Mr Burnaby accompanied Maisie downstairs.

She had already said goodbye to Prudence and the others, and a special goodbye to Rosemary who, although uncomprehending, accepted a kiss with a beaming smile.

At the front door, Mr Burnaby mentioned the wedding reception. Maisie told him where she was going to live and that the reception was to be at Dr Graham's house.

'I'm delighted, then,' said Mr Burnaby. 'I've a feeling that when someone had the courage to tell Mrs Carpenter it was going to be here, she – ah – yes, she might well have refused permission. Dear me, Maisie, I find myself constantly at odds with the lady. However, enough of that. Here is a month's wages for you in lieu of you working out a month's notice.'

'But, Mr Burnaby—'

'Take it, Maisie, I still have control of expenditure, and can easily justify this payment.'

'Oh, I'll share it with Alexander,' said Maisie, 'he's only had this week's wages.'

'No, no, give him this, to make up his own month's entitlement,' said Mr Burnaby, and handed her another fifteen shillings.

'Oh, me and Alexander won't ever forget how kind you've been,' said Maisie, fervent with gratitude.

'You are both very deserving,' said Mr Burnaby. 'Now, I will see you at your wedding, and may it be a happy, happy day for you.'

'Mr Burnaby, I don't know I'll ever meet nicer gentlemen than you and Dr Graham.'

'Thank you, Maisie, you're a splendid young lady, yes, indeed. Goodbye now until next Saturday.'

'Goodbye, sir, thanks ever so much for everything.'

Maisie departed, her reticule containing what were lovely windfalls for herself and Alexander. Mr Burnaby watched her descending the front steps. Waiting for her on the pavement was Alexander, holding a canvas bag containing his meagre belongings, while standing guard over Maisie's portmanteau. Mr Burnaby smiled. Alexander waved to him.

'Goodbye, Alexander, good luck, my boy.'

'Same to you, sir.'

Mr Burnaby closed the door, sighed and went back upstairs to cross more swords with the dragon.

Away went Maisie and Alexander, a new life in front of them.

Chapter Thirty-one

It was Friday, the day before the wedding, and District Nurse Maud Galloway was in Dr Graham's surgery, talking to him.

'You are quite mad,' she said.

'I don't count it as mad to do a favour for such a pleasing young lady as Maisie Gibbs,' said the doctor.

'Well, if the afternoon ends with your house turned upside down, you'll have only yourself to blame,' said Maud. 'However, since I'm sure your housekeeper will be unable to cope on her own, I shall come and help.'

'Upon my soul, will you?'

'I am suddenly determined to save you and your house from disaster, Charles.'

'A man is fortunate to have such a finely determined friend as you, Maud.'

'Fortunate indeed,' said Maud.

'By the way, I've consented to drive Maisie to the church and to give her away,' said the doctor.

'How gallant,' said Maud. 'Such a fatherly

gesture prompts me to suggest you're not too old to have children of your own.'

'Good God,' said Dr Graham.

'Need I say more?' Maud departed smiling. She wasn't too set on delivering other women's babies well into her old age.

Saturday morning, with the weather representative of October's occasional gift of an Indian summer.

Maisie, enchanting in her wedding finery, bridal bouquet of crimson carnations splashing the white gown with vivid colour, was on her way. The bouquet had been a gift from Alexander, and had cost him as much as a half-crown. He had collected it from florists in Walworth Road, and paid for it without begrudging a single penny. In his boyish way, he adored Maisie.

He had gone on ahead to the Kensington church by tram and bus, leaving Maisie to travel with Dr Graham in the pony and trap. The light vehicle threaded its way through the London traffic, the pony trotting and Maisie hiding her flushed face behind her veil. But her brown eyes were bright with happy excitement. Also, she felt wonderfully privileged to be seated beside Dr Graham, he in a dapper morning suit with a carnation in the buttonhole. Oh, I wish Daniel could see me riding like this right now, she thought.

People saw her. Pedestrians stopped and called good-luck greetings. Women waved. Maisie melted.

'Oh, ain't it grand, doctor?'

'Delightful, Maisie, delightful. And you look lovely.'

'Jack, you sure you've got the ring?' said Daniel, a dashing bridegroom in his best uniform and his moustache newly trimmed.

'For the umpteenth time, of course I'm sure,' said Sergeant Jack Lee, best man. 'What's up with you?'

'I'm nervous,' said Daniel.

'Don't talk like a Chinese washerwoman riding a camel, you've been in church before, ain't you?'

'Not to get married,' said Daniel. 'This is my first time, and my only time, I tell yer.'

'That's no excuse for a West Kent corporal, so stop acting like a pansy out on a windy night.'

Daniel composed himself. They were riding to the church in a hired hansom cab and the church wasn't far off. The cabbie brought the vehicle to a stop a minute later.

'We're there, gents.'

The best man and bridegroom alighted. The best man paid up and added a tip. The cabbie thanked him, wished Daniel good luck, and hoped it would be a happy-ever-after occasion and not another Battle of Waterloo. Then he drove off, whistling 'Fight The Good Fight'.

Bystanders outside the church eyed the two red-jacketed NCOs with interest. Young women sighed romantically. Romance was the stuff of life in this long-established Victorian era. Sergeant

Lee and Daniel, tucking their helmets under their arms in correct regulation fashion, walked into the church. The vicar smiled, welcomed them, and shook hands with them. The verger led them down the aisle to their allotted places in the right-hand front pew. In the pews on the left were Prudence and the other house servants, Bill Townley, some old Walworth neighbours, young Alexander, Mr Burnaby, Mr Hubert Smythe, and some lady bystanders who had wandered in to enjoy the proceedings. In the pews on the right were six members of Daniel's platoon, and none other than Company Sergeant Major Albert Sawyer with Mrs Sawyer, plump and jolly, in her best outfit and a hat as high and wide as a birdcage.

The time, seven minutes to noon. The bridegroom, nervous. The best man, feeling for the ring.

She arrived, the bride, on the dot, and the organist greeted her with a fanfare. The congregation rose, and Maisie, preceded by the vicar, moved gently down the aisle on the arm of Dr Graham. Daniel, on his feet, watched her slow advance, her back straight, her figure as neat as ever, her white gown shimmering. You sweetheart, he said to himself, you sweetheart.

On that sunny October day in 1894, Miss Maisie Gibbs of Walworth was given away by Dr Charles Graham of Kensington in marriage to Corporal Daniel Adams of the Royal West Kents.

*   *   *

Six o'clock. The reception, highly successful, had ended an hour ago. Bride and groom had departed, and so had all the guests. Dr Graham and his housekeeper, together with Maud, surveyed the results of their clearing-up work.

'I think we can say we've escaped actual damage,' said the doctor.

'Mind, I thought the house was coming down when they all did a knees-up,' said Mrs Dumbarton, his widowed housekeeper, still active in her sixtieth year.

'Oh, I'd have accepted a few broken tiles and a displaced picture or two just for the sake of the joyful look on Maisie's face,' smiled Dr Graham.

'Well, there went a young lady happy and radiant,' said Maud. 'I feel happy myself on her account.'

'I think I'll go and put the kettle on,' said Mrs Dumbarton, 'I'm sure we'd all like a refreshing cup of tea.' Away she bustled.

'Well, Charles?' said Maud.

'Yes?'

'Did the wedding inspire you?'

'Yes, indeed. My word, I feel there should be another. Will you do me the honour of marrying me, my dear Maud?'

'Happily, my very dear Charles.'

Maisie and Daniel had travelled to their home in Walworth after the reception. Alexander was still nearby, as Mrs Flo Godsby had offered to have him. On Monday, he was going to the army recruiting centre in Chelsea, to hand in the form and ask if he could join up straight away.

Sunday morning.

Maisie awoke, and lay in dreamy vagueness before clarity dawned. It made her hot all over. Practical, and not at all a Victorian ignoramus about what occurred between a bride and groom, she nevertheless coloured rosy red at that which had happened between Daniel and herself. Oh, help, she'd never thought any bridegroom could be so saucy.

Or so exciting.

Not just the once, either. Twice. And even a third time right in the middle of the night. She was sure no other bride had been so put upon. Still, it was all legal, and she didn't feel she wanted to complain. That third time, though, oh, that Daniel.

Still blushing, Maisie cautiously turned her head to see if Daniel was awake. He was, but not in the bed. She heard him then, coming up the stairs of their cosy house. He entered the bedroom, carrying a tray on which were two cups of tea. With the bedclothes drawn up tightly around her neck and shoulders, Maisie looked up at him. He was wearing just his Army shirt. It reached to his thighs. His long legs were firm and muscular, his smile easy and familiar.

'Hello there, Mrs Maisie Adams, top of the morning to you, and how's yer sweet self?'

'Daniel Adams,' she said, 'I've been wondering what I've let meself in for.'

'Heigh-ho,' said Daniel, obviously as happy as a bloke could be, 'here's what you've let yourself in for now, your first cup of tea on your first morning after.' He placed one cup and saucer on her bedside table, with Maisie watching him warily. He smiled, leaned and kissed her forehead. 'Love you, you sweetheart.' He went around the bed, and put the other cup and saucer on his own table. Then he lifted his corner of the bedclothes. Maisie uttered a shriek.

'What're you doing?'

'Getting back into bed.'

'Daniel, you can't! I ain't got nothing on!' Her wedding nightdress had disappeared in the night. Well, almost at the beginning of the night, actually.

'Well, I've only got me shirt on, and I'm not hollering,' said Daniel.

'Well, I am,' said Maisie, 'it just ain't right, not in daylight.'

'But you can stay under the bedclothes.'

'Never mind that, you're not to get back in – oh, no, don't you dare – Daniel!'

Daniel was back in beside her.

'Maisie love, drink your tea,' he said, 'I'm not here to make you yell for help, just to enjoy our first morning cup of tea together. You're safe, take my word.'

'Oh, bless you, Daniel, I just don't want to feel shameless.'

'Understood, Maisie. Mind, I'm not sure what might or might not happen during our first day home together. Tell you what, wear something that'll put me off, something like a sack.'

'Well,' said Maisie, 'well, I just don't know how you can be so airy-fairy after what you got up to in the night.'

'Couldn't have managed it without your help, Maisie me darling,' said Daniel, and laughed.

Maisie little knew that her first-born, a son, was going to turn out as airy-fairy as his father.

After breakfast, they opened up the many wedding presents they'd received, most of which were domestic items, like cutlery, saucepans and tablecloths. All were a delight to Maisie, and she made Daniel do his share of writing letters of thanks.

They spent the week at home, getting to know their immediate neighbours, and getting very much to know each other. Daniel proved useful at doing odd jobs, and Maisie proved to be queen of the kitchen, which added to her worth in Daniel's eyes. They went shopping in the East Street market, a friendly, noisy and bustling centre for families always on the lookout for bargains in the way of fruit, vegetables and other foods. Maisie, in company with Alexander in the days before her wedding, had been renewing acquaintance with stallholders she had known since her years as a girl. Now she introduced them to Daniel.

''Ello, Bert, meet me soldier husband, Daniel.'

'Pleasure, I'm sure. So you've got spliced, 'ave yer, Maisie? Well, he looks a bit of all right, but I ain't recognizing 'im as a soldier.'

Daniel was in civvies.

'Well, he is,' said Maisie with a fair bit of pride, 'he's a corporal in the Royal West Kents.'

'Royal, eh? He guards our old Majesty, does 'e?'

'Not yet,' said Daniel, smiling. 'The Household Cavalry have got that job at the moment.'

There were similar dialogues of that kind with other stallholders. Daniel had put Maisie in charge of the household budget. She still had quite a residue of the cash he had given her weeks ago, and all of the twenty-five pounds he had sent her just prior to the wedding. But she didn't intend to spend more than was ever necessary, which was what her late mum had practised and why she had always managed to keep the family heads above water. Maisie knew that Daniel's pay as a married soldier meant she had to watch expenditure.

But she had never felt happier, or more secure. Daniel was a strong and resolute man, and a tender and considerate husband. Provider and protector, that was Daniel, and that was what God had made a man to be. A wife's duty was to care for him, keep him out of trouble, and not let him get too big for his boots, which some men did. Like Prime Ministers. But everyone knew Queen Victoria soon put them in their place.

What Maisie wholly disagreed with was the way some husbands bullied their wives. Her mum had known a neighbour, a Mrs Heeley, a very meek and mild woman, whose husband was a real brute. So Mum went round one day to give him a piece of her mind, against Dad's advice. Mum must have been a bit upset, because normally she'd have said it wasn't her business to interfere, but round she went. And she did give Mr Heeley a piece of her mind, which made him puff up as purple as a turkey, and he actually pushed Mum off his doorstep so that she nearly fell.

Of course, as soon as Dad heard that, round he went himself to set about the bloke. Mr Heeley bawled at him, and aimed a blow which missed. So Dad said, 'That's it, come on, try hitting me because I'm going to hit you and that's gospel.' He wasn't a railway porter for nothing, and Mr Heeley received a hiding on his own doorstep. The alarm was sounded, and round hurried a copper, by which time Dad had gone back home. The copper told Mr Heeley that he'd heard disorderly conduct was taking place. Mr Heeley said it was a bleedin' porkie. So the copper asked him what had happened to his face, then?

Mr Heeley said, 'I fell over in me back yard, didn't I, when putting something in me dustbin, and if yer don't believe me, go and look and you'll find a newspaper in the dustbin wrapped round pertater peelings. Ain't that right, me love?'

'Oh, yes,' said his meek and mild love, but the incident did her a bit of good because everyone soon got to know it had happened on account of him treating her very uncivilized. It calmed him down quite a bit. Mum told Dad he shouldn't have started a vulgar brawl, but she couldn't have been really cross with him, because she baked one of his favourite fruit cakes for Sunday tea.

Maisie was very much her mum's daughter in how she regarded a marital relationship.

She was happy about herself and Daniel. If she had things to say to him at night, they were only what one could expect of a bride who still claimed to be a respectable young lady.

'Daniel, oh, if you don't stop that, I'll die blushing.'

'Don't do that, Maisie, wait till you're ninety.'

Oh, that Daniel.

They received a postcard from Alexander. He was at Maidstone barracks, the learning ground for all recruits to the West Kents. He hadn't been given a drum yet, he said, just a close haircut, a pair of hobnailed boots, a lot of drill and a lot of talking-to. But he did have a uniform, declaring himself proud of it. He hoped they were enjoying a grand honeymoon in their Walworth love nest.

'Oh, Lor',' said Maisie, 'fancy writing that on a postcard for the postman to see.'

'Oh, postmen know all about their customers without having to read postcards,' said Daniel.

'Well, it shouldn't be allowed,' said Maisie.

This was something she meant seriously, and it was typical of her outlook.

Chapter Thirty-two

The newly-weds were up very early on Saturday morning. Daniel had to be back at barracks by nine. His week of special leave was over, and Maisie was biting her lip at the prospect of not seeing him again until, as a married man, he was allowed weekend leaves while the battalion was still stationed in London.

'I'm going to miss all this and I'm specially going to miss you, Maisie love.'

'Daniel, oh, can I come with you to the barracks?'

'Why not, Maisie? We'll enjoy another ride together by tram to Westminster Bridge, and take a hansom cab from there, shall us?'

'Daniel, we can't really afford hansoms.'

'Well, just this once, eh? We can have a cuddle in a cab, which we can't on a tram or bus. Well, we could, but it wouldn't be private.'

'Nor in a cab, neither, so don't get saucy.'

They had their ride, and in the hansom cab Daniel went no further than holding her hand. Maisie talked about what she was going to do about making the house really nice, and Daniel talked about stripping the kitchen wallpaper on his first weekend leave. Before they reached the barracks, he handed her what was left of his savings, about sixty pounds. It was hers, he said, as a nest egg. On top of that she'd be getting her allowance from the army every month.

'I know you'll manage, Maisie.'

'Daniel, it's all your savings, you don't have nothing left.'

'My savings, Maisie, were always intended for my dream girl, which I knew you were the first time I met you, even if you did give me me marching orders. As for having nothing left, well, I've got all I ever wanted, which is you, and I couldn't speak more true.'

It wasn't surprising that despite all her common sense and her acceptance of what life would be like married to a soldier, her eyes were wet when she said goodbye to him outside the gates of the barracks.

'Oh, take care, Daniel.'

'Rely on it, Maisie, the army don't allow its men to get wounded while in barracks.'

'That's not funny.'

'True, though. Give us a kiss now.'

The guard at the gates looked on with a grin as Corporal Daniel Adams kissed his newly-wed wife goodbye. Maisie didn't complain about it happening right there in public.

She felt lonely for the rest of the day, and more so when she went to bed and there was only empty space next to her.

After breakfast the following morning, she tidied up, then wrote a letter to Daniel, telling him what a wonderful wedding day she'd had, and what a lovely week at home with him it had been. She was looking forward ever so much to his first weekend with her, she said, and hoped it would be soon because when he was there it was much more like home. She sent him her love. Then she went to the morning service at St John's Church, which she'd often attended with her mum and dad.

Daniel received her letter on Tuesday morning, at a time when, much to his disgust, that persistent rumour had become fact. The 10th Battalion had been ordered to commence a spell of duty in troublesome Ireland. All officers, non-commissioned officers and other ranks were to travel to Holyhead the next morning and embark for Ireland the day after. For the very first time, Daniel wished he hadn't joined up.

'What're you swearing about, Corporal Adams?' asked Sergeant Lee.

'My bloody hard luck,' said Daniel.

'Same for everybody,' said Sergeant Lee.

'Not much it ain't,' said Daniel, 'I've just got married, haven't I, and these orders are striking me a personal blow that's making me gorge rise. How am I going to tell Maisie?'

'See your point,' said Sergeant Lee, 'you'll have to send her a postcard.'

'I could do with a bucketful of commiserations,

not a comic remark. I tell you, Jack, Maisie won't like this Irish lark, which is no lark. Gorblimey, how long a spell is it?' Daniel demanded.

'NCOs ain't been informed, but my guess is six months,' said Sergeant Lee. 'Anyway, write your Maisie a kind letter and get it posted.'

Daniel adjusted his thoughts. A born soldier, he put aside any idea of going absent without leave for the day, and joined with Sergeant Lee in informing the men of their platoon of all they had to do to prepare themselves for tomorrow's train journey. And he found time during the midday break to write to Maisie, and he also found an opportunity to catch the afternoon post.

Maisie received the letter on Wednesday morning. Daniel acknowledged her own letter, which he declared read like a song, and ought to be set to music. Then he informed her of the battalion's imminent departure for Ireland.

It's a blow, I tell you, Maisie, and it wouldn't surprise me if it made you feel sorry at having married a soldier. It's the sort of thing that could only happen to a soldier's wife just a week or so after the wedding. I feel now that I didn't do you any favour by getting you to the church, but I couldn't help myself, I fell in love with you the day I met you. All the same, I'll understand if you want to fire some burning arrows at me. I'll write to you again as soon as we're settled, which I hope will be in a field of lucky four-leaf clover, you bet.

All my love, sweetheart. Daniel.

The news upset Maisie, very much. It took her some time to pull herself together. Well, there wasn't much she could do about the army ordering him to Ireland, she could only wait for his next letter, and she refused to mope. Being unhappy didn't mean she had to sit in a corner and cry. Daniel wouldn't want her to give in like that. As for rowing with him about his duties as a soldier, the thought never entered her head. Their marriage was for better or worse in the sight of God, and she'd never go against that.

It was just a bit unfair, the worse happening so quickly.

She put her hat and coat on, picked up her shopping bag, and went to the East Street market to take in its exuberant hustle and bustle and to buy some freshly harvested English apples. Cox's orange pippins.

'How yer doing, Maisie? Where's yer soldier husband?'

'With his regiment.'

'Hard luck, Maisie. Would yer like me to come round this evening and console with yer?'

'That's ever so kind of you, Alf, but I think you'd best stay home with your grandchildren.'

She heard from Alexander again two days later. He wrote to say he was now getting on fine, that he was learning the drums, that the grub was plain but plentiful, and that he'd had a letter from the girl Patty of the orphanage in reply to one he'd written to her. She sounded sort of fond of him, and she asked when he was going to come and see her again. So he'd written back to say he'd go and visit when he had his first leave.

Maisie replied to tell him he could stay with her, and take a trip to the orphanage one day.

Daniel's first letter from Ireland arrived, giving her his address at the army's Dublin barracks. He didn't say much about what his battalion was doing, only that it was patrolling the streets and keeping an eye on Dubliners who could get a bit noisy when they turned out of their pubs and needed help to find their way home.

But Maisie knew, of course, that the Irish he was talking about could be much more than a bit noisy.

It was a long letter, telling her how much he was missing her and that he'd give a month's pay to have the chance of meeting her in Kensington Gardens, and then riding home to Walworth with her. How was she coping, had she deposited the money in a savings account or was she keeping it in her portmanteau, and was she making firm friends with the neighbours? She needed friends, friends she could invite to tea, friends she could spend time with. He was on the roster for home leave in four months, which would be in the New Year. He was looking forward to that.

He closed by saying, 'Keep the bed warm for

me, Maisie love, yours ever with a hundred kisses and a longing to see you, Daniel.'

A regular correspondence began between Maisie in Walworth, London, and Daniel in Dublin, Ireland.

Dublin, December, the night dark, rainy and misty, the streets seemingly deserted except for a patrol of British soldiers. Sergeant Lee and Daniel were at the head of six members of their platoon. A few lights appeared in pub windows, behind which roistering Irishmen were downing their usual tankards of foaming beer.

The patrol, entering a long street, was due to rendezvous with another approaching from the opposite direction, an officer at its head. The rendezvous was to take place outside a house, number forty-seven. There, according to whispered information, a certain Irish gentleman was in hiding. This was one Jimmy Vaughan, a Republican, wanted for wounding a West Kent lance corporal with a rifle bullet. The informant had been Kitty Connolly, a strange woman who slipped in and out of Dublin's turbulent scenes like a shadow.

Dublin was the centre of Irish Republicans who wanted nothing to do with proposed Home Rule, but a united and independent Ireland. Furtive but hot-blooded characters committed regular acts of lethal intent against British soldiers, and were always difficult to catch, for they had boltholes everywhere in and outside the city.

Tonight one was going to be run to earth, if Kitty Connolly's information could be trusted, as it invariably could. In the darkness, the two patrols converged on the house she had pin-pointed. Its window blinds were drawn, but showed a pale glow of gaslight. The officer in charge, Lieutenant Watson, raised the lantern he was carrying to check the house number. He stiffened. Lying outside the door was the inert body of a woman, a thin white cord around her neck and biting into her flesh. Lieutenant Watson let the light of the lantern fall fully on her.

The strangled, lifeless body was that of Kitty Connolly. Lieutenant Watson swore. Daniel whispered an impulsive warning to Sergeant Lee.

'Watch out!'

'Break that door down!' hissed Lieutenant Watson.

Boots and rifle butts smashed at the door until it crashed open. A stream of light from passage mantles illuminated the swarming soldiers.

A rifle began firing. A bullet smashed a window, a second dug a burning hole in Lieutenant Watson's shoulder. It spun him round. Men flung themselves flat on the pavement. Sergeant Lee and Daniel took themselves out of the stream of light and pressed their backs to the front wall of the house. Lieutenant Watson, incapacitated, ordered four men to get to their feet and invade the house.

The rifle fired again. Daniel spotted the tiny flash. It came from the other side of the street, a little way down. The bullet ricocheted off the brickwork only a foot from his head. He brought his rifle, his new Lee-Enfield, to his shoulder. Another tiny flash signalled the despatch of another bullet. It scored the scalp of one of the men charging into the house, and felled him.

Daniel fired in the direction of the flash. He heard the clatter of a dropped rifle. He ran, bent double, across the street, knowing that if he'd wounded his man, other Republicans would materialize out of the night and carry him off at speed. At this moment, another rifle opened fire from a little way up the street. He felt a stinging blow to his left thigh. He staggered, but continued his run, with Sergeant Lee coming up fast behind him. His left leg collapsed and he fell.

Other members of the patrol charged across the street. The enemy melted away. And the men investigating the house found it quite empty except for an old couple who were of no use at all.

The patrol was left with a wounded officer, a wounded corporal, a head-bleeding private, and a cruelly murdered woman.

A letter arrived from Daniel.

Dear Maisie love,

I'm in hospital here. We had a bit of an argument with some of those unfriendly Irish you read about. I took a bullet in my thigh and it made quite a hole. It's plugged up now, and I'm feeling it was a lucky strike because it means I'm being sent home to convalesce, and I'll actually be with you for Christmas. What do you think of that, sweetie? Talk about luck of the Irish, well even if I'm not Irish I'm Irish-based and I suppose that counted in my favour. How are things with you? And how's our little house in Walworth? Wasn't that another piece of luck, finding it and being given the tenancy? I think the good Lord's smiling on us, well you're deserving of a heavenly smile and that's gospel.

I'll be able to let you know in good time the date I'll be with you at Christmas. Could you manage to come up with a fruity Christmas pudding? I can't wait to see you and enjoy Christmas dinner with you.

All my love, sweetheart, yours always, Daniel.
PS. Don't forget to keep the bed warm.

Upset though she was at knowing he'd been wounded, the news that he was coming home, and for Christmas, brought a rush of joy to Maisie. Today was 17 December, which meant he'd be home inside a week. She sat down and wrote an immediate reply, addressing it care of the hospital.

Dear dear Daniel,

I'm really upset about you being wounded, it wasn't because you were careless and airy-fairy, was it? My dad used to say the first thing a soldier's got to learn is when to duck and not to leave himself carelessly in the way of a bullet. But I'm so happy you're better and I can't tell you how rapturous I am that you'll be home for Christmas, it seems like years since you left. I've just had to busy myself around the house, especially in the parlour. I got rid of the aspidistra, it was so big in the window it was hiding the light and then I thought the curtains were a bit yellow with age, even if there weren't any rips or tears. So I bought yards of new curtain material at the shop in the market which they were selling at a real bargain price and I've been making new curtains for a whole week now and they'll be ready to put up before Christmas.

I'll cook us a lovely Christmas pudding, you see if I don't, and perhaps we could afford one of them little bottles of brandy which you heat up and pour on the pudding and then light it. Did your family used to do that? My mum and dad did if they could afford it which wasn't every Christmas.

Come home soon, Daniel, I'm longing to see you even if you are shocking saucy about me keeping the bed warm, lots and lots of love from your Maisie.

When Daniel received and read the letter he was a walking patient and able to ask a nurse if she'd like to do a celebratory knees-up with him. The nurse said the idea was wishful thinking on his part.

Chapter Thirty-three

It was 21 December, and the weather, dismal for a week, suddenly cast crisp winter sunshine over London. It put a spring into Maisie's step, and an impulse sent her travelling to Kensington Gore. There, from a little way off, she spent a few minutes observing the house where she had come to know the kindness and twinkle of the late Mr Fairfax, a lovely old gentleman. She experienced a little stab at the heart at his tragic demise. She would never know whether it was accidental or otherwise.

After some minutes, she walked up to the house and down to the basement door. She tried it. As usual, it wasn't locked. She opened it and listened. Everything seemed quiet, except for a faint little hum from the kitchen. Silently, she went through. The kitchen door was ajar and she heard Prudence talking, and Agnes responding. She knocked gently on the door and it was pulled open by Daisy.

'Crikey,' gasped Daisy, 'it's you, Maisie. Look, everyone, Maisie's here.'

'Come on in, Maisie,' sang Prudence, 'come and sit down and talk.'

'Is it all right?' asked Maisie, stepping in. Edie and Agnes were sitting at the table with cups of tea.

'Oh, d'you mean Mrs Carpenter?' said Agnes. 'She went out ten minutes ago. She's gone shopping, Mr Townley took 'er in the carriage.'

'And she won't be back for an hour at least, like always,' said Prudence. 'We're 'aving our morning cup of tea. Come on, Maisie, sit down and 'ave one with us.'

'And tell us all about yer married life,' said Edie. 'Milly's got the day off, so she'll be sorry she missed yer.'

Maisie sat down and Prudence poured her a cup of hot tea. Maisie asked if they'd first tell her what had happened since she left. Prudence said all kinds of things had gone on.

Firstly, they'd all thought about trying to get new jobs, but Mr Burnaby had persuaded them to stay on to make sure the house didn't get run-down until it was sold, when he'd help them to find new positions. He knew the families of many a grand residence in Kensington. So they stayed on that promise and out of respect for poor Mr Fairfax, who always liked the house to shine and sparkle. And what happened then, you might ask, said Prudence. Well, Milly got herself engaged to her gentleman friend, then Miss Blisset met a gent who said he'd be a father to little Rosemary, so the cook went off and married him. They all thought Mrs Carpenter was pleased to see her go.

All the time the housekeeper was getting on to Mr Burnaby about executing the will in her favour, and then one day Mr Burnaby called to say he'd heard from Mr Fairfax's cousin in South Africa. He was coming to London to dispute the will. That was weeks and weeks ago, and then the cousin arrived, and what happened next, you might ask again, Maisie.

'Go on, tell 'er,' urged Agnes.

And Prudence said he showed Mr Burnaby a letter he'd had from Mr Fairfax a year ago, in which Mr Fairfax told his cousin he was to inherit everything apart from small bequests to the staff.

'Mr Burnaby told you this?' said Maisie.

'Yes,' said Prudence, 'and what else, would yer believe. That Mr Fairfax wrote that if he was persuaded to alter 'is will in favour of someone else, 'is cousin wasn't to take no notice of it, but to keep the letter. Mr Burnaby said it might not actually count as legal, but it was as good as it could be for contesting the will. And it's all going to be decided in court, and Mrs Carpenter, well . . .'

'She's steaming about it,' said Agnes.

'Sometimes you can almost see smoke rising,' said Daisy.

'Steam,' said Edie.

'There ain't no difference in 'er case,' said Daisy.

'We met the cousin when he came to look the

house over,' said Prudence. 'Mr Wilfred Allen, that's 'is name, and a really nice gent, but not as old as Mr Fairfax was. More like middle-aged.'

It all brought forth long minutes of chatter, with Maisie joining in, leaving her only a little time to talk about her marriage and how she and Daniel were getting on. She wanted to make sure she departed before Mrs Carpenter returned, so she didn't go on about Daniel being wounded, she only said he'd be home on leave for Christmas, which made Agnes giggle and say don't drink too much port, then.

They all wished her well when she did leave and begged her to come again any time she could.

It was when she was on a horse bus on her way home that she remembered something, the time when she'd heard Mrs Carpenter talking to someone in her suite. She remembered the housekeeper saying she'd already done as much as she could for the person in question, and to be patient.

Had that person been her niece Fanny Blisset, and did being patient mean Fanny was to wait for something to happen? Like the reading of a certain will?

Oh, Lord above, thought Maisie, then thrust it all to the back of her mind again, but not without a wish that everything would go to Mr Fairfax's cousin.

*   *   *

Christmas Eve. Daniel arrived in London on a train from Holyhead. The weather was wet, very wet, but he couldn't have cared less if cats and dogs had been raining down. He was on his way home to see Maisie.

Sergeant Lee, who had travelled with him, watched him alight, putting his good leg down first.

'Fair, fair, Corporal Adams, you've stopped wobbling.'

'Give over,' said Daniel, hefting out his kitbag.

'Listen, sunshine, me orders are to see you get home without falling down, and I'm going to see self-same orders are carried out to your door-step,' said Sergeant Lee. 'Give us your kitbag.' He was willing to carry one on each broad shoulder, for Daniel still had a painful limp and a bandaged thigh.

Up came a porter.

'Want to use me trolley, soldiers?'

'You beauty,' said Daniel, and he and his sergeant deposited their kitbags on the trolley, which the obliging porter wheeled from the plat-form to the bus stop outside the station. Daniel tipped him a whole tanner.

'Well, thanking you gents, and a merry Christ-mas to yer both.'

It was three in the afternoon when Maisie, wear-ing her apricot frock, opened the door to her husband and his sergeant, the sergeant she had met at the wedding.

'Here he is, Maisie, all safe and sound, except for a bit of a hole in his leg,' said Sergeant Lee. 'Don't let him jump about.'

Maisie couldn't help herself, she flung her arms around Daniel, who received his first Christmas kiss from her with a great deal of pleasure.

'Daniel, oh, it's lovely you're home,' she said, eyes shining, 'and bless you, Sergeant Lee, for bringing him.'

'I dispute that,' said Daniel, 'I brought meself. Jack just came along for the ride.'

'Well, stay for a cup of tea and some cake, Sergeant Lee,' said Maisie.

'Jack,' said Sergeant Lee. 'But I can't stay, thanks all the same, got to get home to me granny.'

'Oh, you're spending Christmas with your grandma?' said Maisie.

'Can you believe she's only twenty-one?' said Daniel.

'Beg pardon?' said Maisie.

'Take no notice, Maisie, he's a bit off balance,' said Sergeant Lee. 'It's his leg. Stay on his left side, or he'll fall over. Have a happy Christmas, both of you. See you here in seven days, Corporal Adams. Keep him in order, Maisie.' Sergeant Lee delivered a kiss on her cheek, hefted up his kitbag and departed.

Daniel took hold of his own kitbag and stepped into his home and back into Maisie's life.

*　　*　　*

They had the happiest reunion, and Daniel found a hot-water bottle in the bed that night. He also found Maisie, so after only a few minutes, out went the hot-water bottle as surplus to requirements.

'Oh, you Daniel, you're saucier than ever!'

'Tell you what, Maisie, you're doing wonders for me injured leg, you sweetheart.'

Their Christmas week together was as happy as their reunion, but it was another rotten day for Maisie when Sergeant Lee turned up and he and Daniel departed together. She'd never imagined she could miss a man so much.

Time moved on. In April, after a six-month spell in troublesome Dublin, the battalion was posted to Egypt, where British troops were required to settle disturbances there and in the Sudan. The men were given four days' embarkation leave, and again Maisie and Daniel enjoyed a joyful reunion. When he left, she realized exactly what her life as a soldier's wife was going to be like. But Daniel was her man, and she wouldn't have changed him for a bank clerk or a bricklayer home every night.

Wonderfully, the battalion was back in early October, and there was one more reunion, the kind that suggested each was starving for the other. In love, their togetherness was exceptionally ardent, Maisie no longer afflicted by the blushes of modesty, Daniel's muscular thighs now in harmony, except for a small scar on the left one.

'Daniel . . .'

'Maisie . . .'

'Oh, ain't marriage lovely?'

The year 1896 arrived, and with Daniel away again, new neighbours moved in next door to Maisie. Mr and Mrs Castle were a jolly couple, he a burly but breezy bloke in his late twenties, she a plump, rosy-faced woman of twenty-four. They were both fond of a little bit of what they fancied, beer in his case, a nice glass of port and lemon in hers. Although Maisie didn't think they were the height of respectability, they were so cheerful and friendly that she found it uplifting to have them living next to her.

Two doors down on the other side of her lived a widow, Mrs Chivers, and her young daughter, Elsie. Mrs Chivers was reclusive, bitter and possessive, rarely letting her daughter out of her sight except to go to school. Elsie was fifteen and, in Maisie's eyes, a sweet and pretty girl, even if she did wear glasses. Her mother ruled her life in a way that kept the girl repressed and chained, which Maisie thought a shame, because young people ought to have the freedom to go out and about with friends, as long as they behaved themselves. Often in the morning, when Elsie was on her way to school, her mother would put her head out of an upstairs window to watch her daughter, and make sure she didn't stop to speak to anyone, especially boys. She was totally against any boy coming within ten yards of Elsie. Neighbours said Mrs Chivers had never forgiven Mr Chivers for going to his grave and leaving her to bring up a young daughter on her own. When she was getting at Elsie, they said, she was actually getting at her husband's ghost.

A moment arrived in Maisie's life that delighted her and inspired her to write at once to Daniel, up in Yorkshire with his battalion. When Daniel received the letter he went straight to Company Sergeant Major Sawyer.

'Sarn't Major, could you do me a favour?'

'No.'

'Could you get permission from the OC for me to have a week's leave?'

'Only a week, not fourteen days?'

'Just a week, Sarn't Major.'

'No.'

'Look—'

'I ain't looking, Corporal Adams, I'm informing you. Battalion's on manoeuvres and you're stuck with it, like everyone else. But might I enquire why you've got the impertinence to ask?'

'I'm going to be a dad,' said Daniel.

'Well, as my old dad said to me when I passed my writing exam, "Who's a clever boy, then?"'

'I am,' said Daniel, 'so I'd like some leave to make sure Maisie's putting her feet up reg'lar and not overdoing things.'

'She'll manage. Give her me regards when

you write, and now get your platoon ready to march.'

'Well, an order's an order,' said Daniel.

'This one is, definite,' said Sergeant Major Sawyer.

Daniel, of course, wrote a very wordy and loving reply to Maisie. He noted the baby was due in July. She was to take things easy, lie down a lot and not to run to catch a tram or bus. Or carry heavy shopping bags. And so on. (Like a typical male fusspot.)

The happy event came to pass, and Maisie was delivered of a baby boy. Daniel, given a week-end's leave, arrived at the hospital on the day she was due to return home, so he had the great pleasure and privilege of accompanying her and the swaddled babe. Maisie was flushed and joyful, Daniel upstanding and proud. They named the infant Robert Alfred, and when Daniel went back to camp his comrades wet his head in lieu of the baby's, as it were, and he might have got charged for being drunk had his constitution not been such as to prevent that kind of condition.

A month later, cousin Victoria, just married herself, came to see Maisie, bringing with her a pair of blue knitted bootees that were to be worn by the child as soon as its feet were firm enough. That eventually led to her cooing sweet words to the infant on regular visits.

'Who's a pretty boots, then?'

And that, in turn, led to young Robert Alfred Adams being nicknamed Boots.

*   *   *

In June 1897 Queen Victoria celebrated her
Diamond Jubilee. London was a place of colour
and excitement. Flags, bunting and decorations
streamed in the breeze, kings, queens and princes
from all over Europe attended the revelries,
thousands and thousands of her subjects giving the
majestic old lady a right royal welcome as she left
Buckingham Palace in her coach to drive to St
Paul's Cathedral. Among the many army and navy
escorts was a platoon of officers, NCO's and other
ranks from the Royal West Kent Regiment. It
included Daniel, his red jacket ablaze in the
sunshine, his bearing that of a privileged soldier
who was also a proud dad, as well as the kind of
husband Maisie had thought right and proper.
That is, protective, providing and not too big for
his boots, army issue.

Chapter Thirty-four

Time went by, Daniel's battalion serving alternately at home and overseas. Sometimes Maisie did not see him for months, but there were always reunions of a heartfelt kind and, on occasions, of a productive kind.

In July 1898 Maisie had been delivered of a baby girl, named Eliza. Daniel was delighted, and Maisie was reminded of the days when she had hoped she would have a daughter as lovable as little Rosemary. She had received Mr Fairfax's bequest of a hundred pounds from Mr Burnaby, together with the information that the court had ruled in favour of Mr Fairfax's cousin, providing Mrs Carpenter was allowed a compensatory sum of two and a half thousand pounds, a ruling Mr Burnaby declared most unusual. All the servants now had new jobs, Mrs Carpenter had departed, and the house was to be sold. That left Maisie with a hundred pounds extra in her savings account, and only memories of her time in the service of a charming old gentleman she would never forget.

Little Eliza soon came to be called Lizzy. Next door, jolly Mrs Castle presented breezy Mr Castle with a baby girl, Emily, destined to become Lizzy's best friend. A second son, Tommy, was born to Maisie in April 1900, by which time the country was at war with the Boers, whose grievances over the expansion of British interests in South Africa were many. Infant Tommy seemed a lusty specimen, but there were immediate post-natal complications for Maisie that kept her in hospital for several days longer than expected. Daniel, home for the weekend, overstayed his leave, visiting his wife and new child every day until he was finally able to bring them home. There, Maisie's cousin Victoria was doing a Christian deed by looking after the other children.

Daniel was four days late in returning to camp in Yorkshire, where the battalion was on manoeuvres prior to embarking for South Africa and the Boer War. He was charged with being absent without leave, and although he offered what he considered a good reason for this, he lost a stripe and was reduced to lance corporal. Maisie, furious when Daniel wrote to tell her, wanted to send his OC the letter of an outraged wife, and threatened to do just that. Daniel, in reply, asked her not to. Dutifully, Maisie complied.

Just as dutifully, in June, Daniel embarked with the battalion for service in the war against the stalwart and obdurate Boers, where the West

Kents discovered that the might of Imperial Britain was suffering humiliating defeats at the hands of the sharp-shooting Afrikaners. It was a war fought in the heat and dust of a terrain much more suited to the hard-riding enemy cavalry than to the fixed formations of British units.

The West Kents, like other regiments, took casualties, but soldiered on in the typically resolute fashion of their kind, occasionally excelling themselves whenever they were able to launch impromptu surprise attacks on the hit-and-run Boer commando units. In the heat, they turned red at first, which made the hairy Boers call them Rednecks, but they gradually took on a nut-brown hue.

In January 1901 Her Enduring Majesty, Queen Victoria, failed at last. Her passing was mourned by the whole country and its dominions, while the monarchies of Europe, over which she had held sway for many years, bowed their heads in homage. The Prince of Wales, inheriting his mother's throne, became King Edward the Seventh.

Daniel, distinguishing himself in a running battle with the Boers in May, won back his lost stripe to become a full corporal again. And in August, after fourteen months of war service, the West Kents returned to Britain and to Maidstone. Casualties and exhaustion required the regiment to be rested, re-equipped and made up to full strength again. Among the reserves who entered the ranks was twenty-two-year-old

Alexander Beavis, he having gravitated from drummer boy to private some years before.

Again, Maisie and Daniel enjoyed an ardent reunion, this time of fourteen days. Daniel renewed his paternal relationship with his son Robert, nearly five and invariably called Boots, and his three-year-old Lizzy. And he came to know little Tommy, now over a year old. For fourteen days he doted on all three, and brought happiness to their mother, who thought that his tanned appearance made him handsomer than ever.

In late October the regiment returned to the war in South Africa, to rejoin the British forces now under the command of Kitchener. The troops, having learned from bitter experience how best to fight the courageous enemy on the dusty plains of Africa, were beginning to get the measure of the Boers.

That August reunion resulted in Maisie giving birth to her third son, Sammy, in May 1902. Sammy was a child of noise and energy, and Maisie, when writing to inform Daniel of the infant's arrival, said she thought he was going to be what her dad called a little perisher.

The Boers finally surrendered on the last day of May, but Britain made up for its original intransigence by offering such generous peace terms that General Smuts, one of the Boers' outstanding leaders, became a lifelong friend of the Empire.

The West Kents finally shook the dust of South

Africa from their boots in July to return home to a well-deserved long leave, and Maisie and the children greeted Daniel's arrival with joy and exuberance, although Maisie didn't actually emulate Boots and Lizzy by jumping up and down. She still practised what Daniel saw as ladylike behaviour. But that didn't prevent her exhibiting delight.

The West Kents, along with other regiments, took on a peacetime role, while knowing they were always liable to be despatched to trouble spots in the far-flung Empire. Daniel was home regularly, watching his children growing up, taking them to his heart, and arranging excursions to places like the London Zoo and the royal parks, as well as their own playground, Ruskin Park.

Maisie knew his regiment might be called on for new overseas service at any time, but that was the way of it for a soldier's wife. It inevitably happened when, in the spring of 1905, the West Kents sailed for India and the troubles on the North-West Frontier. Maisie consoled herself with the knowledge that next year, in August, Daniel had promised to leave the army. He had promised he would not sign up for more.

The troubles on the North-West Frontier were mainly with the wild and unruly Pathans. Maisie suffered the most terrible blow of her existence when, in a violent affray with these fierce men of the Frontier in May 1906, Daniel, his sergeant's stripes at last about to be conferred, rushed to help a fallen comrade, none other than Private Alexander Beavis. A shell from an ancient cannon exploded and blew Daniel's life away.

A telegram brought the unbearable news to Maisie. For all her fortitude, she collapsed. Cousin Victoria, known as Aunt Victoria to the children, came rushing over, and although she was turning into a rather critical woman, she showed nothing but deep sympathy and compassion for the suddenly bereaved family.

It took Maisie many years to adjust to her loss. Young Boots, so like his late father in looks and character, was a tower of strength to his mother by the time he was fourteen in 1910. He and Lizzy, with Tommy and Sammy, were all very much the children of their parents. All had inherited the good looks of their father, and all reflected the 'proper' behavioural patterns of their mother, whom they came to call Chinese Lady, an unusual nickname, but Maisie did not mind it at all.

With only her war widow's pension, she was always short of the ready, very much so. This meant that although she was also hardworking and enduring, in common with most Walworth housewives, she really did have to scrape for spare pennies.

It was in October 1910 that a potential financial lifeline arrived at her door, in the shape of a uniformed river pilot who, having just moved from duties in Southampton Water to the Port of London, was looking for a lodging, preferably in

Walworth and not around the slumlike dockland area. Maisie liked his air of manliness and respectability, and entertained him in her parlour before she realized that with four children, she could offer no lodging accommodation. The three bedrooms upstairs were occupied, one by Lizzy, one by Boots, and one by Tommy and Sammy, who shared a double bed. Maisie herself slept in the downstairs room situated between the parlour and the kitchen.

'I'm ever so sorry I can't help you,' she said to the visitor.

Young Boots was present. Fourteen and already long-legged, and knowing how much his mother needed extra income, he put in a helpful comment.

'Well, you could, Mum,' he said.

'You'd best tell me how, then,' she said.

So Boots asked the visitor to excuse himself and his mum for a minute while he spoke to her in the passage. He pointed out he could move his bed in with Tommy and Sammy.

'That would leave my room, the upstairs back, free for a lodger,' he said.

'You wouldn't mind crowding in with yer brothers?' said Maisie.

'Not a bit,' said Boots. 'Mum, you need some rent money.'

'Well, I can't say I don't,' said his mum, 'and I can't say it wouldn't be a real help.'

'There you are, then,' said Boots.

So they re-entered the parlour and told the

394

visitor they could manage to let him have the upstairs back.

'Are you sure?' said the visitor, a man of maturity. 'I really wouldn't want to inconvenience you.'

'Oh, a blocked-up chimney is a lot more inconvenient than making room for a lodger,' said Boots airily. Presently in the middle of a grammar-school education at West Square in St George's Road, not far from the Elephant and Castle, he was given to exercising his mastery of English in an airy-fairy way. On this occasion, it made the visitor smile.

'Well, if you're sure, let me say a lodging here would suit me admirably,' he said, and Maisie thought him a proper gent in his manners and speech.

'About the rent,' said Boots. An upstairs back could fetch anything from a mere three bob a week to six, depending on location. Across the river, in some East End districts, it could be even lower than three bob.

'Oh, I don't know we want to be embarrassing, Boots,' said his mother who, despite her daily round of hard work, still dressed neatly, and still had an upright carriage.

'It's not at all embarrassing,' smiled the visitor. 'May I offer six shillings a week, with two weeks in advance?'

'Well,' said the lady of the house, 'I just don't know we ought to ask—'

'We accept,' said Boots, 'and I'll take you up to

see the room. I'll also get a rent book, and make it out in your name. Fair?'

'Very fair, young man,' smiled the accepted lodger.

So from that day in 1910, with the welcome rent of six shillings a week entering her purse, and the lodger proving a proper gent indeed, a better if still stringent existence began for Maisie and her family. Over their lives hovered the invisible spirit of Daniel, giving them encouragement to meet all their adversities with the same kind of resilience he himself had shown during his adventurous but cruelly short span.

The lodger's name that Boots entered in the rent book?

Finch, Edwin Finch.

THE END

DOWN LAMBETH WAY
by Mary Jane Staples

The Adams family of Walworth were poor, cheerful, and above all respectable – even though they sometimes had to seek a little help from the pawnbroker.

Mrs Adams – affectionately called Chinese Lady by her children – was a widow, her soldier husband having gone, rather carelessly, to a hero's death on the Northwest Frontier. There was Boots, the bright one, and Tommy, the quiet one, and Sammy, the nine-year-old wheeler-dealer of the family. There was Mr Finch, the lodger, and dreadful Em'ly next door, and genteel Miss Chivers with the terrible old mother, but above all there was Lizzy.

Lizzy was one of the prettiest girls in Walworth. She was young, and always sounded her aitches, and she cared terribly about being clean and neat and . . . *proper*. Lizzy was a peach of a girl.

When Lizzy fell in love it was 1914. Everyone was going to be affected, things were going to change. But whatever happened, the Adams family – gutsy, tough and cheeky – would come through.

Down Lambeth Way is the first book in a wonderful saga featuring the larger-than-life Adams family of Walworth.

0552132993

CORGI BOOKS

ON MOTHER BROWN'S DOORSTEP
by Mary Jane Staples

The big event of the Walworth year was to be the wedding of Sammy Adams, King of Camberwell, to Miss Susie Brown. Everyone was looking forward to it, and Susie was particularly overjoyed when her soldier brother suddenly turned up on leave from service in India in time for the approaching 'knees-up'. The reason for Will's extended leave wasn't so good, for bad health had struck him and he didn't know how long the army would keep him, or how he could find a civvy job in the slump of the 20s. When he – literally – picked Annie Ford up off the pavement in King and Queen Street, his worries were compounded, for Annie was a bright, brave, personable young woman and Will knew that if he wasn't careful he'd find himself falling in love.

And over Walworth hung a greater anxiety – the mystery of three young girls missing from their homes – a mystery that was to draw closer and closer to the Adams and Brown families, and finally culminate – along with Will's personal problems – on the night of the wedding.

Here again is the Adams family from *Down Lambeth Way*, *Our Emily* and *King of Camberwell*.

0552139750

CORGI BOOKS

A FaMILY AFFAIR
by Mary Jane Staples

The Adams family of Walworth are back – in a new, irrepressible saga of cockney life.

1926 was the year of the General Strike, but Adams Enterprises, under the wily management of Sammy Adams, youngest entrepreneur in Walworth and Lambeth, was doing very well. All the Adams brothers worked in the business, and so did two of the wives, Emily and Susie. There was just one dark cloud on the horizon – the impending trial of Ronald Ponsonby. Boots had been the one responsible for catching the murderer, and Ponsonby hated Boots and, indeed, the entire Adams family. He was determined to get his revenge and make them suffer.

When a dapper, quiet, but rather odd lodger turned up at Doreen Paterson's house, nobody thought anything was amiss. It never occurred to Doreen – who worked for Boots in Adams Enterprises and thought him just wonderful – that the strange lodger might be plotting the downfall of the irrepressible, outrageous, and larger-than-life Adams clan.

Here again is the Adams family from *Down Lambeth Way*, *Our Emily*, *King of Camberwell* and *On Mother Brown's Doorstep*.

0552141542

CORGI BOOKS

A LIST OF OTHER MARY JANE STAPLES TITLES AVAILABLE FROM CORGI BOOKS

THE PRICES SHOWN BELOW WERE CORRECT AT THE TIME OF GOING TO PRESS. HOWEVER TRANSWORLD PUBLISHERS RESERVE THE RIGHT TO SHOW NEW RETAIL PRICES ON COVERS WHICH MAY DIFFER FROM THOSE PREVIOUSLY ADVERTISED IN THE TEXT OR ELSEWHERE.

All Transworld titles are available by post from:
Bookpost, PO Box 29, Douglas, Isle of Man IM99 1BQ
Credit cards accepted. Please telephone +44(0)1624 836000, fax +44(0)1624 837033
Internet http://www.bookpost.co.uk or
e-mail: bookshop@enterprise.net for details.
Free postage and packing in the UK.
Overseas customers allow £2 per book (paperbacks) and £3 per book (hardbacks).